THE FIRST JET

showed some of its belly in pulling away, and
then Tindle saw the clumsy eggs, the napalm
tanks, lobbing end over end toward the slope.

They struck. Tindle felt the sudden heat. The
air was scorched and thin. A great spreading
blob of fire grew, and black smoke peeled like
citrus rind from the surface of the solid fire.

Through his binoculars, Tindle watched the
Chinese. A number of them rose and gasped,
and some of those nearer the flaming protoplasm squirmed and fell, clothes and flesh afire.

He could smell the oily napalm and the salty
sharpness of the explosives. Then, the jets
came in again . . .

TROUBLING OF A STAR
A Brutal Novel of Men in War!

TROUBLING OF A STAR

BY WALT SHELDON

BANTAM BOOKS · LONDON · TORONTO · NEW YORK

TROUBLING OF A STAR

*A Bantam Book / published by arrangement with
J. B. Lippincott Company*

PRINTING HISTORY

J. B. Lippincott edition published January 1953
People's Book Club edition published March 1953

Bantam edition published July 1954
2nd printing .... June 1968

TO VICTOR WHITE . . .
who couldn't help teaching

... Thou canst not stir a flower
Without troubling of a star.

—Francis Thompson
"The Mistress of Vision"

CHAPTER ONE

1

THE answer came by morning, before Colonel Straker was quite awake, but in this state he swung from the bed to jot it down. He kept a pad on the night table for just this sort of thing.

He straightened, stretched, rubbed his eyes. Already light outside. He went to the window and stood there for a moment, looking past the tile cottage tops at the silk water-color mountains that surrounded Akuni Air Force Base. The sky was clear today, laundered by a week of May rain. Flying weather, thought the colonel—now we get started. And he'd get in a mission or two himself, because it always helped to have them see the old man flying right along with them—

Old man. Bill Straker laughed: he was actually only forty-four, and he'd been a colonel now, a full colonel, for seven years. His torso above his pajama waist was firm fleshed, with the luster of white marble. His hair was gray and skullcap cut, but none of it had receded.

And when he breathed deeply—like this—his chest still had a good four-inch expansion.

And now he was fully awake, and he turned from the window and went back to the night table to read the note he had scribbled, for he had already begun to forget what it said. He was pleased to see that the writing, though swift, was neat and legible, and he leaned over the pad, squinted slightly, and read:

Singl idea. 1 thing publ remember. Maybe Wing noted kill troops. Keep count.

He read it again, frowned, then nodded and smiled. He moved his lips. "That's it," he said.

He went into the small bathroom now, turned on the light, and carefully laid out his shaving things. The image of his smile was still with him. Straker was proud of what he'd done, because he knew people would not ordinarily think of him as an imaginative type, but here, by sheer ap-

1

plication, he had pulled an idea right out of a hat, and there was no denying that. Application, and self-discipline. That last was the real secret. Last night he'd gone over the figures from stat control—sorties mounted, hours flown, ammo and fuel expended, evaluated strike results—at least a dozen times. Saturated himself with them. He'd paced and scribbled and diagrammed and re-read and paced again —all till past midnight. Then he'd simply gone to bed and let his subconscious take over. It all worked so magically that you could hardly help but sense the existence of a Higher Power involved somewhere.

He shaved slowly and deliberately, going over his beard twice. Although he was anxious to get to the office this morning and put his new plan under way, he disciplined himself to go at his usual pace. He rubbed a deodorant under his arms. He washed his hands again, then clipped and filed his nails. He selected a freshly starched khaki shirt, and carefully pinned his silver eagles to the collar.

Now, before he went downstairs, he took a small olive-drab New Testament from the bureau top and opened it to where a small string marked his place. Some time ago he had set himself the task of memorizing one verse from the New Testament each morning, and by now he had become very skillful at quick memorizing. He was nearly finished with Revelations.

This morning he had reached the first verse in Chapter Nine, and he memorized:

And the fifth angel sounded, and I saw a star fall from heaven unto the earth: and to him was given the key of the bottomless pit.

He liked this morning's verse. He liked it particularly. He liked the picture of a star falling from heaven unto the earth, and the bottomless pit seemed a very satisfactory fate for all the godless.

He tucked his tie into his shirt front and went downstairs.

Saburo had orange juice, dry toast and one cup of black coffee ready in the breakfast nook. Straker ate slowly, scarcely looking at his food. Funny, how everything fell into place now that he had the key idea. Last night he'd missed the salient point: that the 66th Fighter-Bomber

2

Wing led every other outfit in the number of enemy troops directly killed by air action. But this morning it was so clear, he wondered how he had ever overlooked it.

When he had finished breakfast, Colonel Straker went into the living room and checked his wrist watch against the electric clock. 0715 hours—right on the nose. Saburo opened the front door for him and handed him his senior officer's hat, with the silver clouds and lightning bolts on the visor.

He said, "Thank you, Saburo," and Saburo bowed and shut the door behind him.

He swung off down the housing area street toward headquarters, which was near the edge of the airstrip, three-quarters of a mile away. His predecessor, Colonel Vann, had driven every morning in a staff car, but Straker preferred both the exercise and the mild inconvenience.

The May sun was warm upon his cheek and forehead.

At 0718 hours—still on schedule—the colonel passed Major Ronsdale's cottage; he turned his head and saw Ronsdale at the door, just coming out. Good man, Ronsdale: he evidently thought enough of his job to be punctual all the time. Of course, after only three weeks you couldn't know all there was to know about a man, but Ronsdale had certainly made a better impression than most of them. *Looked* like an officer. Might be wise to groom him for better things—take him out of Wing ops and give him a squadron command to start him off. Later, when he was a general officer, Straker could call upon somebody like Ronsdale, and Ronsdale presumably would remember who gave him his first command, and be grateful. You had to look ahead: pick your men early. And, if things worked out, it was just possible that Straker would earn that first star right here in Japan, with the 66th . . . and the idea he'd had this morning might very well be the beginning. Brigadier General William A. Straker—he liked the full, rolling sound of it.

Meanwhile, as he waited, Major Ronsdale was pausing to kiss his wife. Straker could see Esther Ronsdale behind the major's tall frame, and he could see that she wore a kimono, wore it loosely, and, he was rather sure, wore nothing under it.

3

Straker frowned. He wasn't so sure about Esther Ronsdale. He'd watched her desultorily about the base in the past three weeks; he'd small-chatted with her a few times at the Officers' Club, and she had struck him as perhaps a mite talkative, and noisy in her talk. Not quite settled with herself, that was it. He'd also noted that although Esther Ronsdale was slightly plump, she was basically a very pretty woman. And spoiled her prettiness with a little too much make-up. Wife like that could possibly be a handicap to an officer trying to get ahead—

Harriet, thank God, had always been a credit.

Harriet.

He began to wish again that Harriet were alive, and here at Akuni with him. What a help she would be! He remembered her so clearly: Harriet, thin and clean, and always reserved, and never ruffled, and it was she, in fact, who had been largely responsible for his full colonelcy back in the Pentagon. She had made the real impression. She knew always exactly how to dress and what to say: she was invariably at ease, whether at church, on the golf links, at a cocktail party, or formal dinner.

He remembered how fine she had looked sitting in the front pew when he had talked from the pulpit. That had been her idea, too: his becoming a reader for the small Protestant mission in Virginia that had no regular minister. She had sensed that he needed something like that.

And Harriet had died in pain, God bless her, and the way she bore it when they had taken out her insides, and even the morphine didn't do much good any more, the way she kept her face thin and drawn, and without a trace of expression, the way she smiled—a half-smile, really—when he kissed her lightly upon the forehead: oh, God bless her; God keep her fine, clean soul.

Esther Ronsdale slipped away from her husband as Straker watched, and Straker saw some of her thigh, where the kimono skirt slipped away, just before the door closed. His cheeks became warm. He fought that, trying to control it, and only became redder and angrier when he could not.

Ronsdale came down the walk and saluted. No sign that he noticed Straker's flush. "Good morning, sir." He placed himself on Straker's left and fell into step.

4

A handsome devil, Straker thought, glancing at him; probably darned attractive to women. He had a clipped mustache and the perfect chiseled lip for it. He had glossy dark hair and light gray eyes.

Straker cleared his throat and said, "I went over our effectiveness reports pretty carefully last night."

"Yes, sir?"

"The 66th has done mighty well in its close support work."

"They're good boys, Colonel. You won't find a better bunch of boys."

Straker smiled. "I should imagine any hundred pilots taken at random would be potentially a good bunch of boys, as you put it. No, Ronsdale, there's another reason for it. Largely the staff work—largely your end of it, in ops. You've done a good job."

"Thank you."

"But the outstanding fact is this: the 66th seems to be particularly good at hitting troops. It's done more damage in that respect than any other wing in the theater."

"Well—we've been concentrating on accurate napalm bombing," said Ronsdale. "The boys've been getting pretty sharp at it."

"Yes. Concentration." Straker nodded. "That's the secret. And I see no reason why we can't use concentration on the over-all picture."

"Sir?"

Straker rubbed his hands. "Let's imagine a man who is going out to hunt," he said. He enjoyed making little allegories. He'd always worked rather good ones into his sermons back at the mission. "If this man is after a large, fast-moving target, such as a flushed bird, he'll use a shotgun. He'll waste ammunition to be sure some reaches its mark."

"Yes, sir," said Ronsdale—a little guardedly, Straker thought.

"Now, if he's after small game like rabbit or squirrel, he'll use a twenty-two. No waste there, especially if he's confident of his own marksmanship. You follow me?"

"Well, yes—"

"On the other hand he may be hunting elk or bighorn. That calls for a heavier slug, with a high muzzle velocity.

5

In other words, a different weapon for each purpose. The most efficient weapon for the job at hand."

"I see." Ronsdale managed a noncommittal tone.

"Now, then, we have several kinds of targets in Korea—vehicles, buildings, rail lines, bunkers and so forth. Every day several of these are attacked. And the Joint Operations Center calls in the nearest air element when it has a target'—without regard to the special efficiency of that particular air weapon."

A flight of four F-80s passed overhead, blistering the air, and both men lifted their heads to watch as the planes made their breakaway at a thousand feet, one after the other. They were presently strung out, in single file, in the landing pattern. Numbers two and three were slightly lower than the rest.

"Pretty sloppy on altitude," said the colonel. Precision in flying had always come easily to Bill Straker, even in the first days of primary school, and he could never quite understand the lack of it in other pilots.

Ronsdale said, "That's Kingsley's flight, sir. They had a pre-brief mission before dawn, and they didn't get back from their JOC alert last night until almost dark. I imagine they're pretty tired."

"That's just when a man ought to tighten up a little more—when he has a handicap," said the colonel. Then he took his eyes from the airplanes. "But to get back to this idea of concentration. Just what is the 66th Wing best adapted to?"

"What's that, sir?"

"What do we—as an air weapon—do best?"

"Well, as you said, we hit troops pretty effectively."

"Right." Straker nodded. "Then why not use the 66th for that, where feasible?"

"Just how do you mean, Colonel?"

"Look. We have several targets on a particular morning, all waiting to be hit. One's a truck convoy, one's an artillery position, and one's a troop concentration. JOC looks on its plotting board and sees several fighter-bomber flights in the area, and calls in the nearest one to the target. Perhaps the planes from the 66th draw the truck convoy. They destroy it, of course, but any of the other air elements

6

might have destroyed it just as well. That other element, meanwhile, is directed to the troops—and does perhaps seventy-five or eighty percent of the damage the 66th would do. Do you see what I'm getting at?"

"Why, yes," said Ronsdale. "Why—yes."

"How's it strike you?"

"It's good, Colonel. Simple and logical." He laughed. "Maybe that's why nobody thought of it before."

Straker laughed, too. Ronsdale had another talent—he could deliver a compliment, and make it sound sincere. Doubtless, he actually was sincere, but even so he spoke with poise and restraint. Straker turned his head. For the first time he addressed the major by his first name. "Pete," he said, "how would you like to have a tactical command?"

"A command?"

"You've always been on staff work, haven't you?"

"Well, yes, sir. I didn't have a chance to fly any missions last time—though I kept asking for it. I know you got in a good fifty-three yourself, sir."

"I know how you feel about it, Pete. A good staff officer, of course, is a mighty valuable man, but for the sake of your career you should show some tactical command on your record. How would you like to take over the 109th Squadron?"

"Why—naturally, I'd like it very much," said Ronsdale.

"All right." Straker liked to make quick, positive decisions. "It's yours. You can start the paper work this morning."

"Well, thank you, sir. Thank you very much—"

"Don't thank me. It's not supposed to be a favor. Anything I do, Ronsdale, you can be sure is for the best interests of the Wing. And I think this move is." Then he smiled, and added, "You'll get a crack at a few missions now."

"Nothing I want more, sir."

It struck the colonel that Ronsdale said that last a little too quickly and eagerly. But that, of course, might have been a false impression. He said, "I want you to take over as soon as possible. You'll have plenty of desk work at first, cleaning up Czernak's administrative mess." Lieutenant Colonel Czernak had been the 109th's commander, and of the three tactical squadrons, the 109th had shown the least combat effectiveness.

"I was thinking about that, sir," said Ronsdale. "It'd be June before I could get away to fly—and I haven't got my flying time in for this month yet. I had a C-47 set up to take to Tokyo this afternoon. The regular base flight."

"Well, all right. Get your time in, then. Start with the squadron as soon as you get back."

"Then there's one other little thing," said Ronsdale.

"What?"

"It's this Wing party tonight. The Wing-Ding."

"Oh, that," said Straker.

Ronsdale cleared his throat. "I don't particularly want to go to the damn thing, but Esther does."

"Mrs. Ronsdale?"

"Well, you know how it is. She's been looking forward to this party ever since they started talking about it. Been on the committee and everything. I mean, after all, Essie is used to a lot more than she's been getting over here in Japan the last eighteen months. Not that she complains or anything—she's a mighty good sport about it."

Straker heard, but didn't entirely absorb what Ronsdale was saying. These domestic troubles irritated him, for some reason. Always. Perhaps because they reminded him of Harriet, and it was less painful not to start thinking about Harriet again. He kept his eyes straight ahead and began to develop new plans for the Wing. First he'd have to entice some correspondents from Tokyo to Akuni. Captain Gorgas, his public information officer, could think of ways to do that. Gorgas had worked in a Chicago advertising agency—he was another of these disgruntled reservists called to active duty—and if he would only discipline himself and operate at peak efficiency he would probably be a pretty good man. Perhaps he could think up a nickname for the 66th. The Red Killers, or something like that. Something to catch everybody's notice. Then plug the thing. Colonel William A. Straker's Red Killers scored again today as they struck at troops on the central front. Make high brass sit up and take notice. . . .

Ronsdale was saying, "Tonight's flight was the only one I could get. They've got a pretty busy schedule taking care

8

of flying time for all the staff officers. Well, Essie was pretty unhappy when I told her—naturally, she doesn't want to go to this party all alone. So I thought, well, if you didn't have any other plans—"

"What's this? What's this, now?" Straker came out of his reverie.

"Well, I thought you might do me a big favor and take Essie to the Wing-Ding tonight. Just so she doesn't feel alone."

Straker frowned. "I'd only planned to go early—make an appearance."

"Well, in that case, sir—"

"No, no. It's all right. I'd be delighted to take Mrs. Ronsdale. You make the arrangements, will you, and let me know what time to call?"

"I don't know how to thank you, Colonel. This means an awful lot to her—"

"Forget it, Pete," said Straker.

Yes, it was a fine morning, and the colonel was altogether pleased with himself. He felt a strong sense of things beginning, seed coming to fruition, buds breaking forth.

"Looks like a nice day," said Ronsdale, examining the sky.

"Yes," said Straker.

Turbine blades whistled as a flight of F-80s down on the line moved toward the runway for take-off.

2

One hundred miles east of Akuni a four-engined C-54 droned over the Sea of Japan, eastbound. In the waist there were some thirty passengers, men of all branches of the service, and of a number of ranks and grades. They sat along the canvas benches that ran lengthwise with the fuselage. Most of them were partitioned off by their own thoughts.

Captain Richard Tindle, United States Air Force, sat near the tail. He had picked this seat before take-off so that he would have a view of the ground unobstructed by the wing and the engines. He wanted very much to see the Korean coastline fade away, and later, the coast of Japan

9

come into view. This would be his first look at Japan in over sixty days.

A sixty-day nightmare, he thought, and nodded.

He twisted in the seat and looked earthward. Wads of cloud blew across the dark water. His cigarette burned down nearly to his knuckles, and he lit another from it.

You had so little to say about it all, he thought; *you couldn't even pick your own nightmare.*

A yawn caught him, and he let it run out, then stretched his legs into the aisle. He was dressed in grimy fatigues; he hadn't had a chance in the last two weeks to get his laundry done, and these fatigues, grimy as they were, were about the cleanest things he owned at the moment. He'd change as soon as he got to Akuni. There should be a clean uniform in his room in the barracks, if his roommate hadn't borrowed it. He wondered if he'd still have the same roommate. He wondered, altogether, how many of the old faces would be left in the 66th. Two months he'd been gone, and there on the ground he'd watched the F-80s that were struck by flak, and sometimes small-arms fire, clobber into the earth like falling stars. He would always wonder who was getting it. Sometimes word would reach him up there, but not often.

Tindle's neck became stiff and he turned away from the window. There were a couple of sleepy-looking infantrymen across the aisle; one of them, a dark, Italianate fellow, caught Tindle's eye and smiled, and Tindle smiled back. Maybe the guy knew. Maybe he could recognize someone who had been through the same thing on the ground: there on the crawling land with the burrowing creatures who were so different from the creatures of the sky. Maybe he knew from the grimy fatigues, or maybe just from a certain tiredness about the eyes.

And then again maybe the guy just smiled because, like everybody else, he was lonely.

Tindle had the space of two empty seats on either side of him. He arranged a parachute for a mattress, a Mae West life preserver for a pillow, and lay down, folding his long legs to make them fit. He clasped his hands behind his head and stared up at the fuselage. In an hour or so they'd land. Take him another half-hour, perhaps, to clear through

10

Base operations and scrounge wheels to the other side of the field where the 66th Wing roosted. Another half-hour in a good hot shower, and then a long, quiet drink. Somebody around the B.O.Q. would have a drink.

And after all that he'd make his courtesy call on this new colonel, Straker, whom he had never heard of before, and after that he'd look for a flight to Tokyo and take the seven days' leave that was his right reward for a two-month tour on the front lines as a forward air controller.

He might get out this very night if an odd Tokyo-bound flight came along. He could check with Base ops. If he made Tokyo tonight he could find a sack in one of the G.I. hotel billets there, and then he'd be all ready to shop in the Main PX, and along the Ginza in the morning. He'd almost forgotten what a busy street with traffic and people and sounds and smells could be. Good to see one again. He had to admit that now, even though a few years ago he'd fled from a busy city and sworn he never wanted to see one again.

Lord, that seemed long ago, that September, with the soft and faded summer still about, that he and Martha had struck for New Mexico. . . .

Funny that he hadn't missed Martha more in the last six months. Even without quite loving her the way he once had he should have missed her a little more. It would have been only decent to miss her a bit. (He smiled to himself as that idea came into his mind.) The truth was her letters, which she wrote so faithfully every two days, had begun to bore Tindle; he had only read them closely up there on the front line because there wasn't much else to read.

It was hard to say precisely why things weren't the same between him and Martha. You could not pin down any one cause. The money problem may have been the main cause; on the other hand perhaps their financial difficulty was only the main irritant to a wound already begun.

There were times when he believed that he might have surmounted that financial barrier without volunteering to return to active duty with the Air Force. In such moments he tried very hard to find the truth of the thing. Why, actually, had he come back into uniform? Why, honestly? Well—perhaps he remembered that once upon a time he

11

had not been such a failure. Such a dud. Once upon a time he had been fêted and praised and called a hero, and never worried about the budget's ability to withstand real butter or sirloin steak. Perhaps he forgot the hell of the missions he flew in the big war, and remembered only how easy and agreeable everything was later, when he did administrative work. Perhaps he really wanted to re-create all the conditions of those happy times. Yes . . . he must be honest . . . much of the difference between him and Martha stemmed from his own belly, not hers. He must be honest about it.

So Captain Richard Tindle closed his eyes and listened to the engines. Thrum, steady thrum; fine, throaty and in phase. He may have slept; he wasn't sure. He may have dreamt. He saw images, but they were true images out of the past, not composite, not fantasy. Perhaps it was all somewhere between a memory and a dream. At any rate, he saw and heard clearly—as he had then—

3

He was standing by the jeep and he had a T-17 mike in his hand. They had pulled off the road into the cover of some scrub trees.

Noonan whispered. Noonan was the infantry officer who was his partner. "I don't know, Dick, I don't know," said Noonan. "If the bastards hear us—"

"Your idea, buddy, getting this close." Tindle whispered, too.

"Yeah, yeah, I know. But we had to see, didn't we?"

They were on the north side of a hill. They had come over the top an hour before. Not much more than a hundred yards away, when they looked through the trees, they could see the Chinese in their shapeless sand-colored uniforms. Most of them sat in a scattered oval, in the center of which about a half-dozen worked on the broken wheel of a howitzer. There were about sixty of them.

"All that friggin' platoon leader said was there was a fieldpiece over here," whispered Noonan. "He didn't say anything about sixty gooks."

"Maybe they weren't there when he looked."

"For Christ's sake, keep your voice down!"

One of the Chinese had sprung to his feet; he stood

12

there with his thin rifle ported across his chest, and he looked around, swinging his eyes in a slow, wary azimuth.

"He can't hear me," said Tindle. "What makes you so goddamned jumpy?" And Tindle knew perfectly well, of course, that he was jumpy himself, snapping back at Noonan like that. Only he'd been with Noonan nearly twenty-four hours now, scarcely speaking to anyone else, and that was plenty of a guy like Noonan. Back at the Division C.P., where they based themselves between strike calls, he at least had his pick of a few others to talk to. This time somebody had gotten the wild hair idea that they ought to go out and work from the battalions, especially in this sector where there wasn't much artillery cover. And then for another thing Tindle was hungry. They'd killed their C-ration for breakfast, Noonan cooking the canned pork and vegetables in empty cans bent around the edges to support the full cans, and filled with gasoline from the jeep, which he lighted. Tindle, knowing very well he might miss lunch, had tried to eat plenty. But he never could stomach the cloying, overrich stuff in C-ration.

Driving instead of walking here hadn't helped much: he was still tired. They'd had to drive cautiously all the way, without raising a feather of dust that might draw enemy artillery fire from over the next ridge. Several times they'd sought temporary cover behind native huts while Noonan scouted ahead. In one of the huts a woman had offered Tindle kimchi, but he'd burned his throat raw on that stuff before. He'd pretended to the woman that he wasn't hungry.

So now he was hungry, and tired, and jumpy, and altogether low. He scowled.

"Who's jumpy?" asked Noonan.

"You."

"If you'd had it like an infantry soldier you'd be jumpy too," said Noonan darkly. He kept his eyes on the Chinese. There was a long silence. Finally he said, "Well, what do we do?"

"You decide," said Tindle. "You're the commando around here."

Noonan spat. He chewed tobacco all the time in the field. Some people could chew tobacco, reflected Tindle, and it wouldn't bother you, but Noonan had a round pink face and eyes that always became red in the dust or from drinking, and he didn't look a day over twenty years old sometimes, but he always chewed tobacco more indecently, somehow, than anyone Tindle had ever seen. Little thing. Silly thing. Little, silly things bothered you up here. Noonan said, "You want to take a chance? Okay—go ahead. Call your airplanes in. I'll watch the gooks. The minute they show signs of hearing us we'll take plan How Able."

"Plan what?"

"How Able—haul ass, brother. And fast. I'll cover ten seconds, pass you, and you cover me. And on foot, because we'd never get the jeep back to the road on time."

"Maybe we can get further away for our observation."

"Look, stupid, we'd have to go back over the hill. Then we wouldn't be able to see them at all. Use your head."

"All right, all right," said Tindle.

"Don't forget what I told you about covering each other when we bug out."

"I heard you the first and the twentieth time," said Tindle. They'd worked it all out before. Or Noonan had. Whenever it was quiet Noonan had made plans for various things that might happen. Once Tindle told Noonan he worried an awful goddamn lot for a guy who was a veteran combat infantryman, and Noonan had looked at him disgustedly and said, "I'm still alive, ain't I?" He'd had a point. Only the thing stuck in Tindle's mind because it was another case of something turning out differently than he'd expected. He'd thought a typical ground pounder would be a cool, fearless Daniel Boone kind of character, and Noonan had fooled him. And then another thing that had fooled him—and even disappointed him a little —was the way the front looked when he saw it for the first time. It wasn't a front at all. It wasn't a neat, handy line like on the maps in newspapers and news magazines. It was just a big quiet area stretching for six or seven miles; open fields and bare mountains, smoke coming away from semi-distant slopes and crests, and a yellow road winding through a valley. Nobody in sight. Because, as he learned later, nobody wanted to be in sight. And that first day at the front, that first sunny day when he came upon it and

14

stared at it, there was a goddamned bird singing some-where.

Tindle pressed the hard rubber button on the side of the mike. He spoke very softly. "Hello Black Beauty, Hello Black Beauty—this is Lucifer Item."

The answer came after a moment. For an instant, as the voice of the rear controller sounded in his headsets, Tindle had the wild fear that he had left the little boxlike speaker on the windshield post switched in. He whirled and glanced at it, and then was loose-kneed with relief when he saw that it was off. The tinny voice said, "*Beauty here, Lucifer Item. Go ahead.*"

"Here's my position," whispered Tindle. "Baker Tare seven-seven-six-three-zero-four."

"*Say again, Lucifer Item. A little louder. You're coming in about R-3.*"

"Can not do. Repeat not—negative. Too near target."

"*Er—understand. Where's your target?*"

"In my lap, buddy," said Tindle. "One old maid and sixty jokers."

"*Roger. Understand. One old maid and sixteen jokers.*"

"Sixty, for Christ's sake. Six Zero," said Tindle. Damn, he was jumpy.

"*Roger. Six Zero. I have a flight of four Fox eighties near there on road reccy. I'll divert immediately.*"

"Divert damn quick immediately, will you, old buddy?" said Tindle. "I don't like it here without help." He glanced at Noonan. "Air help."

"*Roger, Lucifer, will do.*" The controller sounded bored.

Noonan, still staring toward the Chinese, said, "The sons of bitches must be deaf they didn't hear you. Do you have to shout like that?"

Tindle, who had one earphone on his temple instead of his ear, heard Noonan and said, "You want airplanes, don't you?"

"Ah, frig it," said Noonan.

Tindle laughed, not pleasantly. He heard a faint signal and he put his hands to his head and slipped the second earphone into place. He held the earphones tight. Someone was saying, "*Hello, Lucifer Item, this is Cuckoo Tare Able. Do you read me?*"

15

"Roger, roger—I read you about three square!" Tindle's voice rose in his excitement. Noonan whirled toward him, finger to lips, eyes wide and sharp.

The headsets said, "*Do you have a mosquito, Lucifer Item?*"

"Pinky Four's own mosquito," said Tindle. "He should be on this frequency."

"*Pinky Four here,*" said another voice. English accent. One of the South Afs, probably. "*Been eavesdropping on you chaps all the time. Can't get rid of me, you know.*"

"Okay, Pinky Four," said Tindle, a smile in his voice. "Do you have our coordinates?"

"*Yes. Know the place quite well. Just east of that three-peaked mountain, isn't it? Right near the cricket grounds.*"

"Near the what?"

"*The Kimchi cricket grounds. Chorwon Public took a frightful drubbing there from Pyongyang Technical Institute last week. Surely you remember.*"

"All right," said Tindle. "I'm slow on the uptake. But you'd better be fast on the arrival. Try to come over our position on a heading of three-nine."

"*I'm only a few miles from you now. Cheers and over.*"

Tindle slipped the right earphone off again. Noonan said, "You guys talk more like a couple of old women."

"Relax, Noonan. For Christ's sake, relax."

"Relax around here and you've had it," muttered Noonan. He moved a branch of the scrub oak for a better view of the Chinese just down the slope.

A few minutes later they heard the saucy snarl of a T-6 engine.

Noonan said, "What's that?"

"The T-6," said Tindle. "Can't you tell 'em by the sound yet?"

"It makes an awful lot of goddamn noise for a training plane."

"So it does," said Tindle. "So what?"

Noonan didn't answer.

A new voice in the headsets said, "*Bogie—ten o'clock low.*"

"*Little friend, little friend,*" said someone else. Then:

"Cuckoo Tare Able here—four Fox eighties. Is that you we have in sight, Pinky Four?"

"Roger," said Pinky Four.

The Chinese had heard the T-6. They skittered, each in different direction, and several seconds later most of them had disappeared. They were part of the hillside.

The T-6 with its round, belligerent nose and stubby wings came in over the shoulder of the slope, across Tindle's line of vision. Loud—loud and nasty. Tindle saw the shape of two helmets under its long greenhouse canopy. Lucky bastards, flying. He laughed. He was remembering how he'd been glad to start this tour as a forward air controller, thinking it would be a vacation. Sixty days, he had thought, seeing something new, doing something different, and then back to finish his allotted hundred missions—

But now he wasn't sure that he would ever be able to make himself fly another combat mission.

He'd never be able to explain why: at least not to the people who would expect an explanation. Martha might have understood. But he didn't have Martha, now; he didn't have anybody but himself. Well, they'd want him to fly combat again when he returned, and they would order him to do it. He would have to try. He would have to risk letting them see him fail. He hated thinking about the moment when they'd want an explanation he wouldn't be able to give, though.

Tindle ticked the mike button and said, "You're over the target now, Pinky four."

"Got it. Got the old maid in sight," Pinky Four answered.

Noonan looked inquisitive.

"He sees the fieldpiece," explained Tindle. "We better get out now."

In the earphones: "Pinky Four, this is Cuckoo Leader. Make a pass with your smoke rockets, will you?"

"Roger, roger."

Tindle removed the headsets and picked up his carbine.

The mosquito plane banked away from the hillside and rose, clawing at the sky with one wing. It moved out of sight for a moment, and its snarl faded, and then Tindle heard the waterfall roar of the jets coming in.

17

Noonan was still squinting at the fieldpiece.

"Let's go." Tindle tugged at his sleeve. "He's going to throw a rocket. It won't be so damned accurate it might not hit us."

"Okay," said Noonan. He moved reluctantly. "I wish I could watch the bastards get it."

They crouched and started off at a trot. Tindle's navy binoculars in their leather case bounced back and forth over his chest. They ran upslope and diagonally to the right. Shots broke out behind them. A bullet struck a few feet from Tindle and lobbed off in a screaming ricochet. Tindle flinched, swallowed, and kept running. His legs were rubbery.

"Down!" yelled Noonan.

Hit dirt.

Tindle squirmed after he was down, so that he could look toward the fieldpiece again. Funny, from this further point, he could see the hidden men more clearly. He saw the T-6 diving in shallowly, and then the rockets began to fall away, stretching two lines of white yarn in the air. When they struck, creamy smoke bellowed upward. A Chinese came out of the smoke, running and screaming.

"The bastard," said Noonan.

The jets suddenly appeared over the far ridge, the long blue flint edge across the valley. They came in single file, twisting and squirming. They were tiny at first, but they grew swiftly.

The first one showed some of its belly in pulling away, and then Tindle caught the movement below it, and saw the clumsy maroon eggs, the napalm tanks, lobbing end over end toward the slope. They struck, and there was a sound like the tearing of silk amplified a thousand times. He felt the sudden heat; the quick orange glow hurt his eyes. He smelled the heat. He breathed with difficulty, because the air was suddenly scorched and thin. A great spreading blob of fire grew where the napalm tanks had struck, and black smoke peeled like citrus rind from the surface of this solid fire. A huge cloud rolled upward, a cloud with a big clublike knob on its top.

The napalm tanks struck perhaps a hundred feet to the right of the Chinese. In his binoculars, Tindle saw a num-

18

ber of them rise and gasp, and some of those nearer the flaming protoplasm squirmed and fell, clothes and flesh afire.

The next two tanks, one yellow, and one maroon, dropped some distance down the slope. The third and fourth were direct hits on the fieldpiece. Chinese broke from cover and began to run. Everywhere, anywhere. Most were screaming, but there was also now and then the deep, hoarse, sobbing utterance of pain completely unbearable.

"Oh, Jesus, oh, God," said Tindle. The lining of his mouth was dry.

Black smoke kept rising, unraveling in the wind.

The jets came in again toward the black smoke.

High explosive rockets. They flashed brightly when they struck. The sound numbed Tindle's eardrums. He could smell the oily smell of the napalm, and the sharp salty smell of the explosive. Jets number three and four laid their rockets directly on the fieldpiece, knocking it over.

Tindle heard a sharp crack right beside him, and then he saw a running Chinese soldier far down the slope fall suddenly as though he had merely stumbled.

Noonan grinned and lowered his carbine.

Tindle swung his glasses back toward the crippled fieldpiece. Near it, now, a fat Chinese was sitting on the ground and staring at his intestines, which were extruded, like red toothpaste, from a great hole in his belly.

Once more the jets came in, at first straight and level, then rolling suddenly, curving down upon the hill, completing the maneuver called the split-S. The machine-gun fire from six guns was incredibly loud as each one passed. Brick wall explosion. The hillside shook. A Chinese began to run, and some of the slugs caught him and thoroughly cut him in half. His chest and head fell one way, his legs and belly the other. Blood sprayed.

The F-80s came in strafing twice more. The air was so full of the smell of powder now that Tindle's nostrils smarted. Then the jets turned off and climbed away. The mosquito came back and swung over the scene, banking vertically to observe the damage.

Finally, when the T-6 had gone it was suddenly, unbelievably quiet.

"Don't get up yet," said Noonan.

Noonan was using his own binoculars. He swung them carefully and took his time doing it. Tindle wanted to laugh—or maybe cry—but he held himself in. He wanted to throw a rock at Noonan and curse him.

Noonan finally said, "Okay," and rose slowly.

It was midday now, and the sun overhead was perversely hot for early May. The smoke from the hillside petered off into a blue and humid sky.

They walked back to the jeep. "Look at it," said Noonan. The paint on the hood was blistered from the heat of the napalm. "Look at the son of a bitch."

Tindle checked the radio while Noonan stood guard. He tied in the speaker this time. ". . . this is Black Beauty," the speaker was saying, "Hello, Lucifer Item, this is Black Beauty. . . ."

"Lucifer here," said Tindle wearily. "We had to beat it. Too close. Good show. Scratch one old maid and sixty jokers."

"Roger, roger. Understand. Congratulations. Nice going."

"Tell the bastard to go frig himself," said Noonan. He made a prissy face and mocked the controller's voice: "Congratulations! Nice going!"

Tindle said into the mike, "We're going back to the C.P. now. Lucifer Item out."

"Beauty out."

They started the jeep, and by jockeying it back and forth several times, and cutting in the front-wheel drive, they managed to turn it. She ground upslope in first gear. She moved thirty or forty feet and Noonan touched Tindle's arm and said, "Hold it."

Noonan was looking at the crest of the hill. Tindle looked. It took Tindle a moment to see the tiny, insectile silhouettes up there. He said, "Okay. What do we do?"

"Get scarce," said Noonan. He got out of the jeep, crouched, and moved back into the scattered scrub. He found a place and sat down and Tindle dropped beside him. Noonan kept twisting and using his binoculars. He looked for a long time down into the floor of the valley.

"For Christ's sake, what?" Tindle finally said.

20

"Gook patrol," said Noonan. "Along the riverbed. We better sit tight."

"Okay," said Tindle.

Minutes, minutes, hours, aching in the legs and coccyx, and more shifting. The sun, midsky, still hot, still yellow. Noonan always twisting peering—he hadn't spoken yet.

"Any chow left?" asked Tindle.

"Three candy bars."

"Oh, Christ."

"What's eating you, fly-boy?"

"I hate candy." He didn't. He just hated the prospect of spending more time with Noonan. It looked like all night; he could tell from the compressed ridge of fat just above Noonan's eyes that it would be a long time.

"You don't have to eat it then," said Noonan.

Later he did eat it. That was when it was dark, and Noonan, without making any guesses about the length of their stay, broke the first candy bar in half and gave Tindle one piece.

They split two-hour watches during the night. It was a quiet night, except for the tree frogs in the valley. Several times they heard distant artillery fire, and once during his watch Tindle saw pink flashes far into the east on overhanging clouds. He checked the seconds until he heard the sound, and then amused himself working out the distance of the flashes, using the rough figure of eleven hundred feet per second as the speed of sound. The firing was twelve miles away. In the morning there was a chiffon drizzle. They ate the second candy bar, and then Noonan took his binoculars out and used them.

After a while Tindle said, "See anything?"

Noonan was looking toward the crest of the hill. "The bastards are still camped there."

"I wonder where our battalion is."

"Why the hell don't you ask your buddy on the radio? He's supposed to know everything."

"He doesn't know. He'd have to go all the way back to JOC to find out. And JOC takes the dim view of little requests like that." Tindle got up. "The lazy bastards. I I think I'll contact Beauty anyway."

He snapped on the master switch and waited for the filaments to heat, and nothing happened.

"What's the matter?" Noonan stared at him coldly.

"I don't know." He started to check. Halfway through the check he knew. He looked at Noonan, then pointed to the ignition switch. It had been on all night. He tried the starter and it wouldn't turn.

Noonan stared for a moment, then turned angrily upon Tindle. He glared. Tindle glared back. Noonan said, "I didn't leave the son of a bitch on."

Tindle shrugged.

"One of us must have bumped it with our knee or something," said Noonan.

"Sure," said Tindle.

The sun came up and it was hot again. You never knew exactly what the weather was going to be in May here. Their fatigues darkened with sweat. Noonan smelled like unwashed feet, and Tindle supposed that he did, too. They had another candy bar at midday. They heard airplanes in the next valley working something over, nose guns belching powerfully.

"You couldn't get me up in one of those bastards for a million bucks," said Noonan.

"Better than this. Better than crawling in the mud," said Tindle.

"Sure. It's the easy way. That's why you guys fly 'em."

"Maybe."

"No maybe about it. I've watched you johns on forward control. Okay, some of you have guts. But you aren't really made for this stuff. You're like a bunch of Boy Scouts in a whorehouse."

Tindle stretched himself. "Listen, Noonan, none of us begged to come out here and play hero with you. It was all some brass fathead's idea to have us call in a hundred thousand dollars' worth of airplanes to knock out four gooks on a hill holding up one of your whole goddamn battalions with a lousy machine gun." He didn't really mean it; he knew it sounded ridiculous as he said it. But he wasn't particularly sorry for saying it, either.

"Horse crap," said Noonan.

Tindle didn't answer. He moved off a bit, sat down,

22

and stared out over the valley. Noonan, in a way, was right. He wasn't fit for this duty. The fact was, he wasn't fit for much of anything except flying a combat airplane. He'd spent more time learning that, after all. And he had the feeling that he had never really properly learned another goddamn thing in all his twenty-one years of existence. So what kind of a life was that, where a man learned only one thing, and spent his whole time doing just that, doing nothing but getting better at that one thing? Here he was, a good pilot. A pretty damned good pilot, actually. He knew engines, he knew the magic of weather, he flew on instruments as though they were his own sharpened senses. And was that something, that he was a good pilot? No, it wasn't so much. Most people were awfully damned good at what they did these days. They spent their lives at their single, narrowed-down trades and businesses and professions and crafts, after all. The standard was high. You had to meet that standard just to be average.

Of course he'd once tried to be good at something else. That was probably the real beginning of the trouble between him and Martha. He'd always liked drawing and sketching and he'd been a showcard writer for a chain of drugstores when the war came along in 1941. He was just out of high school then. Then, four years later, a flying captain (at the age of twenty-three), he made three times as much and knew nothing else to do. Then he met and married Martha, and Lord knew, he tried. He tried to get flying jobs—airlines, first, where they simply laughed at him, and later small airports where they shook their heads and said they had all the instructors they needed. Then he tried to go back to showcard writing, but he'd lost his hand with a chisel-edge brush and Speedball pen, and the best offer he got was fifty a week. He took it. They tried, Lord knew, they tried to get along on it.

It was Martha who suggested the idea of studying painting. There was the GI Bill of Rights, she said, where he could get subsistence, and she could work, and actually between those two sources of income they wouldn't be much worse off than they were now. And he'd be making some kind of a career for himself. He had talent, didn't he? And he didn't have to be a long-haired starving painter;

commercial artists could afford whiskey and cigarettes, and even if he never became what you would call rich he would at least have a *direction*, and not be so restless. Martha could be very convincing and earnest once she started. It sounded like a wonderful idea at the time.

They went to New Mexico; to a little art colony in the mountains, and there Tindle enrolled in a GI-approved art school and began to draw and paint.

The instructor said encouraging things. Martha raved. But Tindle (and he realized this now that he looked back upon everything) knew all the time that he wasn't very good. He was perhaps just a little short of lousy. Maybe if, in his formative years, he had spent a little more love and time on the thing—but there was no use speculating about that. You could argue all night about just what talent was, and where it came from, without getting anywhere.

Then the Korean War came along and he filled out a form 125, which was how a reserve officer volunteered for active military service. Martha went back east with her family. Neither of them could work up much tragic emotion at the parting. Martha walked with him to the bus that night.

"Well, Dick, I guess it will be a long time," she said. She had a positive, unhesitant way of putting her words together, like a bright child, and by now Tindle was irritated by the mannerism.

"Maybe a year. Maybe a couple," he'd said.

"It'll give us time to make plans for a new start, anyway," she said.

"Sure," he said.

Then she cocked her head, another bright-child gesture of hers. "I've had the funny feeling in the past few days I may never see you again, Dick."

"It *could* happen—but I'm not expecting it." He grinned.

"No, I guess I'm not really expecting it, either. Not really."

"Everything'll be all right in time," he said. "Everything'll work out." He knew he sounded fatuous.

"Of course," she said.

He stared at her, and wondered how, several years ago,

24

he had ever loved her so. He was fond of her, yes; he would miss her, simply because you couldn't live with a person that long and then leave and not feel some kind of emotion. But even while he was thinking how much he hated to go, his desire to get into uniform, into a cockpit, was becoming stronger and stronger. For flying a military airplane was the only thing he'd really learned to do well; it was the only thing he could do as well as the next man. . . .

And now he had flown again. He had flown seventy-nine missions, and had seen war as a forward controller; he had seen the stinking mud and dust of war.

He must return and fly an additional twenty-one missions in a few days.

He must make himself do it, somehow, because he was caught in the whole thing, and there was no end to it. "You can't even pick your own nightmare," he said.

Noonan said, "What?"

Tindle looked up. "Hm?"

"You said something."

"Did I?"

"You surer'n hell did. For Christ's sake, now you're talking to yourself."

Tindle shrugged.

Noonan said, "How old are you, anyway, Tindle?"

"Twenty-nine."

"Christ, the same age as me and I'm only a first lieutenant. You guys in the Air Corps really have it fat."

Tindle said, "I've had enough of you, you bastard."

"What?"

"You heard me. Get up and fight." Tindle had risen.

Noonan looked surprised. "What do I want to fight for? You going apeshit?"

"Then lay off the cracks if you don't want to fight."

Instead of answering, Noonan sniffed the air. "It's started."

"What?" Tindle realized that he too had been sensing a vague stench for some minutes.

"The gooks. The dead ones. There's only one thing smells worse than a gook, and that's a *dead* gook lying in the sun."

25

By noon the next day they could scarcely breathe. It increased their thirst; they got dangerously near the bottom of their water container.

Noonan finally said, "Look, we can't go this much longer."

"Got any ideas?"

Noonan didn't have any ideas.

It darkened after twenty hundred hours and the cloud cover filled in. It was suddenly cold. The wind came through the valley with a low humming sound. "Okay," said Noonan, "maybe we can get past them in the dark."

They crossed the ridge, veering widely to avoid the encampment near the road. It seemed hours, but later, when they were well down the other slope Tindle looked at his watch and saw that they had done it in about forty minutes.

"They must've moved out when it got dark, too," said Noonan. He spat. "The bastards."

They spent the rest of the night at the foot of the hill, and the next morning they circled back to the road and walked toward the Command Post. On the road they passed a smoking shack in a nest of rice paddies. The earth around it was black from the burning of napalm; fifty caliber fire had crumbled one wall. There was a body near the shack, a woman in a billowy green dress and a white silk jacket. One-half of her head was blown away. The flies were black on the caked blood and they buzzed loudly. An infant with the glossy black brushstroke hair of oriental children sat there and played with the dead woman's hand. . . .

Humming in Tindle's ears. His head rocked. He seemed to look at the world through a film of oil. He laughed, sobbed, screamed, not quite knowing why. Somebody slapped his face and then shook him, and he didn't care; then the sound of his laughing and sobbing seemed to float away.

"You okay, Captain?" It was the swarthy GI who had been sitting across from him in the transport plane. Some of the other passengers stared fearfully.

Tindle said, "Thanks, buddy. I'll be all right."

26

"I get dreams like that myself sometimes," said the soldier.

"I know, I know," said Tindle.

4

Now, after two months, he stood again before the low building that housed the 66th Fighter-Bomber Wing's headquarters. He was in clean, starched khakis. He was surprised that the bright sun on his cheek was not unbearably warm, and then he remembered that sometimes at Akuni the well-mannered breeze came in from the Sea of Japan. He looked up, following the twin flagstaffs, and saw the flag of the United States, and the blue flag of the United Nations. The sounds of jet engines came from the flight line, only a few hundred feet away. They sounded cheerful over here: in some fashion they didn't sound as choleric as they did in Korea. He looked at the headquarters building again. It had recently been painted white. It was so clean here; everything was so naïvely bright and clean.

Two sergeants, young lads with undergraduate looks, came out of the front door, smiled, saluted, and one said, "Good morning, sir," in a well-modulated voice.

Tindle saluted back in a perfunctory way and then wondered if he had appeared surly. He was still tired, if that was any excuse. Even after a hot shower and a drink and a change of clothes he was tired. He yawned and went into the building. A full-length mirror stood just inside the door, and a sign over it said:

IS THIS A NEAT AIRMAN?

Tindle saw that he was thinner and browner than he remembered himself. His eyes seemed more sunken.

He walked the corridors, found Colonel Straker's office, and went into the anteroom. The exec, Colonel Worrel, was a chubby man with fair skin and baby-pursed lips, and he got up when he saw Tindle and said, "Well, well, look who's here! Glad to see you back, Captain!" Colonel Worrel had already outlasted two wing commanders in the 66th. He was one of those neither outstanding nor unsatisfactory people that commanders seemed to like to have around. Tindle always felt that he must have only a few

27

years to retirement, and was just killing time in the meanwhile. At the moment he seemed faintly ashamed to be glad about anything.

"How are you, sir," said Tindle without enthusiasm, and shook hands.

Worrel said, "Well, the old man's expecting you." He jerked his thumb toward the wing commander's office. "He's got Andrews, of stat control, in there now. I'll buzz him."

"I'll wait," said Tindle, but Worrel had already buzzed.

A strong, even voice, somewhat high-pitched, said, "What is it, John?"

"Captain Tindle, back from forward control, Colonel."

"Oh yes. Tindle. Send him in by all means, please."

It was the same office that Tindle remembered from Colonel Vann's regime. Straker hadn't even bothered to change the desks around. Major Andrews of stat control was in front of Straker's desk, and he turned and stared at Tindle rather blankly. Andrews was a stocky man with thick glasses that hid his eyes. Tindle had the idea he used the glasses as camouflage for his thoughts. Tindle nodded hello, and Andrews nodded back.

Tindle looked at the colonel. Tall, spare man; extraordinarily white skin and chilled eyes. He said, "I'm Tindle, sir. I—"

"Be with you in a minute, Tindle. Let me finish with Andrews here." Straker said this politely enough, but managed to work into his voice a faint tone of rebuke.

Tindle nodded and sat down across the room.

"All right, Major," the colonel said to Andrews. "I just want to be sure you understand everything now."

"I understand, sir." Andrews' voice was dry with nervousness. "A chart showing enemy troops killed per sortie-hour. I'll have it started tomorrow."

"Started?"

"Well—"

"Better have it finished by ten o'clock tomorrow morning, Andrews. I'm sure you can get it done."

"Yes, sir, I'll take care of it."

"Good, Andrews. I like to see a man do a job quickly." Straker's sarcasm was just barely apparent, like the first

28

clear ice on the leading edge of a wing. Andrews saluted clumsily and moved off.

So he likes to bully people, this fine new colonel, thought Tindle.

Straker turned to Tindle immediately, as Andrews left. "Well, how are you, Captain Tindle?" His sudden warmth was disconcerting. He rose, held his hand across the desk, and Tindle took it and found it hard and strong.

Tindle said, "I'm fine, sir."

"Just got back, eh?"

"Yes. A couple of hours ago."

"Fine, fine." Straker began picking at his desk blotter with a letter opener shaped like a propeller. "Sit down, Tindle. We'll have a visit. I haven't had a chance to speak to anyone just back from forward control. I wanted to make a tour of our controllers and see it firsthand, but they wouldn't clear that upstairs." He laughed. "You know how high brass is."

Tindle ignored the cheap attempt at being democratic. He sat down in the chair near the desk and took out his cigarettes. He saw the colonel frown a little, but he lit one anyway.

"Major Ronsdale tells me you're one of our best combat pilots," said Straker.

"Pete Ronsdale's prejudiced. We went to flying school together. I was his best man when he married Mrs. Ronsdale on graduation day."

"I see," said the colonel. He put the letter opener down and folded his hands. "You're assigned to the 109th, aren't you, Tindle?"

"Yes, sir."

"You'll be interested to know Major Ronsdale's taking over command there."

"Pete?" Tindle raised his eyebrows. He hesitated, then said, "Why, that's fine." He wondered if his enthusiasm didn't sound a little forced. It was, as a matter of fact, quite a bit forced. Not that he didn't like Pete, and not that he wasn't glad to see the boy go places—but Pete as a commander, well—

"Think you'll be able to work under Ronsdale all right?" Straker had a sharp way of looking at him. Quizzical, and still faintly sarcastic, as he had been with Andrews.

"Don't see why not," said Tindle.

"Good. I'm expecting some pretty impressive stuff from the Wing from now on. You boys are going to be working hard—a lot harder than before. Now, tell me, Tindle, what's your general impression of our effectiveness in combat?"

"Well," said Tindle, "I guess we're pretty effective. When we hit. When we find a target worth hitting."

"What do you mean by that?"

"Well, it seems a little wasteful to call in four expensive airplanes, and risk the necks of four expensively trained pilots, just to throw a lot of costly ammunition at a couple of Chinese schoolboys on a mountain trail."

"Captain," said Straker, managing somehow to make his smile demonstrative, "we have well-qualified people to decide whether or not the expense of killing enemy troops is worth it. If it takes air power to do the job, we'll use air power."

"I've seen jobs artillery could have done just as well. Of course, I'll admit they don't always have the artillery available."

"You've been talking to those ground warfare enthusiasts, I see," said the colonel, half-chuckling as though he were making a joke, but by the look of his eyes not really joking at all.

"Didn't know it was against the rules."

"It isn't. It's just a little foolish to let yourself be carried away by their jealous complaints, Tindle. Ever since we got this separate Air Force—"

"Well, you asked for my opinion on the thing, Colonel, and I gave it to you."

"Of course. So you did. Don't ever hesitate to speak what's in your mind—I like that in a man." His eyes still didn't like it. He cleared his throat. "But what about technique, Tindle? How would you say one of these four-plane air strikes compares with a battery of artillery on the same target?"

"Depends on the target. When it comes to troops our napalm can't be beat. I've—I've watched it hit at close range. Once there were sixty troops and an artillery piece

30

on a slope out beyond the forwardmost C.P. We brought our jeep up close and called an air strike in." As he talked he could again smell the hot smell and hear the screams and see the human beings blacken and shrivel. He could see the doll-faced child playing with the dead woman's fingers. He could hear the flies buzz again. "The poor bastards never had a chance," he said.

Straker said, "I'm aware of the horrors of war, Tindle. No one could be more shocked and dismayed at war than myself. But I'm also aware that we have a job to do."

"Yes, sir," said Tindle in a blank voice, and with a blank look.

Straker rose and began to pace back and forth behind the desk. "Our Wing has been particularly effective against troops," he said. "I'm going to see that we're used to attack troops as much as possible. It may mean a longer trip to the target sometimes, but it will also mean more damage to that target."

Simple, thought Tindle. If you wanted to be deeply against war, and at the same time wage it well, all you had to do was change the words you used. Not a mass of huddled, terrified human beings—just a target. Not a bewildered poor slob of a man who never wanted anything but a few meals and a woman to sleep with, and maybe a beer now and then, but instead got trapped without willing it into the whole mess, into the nightmare—no, not a man. Call him a troop. So many troops comprised a target. A target wasn't a social entity, and a troop didn't have nerve-ends and a mortal soul.

"So from now on," continued the colonel, "you'll do well to concentrate on your gunnery and low altitude bombing. After this the 66th is going to be known as 'The Manhunters.' "

Tindle raised his eyebrows slowly. "The—what, sir?"

" 'The Manhunters.' Captain Gorgas, the P.I.O. cooked it up. Catchy, isn't it?"

"Yes, sir. Catchy," Tindle said.

"Well, Captain—" Straker had a faraway look now and was getting ready to sit down again—"I guess that's about all for the moment. Glad to see you back, of course. And I know Ronsdale will be glad to have you in his outfit."

"Yes, sir," said Tindle, and started to turn away.

"Oh—one more thing. Did you say a moment ago you knew Mrs. Ronsdale very well?"

"Why, yes. Pete and I—"

"I wonder if you'd do me a favor, Captain."

Tindle's look said that depended on what the favor was.

"Ronsdale's off to Tokyo this afternoon getting his flying time in. I'd promised him to take Mrs. Ronsdale to that party tonight. The—er—Wing-Ding, they call it. At the time I didn't realize I'd have to be so busy with this new project tonight. Now, Mrs. Ronsdale doesn't have an escort."

"I see," said Tindle. He frowned. He had a week's leave coming. He'd hoped to begin it by wandering in the town tonight, the middle-sized town of Korokua near the air base. There were lights and colors in a Japanese town at night. He wanted to see them again. He wanted to try to paint them sometime. Funny, he hadn't picked up a brush since he'd been here in Japan, though he'd managed to fill a small sketchbook in Korea. His stuff seemed to be getting a little better, though of course he was himself too close to it to be really sure. Anyway, he'd have to get around to more of that painting. . . .

"Of course, if you have other plans," said Straker.

And also Tindle had wanted to be in bed early tonight, catch a flight to Tokyo in the morning, and not feel too tired when he got there. He said, "No, it's all right, Colonel. I'll be glad to take Essie to the party."

"Thanks," said the colonel. "And don't forget we're mighty glad to have you back. Best of luck, Captain."

Tindle smiled back just as woodenly, and went off without saluting.

As he strolled back to the barracks he wondered just how the colonel had talked him into it. He could easily have refused. But the colonel had a certain strength, a certain ability to steer things, in spite of his fatuousness. It was to be admitted. Doubtless he was very good at making men give just a little more when they flew missions—as Tindle himself would have to do in another week or so.

He started to think about it. He started to think how presently he would have to kill human beings and burn

32

them and shrivel them and cut them down again. Colonel Straker keeping a cold eye on all of it. Straker, with that curious leaden intelligence of his, probably guessing already that he didn't want to. And the fact was, he didn't know he'd be able to force himself to do it: it might call for strength he didn't have—

The problem was just too much for the moment; quickly he stuffed it back into the bottom of his mind.

CHAPTER TWO

I

TECHNICAL SERGEANT FRANK BRAITH arose that morning with a hangover. There were only a few other men in the barracks at this late hour, and for this, and in a stupefied way, Braith was grateful. His head seemed caught in a cap of shrunken rawhide, and his immense body felt strung away from his neck, grotesque and elongated.

He took his canteen cup and went to the Lister bag outside and drank three pints of water, one right after the other. He belched. He went back into the barracks again.

"Jesus," he said, and sat heavily on his bunk.

He looked up and saw Master Sergeant MacInnes staring at him quietly. MacInnes was fully dressed as usual, neatly dressed, and he had that miniature typewriter of his on the desk he'd made of two footlockers and a board, and he was writing one of those damn letters again. The guy must have a million relatives. And smoking that damn black pipe.

Braith said, "What are you staring at?"

MacInnes smiled, puffed once, and turned back to his typewriter.

Braith started to reach into his footlocker for underwear and socks, and then realized that he was already partially dressed. He'd removed only shirt and shoes before piling into the bunk last night. Last thing he remembered was staggering out of that girlhouse after the other guys had picked themselves a dame and disappeared, and there were

33

three dames left, all standing impassive before him, and waiting for his decision, and he remembered thinking to hell with it.

MacInnes was at his letter again. Each peck of the type-writer was like a blow on the inside of Braith's skull.

"Oh, Jesus," said Braith again.

In his mind he began to construct a fantasy in which he walked over to MacInnes, yanked him up by the scruff of the neck, snatched the pipe from his mouth and said, "You see this pipe?" The MacInnes in his mind nodded. "You smoke this goddamn pipe once more," said Braith, "and so help me I'll shove it down your goddamn throat so hard it'll come out of the other end still smoking." Then the imaginary MacInnes promised meekly to switch to ciga-rettes or maybe chewing tobacco. Braith saw all this quite clearly in his mind, and heard the dialogue as though it actually happened. He could almost believe, now, that it had happened. He'd like to tell it to somebody. He'd like to tell how he'd handled that goddamned Master Sergeant MacInnes, and how he wouldn't take crap from anybody—not anybody, understand?

He smiled, and felt better. He nodded to himself, and then looked around to see if anybody had noticed the gesture. Nobody had. Nobody here but MacInnes, still typing, and a few bunks away Pfc. Marquez lying on his bunk and reading a comic book.

Braith undressed, put a towel around his middle, took up his shaving kit and went outside to the shower building. There he adjusted the water carefully to comfortable warmth, stepped under it, and gradually increased the heat until it was so hot that he nearly cried out with pain. His face became ecstatic. He stood there and quivered under the water for a while, half-smiling, and presently he took the soap and stroked his fat, hairless body all over. He tensed his biceps and examined them several times. Have to take some of that fat off, damn it. Have to cut down on eating. Seemed he never could quite get started cutting down on eating. Hell, he'd have a nice build with-out all that fat—plenty of muscle under it. He was strong as a bull. He could pick two damn Japs up, one in each hand, lift their feet right off the ground, and knock their

34

goddamned heads together. He imagined himself doing this, and smiled and nodded again.

When he got back to the barracks, Pfc. Marquez was sitting on the edge of his bunk, strumming his guitar.

"*Traiga me quarenta y cinco—*"

"What's that, Mex—a love song to your fair señorita?" Braith spoke pleasantly. He felt better now, after taking care of MacInnes and knocking the heads of those two Japs together.

Marquez looked up and his dark eyes were slightly puzzled—slightly suspicious. "No," said Marquez. "It ain't a love song."

"I thought that was all you Mexicans sang, love songs. I thought you were supposed to be the great lovers."

Marquez shrugged and looked at his guitar strings. He had stopped playing.

"Jesus," said Braith, "speaking of making love, maybe you think I'm not on P.W. status this morning."

MacInnes looked around. "What kind of status?"

"P.W. Pussy-whipped. Thought you knew that one." Braith grinned. He had fine, big white teeth, and he had often studied his grin in a mirror, and he knew that in spite of his bulk he could be considered handsome when he grinned. He'd make a hell of a better-looking master sergean than MacInnis. That guy looked as though he'd blow away in the first breeze, or maybe turn to powder the first dry spell. That was the service for you, where a guy like MacInnes, with only three years' time, could get to be a master sergeant, and Braith who had been in since forty-two, could only make tech. You had to get the breaks; you had to be in the right outfit at the right time. Take his present job in the maintenance group. Their Table of Organization was full and always had been, and he'd die decrepit before he'd be a master sergeant with them. But in the same 66th Wing there was the tactical outfit, the 66th Group, and there you could make your stripes. The grease-pushers in the 66th didn't have half the work with jets that Braith had with the piston engines of the C-47, yet they went up in rank like a cat up a drainpipe. Mac-Innes was one of them. By God, Braith would work a transfer to that outfit if he had to go needle Colonel Straker

35

himself to do it. Dreamily he began to imagine his encounter with the old man himself. He was polite . . . but subtly disrespectful. . . .

MacInnes said, "I thought you were the great lover, Braith. I thought you were the guy who could really handle anything that came along."

"Hell, I handled it all right," said Braith. He took clean clothes from his footlocker and began to dress slowly. "And it was plenty to handle. *Takusan*," he added, using the Japanese word for "plenty."

MacInnes grunted and stared at the letter in his small typewriter. Marquez kept looking at the strings of his guitar.

"I waited until the other guys and their dames had disappeared," mused Braith, fictionalizing. "I know these places, and I know how these Mama-sans work—I been here too long just to go get any old piece of tail and let it go at that." He lit a cigarette. He went on, making up the story as he went, reveling in his own fluency. "First she trotted out three stock model mooses and tried to pass 'em off on me. I wave my hand and say, 'Eee-yay!'—that means 'no!'—and tell her in Japanese I'm no GI fresh from the States—I know what it's all about, and she better not try to pull any of that stuff on me."

"You said it in Japanese," said MacInnes, smiling.

"Naturally," said Braith.

"How?"

"I can make 'em understand—don't worry. I said, 'Look, Mama-san, you trot out *ichi-ban* for me—get it? The one you keep in the back for the best customers. That's something most people don't know about these Japanese whorehouses. They keep their best one in back all the time, and you've got to be a regular customer before they'll get her for you. She's usually the one that's the best looking and has all the training. They go to a regular school to learn this stuff, you know."

"I hadn't heard," said MacInnes.

Braith glanced at Marquez. He had lifted his head and was listening to the tale. Braith addressed himself mainly to Marquez. "Hell, yes. I was in one of those schools one time. I'd done a favor for this real wealthy guy—he had a

36

pearl store up in Tokyo—and he liked cigars, and I got him a couple of boxes at the P.X., and after that nothing was too good for me. Nothing. He gave me cameras and silk prints and everything else. You should have seen the stuff he gave me. It's up in Tokyo now, in storage, that's why it isn't here. Anyway, one day he said to me, 'How would you like to see a Japanese Geisha school?' I said I would, so he drives me out in the country, and here's this big, beautiful house, with all these gardens and landscapes and everything around it."

MacInnes said, "I thought the geishas were trained right in the geisha houses, and not as whores."

"Well, you see, there's several different kinds of geishas," said Braith authoritatively. "It's very complicated. You have to understand the Japanese mind. But the best thing, as a matter of fact, is to have a steady moose like I did in Tokyo. That's the deal."

"A steady moose, huh?"

"You bet. You've got it any time you want it for half the cost. You can keep one of these dames for next to nothing. Fifty bucks a month, maybe."

In Tokyo Braith had worked as an administrative specialist before it was rediscovered upon his record that he was a rated mechanic. The girl he was elaborating upon now— one Teriko Katana—was a file clerk and typist in a Japanese company that wholesaled electrical parts. Pretty little thing. He'd taken her dancing several times, then more or less dropped her when she wouldn't come across. Their entire relationship had been immensely innocent.

"This moose I had in Tokyo was named Teriko. Terry for short. Now there was a babe. I bought this house and set it up, and stuck her in it. Well, she just sat there all the time, waited on me hand and foot and followed me around like a goddamned cocker spaniel. I was number one man around there, and that's the ungarbled word. If I wanted it quiet—maybe to read or something—all I had to do was say, 'Shut up,' and she'd squat there on her knees for two hours, the Japanese way, without moving or making a sound."

"Great way to spend an evening," said MacInnes.

Braith barely heard him. Braith was in creative ecstasy

37

now. "They just don't have dames around here like Teri-ko," he said. "Matter of fact, I'll get to see her tomorrow night. Major Ronsdale's taking the gooney bird up to get his flying time in, and I finagled the assignment as crew chief on the flight. If you know how to do things you can get anything you want in this damn Air Force. I could be up in Tokyo every few days if I wanted to take the trouble."

"Look, Braith," said MacInnes, getting up, speaking quietly, "you were assigned to that flight because your name happened to be on the board, and because the regular crew chief for 319 happens to be on sick call. I was there when they shifted the assignment."

He walked out.

Braith's cheeks felt warm, and he looked at Pfc. Marquez. Marquez was smiling faintly. "Hell of a lot he knows about it," said Braith darkly.

Marquez nodded. The nod could have meant anything.

Braith lumbered across the room and towered over Marquez and said, "How do you think the regular crew chief got sick in the first place? Answer me that."

"I don't know." Marquez shrugged.

"Well, just figure it out, buddy. Just figure it out."

"Sure," said Marquez meaninglessly.

Braith smiled and patted him on the shoulder. He could feel the young man's lean muscles. He had a build like a boxer, this kid Marquez; Braith had admired him in the shower a couple of times. "You're okay, Pedro," he said. "You keep on the right side of old Frank Braith, and you won't be a Pfc. long."

"My name is George," said Marquez.

He started to play the guitar softly again as Braith, fully dressed now, went out of the barracks.

Braith went to the messhall and entered by the back door. Sergeant Allan Uline, a cross-eyed redhead, looked up from an old typewriter on which he was laboriously typing the next day's menu. " 'Lo, Frank."

"Hi, Allan. Hoped I'd find you in."

Uline almost came to life. "You get some news?"

"Well, yes, I did hear something as a matter of fact. That's why I came over."

"Are they gonna do it?"

"The colonel himself is thinking about it."

"No fooling!"

"I made a point of seeing him last night. He doesn't like to be bothered at the office, so, when I have something for him, I usually drop in on his quarters right around dinnertime. He wanted me to stay for dinner. He wanted me to stick around for chow and talk about old times at Randolph."

"Where?"

"Randolph Field. Flying school. I was a cadet there, you know, when Colonel Straker was just a lieutenant—one of the instructors. He used to say I was one of the few natural-born pilots he ever met."

"No foolin'!"

"It's the honest truth. Of course, you're probably wondering why I'm not a pilot today. Well, that's a long story."

"Did you wash out of cadets?"

"Me? Not so you could notice it. I got pissed-off one day, that's all. That's my trouble—I can't hold my temper. I just don't like to be kicked around. I told a brigadier general where to get off. 'General,' I said, 'you maybe have that star and everything—' "

Uline was single-minded. He interrupted, saying, "But what about me, Frank? What did the colonel say?"

"He said he'd do it."

"You mean—transfer me to Public Information?"

"Sure. First chance he gets. It may take a little time, of course—because the skipper has to abide by regulations just like the rest of us, remember."

"But didn't you tell him I put in the application five months already?"

Braith laughed. He had a deep, hearty, good-fellow's laugh." "Allan, you don't have to worry about anything when you've got me working for you. I just told the skipper, 'Look, Colonel Bill,' I said, 'you've got one hell of a good writer working as a mess sergeant—writes magazine articles and poetry and everything.' "

"Well, you shouldn't give him the wrong impression. I didn't get any of it published yet."

"Don't let it bother you. All Colonel Bill cares about is whether I say you're okay or not. I told him I thought you could do his P.I.O. section a lot of good. He said, 'Well, Frank, thanks for telling me.' You'll have to be reclassified, of course, before anything can be done, and that takes time. But I'll get the ball rolling first thing in the morning."

"You really will?"

"You're on your way, kid. On your way."

"Well—damn. Thanks, Frank."

"Don't mention it." Braith turned to go, then swung heavily back again. "Say—got any chow around? I was too busy taking care of some of Major Ronsdale's work this morning to get breakfast."

It was one of the cardinal sins at Akuni Air Force Base for an enlisted man to expect food at 0731 when the messhall closed at 0730.

Uline said, "Sure thing! Sure thing, Frank!" He hollered something in Japanese at one of the mess boys; the boy jumped to the stove and began putting together toast and eggs and fried potatoes. Uline himself poured the coffee for Braith to start out with.

Braith sipped the coffee and said, "Ahhhh," fatly and resonantly.

"Say," said Uline, "you wouldn't like to hear this here latest one would you?"

"Latest what?"

"Poem." Uline took two folded sheets of paper from his back pocket.

"Go right ahead, Allan," said Braith grandly. "I like poetry. Did you know I was once assistant literary critic on the New York Times?"

"You were—what?" Uline cocked his head. This was a little too much even for him.

"I know that sounds funny," said Braith, "but here's how it happened. I had this job as a cub reporter, because I barged into Brooks Atkinson's box at the Martin Beck Theater one night and made him look at some pieces I'd done for the Lampoon. That's the Harvard magazine, you know. . . ."

Braith had never been to Cambridge. He had never been

40

in New York, either. He had finished exactly one year and two months of high school. But he went on with his tale, ad-libbing. It became real in his mind as he talked; he lived it; he felt it all vividly, and in some respects authentically. For Frank Braith's head was filled with details about places he had never been: he read and observed omnivorously, and with a kind of restless hunger; he retained everything he picked up; he had a neatly kept mental filing system. Seldom, in these fugues of his, did he pause to construct his phrases mentally before voicing them; seldom did he have to proceed with care for the sake of a consistent narrative. It all flowed. It was, in a way, a great talent.

He had this talent, then, and a kind of intelligence. He was sure about the intelligence. When he'd entered the service he'd taken the General Classification Test, which consisted of math, vocabulary and reasoning ability testing. Your score on this was supposed to be fairly close to your I.Q. Braith had scored only 119—but he had an answer for that. He'd pulled it out of thin air one time when a classification officer was going over his form with him, and by now he more or less believed that it was so. "Hell, sir," he'd said to this officer, "I actually have a 149 I.Q.— 1 point below genius—but I happen to know from a certain friend of mine in the Pentagon—he's a major general whose name you'd know if I mentioned it—that the Air Force is picking its officers from the 110 to 130 bracket, because they've found from experience that a too-intelligent man doesn't make a good officer. Tends to wander away from routine, and be too introverted." Braith had read that or maybe something like it, somewhere.

Uline said, "Well, how do you like it?" Uline was holding the typewritten sheets, and he looked shining and expectant.

Braith realized that Uline had just read his poem. "That's definitely got stuff," said Braith without hesitation, though he had not at all heard the poem. "A little rough in places, technically, but the basic stuff is there."

Uline laughed embarrassedly.

Afterward, when Braith finished breakfast, he wandered out to the line where they were gassing up 319. 319 was a ten-year-old C-47 transport that was assigned to the base flight section of the 66th Fighter-Bomber Wing for general utility—which meant largely providing monthly flying time for the desk officers who still drew flying pay. Four hours per month per officer was required. 319's existence, its frequent journeys, and its thirst for gas, oil and spare parts, were justified by throwing into its hold various press or courier pouches containing unimportant public information home-town releases, or photographs, or long-winded reports and communications that might easily have been sent by mail. Occasionally there was cargo. In Tokyo a friend of one of the officers in Akuni might obtain a hard-to-get Nikkon miniature camera and ship it back via 319. Sometimes there were passengers, drawn from casual personnel who happened to be on the base for any of a hundred reasons when 319 was scheduled to fly.

There were six of these passengers standing glumly around the airplane today. There was a lieutenant colonel of infantry in a green field coat, two seamen in whites, a marine, a large Negro corporal of aviation engineers, and a civilian in a Hawaiian shirt and loud sports jacket.

Major Ronsdale and the co-pilot, Second Lieutenant Morton M. Cohen, were looking at the tail wheels, checking the landing-gear retraction mechanism.

Braith went right to Major Ronsdale. He'd seen Ronsdale around the base, and he was intrigued by Ronsdale's appearance. Here was someone, by God, who looked like a pilot. Tall, dark-haired, gray-eyed, graceful: he filled Braith at once with admiration and envy. Ronsdale was in Wing operations, and up there in brassland he might easily do Sergeant Braith some good someday. Maybe get him a transfer to the jets, where a promotion would be easier. Braith smiled his most open smile, saluted casually, although saluting was neither required nor expected on the line, and said, "She'll fly, sir."

"Got the Form One?"

"I'll be honest, sir," said Braith. "I haven't checked the airplane yet. I just got here." He chuckled with studied openness. "Something of a party last night. A lieutenant colonel I used to know at Shenadoah Military Academy—"

"Oh." Ronsdale laughed. "All right, I understand."

Lieutenant Cohen was looking at Braith expressionlessly. His stare bothered Braith; Braith thought of a tortoise. He couldn't decide whether Cohen's thick-lidded eyes concealed stupidity or immense acuity.

Cohen said, "We'd better check the Form One right away."

"Okay," said Braith. He let his eyes go up and down and his lower lip protrude just a bit—not quite enough to be overt insult, but enough for a sharp kike like Cohen to get it all right. Just so they understood each other. Cohen's face remained impassive.

Braith climbed into the airplane and took the Form One from the plywood map case near the pilot's seat. He glanced at it and saw the red line. Whenever something was not functioning quite properly a red line was drawn diagonally across a little square and a notation made. This time it was the radio compass.

Braith closed the pad carefully, and slipped the rubber band around it again. When he came out of the airplane he walked up to Cohen, casually handed him the pad, and said, "I haven't looked at it yet, but I seem to remember that the radio compass is bad on this airplane. We'd better be sure to check it."

Cohen didn't say anything as he took the pad, but Braith could have sworn that for just a fraction of an instant he smiled sarcastically.

Major Ronsdale looked over Cohen's shoulder as he opened the pad. "Well, well," he said, "you were right, Sergeant." He nodded and smiled briefly at Braith. "That radio compass is on the blink." He looked at the sky. "I think we can make it all right, though, on just the flight instruments."

Cohen said quietly, "Did you see the weather map between here and Tachi?"

"Well, no—I haven't filed my clearance yet."

"There's a front, and a secondary over Nagoya. We'd better make sure of that radio compass."

"Well, in that case, I suppose so." Ronsdale frowned at his wrist watch. "Might make our take-off pretty late, though."

"Yes, it might," said Cohen unconcernedly.

"I'll have an electronics man right up here, sir." Braith was cheerful. "I could fix it myself—went one semester to M.I.T., as a matter of fact, but you know what regulations are. Has to be an electronics man do it. I'll keep an eye on the whole operation, though."

"All right, do that, will you, Braith?" said Ronsdale.

The major and Lieutenant Cohen walked back toward operations as Braith set off for the communications shack. Ronsdale said, "Good man, that Braith."

"I don't know," said Cohen.

"Don't know what?"

"Can't put my finger on it, but I keep feeling he's acting. You know, all the time. Playing *himself*, if you see what I mean."

Ronsdale slapped Cohen on the back and said, "You worry too much, Mort. Take it easy, you'll live longer."

"Sure," said Cohen. "I guess you're right. Anyway, I'm glad you'll be along this flight. We're going to need somebody with experience in the damn thing. I haven't even got ten hours in 47s."

"Relax, Leftenant, relax," said Ronsdale, and hooked an arm in Cohen's. He hoped Cohen wouldn't ask him how much twin engine time he had himself. It wasn't very much.

2

It was early evening when Tindle, walking, entered the gravel road that wound through the dependent area at Akuni Air Force Base. This area encompassed a group of cottages that housed the officers and airmen whose families were in Japan. It was still a clear day—a clear evening, now —and the light had softened, mellow with a full day's age; the outlines and shadow edges were soft, somehow not quite real.

As in a dream, as in early drunkenness, there was a wonderful feeling of irresponsibility. To hell with the demands . . . to hell with them.

And then Tindle looked at the underclothes on the washlines, at the seesaws and kiddy-cars, at the rubber dolls left forgotten on the tailored lawns, at the milk bottles outside the doors, at all the evidence of domesticity, and he frowned.

44

He saw a doghouse with a sign: OFF LIMITS FOR DEPENDENT HUSBANDS.

He did not laugh. It struck him as funny, but he could not make himself laugh.

When he came to Ronsdale's house it was almost dark, and the porch light was on. He'd phoned Essie to say he'd take her to the Wing-Ding, if that was all right with her, and she'd squealed with delight.

"Drinks'll be ready when you get here!" she'd said.

He went to the door and worked the wrought-iron knocker. The door opened almost immediately. A wave of perfume-and-powder smell struck him, and Esther Ronsdale smiled, took both of his hands, and said, "Dick! Dick Tindle! Welcome to civilization—such as it it!"

Ess Ronsdale was of a weight that most of her friends defined as "you know—just slightly plump." She wore it well. She was short-necked, energetic; she had coppery hair and broad, well-shaped lips that always seemed a little moist. She had high, firm breasts. She wore this evening a dress with a low, square-cut neckline, crisp lace edging both neck and sleeves. The dress itself was meant to be demure—on Essie it acquired a decidedly sensual look, somehow. She held a shallow glass goblet, and a cigarette between the first and second fingers of her hand. Retaining both glass and cigarette she grasped Tindle by the arms and pushed herself upward and forward to kiss him.

Tindle started to make it a simple kiss; a gentle brotherly smack. Not Essie. Her lips were wide open; they were very warm. Tindle kissed her hastily—but before he drew back her tongue had touched his.

He felt titillation in his spine. It spread to his coccyx and his thighs. He hadn't expected that. He should have, though, after sixty days in Korea. He was furious with himself to find that suddenly he felt clumsy, embarrassed. He spoke quickly, more for the sake of speaking than saying anything. "What's in the glass—a martini?"

"A stinger," said Essie. "There's one for you inside. Come on in, Dick—my, but you're a sight for sore eyes!"

She virtually pulled him in. Her house (he remembered now, it was always like this) was spotless. The furniture was on the modern side, and throughout everything was

45

the faint powder-toilet soap-boudoir smell that was characteristically Essie.

Out of a frosted cocktail shaker she poured another stinger. He took a long sip and tasted the cool, biting sweetness of it. Good enough—but he would have preferred the jolting of gin or whiskey. Essie went to the sofa, sat down, and patted the cushion beside her. He sat there. He couldn't avoid the warm pressure of her hip.

He laughed a little nervously. He said, "So your husband's run out on you, has he?"

"Dick! You remember that!"

Yes, he remembered. It was a great joke from cadet days in San Antonio. Pete Ronsdale was going steady with Essie then; she worked on the base, and every cadet and officer and enlisted man swore Pete Ronsdale was the luckiest bastard in the world to get her. And Dick Tindle was Pete Ronsdale's best friend, and whenever he'd come out to the tourist court where Essie lived and find Pete not there, he'd laugh and say her husband had run out on her, hadn't he? Probably wouldn't be funny to anybody else, but it had always been immensely funny to the three of them.

"Of course I remember," said Tindle.

Essie bounced, and dropped her palms to her thighs and said, "Well, what *have* you been doing with yourself?"

"Practically nothing."

"I mean over there in Korea."

"Good God, Ess, I don't want to talk about it."

"No. Of course not. I should have realized. Well—well, let's talk about the future. What are your plans, Dick?"

"I haven't any plans. I haven't got a damn plan in my head."

"I doubt that."

"Let's talk about you."

"Me?" said Essie. "Why, you know I never have anything to talk about." She put her hand on his glass, letting her palm rub over his fingers. "Another drink?"

"Did I finish *this* one?"

"You certainly did. Without any trouble."

"A mouse drank it."

"No—not at all. You did and didn't notice it. My drinks are subtle. It's a secret formula."

46

"Tell me."

"All right—but not a word to another soul."

"Not a word."

"I put five-eighths brandy in," said Essie. "Usually they put in too much crème de menthe."

"Who does?"

"They. You know—the same people who always 'say.'"

"They say," said Tindle, and nodded gravely.

"They say another stinger never hurt anybody," said Essie, and poured. When she had filled both glasses the cocktail shaker was empty, and she went out to the kitchen and made a new batch. Tindle sipped and smoked. He wondered how much Essie had drunk before he arrived. He remembered that he'd never really seen Essie drunk: her pattern was to be animated, but coordinated, right up until the last moment, and then abruptly she would curl up quietly somewhere and sleep.

She returned with another shakerful. "I didn't get a chance to see Pete after he left this morning," she said. "He was off to Tokyo by the time I got untangled from all the things officers' wives are supposed to do around here. And at that he was held up. Something about a radio compass. Is that it? Is there such a thing as a radio compass?"

"I invented it," said Tindle, and poured himself another stinger.

"Of course." She sat down beside him again, quickly. She took a long drink. "Why is there always something?" she said. She picked up a new cigarette and put it in her mouth, and he lit it for her.

"What do you mean, always something?"

"Oh—if it isn't a radio compass, it's a landing gear, or a manifold pressure, or a magneto drop—I still don't know what in earth those fantastic words stand for. But I know they're not good. I worry."

"Whoa. Wait a minute, Essie. Don't tell me you still worry about Pete flying. Not after all these years."

"Of course I worry." She turned toward him. "Dick—"

"Yes?"

"What's the honest truth about Pete? About his flying, I mean."

47

"What are you talking about, Ess?"

"You know what I'm talking about. He's just not naturally a very good pilot, is he?"

"Well, I wouldn't say exactly that—"

"No. Of course you wouldn't. You're too nice a guy, Dick. But if I asked you—openly and frankly—"

"Ess, you're putting me on a spot. You know that, don't you?"

"I want to know about Pete, Dick. I have a right to know."

Oh, Christ, he thought.

He said, "Now, look, Essie. I don't know what you've been building up in your mind, but you'd better stop worrying about Pete right now. He knows how to fly an airplane. He might not be another Rickenbacker or Doolittle, but he gets along. He's a good, safe pilot."

"He's got barely sixty hours in a C-47. That's not very much, is it?"

"It can be enough."

"And this boy that's flying co-pilot—Lieutenant Cohen —he's barely checked out in the thing. Is that the right way to say it: 'Checked out'?"

"I don't know Cohen." Tindle killed his third drink. He had relaxed more now—these stingers *did* sneak up on you. He turned suddenly and faced Essie fully for the first time and said, "Look—what is it? What's been going on between Pete and you?"

"Between me and Pete? Why, Dick—nothing!"

"Okay. I'm sorry I asked."

She bounced up and poured an additional drink for both of them.

Essie Ronsdale's face was turned from Tindle's gaze, and so she permitted herself to frown. Now, how in the devil had he known that something was wrong with her and Pete? Of course, Dick Tindle always had been rather sharp in his quiet bookish way, but here he'd been practically a psychiatrist. She knew about psychiatrists, because her father had sent her to one: that was the time she became pregnant and had to have the abortion at Carveth Hall. Seventeen, she was then. Just a little too young

48

and dumb to keep her father from finding out how she'd been playing around with nearly everybody and anybody—and young enough to be terribly frightened by the psychiatrist he hired. The psychiatrist, she always remembered, didn't have a beard, like in cartoons. He looked like a bank teller. She would never forget how shocking it was to have a bank-teller type say that she must be frank with him, and then mutter something about "nymphomaniac tendencies," as though he didn't quite expect her to understand it. She'd like to see that square-faced, pompous, cornfed bastard now. Nymphomaniac tendencies, was it? Well, damn him, she hadn't had another man but Pete in over a year now. She could control herself. She could take it or leave it—when she wanted to.

As for tonight—

She turned and glanced at Tindle now, and saw that he was looking at her. He had a morose way of looking sometimes that was decidedly animal and exciting. Odd that it should be. So as for tonight, and Dick Tindle, well, she needed a fling. She'd come down with the screaming meemies if she didn't do something.

But how in the hell had Tindle known about Pete and her? Or, more correctly, about Pete. Christ knew, her desires were normal enough, and not unreasonable, either, in spite of what the cornfed bastard from Kansas may have thought. You'd think any man would be willing to oblige to the extent of one good one a night. She wouldn't ask for more. She could use more, but she wouldn't ask for it.

And it was funny as hell about Pete, when you thought it over—or it would be funny if it were happening to somebody else and wasn't so damned immediate and real. Sex, after all, was an important part of a marriage. Not everything, mind you, but a very important part. And so it was funny as hell when you looked at Pete—tall, unquestionably handsome, beautifully built, well-mannered—why, you'd think he'd be the best lay in the world.

"Isn't it about time for the dance to start?" asked Tindle.

"Do you really want to go to the dance?"

"Certainly."

"How about one more stinger?"

He stared back for a long moment. "Okay. One more stinger. But then, Essie—"

"Yes?"

"Then we go to the dance."

"All right, Dick."

Essie chuckled and felt deliciously light-headed. Dick was suffering from scruples. She hadn't seen the scruple yet she couldn't break down. Just an old scruple-breaker-downer, that was what she was.

"What are you laughing at, anyway?"

"A joke. But you're too young to hear it."

They had one more drink, and then went outside and walked to the Officers' Club, where the Wing-Ding was being held.

Essie insisted on holding Tindle's arm tightly as they walked, and on bouncing her body lightly against his every once in a while. If he minded, he didn't say so.

3

Paper streamers and orange lanterns decked the new wing of the Akuni Air Force Base Officers' Club.

This new wing, sixty by eighty feet, had cost fifteen thousand dollars and had just been completed. The money came from the club's surplus funds. The fund was by no means yet exhausted, and so, in order to whittle it down a bit, before the end of the fiscal year when the overage would have to be turned into the general officers' mess fund for the entire Air Force, free drinks were being served three nights a week. The drinks were free tonight; so were the canapés and music and paper streamers.

The club's profit came from the bar and slot machines mainly; the machines were permitted in Japan since the clubs was not technically federal property. There were dozens of these slot machines designed to take various size coins, and to play them you bought slugs from the cashier with your Military Payment Certificates, more commonly called M.P.C. Regular United States currency was not permitted in Japan. However, a real dollar would fetch more than the official exchange rate of three hundred and sixty yen, and so there was a brisk trade in dollars. Bills could be easily sent from home by mail. A large number of military people were saving a great deal of money this way, for it did not cost much to live under government aegis in Japan; it did not cost much to live even luxuriously.

Take the bar prices. All drinks were a quarter. A shot of whiskey, a pony of Remy-Martin, a scotch and soda, or a complicated mixed drink. Cigarettes at the P.X. were a dollar a carton. They were rationed, of course, but you got at least six cartons a month. You didn't have to smoke these cartons if you were an average smoker; you could do with a pack a day bought in the bar for fifteen cents. Your dollar carton of cigarettes was worth nine hundred yen on the black market. Nine hundred yen equaled two dollars and fifty cents. Figure, at fifteen cents a pack, a dollar-fifty for a carton. On each carton sold for yen, then, you made a buck. And if you had friends who didn't smoke you could sometimes cajole them out of their weekly ration. Sometimes you could get extra ration cards when people went home. Then there was whiskey, and stockings, and tires and washing machines—

If you played your cards right, you had it fat; you had it made, brother, and, in fact, you never had it so good.

Takes a little war sometimes to stir things up.

Not that I wouldn't rather be home — don't get me wrong.

After all, there's no place like good old Usashima; good old Island U.S.A.

Yes, sir, you can take all these countries; North Africa and India and England and France, and I've been to all of them, but give me good old stateside any time.

And white stuff.

What I wouldn't give to be sitting out in a convertible now with the top down and some little white dame, cute as a button, in a real stateside dress, just cuddled up under my arm.

Not that these Japanese moose aren't pretty good; they know their stuff all right. (Or is it meese?)

But in the long run—

Christ, it's been a run . . . It's been a long, long run.

"Oh, Dick, come on! Let's dance this one! 'September Song'! I *love* it!" said Essie.

"Before we even have a drink?"

"Some things are more important than a drink. Not many, but some."

She danced closely, pressing hard. "The orchestra's wonderful," she said.

"Yes." Tindle glanced at the bandstand. The Japanese musicians wore flowery sports shirts and leis about their necks. They played properly and well, he was thinking, but something was not there. A drive, a beat. He wasn't enough of a musician to know.

"Don't you like to dance, Dick?"

"Hm?"

"I said don't you like to dance?"

"Sure. Why?"

"You didn't look as though you liked it."

"I'm sorry, Ess." He tried a laugh. "I guess I was thinking about something else."

He found a table and they sat down, and she ordered a stinger. He ordered a beer.

"My God," said Essie, "beer—on top of stingers?"

"Anything you drink separately you can drink together."

"Maybe—" she fluttered her eyelids "—but I like to stick to one particular thing for one particular evening."

He lit a cigarette and watched the orchestra. They were now playing "China Night," the current Japanese favorite. It was a strange, chaotic mixture of oriental melody shoe-horned into the occidental scale, and then blurred by fox-trot time. It always made him uncomfortable.

"Dick—"

"Yes?"

"What happened over there in Korea?"

"What? What do you mean, what happened?"

"Something happened to you, didn't it? Inside, I mean. Was it really very bad?"

Tindle shifted uncomfortably. "Oh, I don't know. It wasn't pleasant. I don't know." Someday he'd want to talk about it. Not tonight; not with Essie.

"You need somebody to talk it over with, Dick—somebody who understands you," Essie said.

"Yes." He stared at the band again.

A tall youth came to the table and said, "Hey! How you?"

"Melvin Harold!" said Essie, her voice rising a little too much. "Dick, this is Lieutenant Harold. Mel—Captain Tindle.

"Okay," Tindle said. "Sit down."

Lieutenant Harold didn't waste more than a quick glance on Tindle, and then he sat. He had wavy red hair and a very clean profile. He said to Essie, "You dancin' tonight?"

"Sure am."

He kept looking at Essie and said to Tindle, "You don't mind if I dance with your gal, do you, Cap'n?"

"No, no. Not at all."

"Damn you, Dick, you could mind a *little* bit," said Essie, laughing, but not quite successful in her effort to make it sound entirely a joke.

"All right," said Tindle. "I mind a little bit."

"Well then, let's all have a drink first," said Essie.

"Best offer I've had tonight!" said Lieutenant Harold, and laughed uproariously, as though he had just invented the phrase.

The waiter came and Tindle said, "Another beer, another stinger, and one bourbon and branch water."

"I declare!" said Lieutenant Harold. "How'd you know what I drink?"

"Superior intelligence," said Tindle gravely.

Lieutenant Harold laughed uproariously again, poked Essie's arm and said, "How 'bout that!" Then he turned to Tindle. "Been over here long, Captain?"

"Six months."

"What squadron you with?"

"109th."

"Hell, that's my squadron. You ain't in my squadron."

"I just got back from forward control."

"Oh. I see. Well, I only been here a little over a month. But I'm finally started on my missions. What flight you goin' to be with, Cap'n?"

"I don't know yet."

"Well, if we fly together, I'll be just mighty proud."

"How many missions have you flown, Harold?"

"Just seven. It'd be more if that damned R.T.U. trainin' didn't take so long before you ever get started. Doggone, I didn't come over here to be checked out in 80s all over

53

again. I just came from half a year in 80s at cadet school."

"Like to fly, do you?"

"Rather fly than eat!" Harold's eyes were bright. They shone like newly scrubbed onyx. "And, boy, when you go down on the deck, and let them six nose-fifties go—ain't that just somepin'?"

"It's something."

"I got a real close look today. Just as close! We caught a bunch of 'em just off the road. Must've been nearly a hundred. I let go my napalm on the first pass, and then come around again, about yay close"—he showed how close by holding his hands together—"and I could see them gooks just burn-in' . . . with that stuff stickin' to 'em—man, it was really somepin'!"

"It's something," said Tindle.

The orchestra finished "China Night" and went into a rhumba.

"Come on, Mel," said Essie, "this is my meat."

"Sure you don't mind, Cap'n?" asked Lieutenant Harold.

"Just a little bit," said Tindle.

He was relieved when they moved off. He held the cold beer glass tightly in one hand, liking its fingertip chill, and he watched Lieutenant Harold and Essie rhumba. They rhumba-ed very well. Harold was lanky and graceful, and Essie, in spite of her slight stockiness, was light upon her feet. Her face glowed, and she laughed and tossed her head as she turned, and all the while Lieutenant Harold stood in one spot, moving only from the hips down, with his hand held high to pivot her turn.

Tindle enjoyed it.

The rhumba stopped and there was a slow fox trot and Melvin and Essie continued to dance. He ordered another beer. His gaze wandered, and at the bar just beyond the dance floor he watched a group of pilots gathered into a tight knot, and using their hands for airplanes as they talked. He recognized most of them, but a few, like Lieutenant Harold, had not been here before. A lot of these new second lieutenants had been coming in lately. Nearly all of them were eager, like Harold. Nearly all of them were fine pilots, good young men and bright young men, and they flew as Harold was dancing now, moving only from the

54

waist down. Surely they were born to fly; surely their reason for being was to master the complicated business of flying. They didn't waste much time on other things.

Tindle felt suddenly and indescribably sad. He downed the rest of his beer almost desperately, and then ordered another one.

Essie was across the room now, at another table, charming at least six men. They were toasting her.

Tindle supposed he would have to keep an eye on Essie, and see that she didn't get into any serious trouble. Kind of a responsibility. Damn the colonel, anyway, for wishing it upon him.

He felt worse than sad, now; he was becoming morbid. Drinking never used to do this to him. He wished he had Noonan here to fight with. Maybe a good fight, a fist fight, where you could get in and mix it up and feel the blows with your hands, would do the trick. Why didn't they fight wars with fists, anyway? Be a lot more sensible all around. Not like roaring down, straddling your damned stovepipe like a witch, and sending hot, hard, heavy metal into some poor slob's soft and blood-stuffed body.

He'd be doing it again pretty soon. He'd be right in there after his week's leave, dropping napalm, as Harold had done this afternoon, then coming around for a second pass to see the stuff stick and burn.

"Oh, Jesus," he said softly. He grimaced, as with pain.

He wanted to drop his head on his crossed arms on the table, and grind his teeth and sob, but he didn't. He kept staring around the room.

And what if he were unable—truly unable—to kill again?

But of course he would. There was no other choice. Like the woman had said when rape was inevitable—that was Lieutenant Rossi's remark that day he couldn't pull out and knew he was about to cream into a mountain— "It's inevitable," Rossi had said, "I might as well relax and enjoy it." He'd said it on the radio for all of them to hear. For none of them to laugh. Afterward, Rossi got a posthumous D.F.C.

Tindle wandered into the bar and joined the group where the pilots were making airplanes out of their hands. It was an involved discussion of fighter tactics. Somebody was saying that you could nose over to get away from a MIG on your tail, and the negative Gs you'd pull wouldn't really hurt you; and somebody else was saying he was crazy, but you could kind of pull up and half-stall away, like this —he did it with his hands—and it was just mathematically impossible for the MIG to adjust his gunnery lead in that case. There was a long argument on just why it was mathematically impossible. Tindle didn't take sides.

Everybody had more drinks.

The mathematical argument petered out and they began talking about women.

Major Goff, who was bald and wore a fierce black mustache, said, "Okay, I grant you these Japanese dames got terrific bodies—but did you ever smell their hair?"

"Look," said Captain Kingsley, who was small and thin and looked breakable, "when I'm with a dame I don't waste time smelling her hair."

"Well, their hair always smells like fish," said Goff. "Every goddamn time."

"I had one the other night," said Kingsley, "and after we were all through, do you know what that sweet bitch said? She said, 'Thank you! Thank you for making nice time!' Can you imagine an American dame saying that?"

"White gooks don't show me a thing. Not a goddamn thing," said Goff.

"Me, neither," said Kingsley.

"The art of sex is in its infancy in America," said Goff.

"Right."

"The only trouble is—their goddamn hair always smells like fish."

"My kid had his hair cut the other day."

"What's so goddamned wonderful about that?"

"Well, Christ, he's only two—that's Bobby, my youngest —and he'd never had his hair cut before. I remembered the way it was, all thick and curly like, and here comes this Kodachrome of Helen and the kids, and I'll be a son of a bitch if there he isn't with a GI on his head! I wrote Helen, by God, to grow the goddamned hair back on his head again!"

"Well, you've got to watch 'em, these wives. You've got to keep after 'em every minute."

56

"You said it," said Kingsley.

"Not that I don't think the world of Lurleen," said Major Goff. "Jesus, I'd give anything to be back with Lurleen and the kids right now. Or have 'em over here. These bastards that got in before they put the stop on dependent travel are the lucky bunch of bastards, all right."

"They don't know how lucky they are." Kingsley had taken to staring into his drink. They were all staring at something else now; they were not looking at each other as they had been before.

"One thing about Lurleen," said Goff, "she always looks good. Even in the morning. That kid knows how to dress."

"Helen's that way, too. And smart as they come. She wanted to go to school, can you imagine, and get her M.A. while I was over here. Only what with the kids and everything it's just too much for her."

Goff took a long drink, and there was a short pause, and then he said, "Yes, goddamn it, I'm pretty much in love with my wife."

"Same here," said Kingsley.

"I made up my mind I wouldn't cheat on her when I came over here—and, by God, I haven't."

"You haven't?" Kingsley looked at him suspiciously.

"No, sir," said Goff, running his hand across his fierce mustache. "Since I've been here I haven't touched anything but Japanese girls."

4

Afterwards Tindle joined other groups, always briefly, and he drank and talked and laughed and walked from place to place, and waved across the room greeting this one and that one, and he lost count of the beers. He was not drunk. He was still unspeakably sad, but by keeping on the move like this, by staying animated, he managed to flee a little from his sadness.

He was at the bar, momentarily alone, sometime later, when he felt a hand upon his arm. He turned and saw Essie beside him. Her eyes still sparkled. She held a stinger in her hand. "I've tried the rest, now I'll try the best," she said, and squeezed his arm.

He wanted to acknowledge her pleasantry with some

57

kind of smile, no matter how slight, but it was difficult to shift over into her mood. He had been thinking about something, and the track of that thought was still with him like a fading contrail. He had been thinking about Goff and Kingsley and all the others, and trying to picture them holding the same conversation back in Albuquerque or Walla Walla or San Diego or Portland. Oh, they'd discuss sex there—it was after all a topic of certain interest—but their talk wouldn't be quite as intimate, nor quite as detailed. Something over here changed them. Something in the air, perhaps; something about the country itself . . . perhaps the fact of its being so far away, or perhaps because sex was so free and easy here, so prevalent, so naturally a part of the place, and of the lives of the people, for they were a naked people, the Japanese, they were really a naked people. But that wasn't exactly it, either.

He pushed aside these thoughts reluctantly. He patted Essie's hand and said, "Well, ready to go?"

She fluttered her eyelids in that lewd way again. "If you're ready, I am." She dropped her voice and added, "Any time."

He could have slapped her.

He led her, instead, almost roughly, through the islands of partygoers. Wing-Dingers. Most were in small groups by now, arguing, agreeing, singing, shouting, and Kingsley and Goff had begun to make airplanes out of their hands again. Essie moved just a little unsteadily. Tindle hoped that his firm, no-nonsense grip would tell her that he had no intention of having an affair with her, but it didn't seem to work out that way. On the contrary, she seemed to take encouragement; she pressed closer to Tindle and looked up at him and smiled, and kept her eyelids going.

He took her down the road to the cottage area. She slipped her arm around his waist so that he was forced to place his own arm about her shoulders—no place else to put it. He scowled when he discovered that her shoulders felt soft and warm, exciting to the touch. Essie was warm and flushed, and this intensified her powder-perfume-woman smell. . . .

A few blocks away from the club, the quietness of this night asserted itself. There was a half-moon, soapy and

58

bright, charging the faint overhead haze with light. Frogs croaked from the rice paddies. The shaft of the tower marker light swung like a carrousel beam around the awning of the sky. The red port light of a distant plane, whose engines they could not hear, crawled southward near the horizon.

Essie stopped under a willow tree. She turned and faced Tindle, put her palms at first on his shoulders, and then slid her hands up and around his neck. She closed her eyes, parted her lips slightly, and held them ready. He looked at her face for a moment. Then he slid his arms around her and pulled her toward him, and felt the cushioning of her breasts . . . the slight crushing, the ample, firm flesh of her back. Her lips were moist. She opened her mouth wide as their lips came together, and her hot tongue came forward cobra-like, darting and striking at his.

They broke apart some moments later.

"Oh, Dick . . . Dick," said Essie. Her eyes were still half closed. She had him by the arms, working her fingers into his flesh, clawing at him.

"Now, look, Essie," said Tindle—

"Take me home, Dick. Please. Quick. Come home with me."

He pretended not to understand her real meaning. He took her arm again, holding it so that she could not slip it around his waist this time, and he led her in silence to the cottage. At the door he said, "Good night, Essie."

"Good night?"

"Go to bed, Essie. Have a good sleep."

"Dick—you know how I feel. Oh, Dick, you don't know—"

"Never mind the reasons, Essie. We've both had a few drinks, and a nice time. Let's let it go at that."

She changed her expression suddenly, and looked sober, matter of fact, understanding. She straightened her shoulders; she stepped back, and stopped pressing at Tindle. "All right, Dick. We'll be good kids. And you can come in and have breakfast."

"No, I'd better—"

"Scrambled eggs. Toast. Coffee. Can't you taste it already?"

"Well—I can smell the coffee."

"Come on." She laughed, took him by the hand, and pulled him inside.

Her kitchen was bright, colorful and spotless: Essie's kitchen would be. Her frying pan was shiny. She took two eggs from the cupboard, not the icebox. "I put them here before we went out. I thought we might want scrambled eggs, and you should never scramble them right out of the icebox. Always room temperature. It's an old French secret." She smiled wickedly. "I know lots of French secrets."

"Sure," said Tindle, studiously not looking at her. He was spooning out the coffee.

Essie chattered as she worked. "I wouldn't let anyone else know my secrets like this. You like your eggs glossy, don't you?"

"Glossy," said Tindle.

"Thought I remembered. Here's how you do it. Pan hot first. Good and hot—as though you were going to make pancakes. Now—watch."

She poured the beaten eggs from the bowl quickly into the pan. She held the pan several inches above the flame, and began to swirl it with a deft wrist motion. The eggs oscillated about the rim. A moment later the mass folded back upon itself into a fluffy cake. She took the pan away from the stove quickly, dumped the eggs on a plate, and then divided them into two portions. As she did this the toast popped from the toaster.

"Neat," said Tindle.

"Yes, I'm a good cook, damn it," said Essie.

"That you are." He began to butter the toast.

She sat down across from him. "As a matter of fact I'm a pretty damned good all-around wife."

He looked up mildly. "Did somebody say you weren't?"

"No—not exactly."

"What, then?"

"It's just that—oh, hell, I don't know. I don't think Pete knows what a good wife I am sometimes."

He didn't want to hear intimate revelations. He made a great show of buttering the toast and then, to bring the talk back to generalities, he said, "Well, I guess most husbands never realize what good wives their wives are."

"Most wives aren't," said Essie, quickly and positively. "You'd be surprised how damned frigid some girls are. You'd be surprised how many of them just pretend to enjoy it. Go through all the motions, and everything. I've— I've done it sometimes with Pete."

"Wonderful eggs," said Tindle, a little awkwardly.

"I'm sorry, Dick. I'm embarrassing you. I'm not very well-behaved, am I? Maybe it's this country. Maybe it's this being so far away from home and everything. Oh, God, Dick, I don't know what it is."

He looked at her, cocking his head slightly to one side. Funny, he'd been thinking along those lines not long ago himself. He'd been wondering, too—and rather stuffily, he saw now—why he himself hadn't succumbed to this thing in the air. Whatever it was. And then, when he'd kissed Essie out there, and his loins had tingled, he'd been forced to admit that for one hot pinpoint moment he'd wanted her, wanted her badly, and hadn't given a damn about the cost or consequences.

When they had finished breakfast Tindle started to gather up the dishes and take them to the sink, and Essie said, "Don't bother. Atsuko will be here in the morning. I gave her the night off."

"Okay," said Tindle. He got up, stretched, then walked into the living room, and picked up his hat from the chair.

"Dick—"

"Yes?"

"Please. Just stay for a nightcap. I want to talk to somebody. I've got to talk to somebody."

He frowned, but said, "All right."

She brought brandy in a pony glass, then sat on the sofa beside him. She didn't move too close to him. She lit her cigarette rather nervously. She began to talk, and instead of looking at him, she stared at an imaginary point on the coffee table.

"What is it about Pete?" she said. "God—to look at him you'd think . . . well, you know how he looks. He looks like the hero in a movie about the Air Force. He looks like a recruiting poster. But—he just hasn't got it, Dick. He just hasn't got it."

61

"Now wait a minute, Essie. Pete's all right. Are you sure you aren't imagining a lot of things about Pete? Are you sure whatever you think is wrong with Pete isn't in your own mind?"

"I've never had any satisfaction with Pete. Do you know what I mean, Dick?" She was still staring at the table, and she was a little pale, he thought.

"Well—that could be in your own mind, too."

"He's—he's on and off. Like a jackrabbit."

"Essie! Damn it, I don't want to preach, but this stuff ought to stay inside the family. I mean, what the hell, we're civilized people, I suppose, but we're not *that* damned civilized."

"Yes we are. Or we ought to be. I read about Pete's trouble in a book on psychology. Premature ejaculation— comes from mother attachment and excessive masturbation in youth."

"Oh Essie, for Christ's sake—"

She was suddenly upon him. She twisted, rose, and at the same time thrust her cigarette into the ashtray with all the decisiveness of someone stepping upon a spider, and she sprang upon Tindle, grasping his shoulders, and by her weight pushing him down upon the sofa. She smashed her lips into his. She moved her head spasmodically, wrenching, smearing her kiss upon him, and pressing so hard that the feel of her teeth was painful. She ran her fingers up and down his neck, into his ear, and out again. She moaned slightly and very softly as she did this.

"Please, Dick," she whispered. "Give it to me. Oh, God, give it to me—let me have it just once . . . just once. . . ."

He trembled. He nodded automatically. He put one hand upon her buttocks and ran his palm up and down the soft curve; his other hand fumbled at the neck of her dress in a cramped, awkward gesture, and he slipped his fingers inside her brassière, and took hold of the hardening nipple of her breast.

"Oh, God . . . yes, yes," said Essie. Her eyes went up under the lids.

He twisted away for a moment to reach for the lamp chain.

62

"No. I want to see." Essie rose quickly from the sofa. I'll pull the blinds." She did that, and then began to slip her dress up over her shoulders.

It was that gesture. It was something in the soft, plump wriggle of her body, in the tightness of her dress, in the slight difficulty she encountered in pulling it over her head. It was something that had to do with the fleshiness of her thighs, and the queerly artificial look of her girdle and garter straps . . . she was no longer a woman, but somebody's wife: more than that, she was abruptly a symbol of the American married female, essentially soft and selfish and pampered, worshipped and overrated, powerful and corrupt with her power, soulless, well-fed, and treasured—she was not a woman, now, but a household appliance.

Tindle got up and said, "Good night, Essie."

He would never forget how she stood there with her dress crumpled in her hands and held in front of her, dangling from the pit of her neck, and her eyes wide, blank, uncomprehending.

CHAPTER THREE

1

SHORTLY after dark, about an hour and a half out of Akuni, 319 ran into a frontal passage. Before they hit the stuffed cloud there was still a trace of daylight, and Major Ronsdale, in the left-hand pilot's seat saw this cloud as it came. It was a vast black wall.

Ronsdale thought of the fear in his belly as a pale green glow; he was angry for having it there. But he could not control it.

He glanced at Lieutenant Cohen, who was staring moodily out of the right-hand window. He wondered if Cohen was really unconcerned: or was he frightened, too? Probably not. Probably he believed Ronsdale could handle anything that came along. Ronsdale turned his head further, and saw Sergeant Braith standing behind the pilot seats, leaning with his elbows on the chair-backs, looming there, filling the narrow passageway. Braith was watching him.

Ronsdale stared back for a moment, then said, "Everything okay?"

"Yes, sir," said Braith.

"You'd better tell the passengers to fasten their seat belts. Don't alarm them, though—just explain that it's a little weather, and—"

"I already did, sir."

"Oh," said Ronsdale. "Okay."

The airplane began to pitch and thud. There was utter darkness before the windshield; looking to the left Ronsdale could barely make out the blinking port light on the tip of the wing. A soft glow of exhaust flame tinted the wing with a glowing salmon color near the engine nacelle. Precipitation now made a soft purr on the metal skin of the ship.

Ronsdale made himself smile, and glanced at Braith again. "Getting a little rough."

Braith nodded absent-mindedly, and Cohen turned and stared for a moment in that heavy-lidded way of his.

Ronsdale wished now he'd said nothing: they must sense his nervousness now. He had taken a multi-engined aircraft through rough weather only a few times in the past. He had been trained originally as a single engine fighter pilot, but in order to log his flying time each month, after being assigned to an administrative job, he had thought it wise to check out in a C-47, and have this fact entered upon his Form 5.

Anxiously now, but hoping his anxiety would not show, he checked his panel instruments. He had to look at them one by one, staring at each gauge or dial separately, while he tried to adjust his fear-disturbed mind to its meaning. He rationalized that it was not fear which made him do this. He told himself that in this clumsy workhorse of an airplane you could never read your instruments with a quick glance, as you did in a fighter. And too many things to think of all at once, too much airplane to wrestle around. And too many other people to worry about—co-pilot; crew chief; six passengers in the waist. All trusting him. All believing in Pete Ronsdale.

But everything *did* seem in good shape: airspeed, 140; rpm, 1850; 28 inches of manifold pressure, the engines healthy and even. Just the same he dreaded this black cloud; he dreaded it as he had never dreaded anything before.

There was another sickening drop—heavier than those before—and the altimeter needle countered a hundred feet. Immediately after that Ronsdale felt his bottom pressed to the seat as an updraft tossed the airplane back.

Cohen held his hands to his earphones for a moment, then glanced at Ronsdale. "We're off course—we better take about three degrees right."

Ronsdale hadn't noticed, but now he realized that the steady tone of the beam that guided them was broken into faint pulses: long and short, long and short. He nodded, and swung the airplane back, watching the compass.

Braith leaned clumsily across the back of Cohen's seat and looked out of the right-hand window. Ronsdale heard him whistle.

Ronsdale said, "What is it, Braith?"

"See that ice, sir?"

Ronsdale looked at the leading edge of the wing. He could see a thin white line, reflecting at one point the light from the cockpit. "Yes, I see it." He started the de-icing boots; they throbbed, putting spiderweb cracks into the ice.

"Clear ice, not rime," said Braith. Unnecessary talk: Braith was showing his knowledge, and this was clear enough to the major. "Pretty bad. Rime breaks easy, but not this stuff."

Ronsdale had a momentary impulse to swing his head around and tell Braith to shut up, tell him sharply and firmly. But he didn't really want the sergeant to dislike him. He didn't want anyone to dislike him.

"Nothing to worry about," he said cheerfully.

He must remember to seem calm; above everything else he must remember that.

The plane fell, rose again. It wobbled off to the right, and he brought the wing back, overcompensating, so that it went to the left. He finally righted it.

"Carburetor temperature's in the red," said Braith.

65

He looked and it was. Damn that Braith; damn him for his tone of voice, his overplayed obsequiousness. Funny how he could make a simple matter of fact statement like that sound smug. Cohen must have sensed it, too. Cohen was glancing at Ronsdale with that heavy-lidded sardonic eye again. Ronsdale put his hand on the throttle quadrant and eased the carburetor heat in. The airplane continued to dip and buck.

"Major?"

"What is it, Braith?" Ronsdale managed some sound of impatience.

"Airspeed's up to one-forty again."

"Oh. Yes. So it is. Thanks, Braith." Damn him, again. The airspeed had never been *below* one-forty—this was just Braith's buttery way of reminding him that he was going too fast through the storm's turbulence. He took the power down a bit.

The engines began to clatter.

Why? Ronsdale shot glances both right and left, and then scanned the instrument panel. The airspeed needle was quivering at 125. The plane began to shake.

Ronsdale turned to Braith. "Uh—Sergeant, you'd better go back and check those engines from the waist window."

Braith said, "I think you're getting prop ice, sir. The engines are all right."

"Yes, I know that," snapped Ronsdale. "But I want those engines checked just the same."

"Yes, sir." Braith smiled, held it for a moment, then moved off.

Ronsdale cut in the de-icing fluid. This would squirt from the hubs of the propellers along the blades. He waited for some seconds, and the engines, instead of running more smoothly, clattered further.

"Can't understand why that stuff on the props isn't breaking up," he said to Cohen.

Cohen looked out of his right-hand window, looked back, shrugged, and settled in the seat again.

Ronsdale stared at the altimeter. It was falling slowly and steadily. He shoved the power up; the airplane shuddered and would not climb. There were mountains not far below them here; seven- and eight-thousand-foot peaks,

66

dozens of them. If he could stay at his assigned airway altitude of ten thousand five hundred feet he would be all right; the airplane would hold itself together . . . but these engines . . .

He was thinking now in frightened scraps of thought.

He was suddenly cold and lonely.

2

Just as cold is the absence of warmth, and not a thing in itself, so is loneliness the absence of existence. The wet chill of loneliness, thought Ronsdale. Ever since he could remember he had been lonely. Ever since he was the man child with the name and the consciousness that separated him from any others.

Young Pete Ronsdale's father had been a stockbroker in the twenties. There was a house on Long Island, and Pete's world at first was this English-style suburban area with with its cross-beam houses, great trees, clipped hedges and winding drives. Occasionally there was a glimpse of another world when he was taken into New York City on the Nassau Line for shopping or a show. But mainly it was this lovely, secure ordered place he knew.

Hard to remember his father now. Exactly, anyway. Tall, well-groomed and, Pete supposed, handsome. Everybody always said how handsome Henry B. Ronsdale was. How young Peter resembled him. Formal man . . . had to call him "sir" for the longest time, and even afterwards, when youth and father gripped hands man-to-man fashion, "Dad" sounded awkward and out of place. Young Ronsdale always had the impression that his father was bored with him and would like to get away. It was like a man talking to you and glancing at his watch all the time. Mother was always busy, too. Mother always smelled of perfume and powder and the lingering bath—something like Essie, come to think of it. Well, for that matter, Pete himself always had something to keep him busy.

First there was school. They always expected so much of him in school; fixed him with a washed-out righteous eye, and read him long lectures on duty and discipline and noblesse oblige. Beyond school there were always

67

things like the Boy Scouts and the hobbies they permitted him. Dad liked constructive hobbies, he always said. Peter was never sure what Dad meant by that, and in a child's penetrating way, he had an idea Dad wasn't so sure, either. He remembered one time, when he was ten, he wanted an Erector set. Dad got him a whole machine shop in the cellar. He would have preferred only the Erector set—that was his own idea—but he couldn't hurt Dad's feelings by admitting that, and so he'd thanked Dad profusely. And Dad had said fine, fine, and nodded, as though to a board of directors. Every lad should learn to work with his hands, Dad had said.

And then there was the choir. Two nights a week they rehearsed, and they sang all the services on Sunday. Dad bragged about Pete's making the choir: he never failed, when he brought his friends home, and introduced Peter, to say: "Stands on his own two feet, this lad—makes his own spending money singing in the choir. Four bucks a week. That's as much as I made when I started out in life. Betcha he'll have his first million before he's thirty."

But the choir at the family church was more to Peter than four bucks a week. It was the bright hub around which his life revolved. It was the glowing nucleus, the Godhead, the yardstick, and the motto on the wall. It was week-end, reward, vacation, candy. Pete loved the choir above all things . . . the sound of it, even now:

We praise Thee, O God: we acknowledge Thee to be the Lord. All the earth doth WOR-ship Thee: the Father ever-lasting. . . .

Not the words, not the nonsense syllables. The great ceiling, and the live sound of young heavenly voices—his own among them—and the smell of church, especially on Easter morning. The Church of the Inviolate, it was called. Until he learned the word later, Pete always thought it had something to do with a flower.

To Thee all Angels cry aloud; the heavens and all the POW-'rs therein;

To Thee Cher-u-bim and Ser-a-phim: continually do cry. . . .

The choir rehearsal room was downstairs. The voices never made such sorcery in this smaller room as in the

68

great main vault. The male altos and the tenors and basses were always too close behind the boys; the young springwater voices were then corrupted and impure.

It was Wickelly, the red-headed kid from Hempstead, who took him into the crypt one evening during recess, and showed him how to masturbate.

Hea-v'n and earth are FULL of the Maj-es-ty, of Thy-y glo-o-ree!

End of boy.

His voice cracked and they stared at him, every one of them there in the great church, all that company of demons, and he knew that his face was red against the stiff white collar and lacy surplice.

But then he became a youth, and as a youth he looked fine in the summer in a white dinner jacket. They'd just come in that year. Princeton. "School of hard knocks, myself," said Dad, possibly convinced that it was his original phrase, "but I always said a college education never hurt anyone."

Pete was the hit of the Triangle Club show that year. Several Broadway critics said kind words about his light baritone voice—possibly even meant them.

Then a year in the office, to groom him for a customers' man. He was still pretty young; he'd skipped a few grades in elementary and high school. The racket, Dad said, meaning the stock business, was tougher now than when Dad had started, what with taxes and the S.E.C. and one thing and another . . . still, a man could get somewhere if he would be single-minded about it. Have a goal of some sort. Swear he'd make a million before he was thirty, that was one way to go about it. "When you get a little older, son, you'll stop running off so early on week ends to fly that airplane of yours, that Piper Cub, or whatever you call it, and later on, when you've got yourself set, why, then you can enjoy life. Look at me. I'm exactly twice your age, and if you think I don't enjoy life—"

We therefore pray Thee . . . hel-l-lp Thy ser-vant: Whom-Thou-hast-re-deem-ed with Thy pre-cious blood. . . .

"Yes, Dad. I signed up with the Air Corps this morning. I—I hope you're not angry, sir."

69

"Angry? My boy. My boy."

"Well, I thought you might be—the business and everything—"

"The business can wait. Go give 'em hell, boy."

Dad gripped his shoulders. But even then he looked as though he wanted to hurry and get this over with so he could go and keep an appointment.

3

Braith came back. He put his hands again on the backs of the pilots' seats, and thrust himself forward.

"How are the engines?"

"They're okay, just as we thought. It's something else."

"What?"

"No de-icing fluid in the prop tanks."

"Why the devil not?"

"Well, sir," said Braith, "if I were taking care of this plane regularly this kind of thing wouldn't happen. I instituted a check-off system when I was a technical expert at Wright Field. I was a civilian then, and—"

The plane pitched violently, and Ronsdale felt it in his stomach. He racked the wheel to one side, fighting the turbulent air, his gullet drawn and empty.

They were still losing altitude.

"Look, Braith," said Ronsdale, "can't you transfer the fluid or something? Isn't there another tank—the windshield tank?"

"Take pretty long," said Braith. "I've got a better idea, Major."

"What? What then?"

"Jazz your engines back and forth," said Braith. "Get 'em out of synch. That ought to shake the prop ice off. Here—like this."

Braith reached forward to the throttle quadrant, and worked the levers against each other. The engines went VROOM! VROOM! VROOM! The plane shook, fishtailed. Braith did this for several seconds. Ronsdale sat there with his hands tight and cold upon the wheel; he stared at Braith in a fascinated way.

"Now we'll even 'em up," said Braith.

70

Once again the big sergeant synchronized the engines. They purred more smoothly. Ronsdale took the throttles from him, and jockeyed them forward until both needles on the manifold pressure gauge rose together. The ship was still pitching, dropping sickeningly, bumping, rising sharply—but on the whole, now, she was climbing.

"We ought to be through the front in another few minutes," said Braith.

"Thanks to you, Sergeant. Nice work."

Braith laughed. "Well, it was just a trick I learned from a transatlantic pilot when I was flying Clippers."

"When you were what?"

"Oh, I wasn't a pilot—I was a steward on British Overseas Airlines for a while. I didn't really need the job, but I wanted to do some research on a history I was writing, and London was the only place I could get the dope I needed. So I had to figure out how to get to London. . . ."

Ronsdale was listening not to the words, but to the tone and manner of the sergeant's voice. There was a subtle difference, now. Nothing you could put your finger on, but a few moments ago there had been the usual overtone of rank—the kind of thing that always pervades the talk between two military men of different rank—and now the sergeant spoke to Ronsdale, in some intangible way, quite as an equal. Perhaps he was even a little lofty.

Cohen, with his heavy-lidded eyes, looked once at Braith, once at Ronsdale, holding each look for a moment, and then he pretended to be very busy studying the instrument panel.

Braith said, "Say—how long do we spend in Tokyo, Major?"

Now, Ronsdale told himself. Slap him down now—nip this thing in the bud. Be strong for once. Do it the way all the people who look at you, and see the very picture of an officer and a fighter pilot and a man of strength and courage, would expect you to do it. Now, he thought.

Then he drew his breath and spoke, and his voice came out as a stranger's voice. It was civil—even pleasant. "We'll be there all day tomorrow. Probably leave the day after."

"Be good to get to Tokyo, all right," said Braith.

"Yes."

71

"Guess you'll be doing some shopping and everything, hm?"

"Yes. I'll get in some of that."

"Any particular plans for tomorrow night, Major?"

"Plans? No. Why?"

"Well—I was wondering. I was just thinking you'd get a big kick out of Teriko. I'll bet you'd really go for it."

"Who's Teriko?"

"She's just the best-looking dame in all of Tokyo, that's all. She works at a radio parts place there. I used to keep her on the string when I was stationed at FEAF. She's got—you know"—Braith outlined breasts on his chest—"as big as a white woman's. Magnificent bazooms. And passionate. Very passionate."

"Is that so?"

"I mean, don't get me wrong or anything," said Braith. "She's no tramp. She's a hell of a nice kid—but if she likes you, and everything clicks, you can probably get in."

"I wasn't planning on that kind of entertainment," said Ronsdale. His throat was suddenly dry, and he swallowed. Often he'd thought about taking a fling in Tokyo; often he'd catpawed the idea in his mind. He did so miserably with Essie. Why was it they never quite managed to hit it off in bed? Lord knew, they tried. But they were always like two people singing the same song in different keys. And maybe he needed a change; maybe he needed a really successful affair. Maybe that would kind of break the log jam.

Braith was saying, "Well, there's no guarantee she'll come across or anything, but I just thought we might have some fun. Maybe go out to a Jap night club. I know all the joints in Tokyo. I got a half-dozen dames to pick from, actually, but I thought you and Terry would really get along. You'd look good together. So what do you say?"

Why was Braith doing this? Ronsdale turned to study his face, saw only round innocence, and turned away again. If he accepted Braith's offer, Braith would have even more of an upper hand, a kind of claim upon him. Maybe that was the idea. Ronsdale ought to tell him sharply, once and for all, that he had no intention of—

72

But, Christ, he needed a really satisfying sexual experience for a change. He needed it badly.

"Well, we might try it, Braith," he said, pleasantly, laughing as though somewhat mildly amused.

"Good," said Braith. He rubbed his large, meaty hands.

The airplane nosed out of the clouds, and they saw the pearl lights of the villages on the shore eight thousand feet below. There was a half-moon.

CHAPTER FOUR

1

IT WAS morning in Tokyo. Only the edge of the storm had touched the city the night before; now there was a blanket of cloud rapidly becoming threadbare under the sun. It was humid, and the invisible moisture was already greedily hoarding the warmth.

The day's traffic was becoming heavy upon Avenue A (named this by the Occupation; the Japanese do not name their streets) which ran parallel with the east moat of the Emperor's palace grounds. There were stock model American cars, bandy-wheeled Japanese Datsuns, British Morrises, French Renaults, trolleys, buses, handcars, pedicabs, and every great now and then an old-fashioned rickshaw. There was a prevalence of jeeps.

Among these vehicles this morning was a low, two-place yellow M.G. with red wheels. It joined the southerly flow near the Meiji Building, where the Far East Air Forces made its headquarters. The driver was a rotund, toadlike little man who wore a flowered sports shirt. His arms were thick and muscular, and a matting of gray-shot hair oozed from his open collar. He was wall eyed, but this was partially concealed by his thick, horn-rimmed glasses. His name—John Pendermeyer—was lettered in gold leaf on the side doors of the car.

Swinging from lane to lane on Avenue A, he wove past Supreme Headquarters in the Dai Ichi Building, past the yellow-drab brickpile of the Imperial Hotel, past massive Radio Tokyo. Every once in a while he looked down upon

73

the seat beside him at a large, square package, which was wrapped in plain brown paper. Each time he saw it he nodded to himself, reassured that it was still there.

Several blocks past Radio Tokyo he turned off the main street into a narrower thoroughfare that was lined on both sides by flimsy shingle and panel houses, most being shops with open fronts. This street was crowded, and here the people dressed less in western and more in Japanese style. Many men wore summer kimonos, some short cotton jackets and cut-off trousers, a few no more than loincloths. There were more wooden geta than shoes. Red and white flags and streamers fluttered, advertising wares; the big Japanese characters in broad commercial calligraphy seemed festive. There was a strong smell of fish.

Johnny Pendermeyer arched his thick nostrils and rolled his cigar to the center of his mouth. By God, these Japs were a backward people, he thought, and that was something you just couldn't get away from. They were just different, that was all. Same way niggers and spicks were different: darker, dirtier and dumber. Give 'em all the schooling you wanted, and you'd never change that. Born into 'em. By God, these Japs were damned lucky to have the Americans come over here and straighten 'em out like this. This Occupation was the best thing ever could have happened to 'em.

Of course they had their points.

They were great at fixing up little fancy things, and they did pretty good woodwork, and they were like a bunch of cocker spaniels the way they tried to please you sometimes. And as for Japanese women, well, there was an awful lot to be said for them. Damned nice bodies most of them, except for an oversupply of flat chests, and, even more important, they knew their place. They really knew their place as women.

Take Sachiko. Sachiko was really a looker. He'd been keeping her in a little cottage out around Azabu, in a section of trees and high walls and narrow streets and bamboo fences, out where all the embassies and missions were. Sachiko waited on him hand and foot, and watched his moods with a falcon's eye, so that she could immediately mirror any change. Often she patted his fat gut and

74

said it was cute. *Ho-tei Sama*, she called him sometimes, after the potbellied god of laughter.

He laughed to think of it.

But if it came down to cases, he went on thinking, he wouldn't trust Sachiko any further than he would a rattle-snake. After all, it was just the way of these Japs, for all their smiling and polite hissing, to doublecross you in a minute if they got the chance. Real honesty just wasn't born in people like these, and that was something you just couldn't get away from. . . .

He drove several blocks along the side street, and then pulled the sports car to the curb in front of an establishment that bore the sign:

YAMAMOTO WHOLESALE PARTS, Ltd.
Parts of the Radio all assorted. In addition English spoken.

The place was a long, low building with a glassed-in front. An office filled with close-jammed desks showed through the panels. Japanese men and women worked at these desks. Behind the office was another room, parti-tioned off, and here were lines of bins containing parts and supplies.

Johnny tucked the plain-wrapped package carefully under his arm and went in.

A girl in a white, off-the-shoulder blouse sat at a desk near the door. Johnny avoided looking at her directly, but from the corner of his eye he noted with satisfaction that she glanced up quickly as he passed, then looked down at her typewriter again. Her shoulders were remarkably broad —like a swimmer's shoulders—and she was tall for a Japanese girl. Her hair was like darkest mahogany, but not quite black. Its natural wave gave it a thick, piled texture. Her face was angular; her eyebrows were plucked and pen-ciled into exotic arches, and her lipstick was drawn upon her lips in a way that gave her mouth a moist, somewhat spoiled-child look. In her slightest movement—typing, turning a page, leaning back, leaning forward again—she had all the grace of a ballet danseuse.

Johnny walked toward the largest desk at the end of the room, where sat a painfully thin Japanese with long, straight hair that was parted in the middle and hung in ropy strands down the sides of his head. This man was smoking a cigarette in an ivory holder. As Johnny approached, he got up, smiled, and showed several sickly gray aluminum teeth in front.

"Hello, Johnny," he said in excellent American-English. "How're you feeling today?"

"Fine, Dan, fine. How's yourself?"

Dan Yamamoto nodded. "Same." He had American cigarettes and he offered them absent-mindedly. Johnny shook his head and waved his cigar. Then he stuck it back into the corner of his mouth, sat down, and dropped his hands to the square package in his lap.

"How's business, Dan?" asked Johnny.

"Coming along." Yamamoto had spidery fingers; he folded them on the desk. On his face was an odd, sharp smile.

Knows I'm not here on just a social call, thought Johnny; old Dan's pretty sharp, all right. But not so sharp I can't handle him any time I want to. Johnny said, "Just thought I'd drop around and say hello."

"Well, nice to see you. Nice to see you any time." Yamamoto tilted his head in a faintly wary gesture.

"Not interrupting your work, am I?"

"Not at all. I've got plenty of time. Maybe not so much money—but plenty of time."

Johnny laughed. "Dan, you bandit—you've got more time and money, both, than the Bank of Japan, and you know it."

Yamamoto laughed politely.

"But that's the way it goes," said Johnny. "Fellow with a little scratch always has a chance to make a little more. Course I'm in a different boat myself. I got to pick up a little here and little there—whenever I can."

"Of course." Yamamoto had a slightly patient air, now.

"Meanwhile I want to do my job right up at FEAF."

"Naturally."

"We tech reps don't have it as easy as some people think." Johnny leaned back in his chair. "For a while we couldn't get the equipment we wanted nearly quick enough. Had to build things out of spit and bailing wire.

76

Had to buy stuff out of our own pockets, sometimes. As you well know."

"Mmhm," said Yamamoto.

"Well, that's changed now. We finally got authorization to make local purchase here in Tokyo on items out of stock. And I'm the lad who's going to do the purchasing."

"I see," said Yamamoto. And looked more interested.

Johnny held his cigar before his eyes, and turned it this way and that, and studied it. He liked the pose. He liked the dialogue with Yamamoto—it gave him the feeling of being a slick operator. He'd always admired slick operators. He was convinced that he was not wealthy today because the luck factor was negative in his own particular case: all the talent in the world wouldn't do you much good if you didn't happen to get the breaks.

He was fifty-two now. He wondered sometimes where all the years had gone, for it seemed only yesterday that he was a hustling kid in South Philadelphia turning a half-buck here and a half-buck there. Funny how he'd gotten sidetracked into radio. He and a friend had rented a store cheap with the idea of setting up a betting place. A couple of well-dressed toughs had dropped around one night and managed to discourage them from that idea. But they still had the store. At that point Johnny's friend had discovered that a cousin of his was making a potful in the radio repair business—a simple little soldering job could be passed off to a customer as a major repair job costing ten or fifteen bucks.

Johnny and his partner bought up some junk and opened the shop. The really tough repair jobs they farmed out; meanwhile Johnny, who always worked hard at whatever he did, began to learn a few things about radio repair in spite of himself. He took a correspondence course, at this point still convinced that he was only doing it because it would help his racket. Eventually he got his first-class license, and through the years, after one thing and another (still never having made that big, smart killing) he ended up with the Civil Aeronautics Administration. Sucker's dough, working for the government, but the security of it couldn't be beat. Not that he wasn't still waiting for his big break—but meanwhile—

Time went by behind his back. He wasn't paying attention. Sixteen years ago he had started with Continental Radio Corporation. My God, was it sixteen years ago? He counted the dates. Good grief. Well, anyway, he'd get a pension now in another four years, and extra for this overseas time he was serving now. To say nothing of the little deals a man could work on the side over here in Japan.

Yessir, this tech rep business wasn't too bad, after all. Figuring extras and everything you could knock down eight grand a year, living cheap over here and saving what you made. And by living cheap he didn't mean scrimping either: like a king, you lived cheap. As for the work—there was nothing to the work. A dope could breeze through it with both eyes closed and his hands behind his back. Assist and advise, said the directive, and that could be just about anything you wanted to make it—or didn't want to make it. The only mandatory duty was to write out a report for the company every month on what kind of equipment the Air Force was using, or would be likely to use in the near future. The company had nearly fifty technical representatives over here now, scattered all around the theater. It didn't cost Continental much, because they could deduct the expense from their corporation taxes, and for their pains they got maybe millions of dollars' worth of influence and good will. Smart operating. Johnny admired smart operating.

"So you see," he said to Yamamoto, "just where we buy this local purchase stuff depends on a lot of things."

"I understand," said Yamamoto. "Just how much kickback do you want?"

Johnny laughed; shook with it. "Dan, you're a sharp one, all right! You're really a sharp one!"

"Well, Johnny, you understand I can't give you too much commission."

"What do you think is too much, Dan?"

"You've got to realize that I don't have a high margin of profit. On some items a commission would hardly be worth it."

"Don't kid me, Dan. But, hell, we don't have to go into details now. We can do that later. Besides, I'll have to make up a list of the kind of stuff we'll be needing."

"All right, Johnny. Whatever you say. How soon do you think you'll be ready?"

Johnny frowned importantly. "Dan, I'll make it as soon as I can. But they've got me really snowed under up there. Some of the equipment they use is too complicated for them to understand, so they need a tech rep on it. And I'm the only tech rep up there cleared for secret matter—" he chuckled—"I guess there was never much doubt where I stand in this loyalty business. Not that I'm a flag-waver, or anything like that, but I just figure I'm pretty lucky to be born where I was."

"Sure, Johnny."

"And you Japanese—you're pretty lucky to be hitching up with us. Like to see a bunch of you over there in Korea now, on our side."

Yamamoto nodded and smiled; if he was discomfited, he did not show it.

"Well, that about does it, I guess." Johnny rose, seeming to bounce after he got to his feet. He clutched his plain package tightly. "I'll get in touch with you on that matter in a few days."

"Any time, Johnny."

"See you later, Dan."

Five minutes later Johnny met the girl in the white, off-the-shoulder blouse in a little coffee shop less than a block from Yamamoto Wholesale Parts, Ltd. He went to the place first, ordered iced coffee, and then, when she appeared, he rose and smiled.

"Hi, Teriko," he said. He patted her bare arm. "How's tricks? *Ikaga desuka?*"

"I feeling fine," said the girl. She pulled away from his hand, and slipped into the booth, across the table from him.

"Good! Good!" said Johnny broadly. "What do you want to drink?"

"Please—I can have iced coffee, too?"

"Anything you want, baby. The best. You name it, and it's yours."

"So." She nodded, making it seem a curtsy. She put her forearms on the table, and leaned slightly forward so that the parting of her breasts showed under her blouse.

79

Terrific breasts, thought Johnny, for a Japanese girl. Terrific. If he didn't have Sachiko he could really go for this one. Hell, maybe someday he'd have to get rid of Sachiko. She'd been getting like she owned him lately. Be nice to keep this one sort of in reserve.

Right now he'd better stick to business.

"I got the stuff," he said, and nodded at the package beside him.

"So," said Teriko.

"It wasn't easy," he said, "and I had to pay off that kid from communications supply."

"Ah," she said.

"You understand me?"

"I understand."

"I can never tell whether you're following me or not. You look the same when you don't understand as when you do understand."

Teriko cocked her head. Puzzled.

"Okay, okay, skip it," said Johnny. The waitress came and he ordered an iced coffee for her in stumbling Japanese. His cigar had gone out. He re-lit it. Then he leaned heavily across the table and spoke in low tones. "Now, listen, kid, I want you to be real careful getting rid of this. The both of us could get into an awful lot of trouble."

"I understand."

"Sure you do. I always thought you were a pretty smart kid."

"No—I don't have good head."

"Baby, you've got more than just a good head. You've got everything," said Johnny.

She looked impassive again.

Johnny said, "Now, listen. I'll walk out of here first. I'll leave the package on the seat here. You wait maybe five minutes before you go out with it. *Wakari mashita?*"

"I understand. *Wakari mashita.*"

"And when do you think you'll have the dough?"

"Ah—*shiranai.*" She shook her head rapidly. "Maybe— maybe two days, neh?"

"Okay. Two days. But we got to figure out a way for you to deliver it."

"You can't come Yamamoto Wholesale?"

"Not for the dough. That wouldn't be safe. You better meet me at night somewhere. Like you're just meeting me for a date or something."

"Date? You never ask me date before."

"And I'm not now, baby. I didn't mean a *real* date." He dipped his round head. "Not that I wouldn't like it. But Sachiko would take the dim view, I'm afraid."

"Ah, so. Sachiko." Again she nodded.

"You let me figure out the details of where I'm going to meet you, then I'll call you on the phone at Yamamoto's and give you the dope."

"*Hai.* I can do."

"Maybe I can pick you up at your house."

"You can find?"

"I drove you there once, didn't I? Once I go to a place I never forget where it is."

"Ah, so *desuka*," she said gravely.

Johnny studied her, sighed abruptly and said, "I sure hope you know what you're doing on this deal. Trouble is, I can never tell what you're thinking. From your face, I mean."

"You are same," she said.

"Same?"

"I can't tell what you are thinking. Very hard for Japanese to tell what thinking American people, neh?"

"No foolin'. Is that what you really think about us?"

"So."

He laughed. "Where'd you learn English, anyway, Teriko?"

"I learn in school."

"You speak it damned good."

"No, I don't speak so good."

"You're a real smart kid. I knew it the first time I saw you up there in Yamamoto's."

"Not smart," she said.

The hell she wasn't, Johnny was thinking. He could pick the smart ones—he'd picked her the minute he'd seen her pecking away at a typewriter up there in Yamamoto's. Of course, he hadn't figured then that she'd have these black market contacts. But she must have sized him up as a customer all the time. She hadn't rushed things, either.

That first day he'd asked her to duck out and have coffee she hadn't even brought the subject up. Later, she'd started off in a small way. She'd wondered, kind of offhand, if he had any cartons of cigarettes he'd like to get rid of for a nice profit in yen. Then one thing led to another. After a while it wasn't hard to let him know what was bringing a hot price on any given day. But tubes he'd wormed from comm-supply was the biggest deal so far. Even after she took her ten percent, and he figured what he'd paid to get it, he'd still clear nearly sixty thousand yen. Not bad for a couple of days' work. A year's salary for Teriko where she worked. No wonder she played around with the black market, the way wages and prices were for these people—she didn't dress the way she did on five thousand yen a month. That was, let's see, only about fourteen bucks, American. Nope, she must have lots of other sources.

"You got any boy friends, Teriko?"

She looked momentarily surprised and then said, with the air of one answering a foolish question, "I have boy friend. Of course."

"Japanese?"

"Some time Japanese, some time American. Why you ask?"

"Just wondering, that's all." Johnny waved his cigar. Matter dismissed. Not time to follow it up now. He'd have to play close to the vest on this one—and besides he wasn't yet one hundred percent sure he was going to give Sachiko her walking papers. He just wanted to have everything set up in case he did. Hell, it was funny how easy it was to get tired of a dame when you really lived with her, and how quickly it could come about—

He sipped the last of his iced coffee with a noisy gurgle at the foot of the straw. He said, "Ahhh," in the way of a fat man, and rose. "I'll call you later today and tell you where to meet me. Okay?"

Teriko nodded.

Johnny went out humming "China Night."

Teriko sipped her ice coffee slowly, daintily, and without a trace of expression on her face.

82

IT'S THIS WAY

Tokyo (Undated)—It was one of those casual meetings at a bar; just a couple of guys, we were, and both lonely. You can be lonely in Tokyo, as in any big city.

It developed that we both had been radio operators in the last war. That gave us a pretty good common ground; that, and the beer we sipped. After a while we talked about the Japanese language and recalled that the Japanese word for "drunk" was "yoparai," and so we made our first joke. We said we must both have been radio yoparaitors.

We gave this joke much more laughter than it deserved.

This other man was very thin, and, I thought all the time, curiously sad. He was a good listener, so I talked a little more than I should have. Bragged a little, I guess. "I had it pretty rough," I said. "I did my radio operating on B-17s in the E.T.O. One mission over Vienna twenty-four of us went out and nine came back. I'd been a corporal. I was a staff sergeant the next day."

"Yes," said the thin man. He'd told me he'd been in the Navy.

"One thing about the Navy," I said. "You always have it fat. Always good chow—and coffee when you want it."

He laughed.

"Not so?" I asked.

"I was on a minesweeper," he said. "They're not too comfortable. Besides, I did that long stretch in prison camp."

"Prison camp, eh?" I looked at him with both interest and respect.

"Fish," he said. "Fish and rice. That was all we got. And how I hate fish and rice."

"Seems funny that's all you got."

"They appeared to think we could live on it. Well—we did. After a fashion. I lost forty pounds. But that wasn't the worst of it. The beating with the bamboo was what got me. The bamboo cane was an inch in diameter and they used to beat us over the head and across the back with it."

"Really?"

"There's something about bamboo. It's hard, but it has just enough flexibility to whip and sting. I think the welts from bamboo stay longer than any other kind of welts."

"Who whipped you with the bamboo, anyway?"

"The corporal. The louse. Of course, if we stood in the hot sun for two hours without moving a muscle, we didn't get whipped. Nobody quite succeeded in doing that every time."

"Where was this, anyway?"

"In the Philippines. In a prison camp in the Philippines."

"I see." I finished my beer thoughtfully. "We better have another."

"All right." The thin man bought the drinks. He said, "You know, I promised myself if I ever came across the sergeant here in Tokyo I'd buy him the best drink I could find."

"The sergeant?"

"The one who finally caught the corporal whipping us with the bamboo cane. He hit him flush on the jaw and knocked him out with one punch. Only time I've ever seen that done. I think you have to catch a man just right to do it."

"I guess so," I said.

Our second round of beers came and we sipped them. The thin man looked across the bar, into a distance he'd found somewhere. "It isn't a very good story, is it?" he said. "I'm sorry I bored you with it. You see, it was very vivid to me, and I can't quite convince myself that it isn't unique."

"But it is unique," I said.

"No. Hardly. It's the kind of prison camp story you hear all the time."

I took out the old envelopes I use in place of a notebook. "I want to use the story," I said. "I didn't catch your name exactly when we introduced ourselves."

"Yamamoto," said the thin man. "Danshiro Yamamoto.
84

But my American friends call me Dan. That's an easier name for Americans. All the American guards called me that in their prison camp back in the Philippines. . . ."

"You better let me buy the next beer," I said.

3

Teriko left the coffee shop some fifteen minutes later and walked back toward the offices of Yamamoto Wholesale Parts, Ltd. She walked with a lilt, swinging her head from side to side and voicing softly the opening measures of Mozart's *Eine Kleine Nacht-musik*, which she learned in school. So Johnny Pendermeyer, Johnny-san, the fat little American, had wanted to sleep with her. She had seen that, and while she didn't suppose she particularly wanted to sleep with him, the fact of being desired by a man always gave her pleasure.

Teriko Katama was twenty-four years old. Her father, Satoshi Katana, had been an inspector with the government police before the war, and he was already sixty-four when Teriko was born. Her mother was fifty. Inspector Katana had died just before the bomb and the surrender, and Teriko lived now in two small rooms in someone else's house with her mother. She did not believe that she would live like this forever.

Oh, there were so many things she wanted to be other than what she found herself to be! So many things. Often she wanted to be a man. All the way, with the organs of a man, and everything. Then sometimes she wanted to be an American woman—not the fat, brutish women you saw around Tokyo (factory-rejects an American boy friend of hers had called them, and, working in a radio parts company, she understood the term) but those you often saw in American movies.

She knew, of course, that American movie stars weren't quite real. They simply didn't look real, like the people in British and French movies, for instance, and without any real facts to guide her she completely sensed this. But still, she loved the movies. Probably she loved the movies better than anything else. She spent quite a bit of her five thousand yen a month salary upon them.

And then sometimes she believed she would like to be

85

married to an American. She might make it work. Things were changed now—as her mother always kept reminding her in that complaining way of hers. She was not like most of her Japanese girl friends; she was sure of this. To begin, she was not as bashful as they. When she wanted something she asked for it; if an American escort seemed inclined to give her his seat on the street car, or hold the door open for her to go first, she was perfectly willing that it should be this way.

She kept humming Mozart. Now there was within her a curious elation, a meringue of happiness that was wonderfully pleasant, but that didn't quite blot out the heavy melancholy underneath. Always she must admit, eventually, that her future held little she would really desire. It was a matter of being born in the wrong place-time, and of the wrong sex. And yet . . . and yet she didn't want it to be quite otherwise. She had never learned to live with security; real security might make her uneasy, frightened.

The fire bombs, for one thing, had frightened Teriko.

Father was still alive then. They lived in a nicer section of Tokyo, among trees and brooks and rambling stone walls and gardens. The B-29s would come in the middle of the night. They had been shown pictures of slim, knife-winged monsters in school during the day: they knew that this was another inhumane weapon of the enemy. What manner of uncivilized barbarians would send such engines to drop fire bombs on a city of huddled and innocent civilians! They expected her to hate and be frightened, and in a way she did, and was: but for those years these were the only nights she knew, and so she lived with them. In the middle of the night, then: and first the sirens of the early alert, ghosts in the night like the offstage coming of the spirits in a Kabuki play. And everyone would file to the air-raid shelter, not yet going inside, but sitting in the humid summer air and watching quietly, fearfully, the sky. After a while there would be a sound like a tremolo on the samisen, but soft, distant. It would approach; they would seek cover. The guns all over the city would begin to crump. Once in a while the spent shrapnel of the anti-aircraft would fall in a harsh patter around the shelter.

86

Presently the B29s would be overhead. Teriko had slipped out of the shelter several times, curiosity overcoming fear, and she had gazed upward. Once she had seen the bright cross of an airplane caught in a stiff swaying search-light beam. They never saw the bombs fall. They heard them strike sometimes, and they saw the growing, bright-ening flames, and they heard the wails of the wounded and the bereft and the desolated—but they never saw the bombs actually falling.

That dark night she had slipped from the shelter with Giichi. He was slender and handsome and kind: a young man in body, with the strange comfort of an old man's eyes, and had he lived it might all have been very wonder-ful and different. Both families approved the marriage; they were only waiting for it to be financially possible. Everything was understood. She had given herself to Giichi that dark night and she had found her first comfort. . . .

But Giichi had always had that odd, characteristic cough, no more than the nervous clearing of throat, you would think, and he had always had that strange rose color to his cheeks. He had loved the color of the rose, and in his first poem to her, which he wrote in a strong but graceful brush-hand, he said, "*In autumn now the rose leaves fall; I will be buried by the rose leaves, since it is a thousand autumns until I see you.*"

He died in the autumn after the summer of the bomb; he died very suddenly.

Teriko went to her aunt's house in the north country, then, and rested for three months. This was the custom. When she came back to Tokyo she no longer cared about herself, about anything. This marked the change.

But perhaps it had begun long before Giichi—the real beginning, she thought. Perhaps, for instance, something had begun that time she was first kissed. She was seven-teen then, all wrapped up in the Middle School and holi-days and girls' games, as a young lady of seventeen ought to be. She hadn't even known what a kiss was. Oka-san had announced one Sunday that they would visit her uncle whom she had never seen. They traveled a long way, it seemed to Tokyo, changing buses and street cars several times. When she—walking a respectful step or two behind her mother—first approached her uncle's house, she didn't realize it was a house at all, because it was so huge and beautiful it looked more like a school or a temple. She had always liked temples and shrines: they were so green and happy. Not at all like the bony gray Christian churches and the dark mutterings of death that seemed to issue from them all the time. She stared about wide-eyed inside. Oka-san and Oji-sama—who was her mother's younger brother—sipped green tea and talked. She stole glances at Oji-sama. He was a stocky, positive man with a fine squarecut head and a small mustache. He had a deep, pleasant voice. She forgot now what Oka-san went off to do—at any rate, Oka-san wasn't in the room, and Oji-sama came over to her, smiling, put both his arms around her (they felt warm and strong and all-engulfing, like a hot bath) and pressed his lips, soft and moist, to hers.

She was startled, and as she had been taught to do when startled, she looked up at him blankly, impassively. He said that he would do it again, and this time she must open her lips and touch her tongue to his. She did that, and he touched her breast, lightly at first, and finally squeezed the nipple until it hurt slightly. She didn't cry out. He managed to kiss her several times before Oka-san returned. It was an old western custom he had learned in San Francisco, he explained. He warned her to say nothing—absolutely nothing—about this to Oka-san.

Of course, after she and her mother were home, she told Oka-san all about it. Everything. Oka-san cried a little and for the next several days she would think of the incident now and then and cry or sniffle anew. She went into long explanations about the differences between men and women, and the mechanics of reproduction, which Teriko only found confusing, and never really remembered.

No—not everything. There was something she hadn't told her mother. That was that she had enjoyed the sensation of kissing immensely, and that within her now there was desire as glowing and smokeless as a red charcoal ember in the gray ash of a wintertime heating fire.

Maybe it had begun then. Maybe as far back as then she was already moulded to behave as she did when she returned from her period of mourning in the country. When

88

she returned a relative had arranged a job for her in the American P.X. She must work; she must kep busy, they all said. At the P.X. the GIs frightened her a bit at first, but she was used to being frightened, and she felt a strange mixture of terror and pleasure when she made her first date. He was a lieutenant in the artillery. He was a young man—a young and extraordinary pink man—and she suspected he might be even younger than she. She didn't sleep with him, but she kissed him good night in the taxi, remembering how her uncle had taught her to kiss one hot afternoon so long ago. The lieutenant had drawn back in surprise and said, "Wow! Where'd you learn to do *that*?" The next man was a chief petty officer in the navy. He had fed her a sweet drink at an American-style night club, saying it wasn't strong. It made her head whirl, and her knees weaken. Wondering why she was unable to control herself, she had gone to a Japanese hotel for the night and slept with him. After that there were four or five others: she could remember them sometimes individually, but she never counted them. She thought of them as a whole. Oka-san, she supposed, would have thought her wicked and promiscuous, had she known, but, actually, she refused more men than she accepted. She received at least a dozen offers each day in the P.X., and she knew from the gabbling jealousy of the other girls that for some reason she was curiously attractive to Americans, probably because of her narrow nose and broad shoulders, which she had thought at one time something of a blemish.

She knew that in sleeping with a man now and then she was searching for something . . . grasping for security and peace of mind desperately . . . hoping some day one of these men she favored might take care of her . . . playing the longer odds for the higher stakes—and at the same time assuaging the restless thirst of her body angrily, hastily, as one would hush a noisy child. She knew this; but she could not have put it into words.

This May morning she turned into the office of Yamamoto Wholesale Parts, Ltd., after her walk from the coffee shop, and saw a large GI, who was sweating a bit in the increasing heat, standing by her desk.

She didn't fully recognize him until she saw the Air Force tech sergeant's chevrons upon his sleeves, and then she remembered that she had gone dancing with him several times a month ago. She hadn't really liked him, but she remembered him because for some odd reason he hadn't tried, like the rest, to kiss her or feel her body. Maybe that was what she hadn't particularly liked. Now she recalled his name—Frank-san. The last name began with a "B" and she couldn't pronounce it very well.

"Hi, Terry! What do you say?" said Tech Sergeant Frank Braith.

"Hello, Frank-san!" She pretended to be pleased. She curtsied.

"Brought a present for you," said Braith. He put a small package on her desk. "Here."

"Ah, so!" She picked it up, curtsied again and said, "Domo arigato gozai masu!"

"Well—aren't you going to look at it?"

She nodded and began to unwrap the package. It was a bottle of perfume and the expensive kind she had always admired when she worked in the P.X. "Thank you very much," she said.

"Just a little present." He shrugged clumsily, then leaned on the desk. "Say—I just happen to be in town a short time. What are you doing tonight?"

She was doing nothing, but her first instinct was to say that she was. Then she considered. A date with Frank-san would be very strenuous, and she could probably talk him into taking her to a movie. There was an American musical in Shibuya-ku she wanted very badly to see. "I am doing nothing tonight," she said.

"Well, how about going out with me and my friend, Major Ronsdale. I'd sure like to have you meet the major."

"Major—what is name?"

"Pete. Pete's his first name. Pete-san. *Ichi-ban* friendo."

Now she remembered that Frank-san often talked pidgin English to her, and she hated that. She kept smiling, however. "So. I can see you. What time wanting?"

"Well, you could meet us in front of the Ernie Pyle Theater maybe-so seven o'clock?"

That would be a little early; that wouldn't give her

90

much time to get home, go to the public bath, change and take a street car into the center of Tokyo again. "Maybe seven-thirty better, neh?"

"Sure. Seven-thirty. Okay, seven-thirty."

"Thank you very much."

"Hell—you don't speak thank you to me. I speak thank you to you. American. Differento, neh?"

"So," said Teriko.

Braith said, "Wonderful to see you again, kid. Seems like I been away a long, long time."

"You go Chosen?"

Braith looked abruptly grave, and just a shade heroic. "Yes, I've been to Korea. Up there at the front. Kill *takusan* Chinese. General says to me, 'Sergeant Braith, you do *takusan-plenty* now. You one man army,' he says. 'You go Tokyo—take good rest—then come back kill more Chinese.'"

"Ah, so!" said Teriko. Funny that an Air Force sergeant should be at the front killing Chinese, she thought, but then she never did fully understand the mysterious workings of the American service. And if Frank-san said he had been killing Chinese it undoubtedly was so.

"How about ducking out for a Coke or something?" asked Braith.

She nodded. "Please. Very nice. I know place we can have ice coffee, neh?"

Dan Yamamoto scowled a bit as she went out this second time, but she didn't really care. She'd been working hard in the daytime, and sitting at home in the nighttime for more than a week now, and she was feeling just a bit reckless today. . . .

4

It was seven p.m. and Major Ronsdale was still undecided. He stood in front of the big Tokyo P.X.—it had been a downtown department store before the Occupation—and he frowned, looking both ways along the street, hoping that anyone who saw him standing there thus indecisive would assume he was waiting to meet someone. But this wasn't the appointed place. It was time to go to the Ernie Pyle now for the date Braith had arranged.

And he still didn't know about keeping this date; he still wasn't sure that he ought to.

The sergeant had called him at noon at the Meiji Building, where Ronsdale had gone to deliver some papers (the excuse for his flight to Tokyo) to the Far East Air Forces headquarters. Braith had reported that everything was set. He had a date for the major with this Teriko, this passionate babe he'd told him about, and Braith himself had a date with someone else. They would all meet at seven-thirty in front of the Ernie Pyle Theater, go to supper, and then maybe dance a bit at a Japanese night club, and after that—well, said Braith, it was anybody's hassel after that.

Ronsdale thought it all over. On the street called the Ginza the trams bustled along, following each other like cigarbox elephants; taxis blew their horns and charged at pedestrians; bare-legged men on bicycles wove in and out of traffic, swaying, and on the sidewalks Japanese citizens, all looking earnest and important, jostled each other, swirling like electrons around the slower-moving nuclei of GIs and Americans. It was hot; the sky was clear and still. Under the blousing of his shirt Ronsdale felt a trickle of sweat come down his spine.

It was the damnedest feeling . . . he wanted to keep this date, and yet he did not. It caused a sensation in his stomach not unlike that of fear. He felt this fear too often, and sometimes he wondered if he'd be able to stand living with it any longer. It was always born of uncertainty, somehow. Every decision that came along was always so fuzzy . . . it seemed unfair that things weren't more clear-cut; that there wasn't more of a set of rules to go by. He wondered sometimes if his mind was exactly right. Certainly it was burdened. He wondered if some day it wouldn't crack under the burden. Oh, God, it was painful, life was painful, the unavoidable fact of existence was painful, and yet there was a built-in desire to continue it, further it, protect it, reproduce and perpetuate it. That was the basic dilemma—that was the underlying, omnipresent pain. His smaller dilemma now (should he or should he not keep this date?) was only a capsuled dramatization of this greater conflict.

He tried reason. He'd already told himself that in some curious way he'd be better off to be true to Essie. She was a good wife in many ways, even if they didn't do so well in bed. He'd already told himself that this man, Braith, was dangerous and poisonous, and something not quite healthy lay behind his odd behavior in arranging this date for Ronsdale. And then, on the other hand, he told himself that if he wanted to be safe all the time, he'd never get any enjoyment out of life. You had to do something a little wrong, a little dangerous once in a while. If you worried about city traffic you'd never venture out at night to see a movie. You'd never be able to fly, not even cut-and-dried airway flying in a C-47. That incident last night . . . he'd been terror-stricken, but now, in a way, he was glad that it had happened. He was glad he'd gone through it, even though he'd do everything in his power to avoid another incident like it in the future. Perhaps this affair tonight would produce something of the same result, and, because a threat to his immediate person would not be involved, he would find the plunge a little easier.

He would do it.

He had been smoking a cigarette. It was down to a butt now. He took a last drag, dropped the butt to the sidewalk, toed it, faced abruptly to the left, and set off down the street toward the Ernie Pyle Theater.

Having made his decision he felt much better, and even a little licentious.

Major Pete Ronsdale smiled with his eyes, he smiled to himself, as he swung down the Ginza. He had studied this faint smile of his, and he knew that it made him quite mysteriously handsome. He saw people glance at him as he passed—a fine figure of an Air Force officer—and he pretended not to notice them, and was gratified. He was suddenly, inexplicably elated now; quite as happy as he had been sad a moment ago.

He turned off the Ginza, and at the Tokyo Electric Building, which was now an Air Force billet, he crossed one of the innumerable bridges across the rivers and canals of Tokyo. Past the bridge the sidewalk widened into a kind of rialto before a large, round-fronted building that

93

housed a Japanese movie and burlesque theater. A loud-speaker squawked with a popular American cowboy tune. Colored posters depicted more-than-life-size scenes from the Japanese movie (it had something to do with swords and samurai warriors) and glassed-in photographs showed the burlesque girls in plumes and G-strings, their breasts covered only by circles of gold foil fitted to each nipple. Young Japanese girls in garish evening dresses, or in sweaters and bobby socks, stood about, usually in pairs, and eyed the passing GIs hopefully. Several of these girls turned bold, open stares upon Ronsdale as he passed. Admiring stares. Ronsdale felt rakish, and stared back in the same way. He smiled wickedly and knowingly, then laughed to himself and walked on.

Yes, he felt better, much better, now.

He turned into the side street that led to the Ernie Pyle Theater, two blocks away. Everything was crowded and noisy. There was life. It had never seemed to him before that he liked Tokyo, but now he sensed a vitality, a personality, an over-all effect, such as he had felt in other big cities—New York and Paris, mainly.

Braith was at the corner under the marquee of the theater when Ronsdale arrived. Braith wore khakis and a tie—which was not required—and his belt buckle and black shoes were fiercely polished. His stomach seemed smaller; probably he was self-consciously sucking it in.

"Hi, Maj!" said Braith, grinning. "See you got here."

"Good evening, Braith."

"Just call me Frank, Maj—all my friends call me Frank. Funny thing, General Ridgway himself remembered my name one time when I was over in Korea. That was when the Wing had its forward operations over there in Taegu. I was standing on the airfield, not doing much of anything, when in comes this grasshopper plane, and who should step out but Ridgway himself. Well, I had a coupla months' beard, and one of these dog-fur Korean hats, and an M-1, and a pistol on my hip, and a Russian burp gun I'd picked up under my arm, and I guess I looked a sight. I was the only one there. Ridgway stares at me and says, 'Are you a soldier?' 'I surer'n hell am, sir,' I said. He said, 'Who's in charge here?' I looked around, and didn't see anybody

94

else, so I said, 'I guess I am.' Well, he laughs like the very devil, and then he says, 'Soldier, how would you like something to drink?' Well, you can imagine how long it had been since I'd had anything to drink. I told him I would sure like something to drink. So he reaches back in the plane and pulls out something. And guess what it was?"

"What?"

"A bottle of *milk!* Me—he offers me a bottle of milk! I had to drink it right in front of him and look as though I were pleased!"

Ronsdale said, "Where are the girls?" He hadn't really been listening.

"Oh—it's early yet." Braith looked at his wrist watch. "Seven thirty-five. Japanese dames are never on time. And, by the way, I kind of got stood up on this deal."

"Stood up?"

"Yeah, my dame couldn't make it. Only Teriko's coming."

"Well, in that case, Braith, I'll fade out."

"No! Hell, no, sir! She's your date."

"But I'm only along for the ride. Besides, you're already acquainted with this girl, so you'd better take her."

"Naw—" Braith brought his hand down—"I like something new all the time. Two or three dates with a dame is plenty for me. I remember one broad in San Francisco one time who was really crazy about me—believe it or not, she was a Hungarian princess. After I'd gone out with her two or three times, I said, 'Honey, okay, this is it. See you around some time.' Well, you know what that dame did?"

"No." Ronsdale spoke routinely.

"Moved right into my apartment! Bags and everything! I was living in a little penthouse place at the time—working with an advertising agency then. Hell, I had to call the cops to get her out, and even then, they had to carry her. I'm telling you, these Hungarians—"

"Listen, Braith, I think I'll just run along," said Ronsdale. "You meet this girl here and the two of you have a nice time. I'll see you down at Haneda Airport in the morning. We take off about eleven."

"Maj, I just wouldn't think of it! If I say I'm going

to get a pal of mine a date, by God, I'm going to get him a date! I'm a man of my word." He hitched his trousers. "Maj—you've got to take this gal."

Ronsdale smiled. "If you're a little short of money, Braith—"

"Money?" Braith laughed. "That's one thing you never have to worry about with me! I've always got more than I can use. They're all kinds of ways of making the stuff over here if you know how," he added mysteriously.

Ronsdale laughed and put his hand on Braith's shoulder. Funny, Braith was about his size—around six feet—but sometimes seemed to be a short man. Ronsdale said, "No, I'd better not go along tonight. I'm flying tomorrow, after all, and—"

A girl came behind Braith, touched his arm, and said, "Frank-san."

Braith whirled.

Ronsdale turned slowly and as the girl and Braith grinned at each other he had a moment in which to study her. She was tall for a Japanese and her shoulders were broad, like a swimmer's. Her skin was much like ivory; the mass of her long black hair formed a simple, startling contrast to it. She wore a yellow dress.

"Hi, baby!" Braith was saying. He was taking both of her hands and swinging her arms outward. "Lemme look at you!" He wolf-whistled.

The girl smiled and curtsied.

She was so extraordinarily attractive that Ronsdale felt as though he had just taken a drink.

"Baby," said Braith, "I want you to meet my buddy, Major Ronsdale. He's the one I was telling you about. This is Terry, Maj."

Later, Ronsdale was unable to describe what he felt in those first minutes of seeing Teriko. It was a kind of vibration. It was like someone hearing a wondrous passage of orchestral music and knowing that it was superb, but being unable to say exactly what the instrumentation or harmony had been. It wasn't love, not the storybook love Pete Ronsdale still half-believed in—it was plain sexual desire. That much he could recognize.

He must have spoken; he must have acknowledged the

96

introduction, and even made small talk of a sort. He couldn't recall any of it. He knew only the broad facts of the next half-hour: Braith hailed a taxi and they piled into it, and Braith suggested they go somewhere to eat tempura, and Teriko gave the taxi driver the address in Japanese. In the taxi she sat in the middle, and Ronsdale's right thigh, pressed to hers, actually began to tremble. Braith kept babbling away—something about how he'd once cooked shish-kebab for the Shah of Iran—and Teriko, her head partly turned toward Braith, appeared to be listening, but Ronsdale felt that she was not. He was almost certain that she pressed her thigh to his just a little more firmly when she felt his tremble. But of course he couldn't be altogether certain. . . .

The tempura restaurant was in an alley, and they pushed through the hanging banners to enter the place. There was a counter with stools in the front room. They elected to eat here, rather than remove their shoes and go to a private room upstairs. The man behind the counter was cooking in deep-fat utensils. Along the top of the counter, under glass, were his uncooked materials—rose-pink shrimp, angry brick-red octopus, shining gray eels, icy slivers of fish filet, all prettily arranged in beds of cut bamboo leaves.

A very old coffee-skinned man in Japanese summer dress came from the back of the restaurant, and slipped from the elevated floor into wooden geta. He clomped toward them, grinned and bowed. He had a white beard that reached to his waist.

"Hi, Grandpop!" said Braith. "Remember me?"

"Ah, so desuka," said the old man in a cracked voice.

"This is Papa-san," said Braith. "He owns the joint."

The old man laughed as though Braith had said the wittiest thing in the world. He spoke rapidly in Japanese to the man behind the counter, bowed again, then went into the back again.

"Beard, neh?" said Teriko, gesturing at her chin. "We say 'hige'—means beard. So this place called Hige Tempura because have beard."

"The place or the old man?" said Braith, and clapped Teriko on the back and started laughing.

"*Tempura* have beard, same like Hige-sama," she said gravely.

"What do you mean?"

"Make egg and flour on *tempura*, cook in oil, neh? So many piece hang down—so." She showed with her hands how the batter drippings would hang. "So we call beard *tempura*, neh?"

"It's too complicated for me," said Braith, showing mock despair.

Ronsdale said, "What did the old man say to the cook? To give us very special treatment?"

Teriko laughed, and rocked a little on her stool. "Oh, no! He say American people you better charge more money!"

They all laughed, and then Braith asked Teriko to order, since she was an expert. She turned and spoke to the counterman in Japanese. Ronsdale watched the terpsichorean movements of her head and shoulders as she talked. Her hands were long-fingered, almost willowy. The sleeveless yellow dress was a cotton print, and might have been bought for a few dollars in the basement of any department store, but she managed to look smart in it. Ronsdale tried to imagine how she'd look in a really expensive thing. That wasn't hard to imagine. She'd look fine, just fine; she would look like a million bucks. He would walk into a New York night spot with her and heads would turn. The two of them, in fact, would make a pretty smooth-looking pair—

"You eat *tempura* before, Major?" she was asking him.

"Uh—no. Not yet." She'd caught him a little off balance. "Pete's the name. Call me Pete."

"Ah, so. Pete-san," she said. She watched him for an extra moment before she turned away again.

A girl in a brightly colored kimono brought warm, moist towels in little baskets, one for each of them, and then beer. They wiped their hands on the towels. Teriko poured their beer, then filled their individual shallow saucers with *oshoyu* and dropped a pat of horseradish in each. The counterman brought the first small shrimp, hot and golden and crisp. Braith picked it up by the tail, dipped it in his soy-and-horseradish and ate it with a great deal of noisy pleasure. The counterman placed other shrimp, one by one, on the slanting board atop the counter, and they each helped themselves. Teriko picked hers up with chopsticks, and Ronsdale tried to do the same. He dropped the morsel several times.

"I show you!" Teriko laughed. She demonstrated with her own chopsticks, then, and carefully explained how one, firm between the crook of the thumb and the ball of the third finger, was to remain stationary, while the other was manipulated as easily as a pencil by the tips of the thumb and forefinger. Ronsdale caught on to it in a few more tries.

"Pretty good!" said Teriko.

"Seems the hard way to do a thing to me."

"I think knife and fork is difficult," she said.

"Might have known it." Ronsdale grinned and downed another shrimp.

As the shrimp disappeared they were replaced by small fish, cuts of eel, larger shrimp, soy beans in their green pods and sticks of ginger.

Ronsdale was too busy paying attention to Teriko to notice the taste of anything. He must have enjoyed it subconsciously: he ate quite a bit. He downed two large bottles of Kirin Beer, and Braith did away with four. Teriko, Ronsdale noticed, made one small glass last the entire meal.

He tried to make conversation with her. "Look—is this *tempura* really Japanese food? Do the Japanese eat it at home and everything?"

"Yes."

"What else do they eat? *Sukiyaki?*" He pronounced it *soo-kyaki.*

"S'kyaki," she said. "Ah, so."

"Well, those are the only two I know. Do they have other foods?"

"Yes."

Her eyes were so completely expressionless. They moved, and they were clearly alive, but they were opaque to whatever lay behind them.

"Well, *what* other foods?" asked Ronsdale.

"*O-sushi,* neh?"

99

"O-what?"

"*O-sushi*. Is fish and rice." She made small movements with her long fingers, as though putting little cakes together. "Fish not cook, neh?"

"Raw?"

"Ah, so. Raw."

For the first time Ronsdale realized that actually she did not speak much English. She knew the main operating words—be, have, give, take, do, make—and a great many common nouns, but she was unable to explain things much in detail. On a more abstract level she would probably be hopelessly lost. He wondered: how, then, did he gather this impression of keen intelligence on her part? Was it an illusion? Did it have something to do with those impassive eyes? This he knew: she was as intriguing as the very devil.

"Sometimes have Chinese egg," she said.

"You mean those thousand-year-old jobs?"

"*Nani?*" She looked puzzled.

"Chinese duck egg. Old. Very old. *Takusan* old." He was immediately ashamed of himself for speaking broken English so thoughtlessly to her. Patronizing thing to do, damn it. A bad habit of most Americans. But he hadn't been able to help it, and probably he'd do it again. He wondered if she knew enough English to spot the difference.

"No—not old egg!" She was laughing, tossing her head, letting her dark, naturally wavy hair cascade to her neck and shoulders. "No—is Chinese egg cook in pan, neh?"

"Oh. Maybe like Egg-foo-yong."

At that point Braith moved heavily, shifting on his stool. "By God," he said, "I think I'm getting full at last! Never thought it would happen. Christ, but I love this stuff!"

"Shall we go now?" Ronsdale didn't really want to go. He wanted to sit here and continue to discover things about Teriko.

"Where do you want to go, Maj?"

"I don't know. I mean, I'm not familiar around here." Curious that he wasn't more familiar with Japanese food, and Japanese customs—he'd been in Japan almost two

100

years now. Most of that had been spent in the company of his own kind, among the familiar things the government provided for its servicemen overseas. They said it was the British who always dressed for dinner in the jungle, and remained forever British in the damnedest far-off places, but the Americans actually did rather well in bringing with them wherever they went their hamburgers, malted milks, comic books, electric mixers and washing machines. They didn't insist on keeping these things all to themselves, however: they were great spreaders of their culture.

Braith winked fatly. "I know just the place, Maj. Just the place."

Teriko turned to him. "Where we go, Frank-san?"

"Cho-Cho Club."

"Ah, so," she said—but not enthusiastically.

"Don't you like the joint?"

"Oh, I like very much, Frank-san," she said quickly.

"Sure you do, baby," said Braith. "You like any place ol' Frank takes you, don't you? And he fixes you up all right with boy friends, too, doesn't he?" He glanced at the major and winked again. Ronsdale was surprised to see that he was slightly intoxicated—not drunk, just flushed and noisy. Ronsdale would have thought it would take more than four beers to affect a bulk like that.

"I'll call the taxi," said Braith, getting up and heading for the door. "Uh—Maj. Take care o' the bill, will you, ol' buddy? I'll square up with you later."

"All right," said Ronsdale.

Teriko was looking at him steadily. He caught her at it, and she turned away. He had the feeling that she saw inside him, that she sensed weakness, and that she knew already that in some strange way Braith was able to dominate him. He decided to take the offensive. "Terry—you don't really like this Cho-Cho Club, do you?"

"Oh, I like very much."

"Tell the truth now."

She smiled. "Don't like."

"Shall we go some place else?"

"Go away Frank-san?"

101

He gabled his eyebrows, sighed and said, "No, I don't suppose we can leave him, can we?"

"Maybe later."

"All right, maybe later."

Braith's voice came from the outside. "Come on, you two! Got a cab! Pulled him right off the street!"

Ronsdale paid a bill of three thousand yen and they left.

The Cho-Cho Club was a large house in a stone-walled garden in South Tokyo, on the road to Haneda Airport and Yokohama. The light was dim, and there was a check room and a dance floor and tables on a raised circular platform. The furniture and decoration were new enough, but it had an air of cheap imitation about it. A five-piece orchestra played cabaret-type American jazz—not too badly, it seemed to Ronsdale, though he was no judge of modern swing. Braith was expansive with the hatcheck boy and the waiters. He made jokes and they laughed toothily and dutifully. They were seated at a table at the edge of the dance floor.

Now that Ronsdale's eyes were accustomed to the dim light he could see that all of the several couples dancing were servicemen and Japanese girls. At one long table in a far corner sat about eight Japanese girls in evening gowns, all looking slightly bored. A soldier came along, picked one, and led her to the dance floor.

Braith said, "What are you drinkin', Maj?"

"Uh—scotch and soda, I suppose. What about you, Terry?"

"Orange drink, please."

"Orange drink? Come on, now—you want something better than that."

She shook her head quickly.

"Okay. Whatever you say."

Braith said, "Guess I'll have a scotch and soda, too. That's really the drink. One time in Edinburgh I was at this old castle—"

"Dance?" said Ronsdale to Teriko.

She nodded and they rose together, and Ronsdale looked at Braith and said, "You order. We'll be right back."

They danced without speaking. Ronsdale enjoyed that;

102

Essie always kept up a running chatter in his ear when they danced, and sometimes she insisted on singing the tune, in what she probably honestly imagined to be a torch voice. She always sang each note a mite sharp. Funny, Ronsdale had heard of people singing flat, but Essie was the only one he knew who could sing consistently sharp.

But Teriko. Not only did she dance silently, but she pressed close to him, somehow adapting the curve of her body to his and anticipating every move, every step, before he made it. Once, when he drew his head back to look at her and smile, she did the same—simultaneously, he swore. This time, as their eyes met, he felt that for once her impassiveness was gone. He felt that he'd caught her off-guard. When they came together again she pressed even more firmly to him.

They returned to the table, and the drinks were there, but Braith was gone.

"Out powdering his nose, I guess," said Ronsdale. He laughed, pleased with himself. He knew he wasn't often capable of even modest humor.

"Powder nose?" Teriko looked puzzled and doll-like.

He laughed some more, then explained the idiom to her. Instead of responding with laughter when she finally understood, she nodded gravely. By that time he had finished his scotch. He ordered another, sat back, studied her for a moment, then said, "You know, you're a funny one, Terriko."

She sipped her orange drink.

"I guess every GI you meet must try to date you."

"That is what Mr. Yamamoto say. *Takusan* boy friend."

"Don't you like that?"

She shrugged. "*Takusan* boy friend, but have no *koibito*."

"What's *koibito*?"

"Sweetheart."

"No sweetheart? That's hard to believe."

She tossed her head again, and this time with an air of wantonness. It bothered Ronsdale, for some reason. He wondered about her; he wondered whom she slept with, and how often.

103

Her eyes were still again and she said, "You have question ask me?"

"Question?"

"You want ask?"

His heart was beating fast. He couldn't quite believe that she was inviting him to ask her to spend the night with him, and yet her words, the tone of her voice, the very stillness of her look suggested that. He cleared his throat and laughed nervously and said, "No question. Come on, let's dance again."

When they came back Braith was still absent. Ronsdale ordered more scotch. He looked around. "Where the devil is he?"

"Oh, Frank-san always go away. Make me angry some time."

"Habit of his, eh?"

"Habit?"

He had to explain the word "habit" to her. He was sitting beside her now. During the explanation she took his hand and held it for a moment, then began to stroke his fingers with a strangely lascivious motion. He was startled. He kept telling himself that this was an Asiatic girl with a background he could never hope to understand, nor even visualize, and he must not be surprised at any act of hers. But, still, he was startled.

She said out of a clear sky, "You are married, Pete-san?"

"Yes."

"Have children?"

"No."

"So," she said, as though that explained something.

"What do you mean—'so'?"

"I don't think married, you."

"Is that a compliment, or something bad?"

"*Shiranai*— I don't know. Always I like married man best. Why?"

"I don't know why."

"Funny, neh?"

"Yes, funny." He was sure now that he would sleep with her tonight.

The orchestra finished a selection, and then from the

104

cocktail lounge there came the sound of several voices in not-very-good harmony.

Teriko laughed and looked that way. "Frank-san! Always sing."

"He must have done this to you before."

"He like sing very much." She turned and looked at Ronsdale again. "We better go, neh? Just two."

"Well, we can't leave Braith. He may not have taxi fare home."

"You need give him money?"

"I suppose so. I don't think he has any."

"I do. I give to waiter."

"Well—"

"Okay, I do this. Waiter understand."

"Well—all right. But I still don't feel right about it—" he watched her as she rose, watched the sinuousness of her body—"however, I suppose it's the only thing to do."

They paid the bill, made the arrangements with the waiter, then slipped out quickly and quietly.

In the taxi Ronsdale said, "Where to—home?"

She said something in Japanese to the driver. The cab started off. He put his arm around her shoulders and she came immediately to him. He bent his head, intending to kiss her easily this time, and she opened her mouth and worked her tongue against his.

When they had pulled apart again he stared at her. She laughed, pulled him toward her and kissed him again.

He said, "I'll be damned."

She was playing with the back of his neck with her long, light fingers, smiling up at him. "You are very handsome, Pete-san. Not good say this to man, neh? But very handsome."

"You're crazy," he said.

"So," she said. "Sometimes *sukoshi* crazy."

He said, "Tell me more."

The taxi was winding through darker, narrower streets. He'd lost all sense of direction. She said, "Tired talking now. Sometimes talk English making me very tired." They kissed a third time and she curled up her body to press

105

her thighs against his. "Tonight," she said, "I am very excite my body."

"Oh." Ronsdale stared at her again.

"Sometimes happen, body excited. Why?"

"Well, I don't know—"

"Man excited all time, neh? But woman different. Only sometimes excited."

"You—er—get excited often?"

"Not every time. Maybe one time for week, neh?"

"I see. What do you—that is, do you do something about it?"

"You mean give body for man?"

"That's more or less what I meant."

"But only if liking somebody *takusan* can give body. Not always liking man, so I do nothing."

"That's reasonable." He cleared his throat. His collar was tight.

Again she kissed him; he put his hand upon her breast this time and felt for the nipple. She breathed in sharply.

"Er—don't you want me to?"

"More," she said quietly. "More." She kept her eyes shut.

The taxi stopped and the driver turned and spoke in Japanese.

"We here," said Teriko.

"Your home?"

"No, not my home. Hotel."

"Oh. Yes. Hotel. Well, well, well." He clambered from the taxi, worried out his thick wad of yen and laboriously counted off the bills to pay the driver. The meter said six hundred yen. He gave the driver seven hundred. The driver said in English, "Sank you very much," and drove off.

It was a large, one-story house with a court in front. Teriko knocked at the glass panels of the front door, called softly, "*Kon-ban-wa!*" and a moment later a shadow came to the door and opened it. An old woman in a kimono stood before them. There was bowing, polite muttering. Ronsdale, fingering his cap in his hands, felt awkward.

A moment later they were ushered into the vestibule, and they sat on the raised level of the inside floor and removed their shoes. Ronsdale saw several other male American shoes resting by the step. The old woman placed slippers out for them, and when they had stepped into these she led the way down the hall toward the rear of the place. A younger woman appeared, carrying a teapot and two cups on a tray.

The sliding doors to their room were of translucent paper on a cross-hatched wooden frame, and the floor was covered with the usual soft straw mats, black-bordered with cloth, and closely laid. The only decoration was in the niche of one wall: a vase of flowers and a hanging showing a mountain scene. There was a low, square table in the middle of the room. Two cushions were at this table.

"Come," said Teriko, smiling, sitting on one cushion, and patting the other.

Ronsdale obeyed in a slightly dazed way. The maidservant sank to her knees and bowed with her head touching the mat before she placed the cups on the table and filled them with pale green tea. Teriko sipped, and Ronsdale followed suit. The tea was much like hot water, with just the smoky suggestion of taste.

"You like something eat?" asked Teriko.

"Lord, no. I'm full."

"Drink?"

"Well, as a matter of fact—" he did need relaxing— "yes."

"What? Beer or sake?"

He had never tried sake, and asked for it. She spoke to the maid, who faded out silently, sliding the door behind her.

"I—er—this is all a little more sudden than I'm used to." He laughed nervously. "I mean, here I meet you for the first time tonight, and—well, here we are."

"I cannot help body excited." She was squatting Japanese fashion, on bent knees. She swayed toward him.

"No, I suppose not," said Ronsdale. He didn't touch her or lean toward her. He was displeased with himself again. He ought to be able to take all this in stride—casually, and even rakishly—but he couldn't drive away his inner clumsiness. Damn her, she'd caught him off base.

"Maybe later you like bath," she said.

He grinned. "The hot Japanese variety?"

"Hot bath good for you. Also, you have hot bath, you don't make baby."

"That's the first time I've heard that one."

"Japanese people all knowing this."

"Well—I'll try anything once. I hope you're right about not making a baby, I mean."

"I am always careful. I don't want baby. *Takusan* trouble, neh?"

"It could be difficult." That was better. He was being a little more suave now.

She had leaned even closer. "Don't you like kiss me?"

"Can't think of anything I'd rather do more," he said. He took her in his arms and kissed her again, and this time she worked her body around to press it against his.

There was a soft rap on the sliding door. "*Gomen-asai!*"

"*Hai! Do-ozo,*" said Teriko.

The sake was in a small porcelain pitcher and Teriko poured it into tiny cups. It was warm, and tasted at once bland, bitter and sweet. It warmed his chest like whiskey as it went down. Loosened him up a bit. He said, "I suppose you've been to this hotel before?"

"One time."

"With—er—American?" He was morbidly interested.

"So."

"You liked him very much, I suppose."

"Of course. Not sleeping with man I don't like him."

"What happened?"

"*Nani?* Happen?"

"I mean if you like him, and everything, well, where is he now?"

"Oh, he have wife and two child Tokyo. American wife, neh. But he wants one time get away. Very funny man. Says he belongs A.W.A.S. Club."

"What on earth's that?"

"He tell me stand for 'American Woman Are Slob.'" She pronounced it slob-bu. "Funny word, slob, neh?"

Ronsdale laughed and said, "Good God. Terry, you're—you're fantastic."

"I never see this man again." She sighed just a little. "*Sayonara.*" Then abruptly she rose, went to another

108

sliding door and opened it to a closet. She took out two summer kimonos and sashes. "Bath now, neh?"

"At this point," he said, "I guess I'm game for anything."

She turned her back carefully as she undressed, her sudden modesty startling him. He stared at her. She looked over her shoulder, caught him staring, and stared back in that expressionless way of hers. Ronsdale felt his cheeks redden. He got up, then, and undressed, hanging his trousers neatly on the lacquered cross bar in one corner. He donned the kimono and sash.

She was already in her kimono. She laughed when he turned around. He looked down at himself. "Did I do something wrong?"

"I do for you." She stepped toward him.

The nearness of her body, the brushing of her hard breasts against his torso as she fixed the obi was maddening to Ronsdale. She slid the sash around so that the knot was in the back, and then retied the knot.

She led him down the hall, now, to the bath. It was behind another sliding door, and they descended several steps into a sunken room. There was a large wall mirror in this room and several baskets for clothes and towels stood on the floor. Through another door he could see a tile-floored room with a large square pool in the center. Several wooden buckets stood around the pool.

Ronsdale, still feeling awkward, waited.

"You can have bath now," said Teriko.

"Oh. All right." He undid the sash she had so carefully tied. She slipped his kimono off for him.

"Do-ozo," she said, pointing to the tile-floored room.

"You're not joining me?"

She shook her head. "I come after."

Ronsdale shrugged and went into the bath. This girl was simply too hard to fathom—he'd have to stop trying. Dimly, he sensed that her entire emotional reaction to sex must be infinitely different from his own, from any American's, but at the moment he wasn't quite sober enough to analyze the thing.

The water was scalding hot. He compressed his lips and forced himself into it, lowering quickly to a squatting position so that it finally came to the level of his neck. He

109

gasped. Then, to his surprise, he became used to the temperature in a very short time. He looked up to see if Teriko was watching. The outside sliding doors were just closing behind Teriko—she was evidently returning to the room.

"My God, what a screwy evening," said Ronsdale.

His face was hot, flushed. It felt bright pink. His head swam a bit. Perhaps the hot water was intensifying the effect of the scotch and sake he'd drunk. He did not often get drunk—usually he couldn't put enough actual liquid into himself in a short enough time to make him drunk—but he felt pretty drunk now. Pretty goddamn drunk, by golly. He felt free and strong and superior and unchained and happy and sad and a little wicked.

"What a screwy place," he said.

His voice was resonant in the small room. He tried a note in his pleasant baritone. Sounded good.

"What a screwy country."

Then he began to sing.

"The hilllllls of home! The hills of ho—ome!"

By God, he hadn't sung this well in years. Been neglecting his voice, that was the trouble. Essie wasn't so enthusiastic about his voice. She could always be depended upon to come up with a remark like, "Sing Far, Far Away"—Lord, how he hated the banality of that remark, and people who made it with all the bright confidence of an original quip. Which Essie did. Okay. To hell with her.

"The hills of ho-o-OME!"

He was more sober when he finished bathing, but still not entirely clear-headed. He felt a little out of his own control. Somewhat wild. Hungry, terribly hungry in the loins. And now he would appease that hunger. It would be much different than those heavings in the dark with Essie. This girl would enjoy it. Oh, Essie always put on a fine show, and he supposed she was passionate enough, but she didn't really deceive Ronsdale. Fellow can tell over a period of time. Teriko was different: Teriko wanted him, and had picked him, and it had all been her own idea. He would do everything possible to please her tonight—

He stopped drying himself suddenly and stared at his body in the big mirror. It was a good body, lean, muscular, well-proportioned; he was quite as handsome naked as he

110

was clothed. *But could he do it this time? Could he give his partner pleasure?* God, it was so empty and meaningless and agonizing when he could not. It was the most dismal, soul-shaking sensation of failure that he knew: he felt then most useless, most despised. *How could he control his body, though? How did other men do it?* Oh, God, oh, God, oh God. Oh, God, please help me to please her. . . .

He donned his kimono and obi and went back to the room. The table had been cleared away. A mattress lay upon the floor, and there were sheets and a quilt covering on the mattress. Teriko lay there in her kimono with her hands cradling the back of her neck; her dark wavy hair streamed away from her head liked spilled Chinese ink. She was smiling.

"Finish bath, Pete-san?"

"Yes."

"I did have mine, too. In other bathroom."

"Oh."

The overhead light had been switched off, and there was now only the dim light of a paper-shaded floor lamp.

Teriko patted the place beside her, smiled, and said, "Do-ozo." With her other hand she reached for the light switch.

The seizure . . . the glowing all over, as hot metal glows, the grip of it. The prickling of his skin. The illusion that his head was light and large, like a balloon, and his body a strange, scrawny twine that spiraled away from it. A steel strapping for a moment about his thighs.

But he floated all this time . . . much like flying, this; surprisingly like flying.

He tensed his biceps, he drew his belly flat; he would be male and dominant and strong and cruel; he would endure; he would be inexhaustible. He spoke in a low, soft, rich, deep voice. The words didn't matter.

As a jet engine starts, he thought. *At first nothing, at first metal, cold and dead, then the slow grinding, and the rising highpitched whine, the overcoming of inertia, wilder and wilder and now more insatiable, faster, faster, and the whine rising to a scream, and beneath the whine the first*

111

low mutterings and grumblings of surly, awakened power. All this toward the flame, the instantaneous creation, the godlike act—

She didn't complain; she even smiled and kissed him on the forehead.

"Wait," he said. "I'll try again. Just wait a little longer, until I rest."

He closed his eyes while he was resting, and fell asleep. When he awoke again at four in the morning. Teriko and her clothes and handbag were gone.

CHAPTER FIVE

1

AT FIRST the knocking on his door seemed to Captain Richard Tindle part of his dream. It was a falling dream; he had been falling from a great height, his stomach turning over and over with fear . . . but by the time he pushed from the bed and staggered to open the door he had forgotten the dream.

It was a corporal, the Charge of Quarters from the billeting office. "Colonel Straker just phoned, sir. Says you're supposed to get over there right away."

"Over where?" Tindle always felt a little belligerent when he first woke up.

The corporal was not to be intimidated. "Wherever he hangs out, Captain. In his office, I guess."

"All right, all right," said Tindle, and closed the door.

He shuffled into wooden shower clogs, wrapped a towel about his waist, picked up his leather shaving kit and pushed out into the hall again. He went to the washroom. He looked at his wrist watch and it said nine. Nine o'clock, and the sun high; in Tokyo Pete Ronsdale was probably getting up, but not with this painful head, and this hair-coated tongue. He hoped Pete had made it all right through that frontal passage last night. But of course he had; Tindle would have gotten word by now if anything had happened.

He looked at his bloodshot eyes. Lord, what a night. What a drunken, excessive, foolish night. But he hadn't

112

actually been drunk—he'd just drunk a lot. And that whole rotten business with Essie—

He needed a shower now, badly, not only to cleanse himself, but to fulfill an emotional need. He wanted a good hot shower, a lingering one, and he would take his fine time, and Colonel Straker could sit and wait, and to hell with him. That was the way Dick Trindle felt this morning.

Now that he was more nearly awake he began to wonder what the devil Straker wanted with him, anyway. Tindle was supposed to begin his leave. He was to have picked up his orders this morning—seven days of rest and recuperation. He could use the rest and recuperation, all right, but the leave was important to him for another reason. He was rather ashamed of this reason, but in honesty he had to recognize it. The truth was that he wanted to put off as long as possible the job of killing human beings again.

Funny about that. Not a logical thing at all. He'd be perfectly willing to support this war (he felt that it was a deplorable but now necessary war) in some way other than pulling a trigger and watching the result of his handiwork. Maybe it was a kind of cowardice, or a kind of social laziness not to want to do the dirty work. A kind of emotional snobbery, perhaps. He didn't admire himself very much for feeling this way, but he could not simply turn off his feelings as one twists a faucet. Here they were; he had to live with them, like it or not.

"Oh, hell," he said, and turned on the shower.

When he was dressed the mood had passed somewhat, and he felt better. He had taken two aspirins, drunk at least a quart of water, and then he had dressed slowly and carefully, paying much more attention than he usually did to details. He shined his black shoes to a mirror polish, using several drops of cold water to harden the film for a final buffing. He lit a cigarette and set out for headquarters.

It was another bright, still day. Jet engines roared down at the line; occasionally a piston plane rumbled in landing or take-off over the long, steel-mat strip. Jeeps and trucks beetled along the roads, trailing high dust.

It didn't seem like war over here. Akuni might very well have been almost any air base sleeping under the sun in

113

peacetime. Not at all like it had been last time, even in the United States. Maybe that was because people still couldn't quite bring themselves to admit that this was a real war. They didn't go around this time waving the war bonds they had bought, reminding you that loose lips sank ships and telling you how they'd chiseled a tankful of gasoline without ration points the other day. Perhaps he should have been grateful that, being in a war, he could yet escape its atmosphere. He was not grateful; he was disturbed. He was puzzled and uncomfortable.

In Colonel Straker's anteroom, Colonel Worrel looked as chubby and unperturbed as ever. "The old man's waiting for you," he said cheerfully.

Tindle knocked once, as required by military custom, and went in.

There was now a chart on the wall behind Colonel Straker's desk. It was of heavy showcard, four feet long and two high. There were three graphs on the chart: one was TROOPS DESTROYED, another AMMO EXPENDED and a third SORTIES (PER AIRCRAFT).

Colonel Straker had his back turned and his hands thumblocked behind him. He was gazing at the chart. A pose, Tindle thought; transparently a pose.

Tindle said, "You wanted to see me, Colonel?"

Straker turned slowly. His eyes were dry and cold. "You took your time getting here, Captain."

"Yes, sir, I did."

"Why?"

"I was sleeping. I tied one on last night."

Tindle could see Straker bristle, and then control himself. "All right, Captain. The important thing is to get down to business now. But I hope you'll be more prompt next time I ask you to report."

"I hope so, too, Colonel. Ordinarily I stay away from brawls like that Wing-Ding last night. But, then, you know why I went this time."

Straker smiled. "Because I asked you to, wasn't it?" He had a smile which appeared to alter only the ends of his mouth, while the rest of his face remained immobile. "But I don't recall asking you to soak yourself in alcohol so that you wouldn't be in shape in the morning. I'm not against

114

drinking, Captain; I take a cocktail myself occasionally. However, I think it's a moral obligation of a combat flying officer to keep himself in shape physically."

Tindle didn't answer, but he knew his disgust must show in his expression.

Straker said, "Sit down, Captain."

Tindle sat.

"You may smoke if you wish."

Tindle lit a cigarette.

"I suppose the things you saw on forward control are still pretty fresh in your mind, aren't they?"

"Yes. I suppose so."

"You must have had a good look at the effectiveness of some aerial weapons."

"Almost too good."

"What do you mean by that?"

"I don't enjoy seeing men killed."

"Does anyone?"

"Perhaps not. Perhaps not really."

"But soldiers get used to it, don't they, Tindle? And you're a soldier. Sometimes in the Air Force we forget we're soldiers."

"Not after a tour of forward control," Tindle said. "You never forget it after that."

"We won't argue the point. I simply say that I see no reason why you alone should be granted the privilege of feeling annoyed at the unpleasantness of war."

"Is that what you called me in to tell me, Colonel?"

"You know very well it isn't. Your attitude this morning isn't exactly helpful."

Tindle shrugged.

Straker said, "Do you think you could give an intelligent briefing on the effects of air weapons on troops? Do you think you could tell a few pilots about it without fainting dead away at the horrible thought?"

Tindle said, "I guess since you're a colonel, Colonel, you can be sarcastic and I have to take it. I guess that's what you call Rank Has Its Privilege."

Straker reddened slightly. "All right, Tindle, I'll make it brief. I want you to prepare a little talk to the Group tomorrow. The effects of aerial weapons on troops. Think you can?"

"Yes, I can. But I'd like to point something out."

"What?"

"I'm supposed to be on leave. Seven days R. and R., remember? I was going to take a train to Tokyo today. I'll have to put the trip off until tomorrow now."

"Better put it off indefinitely."

"Sir?"

"Better forget that leave. I can't spare men now, Tindle. This is a critical time. You'd better check out again on familiarization in an F-80 this afternoon, and then fly with your squadron tomorrow."

"Fly with my squadron? Now, wait a minute, Colonel!"

"Afraid, Tindle?"

"You know damn well I'm not."

"No, I don't know. I've been watching you, Tindle. I've been around pilots quite a while—I fly a lot myself—and I think I know symptoms. I think I can tell when a man's slipping a little in the wrong direction. Actually, Tindle, flying a mission tomorrow will be the best thing you can do. Nip your fear in the bud."

"For Christ's sake, Colonel," said Tindle disgustedly.

"The blasphemy isn't necessary."

Tindle stared for a moment, then said, "There's a word for a man like you, Colonel."

"I wouldn't say it, if I were you."

Tindle half-smiled. "What would you do, Colonel—court-martial me for insubordination and disrespect?"

"I'd take you down to the gym, put on some gloves and whale the tar out of you," said Straker.

"Colonel, that's corny. They only do that in the movies."

Straker's face became red again. His voice was tight. "Go ahead and say that word, Tindle—I'm hoping you will, now."

Tindle instead smiled, saluted with unnecessary precision, right-faced, and walked out of the room. He remembered that just before he turned he had noticed Straker working his long white fingers into fists at his sides.

116

He laughed and wondered why he felt light-headed all of a sudden.

2

Tindle had a busy afternoon.

First, he left headquarters and returned to the B.O.Q. area to get his pistol, flying suit and paratrooper boots. He wore these boots tightly laced when he flew, feeling they would not snap from his feet with the opening shock of the chute in case he had to jump. Second, he returned to headquarters and arranged with the adjutant general to revoke his leave orders and put him back on operational duty with the squadron. Third, he took out his additional flying gear in the personal equipment room of the Group operations building on the line. He went over the gear carefully, making sure that the mike-and-headset cord to his soupbowl helmet was not frayed, and that his oxygen mask was snug, and that his parachute was properly packed. Next, he checked with operations to have an airplane assigned and scheduled for a familiarization hop. He would fly at fifteen thirty hours. He went down to the line to look over the airplane.

They were arming 861 when he arrived. He was making only a local flight, but a Group regulation called for the arming of all tactical aircraft, even below the bomb line. This was against the rare possibility that one day enemy aircraft might appear over Japan. Tindle saw a small, dark airman in greasy overalls folding a clip-belt of fifty caliber bullets into the ammo can he had removed from the nose of the ship.

Tindle walked up and said, "What's your name?"

"Marquez, sir. Pfc. George Marquez."

"How long have you been an armorer?"

"Jus' three months."

"Well, here's something you might remember. See the way this clip is bent?"

"Yes, sir."

"That could jam the gun."

"A little bend like that?"

"It's happened."

117

"Well, gee—I'm sorry, sir. I saw it was bent a little like that, but I thought it was okay."

"It would probably go through the gun—but I don't like to take even small chances on my airplane. Not any, understand?"

"Yes, sir. Sure, sir. I'll change it."

"Thanks, Marquez. And watch it after this."

"I sure will, sir."

Tindle stood there watching while Marquez filled the can, put it back into the nose, and then pulled the handle that changed the guns. When he was finished, Marquez looked up. Tindle smiled and nodded, and Marquez went off to the next ship in line.

Tindle climbed to the wing of the ship, then, and looked into the open cockpit. It was clean; both the oxygen hose and radio cable were neatly in place. Good crew chief on this one, and that, at least, was a break.

A voice behind said, "You the pilot, sir?"

Tindle turned and saw a small, wiry master sergeant with a deeply lined face and quiet, adult eyes. "Yes. I'm Dick Tindle. You crewing this airplane?"

"That's right. My name's MacInnes, sir."

"Nice cockpit, MacInnes."

"Thanks. It's a damn good airplane—I'd hate to spoil it."

Tindle grinned. "In that case I'll try to bring it back in good shape all the time."

"I'm not worrying, sir. No sweat on that."

"How about the power plant?"

"Good. Takes hold fast. Coasts kind of evenly from twenty-five percent up to about seventy-five, and after that you hardly have to move the throttle at all. You've got to watch it on eighty-five or ninety: you're likely to bring it up to a hundred before you even know it."

"Okay, that's good to know. I'll watch it. When was her last hundred hour?"

"Two days ago. I inspected her myself—every damn rivet, sir." MacInnes hauled a large, black pipe out of his pocket. "Oh, by the way, there's another thing you have to watch. The pressurizing goes out sometimes. Temperamental. It went out at high altitude with Lieutenant

118

Morris—he had it before he went back to the States on a medical. The bubble frosted all over. I'd tear it out and put a new one in, Captain—if I knew where the hell to get a new one."

"Maybe we can make a moonlight requisition some night."

MacInnes grinned. "Been thinking along those lines, frankly. Maybe, after the next crack-up on the field, if we can make it to the salvage yard fast enough—"

"We'll do that." Tindle climbed down again. "Well, thanks for the briefing, Mac. Check my radio—all channels —before I fly this afternoon, will you?"

MacInnes looked hurt. "I always do that, sir."

"Sure you do. I should have known. Sorry I mentioned it."

"That's okay, Captain. Matter of fact, I'm kind of glad you did. Me, I like cautious pilots. I hang on to 'em longer."

"You've got a cautious pilot. Maybe too much sometimes."

"I don't think so, Captain. I get awfully fed up with some of these daredevil kids we're getting in."

"They're good pilots usually."

"Maybe. But if they're not around long we don't get much mileage out of them, do we? There's a second lieutenant in the squadron I had to chase away from the air scoops when we were testing an engine the other day. Another two feet and he would have been sucked in. He said he'd always been curious about how near you could get before it started to grab you, the crazy guy."

"Lieutenant Harold?"

"That's the one. How did you know, sir?"

"Just a wild guess."

"Well, sir, I'm glad to have your airplane, and I'll do the best I can with it. I'll take you older fellows any time."

"Sure," said Tindle, and waved so-long.

As he walked away he thought: well, there's the proof. One of the older fellows. Almost an old man. Airwise, perhaps, already an old man. Maybe he'd seen too much, and maybe he thought too much about what he'd seen. Maybe the crazy kids ought to do all the combat flying—

119

But then again, maybe he was just trying to pile on more reasons why he shouldn't fly a mission tomorrow. . . .

3

The briefing room of the 66th Fighter-Bomber Group was in a building that had once been a gymnasium. Olive-drab folding chairs were arranged theater-like the length of the floor. As Tindle entered the place, other pilots, most already in flying gear were filing in.

Tindle looked at them and was struck with the idea that here was the handful of men around whom the entire Wing was built. Drop a bomb on this old gymnasium and you wouldn't have much of a Wing left. The administrative and service and maintenance and supply personnel—who vastly outnumbered the few pilots—would have no more reason for existing.

They were wonderfully skilled men, these pilots, Tindle reflected: and so, for the most part, were the men who backed them up. There were even more of these specialists behind each pilot than in the last war, the big one only five years ago. There had to be. Long, long ago there must have been a time when every man in an army fought, and was a combat soldier in the strictest sense of the word. But as new gadgets appeared, and as the weapons of war became more and more machines, specialists were required for them. By the time of the Roman Empire there were already soldiers who were experts in transportation or administration, and seldom fought. With each new development the ranks of the second echelon swelled . . . the tank, the airplane, the submarine . . . electronics, engineering, transportation, weather, psychological warfare, special services, public information, finance . . . now a man could make a career of any of these. A man could become mighty good at his job. He could spend most of the waking hours of his lifetime mastering it—it had to be that way, for these jobs were that intricate.

But when, then, could a man find time to study himself and his own soul (if men indeed had souls) and thus have glimpses into the souls of others, and thus look briefly and occasionally upon fragments of the truth, and thus know moments of beauty, and thus touch ever so lightly, every once in a long while, upon utter exaltation?

Tindle thought about all this as he stood for several minutes by the doorway. Now most of the seats in the old gymnasium had been filled. There was a hum of conversation, and a pall of cigarette smoke. The weather officer and the ground liaison officer had already entered, and were busy arranging their map exhibits.

Tindle sat down. He didn't notice the man beside him until the man turned and said brightly, "Hey! How you?"

He looked and saw Second Lieutenant Melvin Harold. "Hello."

"I see you're assigned to my flight, Captain."

"Am I? I hadn't checked."

"You're number three. I'm flyin' your wing."

"Fine, fine," said Tindle absent-mindedly. He looked up at the radio channel chart in the front of the room and said, "What's our call sign?"

"The Group's Candy. Our flight's William flight."

"Thanks." Tindle picked up one of the mission cards that were placed on the seats. This was a mimeographed three-by-five file card, stamped SECRET, top and bottom, and containing spaces for such data as call-signs, mission number, course to target, map coordinates of the target, and course back.

"I reckon you're all checked out and everything now," said Harold, making conversation.

"Mm," said Tindle, and nodded. He didn't feel like conversation.

"Hear you're goin' to make a speech today."

"Well, I'm supposed to."

"You're the man sure ought to know what it does to 'em down there."

"What?"

"The napalm and rockets and stuff, I mean. You can really clue us on that. I'd sure hate to throw a lot o' stuff down there on people and not think it was doin' any good."

"I guess you're right," said Tindle.

Somebody in the back of the room called: "Ten-*hut!*"

Chairs clattered as everybody rose. Colonel Straker

121

marched in, heels clomping on the wooden floor rather loudly in the sudden quiet. Several other officers came along behind him and they all took seats in front. Straker did not sit; he walked to the maps, turned, surveyed everybody for a moment with a blank eye, then said, "As you were."

They shuffled, sat.

Colonel Straker looked pale, thought Tindle, and a little older. Maybe just the effect of the smoke-filled room. His voice seemed less resonant than in his office. His sibilants made an annoying sound, like the scraping of a fingernail across a blackboard. Straker said, "Gentlemen, I don't usually inflict myself upon you during these briefings."

No one laughed.

"But we're beginning a new line of attack with today's effort. And since the most effective soldier is an informed soldier, I thought I'd let you know what was going on."

A few of the men looked at each other.

"In the past—because of our skill in air-to-ground tactics —we've managed to kill more enemy troops than any other outfit in this theater. I've called this to the attention of those at top level. They've now agreed with me that troop-killing is the specialty on which we should concentrate. I don't imagine any of you—" he smiled dryly—"will object to this as an outdoor sport."

He drew a few grins this time.

"All right, then. That's our new assignment. You're all officers, and I expect you to take any assignment you get seriously. Killing troops is now our reason for being here —and I want all of you to be conscious of that twenty-four hours a day. To help that along, the Wing's been given a new nickname, and a new official insignia. This will be reproduced in the daily bulletin tomorrow. It will be authorized for wear on jackets, in signs about the base, on airplanes, and so on. We're going to call the 66th Wing —'The Manhunters.'"

Tindle looked around him. No one had reacted; nearly everybody simply stared at the colonel. Tindle wondered if the nickname had fallen flat, or if they actually liked it, but were too embarrassed to show enthusiasm.

"Captain Gorgas, our P.I.O.," said Straker, "has already
122

sent out a story on the new name. He talked with a correspondent—Herb Oscott, the columnist, whose war stories
you've all probably read—and Mr. Oscott said he would
use the story. AP is sending a photographer down to do a
follow-up on it. Very probably the newsreels and radio
networks will be around shortly, too."

The men stirred in their seats. Definite interest, now,
Tindle felt. He glanced at Lieutenant Harold. Harold was
perched on the lip of his chair, grinning and eager.

Straker continued. "All of our scheduled missions today
—as you'll learn very shortly—will give you a chance to do
some manhunting. The Joint Operations Center is picking
out troop targets for the 66th wherever possible. I want you
to pay close attention to your estimates of enemy casualties
from now on. If necessary, make extra passes on the targets
to get those estimates. And above all, gentlemen, see *how
big a bag you can get.*"

Dramatic pause for emphasis. A little cheap, thought
Tindle.

Straker said, "Any questions?"

There were none.

"All right, then, we'll start our briefing. There's an extra
item on the briefing today. Captain Tindle, whom most
of you know, has just returned from forward control. He's
seen the effects of our weapons. He's going to tell you
about it, and answer any questions you might have. Tindle,
will you do that right after the operations briefing?"

Tindle said, "Yes, sir." He saw heads turn and felt the
many eyes upon him, and wondered if Straker had forced
him to speak like that simply to make him uncomfortable.

Straker said, "That's all, gentlemen," and sat down in
the front row.

Tindle thought: *I'm flying today. Flying and killing.
Without willing it I shall be doing this. Or—shall I?*

The ground liaison officer arose. He was a dark captain
with heavy horn-rimmed glasses. There were three large
maps of Korea on the front wall, each covered with a sheet
of plexiglass. The transparent film was marked differently
on each with grease-penciled, colored symbols. These maps
depicted the ground, weather and air situation. The ground
layout was marked with squares and triangles to desig-

123

nate the various units, the air map showed primary and secondary targets and enemy flak positions, and the weather map bore cloud and precipitation symbols. The ground liaison officer tapped his pointer upon the eastern sector of the front, which stretched roughly across the narrow neck of Korea, and extended further north on the east coast than on the west. "Republic of Korea troops moved forward three miles here yesterday and last night, encountering little opposition," he said in a monotonous, somewhat officious drone. "Further west X Corps held steady with only light patrol action, the dismounted cavalry down here being still kept in reserve. On the central front . . ."

Tindle barely listened. He was trying to decide what to say to them when it would be his turn to talk. Maybe go over the air weapons one by one. Now, take five-hundred pound bombs; if you dislike messiness, they do the cleanest job. They just blow everything the hell to oblivion wherever they strike. Rockets are good on pillboxes and tanks. They penetrate and start everything burning, especially if there's gasoline around. Makes a nice clear flame, gasoline; you can look into a sheet of it sometimes and see the dark specks of bodies before they disappear entirely. Of course, just plain old fifty caliber bullets can't be beat for some things. They make hamburger of human flesh; a spray of them will cut a man in two. Actually saw that happen once. And napalm. Yes, he would have to tell them about napalm, the most exquisitely devilish weapon of them all. No escape from it, that was the main thing. It clung. When it burned men screamed more horribly than anyone who had never heard the sound could possibly imagine. It ran, glowing, into foxholes, and found its way behind parapets and earthen banks. No escape, no escape.

The ground officer had finished, and the weather officer was already giving his briefing.

". . . broken layer of five-tenths strato-cu at nine thousand, visibility unlimited, possible haze in the valleys . . ."

Tindle could retain this without really putting his mind to it. He had noted mentally by now that it would be a good day for air-to-ground attack. Good hunting—that was the phrase.

Now the operations officer, Major Goff. Goff ran his

124

hand constantly and nervously over his bald head as he talked. "These are pre-brief missions this morning, fellas. We've all got definite targets JOC has picked out for us. If we can't find these targets, however, we're to make ten-mile reccy circles in the target area. Unless JOC diverts, of course—and the way those jokers never can make up their minds, that could happen." Laughter. "Okay," said Goff, "take off times for the 107th, 108th and 109th squadrons in order will be thirteen hundred, thirteen twenty-five and thirteen forty-five. You all see your in-and-out courses here on the map. Be sure to check Icicle Control crossing the bomb line, and coming back. And here's a change in the bomb line on the eastern sector. Put it north three miles at this point. Here—I'll read the coordinates."

Tindle felt now that he had never been away. The briefing today was nearly identical with the last briefing he'd attended. Some of the figures had changed, that was all. He wondered now if he would have this same sense of familiarity when, an hour or two from now, he lined up a target in his sights and began to sweep down upon it. Certainly flying had come easily again yesterday during his check ride. His thought then that it was like swimming or riding a bicycle: once you learned you never really forgot.

"One more thing—I almost forgot," said Goff, frowning at some notes in his hand. "Intelligence wants me to pass this on. Doubt if you'll ever have to be concerned with it, but I'm supposed to tell you about it, so here goes. They're real anxious to get a look at one of the MIG pilots, so they can tell whether it's Russians or what who are flying the damn things, so if any of you ever get the chance to shoot down a—"

Goff's words were damped out by the sudden laughter.

"Okay, okay," he said, grinning, when they'd all finished laughing, "I'm just passing on to you what they told me. And that's all I've got to say. So now Captain Tindle'll take over. Dick?"

Tindle rose and walked forward. Everyone looked at him, and he stared straight ahead, then decided he must seem all the more ridiculous trying to avoid their stares. He turned, faced them, cleared his throat uncomfortably and

125

wondered what in the hell to do with his hands. He finally thrust them into the belt of his flying suit. "Er—I'm supposed to tell you about the results you get down on the ground. I'm supposed to tell you how all these things you use affect enemy troops. I'm supposed to tell you all this because I just got back from a close look at it. It's not a pretty sight."

He saw the puzzlement form in their eyes, the way sudden mist sometimes forms in hollows and ravines. He felt a little more at ease. He felt now that he wanted to talk to them; but he didn't want to give just the dry operational facts that Straker expected. He wanted to try to get something across to them. He wanted to get the feel and smell of everything across to them.

He spoke quietly and simply. The words came easily. He told them about the man who had been cut in two by fifty calibers. He told them about the screaming when the napalm ran. He told them about the stinks of corpses in the sun. He told them about the child that had played with the dead woman's fingers.

They were all scowling and squirming uncomfortably in their seats when he was through.

He walked back to his own seat through a thick, embarrassed silence.

He caught the colonel's eye when he sat down. The colonel had turned in his front-row chair and he was looking at Tindle very steadily. The colonel's look was hard as armorplate.

4

After the briefing Tindle went to the 109th Squadron's personal equipment room down on the line. He slipped his bulky Mae West over his neck, and then donned his parachute. The gear was heavy and warm; he sweated under it. He scooped the enameled leather crash helmet from the counter and adjusted the oxygen mask that hung from its cheek flap. The helmet was bright red—that was the 109th's color. His pistol was strapped to his chest, and his escape kit wrapped about his middle.

He was startled to hear Colonel Straker's assured, high-pitched voice behind him. "Got my parachute ready?"

126

Straker was speaking to the equipment non-com. Tindle put the helmet back on the counter and turned.

The non-com said, "Yes, sir. And here's a helmet for you. It was Lieutenant Brechner's."

"I have my own helmet," said Straker. He had been carrying one beside him—it was white, with gold edging. "Throw Brechner's away."

"What, sir?"

"I said throw it away."

"But, sir, we're hurting pretty bad for helmets. Every time we put in a requisition they—"

"Throw it away, Sergeant. We don't want anybody using a dead man's helmet."

"Yes, sir."

Straker turned to Tindle then. He looked at him coldly, as though hoping to make him avert his eyes. He held this stare for a moment, and Tindle met it. Straker finally said, "That was quite a talk you made at the briefing, Captain."

"I guess it wasn't very good." Tindle spoke wearily.

"It would have been passable, at least, if you'd stuck to facts. We could have done without those little sob stories of yours."

Tindle said, "All right, Colonel. Let's get something straight right now. I'll obey orders because I guess it's a habit. But I won't stand here and take guff. There's nothing in the book says I have to."

Straker grinned abruptly, disconcertingly. "Got you mad, have I? Well, that's a step in the right direction. Sometimes being mad will make you forget being afraid."

"So you think I'm afraid, do you, Colonel?"

"I think I've been around pilots long enough to get a pretty good idea of the things that ail them. There are certain symptoms I know when I see them. Of course, I might be wrong, but the chances are I'm right."

"I don't think my record exactly backs up what you think," said Tindle.

"No, it doesn't. For your information I've already checked your record personally and thoroughly. But I'm not interested in what a man has done before—I'm interested in what he's doing now. And if it isn't in the interests of the Wing, I haven't any use for that man."

"Colonel," said Tindle, "a few seconds ago I was mad. You caught me off base, a little. But now I think I see through your amateur psychology, and I don't think I'll let myself get mad at all. Go ahead, Colonel, needle me. I've suddenly got a nice, thick skin as far as you're concerned. Let's see what you can do with it."

Straker's face hardened. He stared quietly for a moment again, and then he shook his head once and turned away from Tindle. Tindle shrugged and walked off. He was halfway to the line before he remembered that he'd left his helmet on the counter. He went back. In the personal equipment room Straker had already donned his parachute and was now putting something into the zippered pocket of his coverall. Tindle saw the object just before it disappeared: it was a small, olive-drab New Testament.

5

The red-tailed jets of the 109th Squadron, earthbound, stood squat and clumsy on the line. A yellow fuel truck moved along the ramp, topping tanks when a crew chief called for it. It was hot in the sun.

Tindle and Lieutenant Harold and Captain Norman Kingsley walked three abreast from Group ops toward their airplanes. A hundred feet ahead of them Colonel Straker walked alone, taking long, assured strides. All carried parachutes, helmets and books of map sections.

Kingsley said, "Damned if I like it, flying behind the old man."

"Well, shoot, man," said Lieutenant Harold. "He's the colonel, ain't he? He's the co-mandin' officer."

"What's that got to do with it?"

"Well, you just don't get to be a colonel any ol' day."

"Enlighten him, Dick," said Kingsley. "Tell him how some colonels sometimes get to be colonels."

Tindle said, "Oh, I guess Straker's good enough as a combat pilot. I've got a funny idea that maybe he's even damn good at it."

"Maybe," said Kingsley. "But I still don't like flying wing on a guy without a lot of combat time."

Harold grinned. "I'll clue you something. You're just jealous, boy, because you ain't leadin' the flight today."

128

"Nuts," said Kingsley.

Harold laughed and swung his bright red helmet.

Tindle wondered if Straker had deliberately had him assigned to his flight. He kept telling himself that there was no real reason for Straker's enmity, and that Straker, for all his bullheadedness, was too essentially fair-minded to let a personality clash matter operationally—but it certainly did seem that the old man had it in for Tindle, plain and simple.

Ahead, the colonel reached his airplane, and began to make his ground check, stooping to peer under the wings, under the tail, and into the landing gear recesses.

Tindle came to his own ship; MacInnes had the fitted ladder hooked over the edge of the cockpit. "See you fellows," said Tindle, and turned off.

"Hey, boy," said Lieutenant Harold.

Kingsley waved absent-mindedly.

MacInnes said, "Hi, sir. She's all set. Ready to go."

"Good. I'll make a check, though—matter of habit."

"Yes, sir," said MacInnes. He had a large, black pipe, unlighted, in the corner of his mouth now.

Tindle stepped to the nose, opened the panel and examined the guns first. They were charged. He glanced at the Pitot tube where it protruded from the airplane, and saw that its cover had been removed. He bent over the tip tanks and tested the filler caps. Tight. A battery cart with two men on it rolled up and Tindle waited until they had connected the plug to the fuselage to feed in the extra power that would start the engine.

He clambered into the cockpit. He donned his helmet and plugged his oxygen tube in. MacInnes came up alongside and plugged the cable from the back of the helmet into the radio line. He helped Tindle with the straps of his Sutton harness, adjusting them to size, and Tindle tested the locking handle beside the seat. He glanced at his oxygen control dial and saw that it was normal, then he reset the circuit breakers, switched his aileron boost on, and cut his gun camera switch to the SIGHT AND CAMERA position.

The checklist was sandwiched into two layers of plexi-

129

glass; he took it from the panel and handed it to MacInnes. "Read 'em off."

"Fuel selector and fluid injection," MacInnes said.

"Off." Tindle touched the switch as he spoke.

"Emergency fuel."

"Off."

"Starting fuel."

"Off."

"Air start ignition."

"Off."

They went through it quickly, and now the feeling of continuity with the past was strong. More than his conscious mind had been trained to this thing. The machine was an extension of his own nerve and flesh.

She was ready for starting now; he nodded to MacInnes, and MacInnes waved to the men on the battery cart. Tindle cut the leading-edge fuel tank in, then lifted the starter switch and held it for a few seconds. The engine sang; the sound was something between a whine and a shrill whistle. He watched the power gauge and saw the needle rise and quiver at ten percent. He started the automatic flow then, and the engine caught—WHOOOOOM! The power rose to twenty percent, then a little more. He brought the throttle to the idling position. After that he changed his feed to the fuselage tank and ran a quick eye over the engine instruments.

All okay.

"Take her out!" he yelled. They disconnected the battery cart.

Tindle brought the power up to fifty-five percent and the ship trundled off. The last thing he saw before he swung to the taxiway was MacInnes standing there, grinning out of his creased face.

Tindle moved the ship quickly toward the runway. Here on the ground she consumed more than three gallons of fuel every minute—enough to take seven or eight miles from his over-all cruising range. He might need that extra power nursing a tattered ship back into the field. There were people shooting back at you up there, after all.

Colonel Straker and Captain Kingsley, in their airplanes, were already at the end of the runway; Tindle was number three man, and Lieutenant Harold was behind him. There were two other flights in the squadron, but these were assigned to other targets today. Tindle, at the end of the runway, made one more check. He was fairly heavy today with full wingtip tanks, each holding nearly 150 gallons of extra fuel, he had a nose full of fifty caliber ammunition and two napalm tanks under his wings. He checked everything very carefully. He brought his flaps down to seventy degrees. He closed his canopy.

Ahead, Straker and Kingsley kicked on to the runway together, and then rolled off, gathering speed. Tindle swung around in their wake. He turned his head quickly, once, and saw that Lieutenant Harold was close behind him.

"Candy William Three and Four," he told the tower.

"Cleared for rolling," the tower said.

He jockeyed the ship for a few feet down the runway to center his nose wheel, then he slowly opened the throttle, watching the tailpipe temperature gauge. The jet vapor simmered out behind; the airplane surged forward. The power rolled to ninety-eight percent, and he turned on the fluid injection switch, so that alcohol and water would give, momentarily, an even hotter flame.

At first he used his brakes, tapping alternately the right and left brake on the top of each rudder pedal, to keep the ship in line. Then, when the airspeed needle had passed seventy-five miles an hour, the rudder took hold. He felt the power gather; he felt it broad upon his back. At one hundred all of his flight controls felt workable. Then past one hundred . . . one-twenty, one-thirty; he rolled back on the stick very slightly, and she was airborne.

After milking his flaps and landing gear back into the airplane he began a long, straight climb. He was on a westerly course. All of the red-nosed, red tailed jets had come into position now; Colonel Straker led a V formation, with Kingsley on his right, Tindle on his left, and Lieutenant Harold tagging along behind.

"Keep 'em at ninety-eight for the climb," said Straker, over the radio.

The four of them rose, graceful now in the air, as the white crane is graceful when he leaves his awkward stance

131

upon the earth. The Sea of Japan was below them, the land was already far behind. Tindle sat back and flew. He floated up through the shredded clouds, kept climbing, and when presently he looked down again they were lint on the dark sea. He held nearly eight tons of power in his fingertips, making all of it respond to his slightest movement. Like a dream, that. It gave him a combined feeling of aloneness and self-sufficiency that added up to a sensation of power. His head was extraordinarily clear, and not merely because he was breathing oxygen. This feeling of bridled drunkenness was perhaps the biggest single thing that made men want to fly. . . .

Now, abruptly, it seemed to Tindle that he might be able to go through with this mission, after all. Everything was suddenly becoming detached, impersonal—the way it used to be. Now he was faced with only a technical problem. A challenge to be precise. Precision had its beauty: there was excitement in a well-drawn fuel consumption chart, an airframe template, a Bach prelude and fugue. No human factor in these things; humans weren't this close to perfection. There was a sense of wonder here, a touch of awe. It seemed to Tindle an experience very much worth having.

Candy William flight leveled off at twenty-thousand feet and the air speed indicator said five hundred miles an hour.

"Back to ninety-two," said Straker.

Cruising. The silence, sealed in by tight headsets, the sun strong upon the canopy; the earth (and earthly futility) miles below. Clear, clean beauty, heady in its purity. Perversely heady. As though the curve of simplicity circled back to move again toward the complicated infinite and unfathomable.

Only a technical problem now.

The whole business was nothing more than that. The mission itself—it began simply with a target, a scattering of camouflaged tents some distance behind enemy lines. The night before a black bomber had flown over this area, releasing bombs of flashlight powder. These, upon exploding, had tripped a photoelectric cell and triggered off an aerial camera in the bomber. In the dark of early morning men had studied these photographs, and noted the tents.

132

The target, neatly classified and numbered now, had gone into the Joint Operations Center. JOC was a room of many maps somewhere in Korea. Plotters pushed tiny symbols over and across these maps to show the whereabouts of planes and ground units. A board of high-ranking air, sea and ground officers decided who should strike at what targets. When a target was picked, all the information— map coordinates, armament desired, enemy opposition— was sent to the appropriate wing by teletype, and the operations officer assigned it there. There were blunders now and then, but on the whole it was a good system, and a clever one. It was a technique, getting better all the time.

Tindle peered ahead, over the lip of his right wing, and saw the Korean coast. It was blue-brown and maplike. Candy William flight entered a steaming cloud then, and the ships bumped along over waves of air. The cloud was like opalescent milk. The droplets of mist focused the sun's rays, making it noticeably warmer in the cockpit. The filtered light burned raw upon Tindle's cheeks.

"Keep 'er on ninety-two," cautioned Straker. They could not see each other too well here in the cloud. And here there was more of a sensation of speed: the white stuff streaked by, sometimes tearing on the wingtips, then raveling away in the slipstream. A lacework of frost appeared on Tindle's canopy.

"Bobolink Control, this is Candy William Leader," said Straker's voice. It was crisper, less formal in the air. Tindle was struck with the idea that Straker, by leading a flight, gained some kind of inner confidence. He sounded younger, fresher and not so labored. And he flew well, all right; Tindle could see this in the way he held the ship neatly on course.

"Bobolink here, Candy William."

"Over your station, inbound, fourteen zero seven."

"Roger, Candy William, you're cleared to Icicle. Check in there before crossing the bomb line."

"Understand. Candy William out."

A hundred miles later they came out of the cloud. There was only a broken layer between them and the ground now. Korea was a wrinkled, blistered land below. From this altitude the green of rice paddies and lower slopes was not

133

evident; the earth looked drab, and sometimes rust-red along the eroded mountaintops. Fires of war burned in dozens of places. The smoke gathered in puddles, filling the basins and valleys.

"Icicle Control, this is Candy William Leader."

"*Candy William, this is Icicle. Over.*"

"Candy William inbound, request clearance."

"*Roger, Candy William. You are cleared to mosquito controller, Ladybird Zebra. He'll give you further instructions. No change in coordinates, and check here on your way out. Over.*"

"Wilco, Icicle. Candy William out." There was a short pause, and then Straker added, "Candy William flight, this is Candy William Leader. Go over to Baker channel."

Tindle switched to another radio frequency—Baker channel—by punching a button on his VHF radio control box. They flew some more; eight or ten minutes perhaps—

"We'll go down on eighty-eight," said Straker.

They throttled back and spiraled earthward.

"Keep your eyes open, pick up that mosquito," Straker said.

It was Lieutenant Harold who spotted it. He didn't recognize it at first. "Bogie!" he called excitedly. "Bogie—ten o'clock low!"

"Little friend," came Kingsley's calmer, dryer voice. "That's our mosquito."

Straker called the smaller plane. "Ladybird Zebra, this is Candy William."

"*Ladybird here, Candy Willie.*" The mosquito controller had a deep, languid voice and sounded bored.

"What have you got for us down there?"

"*Plenty. This place is lousy with troops down here.*"

"All right. Make a run over our target area please, and we'll follow in and get the lay of the land. After that you can mark it for us."

"*Easy,*" said Ladybird Zebra. "*No sweat.*"

They watched the T-6, a toy plane far below them, make a lazy turn, then skim over a deep valley, little more than a cleft in the earth, this valley was. White puffs of flak and a few tracer streaks danced around the mosquito plane.

"*I'm right over 'em, now,*" said Ladybird Zebra. "*They're*

134

on my left. Tents and a few vehicles all over the hillside. On the short slope here, running about two hundred yards."

"Roger. We'll follow in," said Straker. "Breaking left—now."

The colonel brought his wing up sharply, and peeled off. Kingsley came along in his wake, only a short distance behind. Tindle did the same, glancing back to see where Lieutenant Harold was. Lieutenant Harold was right with him.

The F-80s leveled off, one after the other, at about a thousand feet above the mountains. Straker led them in a straight run along the ravine. Over the target he dipped his wing vertically for a better view, and the rest of them repeated the maneuver.

It had been some time since Tindle had tried to see details on terrain far below while passing over it at four hundred miles an hour, but apparently he hadn't lost his knack of observing. You never noticed much the first few missions, then gradually you learned what to look for, and how to recognize it. Now he spotted blurred squares, the lighter spots that were tents, and the rust-colored pimples of earth that were foxholes. He caught the rectangular shadow of a truck. A thread of smoke from a hastily choked campfire still clung to the shrubs at one place.

The bivouac was on the western slope of the ravine. The ridge of this slope was a good five hundred feet lower than the eastern ridge. It was a clever placement, for if attacking planes were to hit this target broadside, they would have to come in higher, over the east ridge, diving at an unusually steep angle. This meant that they would have to pull out sooner to avoid striking the ground. It meant that the point of bomb release and firing would be much further away—thus, less accurate.

Ahead, Straker's plane chandelled and climbed, Kingsley's ship came after it. Tindle led Lieutenant Harold skyward again. The four of them were spread out now, in single file, each several hundred yards apart.

"Hello, Ladybird Zebra, this is Candy William Leader. Will you make a firing pass for us, please?"

"Roger, will do."

Tindle scowled. They had seen the target clearly enough
—it didn't seem necessary for the T-6 to go in and use his
smoke rockets. And it didn't seem right to call for a pass
that wasn't necessary. Straker was just making doubly sure,
he supposed. He watched the T-6, with its slower speed
and narrower turning radius, come in from the south,
about level with the highest ridge, and then slow-roll into
a sharp left turn. This brought its nose into firing position
on the target. Momentary spurts of flame appeared under
its wings as its rockets went off. The missiles trailed smoke
like white yarn. Then they struck: flame showed white for
a moment on the green slope. White puffs and a spray of
ground fire still cluttered the air around the two-place
trainer.

The next thing happened casually, and much too quickly for immediate realization. A black jet of smoke came
suddenly from the T-6's cowling, and the ship winged
over lazily and crashed into the ground. A second later
it exploded.

Tindle stared; his eyes widened slowly.

"My God," said somebody on the radio. It sounded
like Kingsley.

"All right, Candy William Flight," said Straker evenly,
"let's go in and get them."

Straker led the way. A straight, steep approach from the
east this time; they dove at a high angle to avoid the ridge.
Kingsley backed off, putting another hundred yards between himself and the colonel. Tindle and Lieutenant
Harold fell into place.

"Napalm first," said Straker.

Tindle was a good mile behind the colonel's lead plane.
He watched Straker bullet down upon the near ridge, and
instinctively he wanted to pull on his own stick. Straker
kept diving. It seemed that at any moment he might strike
the ridge. The old guy had guts . . . Tindle would give
him that . . . but then, if supply and demand had anything to do with it, courage was cheap enough over here.
Pull out, Tindle thought. For the Lord's sake, Straker, pull
out! Then Straker flared from his dive. He skimmed across
the higher ridge, seeming to brush it with his belly. Tindle
saw the yellow napalm tanks lob away, then lost sight of

136

them. Kingsley came in behind the colonel, flying as close to the ground as the colonel had.

Long masses of flame ran across the ridge and began to spread. Black smoke billowed upward. A tent, some distance from the flame, caught fire and burned suddenly and brightly. Kingsley's tanks struck—

The near ridge was already coming up at Tindle's windshield at incredible speed. Tindle wasn't sure when he should pull out—now, or a few tenths of a second from now. His judgment seemed frozen. Funny, he would have known exactly when to pull out sixty days ago. Now it was as though his brain had flown into a cloud. He wasn't sure, he wasn't sure . . . he couldn't take a chance on knowing, and he would have to pull out *now*.

He ticked his bombs off and brought the stick back. It was done in an instant. He was pressed with terrible force into the seat as the jet curved upward and away. The pressure pulled at his arms, pushing them to his lap, and it drew his cheeks and eyelids down, stretching them. The illusion of thin gray smoke appeared in the cockpit. Then he was climbing again, toward the clean air. From the corner of his eye he saw Straker and Kingsley far to the right, turning to come in on another pass. He lobbed over and followed.

"Candy William Three, this is Candy Leader."

Straker calling him. What the devil for? "Candy William Three," Tindle acknowledged.

"You were way off. Pulled out too soon. Anything wrong?"

"I'll try again," said Tindle wearily.

They threw off their rockets next time around. Tindle saw two of Straker's go off together, sizzle toward the slope, and strike a few hundred yards beyond the bivouac area. For an instant Tindle thought that Straker had miscalculated, too. And then, abruptly, there was a secondary explosion—it seemed to rip the mountainside apart. Tons of smoke came up, up, up, thickening out.

"Man!" yelled Lieutenant Harold. "That's there's an ammo dump!"

Tindle hadn't seen it, but he knew the colonel must have

spotted it and changed his sighting at the last moment. If that were so, it was beautiful shooting.

But now Tindle was coming in again, hurtling toward that ridge wall, and this time he was determined to put his rockets on the target. Not difficult, he told himself. A mechanical matter. Keep the sight on the target, hold it there, wait, wait as long as you could, trigger, and pull out fast. A moron could be taught the motions.

The green earth was fat in his view. There was too much of it. It was coming too fast. He squeezed his stick hastily, the rockets slammed away, and he pulled out: he did this almost in panic. When he came out of his climb he banked and looked down, and saw that his rockets had struck far to the left. A nervous yaw of the plane had thrown them off, perhaps; a reflex in one leg that affected the rudder pedals . . . maybe that had done it. Meanwhile, he saw for an instant the tiny, blackened, shriveled men, the roasted locusts of men, lying in grotesque, curled attitudes. He saw puddles of napalm, still glowing, still spreading over the earth. He swore he could smell the burned flesh again. His lower lip was numb. He had been biting it.

"Candy William Three, this is Candy William Leader." Straker again. "What's the trouble? You pulled out at least a mile too high."

"Roger, William Leader." Tindle's voice was strange and dry in his own headsets. "I'll take another crack at it."

They began their strafing passes. Tindle tried desperately to lay his tracers on the target. He couldn't do it. He couldn't understand why—each time he came in again, he was convinced he'd be able to hold his dive, and each time something other than his own will forced him to break away too high.

The colonel said nothing more about it on the radio.

Candy William Flight raked and plowed and scorched that hillside, and then they flew down the ravine several times, observing their damage. No more ground fire was visible.

"Count 'em! Count the dead!" the colonel called.

They matched estimates. Over a hundred troops, at the very least.

They climbed to twenty-five thousand, found their head-

138

ing, and flew for Akuni Air Force Base in Japan. Tindle knew that the colonel would call him in almost as soon as they landed. He knew, in essence, what the colonel would say. Yellow, the colonel would say, afraid to take that extra chance that made a good fighter-bomber pilot. Then he'd probably get fatherly about the whole thing. Just a state of mind, he'd say; something you can control if you're really determined to. Best thing is to face it. Go up and do it again. Don't let it lick you. Don't let it get you down.

Tindle wondered if he would lose his head and spit in the colonel's eye.

And he wished that the queer thing that had gotten a grip on him—whatever it was—could be something as simple and understandable as plain, ordinary cowardice. . . .

CHAPTER SIX

1

IT WAS the end of the working day for Johnny Pendermeyer. The warmth of the afternoon sun drew a hot towel across his face as he stepped from the air-conditioned Meiji Building, and he stood there for a moment, getting used to it. Other workers from the Far East Air Forces headquarters, mostly blue-clad officers, brushed past him as they emerged. He lit a new cigar.

A younger tech rep, a gangling lad with traces of the Ivy League still clinging to him stopped and tapped Johnny's arm on his way out. "Hi. Going to the billets for supper tonight?"

Johnny smiled knowingly. His face became a pucker of wrinkles when he smiled, and his eyes, narrowing, all but disappeared behind his thick glasses. "Hell, no," he said.

"Seeing your girl again, eh?"

"Wouldn't you?"

"Sure, I guess I would. 'Night, Johnny."

"Good night."

Johnny turned right and walked down Avenue A toward the place where he had parked his sports car that morning. He wore a plain khaki uniform with the U.S. TECH REP patch on one shoulder during working hours, and he knew that this uniform was not the most flattering thing he could wear. The pleatless trousers revealed the bulging shape of his gut, and the shirt was somewhat tight about his meaty chest and shoulders. The blue overseas cap brought his globelike head to an unattractive point. Well, it didn't matter; he'd be out of the fool thing as soon as he was home. By home he meant his little love nest (as he liked to call it) in Kazumicho.

Government personnel were supposed to live in the billets provided for them, various halls and hotels the Occupation had taken over from the Japanese government, and Johnny still maintained an address in a four-man room at Army Hall, paying his service charge of one dollar a month. But he slept there only about once a week. The rest of the time he stayed in the Japanese house that cost him twenty thousand yen—about fifty-five dollars—a month. Sachiko herself cost him not much more than that in addition, and Shoji, his house boy, cost even less. Altogether, he would spend the total on drinks and slot machines if he hung around Army Hall all the time. And not have nearly as much fun.

He swung his car in and out of traffic on the way home, enjoying the near misses. He left a tangle of motorcycles and pushcarts behind him. Served the stupid bastards right for taking up a main thoroughfare the way they did, he thought. He climbed several hills through a well-shaded residential section, wound through some narrow streets, and finally stopped before a small Japanese house in a tiny, fenced-in garden. A sliding door admitted him to the garden, another to the vestibule of the house. The floor was raised above the level of the vestibule, as in all Japanese houses.

"Hi, baby! I'm home!" called Johnny. He sat on the steps and began to remove his shoes.

A woman in kimono and obi appeared. She was fanning herself with a flowered fan. She smiled and showed two gold teeth on the left side of her mouth. She had a double chin and extra flesh folded over on the backs of her arms, just above her elbows. She wore pancake make-up and thick lipstick. She bowed to Johnny and said, "*Irashai mase,*" in that whining, sing-song voice the Japanese use for conventional remarks.

Johnny laughed and said, "Always glad to see me, ain't you, baby?" He clambered to the floor level. She lifted her face as though to kiss him as he passed, and he laughed again and reached behind her and patted her buttocks. He went by her, and into the main room. He took the cigar from his mouth and laid it carefully in the ashtray on the low table. Then he started to strip his clothes off. Sachiko took them one by one as he handed them to her, folded them neatly and hung them over a lacquered wooden rack. When he was peeled to his shorts she handed him a cotton summer kimono.

"Not yet," said Johnny. "Even a *yukata's* hot today. Where's that boy?"

"Shoji!" called Sachiko. "*Ano-ne!*"

A moon-faced lad in a patched white shirt and slacks a size or two too large appeared. He was carrying a basin of water. The water steamed. His eyes were razor slits in a puffy, expressionless face.

"Good boy," said Johnny. "Just what I wanted. Hot water. *Mizu*, huh?"

"*Mizu's* cold water," said Sachiko. "*Oyu* is hot. I told you that last night." She had a throaty voice with only a trace of accent to her English. "Now kneel down, Johnny, and I'll give you your bath."

"Attababy," said Johnny, grinning. "Just what was on my mind." He knelt upon the floor, took his cigar from the ashtray, stuck it into his mouth, and relit it.

Shoji disappeared as quietly as he had entered.

"How about a beer, baby?" asked Johnny.

Sachiko glided to a small, porchlike corridor that was separated from the main room by sliding doors, now open. It looked out over a garden. The icebox was in the corner of this corridor. She came back with a bottle of Kirin beer, opened it and poured a glass for Johnny.

He drank, smacked his lips and said, "Ah!"

She dipped a small towel into the water now, scraped it upon a bar of soap, and began to rub it over Johnny's fat, hairy back.

141

"Attababy, attababy," said Johnny. He poured another glass of beer.

She squeezed the soap out of the towel, dipped it into the warm water again, and sponged the soap away. She worked smoothly and silently; there was a dull look of contentment upon her face.

"Put a little music on, baby," said Johnny.

She stepped to the record player on the floor in the corner of the room.

"Something good and hot."

"Don't you want to hear some Tschaikowsky?"

"For Christ's sake," said Johnny.

"Well, I like Tschaikowsky better. That's what I'm used to."

He looked at her for a moment. "Are you going to start that royal family stuff again?"

"Well, my mother was a baroness. I've showed you the pictures and everything. I don't know why you never believe it."

"I believe it, baby. I just don't go for it."

Sachiko shrugged and picked out a Stan Kenton record. When it was playing Johnny beat time on the floor with his hands, and imitated a cymbal beat with his voice, saying breathily, *"Pagh! pagh! pagh!"*

She began to wash his chest. Johnny puffed happily on his cigar and drank more beer. Whenever his glass was empty she filled it again. He beamed. He looked through the open doors of the garden and contemplated the light of the afternoon sun on the broad palm leaves.

"In some way," said Johnny, "I'm sure gonna hate to leave all this."

"What did you say?"

He looked at her as though interrupted. "Nothing."

"What did you say about leaving?"

"Nothing, baby. Come on—let's get on with the washing."

She washed some more. She patted his chest and said, "Takusan hair."

"Right, baby. Takes a man to grow it like that."

"Like a Hokkaido bear," she said.

"Like what?"

142

"Up in Hokkaido they have bears. We always say a hairy man's like a Hokkaido bear. It's an expression. A figure of speech."

He looked at her again. "Sometimes I swear you speak better English than I do."

"We always spoke English at home. The baroness always insisted on English and French, besides Japanese, because—"

"Baby, please don't make like the baroness again."

"I guess you're right. I guess things are a lot different now. Everywhere."

"Yeah," he said.

She washed down, from his chest to his vast belly.

"You're sure a funny one," he said.

"I am?"

"Yeah. Sometimes I swear you're a hundred percent Japanese. Then other times you're just like an American dame."

"I don't want to be like an American woman."

"Why not?"

"They're all too fat or too thin. And too noisy."

"The hell they are."

"But I see them on the street in Tokyo all the time. And that night you took me dancing at Army Hall. I watched them."

"Hell, they were just factory rejects you saw. They come over here because they can't do anything better back in the States. Or else they're screwed up and want adventure. They got it soft. Bunch o' damn stenographers having all the privileges of officers, billets and everything else. Back home they're different."

"I don't know," said Sachiko doubtfully.

The record ran out and he said, "Put another one on, baby." She moved quickly. "Another hot one,' he said. She flipped the Kenton record.

She came back to him, continued washing, and said, "How did it go at the office today?" She was still washing his belly, but now the strokes of her hand were more like caresses. Her expression hadn't changed, but Johnny knew what was coming. Damned if he'd ever thought he'd get tired of *that*, but sometimes he had more on his hands than

143

he could handle. That wasn't the reason he'd have to leave her, though. She was just plain getting too expensive—chiseling a little more every month, and thinking she was getting away with it. She had another think coming.

He answered her question. "Oh, it wasn't so bad. Easy, in fact. If I didn't have to put my time in I wouldn't even have to show up—and nobody'd know the difference."

"Funny," said Sachiko, "I know a lot of Americans who talk that way. Why do they send them here if there's nothing for them to do?"

"Well, they got to be here to take care of things. Listen, baby, don't worry about the good old U.S. It knows what it's doing. If we didn't have to take care of Europe too, we'd push those gooks right out of Korea in two minutes. Like this." He snapped his fingers. "Get me another beer, will you, honey?"

She got him another beer. She started to wash his gross, hairy thighs.

"Look, it stands to reason," said Johnny. "How can a bunch of natives stand up against brains and science? You got no idea of the kind of stuff our boys have to work with. Strictly scientific. Hell, I saw a design on some equipment today right out of Buck Rogers."

"Out of who?"

"Buck Rogers—he's a guy in the future. Rocket ships and things. You know, a comic strip."

"I don't care for comic strips. Wait—I'll take that back. I like Joe Palooka in the Stars and Stripes."

"You like Palooka, eh?"

"Yes. Because I like boxing."

"And why do you like boxing?"

"I like the blood."

He glanced at her, but her face was innocent.

"Why don't you take me to the boxing matches some night? I think they'll have some at Korakuen Stadium next week."

"Okay, I'll take you sometime."

"You always say that. But you never get around to taking me. As a matter of fact you don't take me anywhere. All we do is sit home."

"Don't you like it here?"

144

"Sure I like it here. But I want to get out once in a while."

"Well, stop squawking about it and maybe I'll take you." He spoke sternly. Had to keep these women in hand. They'd spoil easily if you didn't. Some things he could put up with—like this fairy tale about her mother being a baroness, when he knew damn well she'd been nothing but a foreign traders' girl friend for maybe a good ten years before the last war. She was no chick, after all. Anyway, that was okay with him: at least she was used to foreigners and spoke good American English, and that made everything a lot easier. The only trouble was that just in the last few months, by golly, her age had begun to show a little. More wrinkles around the eyes. A heavier fold of fat at the elbows. She was, frankly, getting just a little too expensive for second-hand goods. He said, "Now what was I talking about before you changed the subject?"

"Roger Bucks."

"Oh, yeah. This radar stuff of ours. It does everything but talk and take care of the baby. Of course, I got a few ideas for improvements on it, but it's like butting your head against a stone wall to tell them anything up there. Anyway, this new electronic camera of ours takes a picture at night from the air and shows every damn detail on the ground. Even puts artificial shadow in by out-of-phase synch. Goddamnedest thing I ever saw."

"I don't understand it exactly," said Sachiko.

"I don't think the guy who invented it does, either," said Johnny. He turned toward the door suddenly.

"What's the trouble?"

"Was that Shoji snooping at the door?"

"I don't know."

"*Shoji!*" he bellowed.

Shoji, bland-faced, stepped into view.

"What are you doing smelling around like a bird dog?"

"Beg pardon, sirrh?" said Shoji.

"Trying to get a free peep show on me and Sachiko, eh?"

"Beg pardon. Not understanding, sirrh."

"Okay, skip it. Better start the rice for supper."

"Rice is cooking, sirrh."

"Then beat it. Scram."

145

"Yes, sirrh." Shoji disappeared.

"You don't have to treat him like that," said Sachiko. "He's just a boy. He gets very mixed up sometimes because he doesn't understand."

"Oh, for Christ's sake, don't you start needling me now," said Johnny.

She looked up at him then. She was breathing heavily. Her eyes had a soft, moist look he knew—that look usually appeared when he spoke strongly to her.

"Now what's on your mind," he said, a little more softly.

"You know."

He grinned. "Okay, baby, close the doors."

Had to keep her happy while he still had her, after all. Actually, sometimes the damned dame was too much for him—but it was a matter of pride to keep up with her. And, everything considered, he didn't do bad. By God, he didn't do bad at all for a man his age.

She had removed her kimono.

She knelt before him and grasped him tightly, pressing her forearm painfully into the back of his neck. She bit him.

"Hey!" said Johnny.

She lifted her face.

Johnny, almost wearily, swung his hand so that the knuckles struck her hard across the cheek. She whimpered, fell away, tears came to her eyes, and then she smiled and was upon him again. She clawed at his back this time with her long nails.

"Goddamn it!" Johnny said. He swung at her, and she dodged, getting to her feet. He grabbed the wet towel from the basin and snapped it hard upon her buttock. She turned then and came back to him, and fell upon him and smeared wet kisses all over his face. "Johnny-san, Johnny-san, Johnny-san. Oh, I love you, Johnny-san!"

"Change the record first," he said. "The record is scratching."

She put on a jazz version of Ravel's *Bolero* this time. He recalled that it was her favorite.

2

Later that night Shoji left the house. Probably Sachiko-

146

san heard him, for he knew that she was a very light sleeper, but as long as Pendermeyer-san didn't hear him everything would be all right. Sachiko was lenient about his going out at night. Undoubtedly she thought he was going to meet a girl somewhere; her mind ran that way. As for Pendermeyer-san, the fat fool was snoring so loud that it shook the shingles. Shoji didn't have to worry about him.

It was eleven o'clock. Shoji walked a long distance, taking short, purposeful strides. He smoked several American cigarettes, stolen liberally from Johnny's supply, and altogether he walked for a little more than an hour, toward the center of Tokyo. No use spending twenty yen on a bus when he had good legs.

He came finally to a small café in a side-warren that was still open. Banners with Japanese characters hung over the entrance. There was a counter with stools, and several tables inside. A few young Japanese men—most of them wearing the lacquered belt buckles of college students—sat at these tables. The barmaid was a thin, tuberculous woman with a pockmarked face. "Welcome," she said to Shoji.

He nodded. "A cider, please."

She poured the sweet, tasteless soft drink into a glass for him. He took one sip, then said, "Where is Wataru-san?"

"Inside." She tilted her head toward the back. The flat-toned picking of a samisen came from there. "Sleeping."

"Wake him up."

"Pardon. He'll be angry. Please pardon. He's always angry if someone awakens him."

"Wake him anyway," Shoji spoke sharply.

The barmaid took a step back, bowed, said, "Pardon," again, and left.

Shoji lit another cigarette. He swung around on the stool and coolly looked at the men sitting at the tables. Two had been staring his way and he saw now that they turned their eyes hastily. He smiled to himself; he had a way of dominating others when he wanted to. He would be a leader someday. Maybe even a great leader; maybe Party head in Tokyo, or even all of Japan. Someday, when things worked out, Shoji would be rewarded for the hard work and patience now.

147

Shoji was twenty-two. He had just graduated from Chuo University with a degree in electrical engineering, and he might have been much more than a houseboy for a slob like Johnny Pendermeyer if he didn't have a mission to perform. Wataru-san and the others had shown how he could accomplish more by taking this menial job and keeping a sharp eye on the American technical representative. There were at least a dozen Party members scattered about in such critical spots now. One was a gardener to a full major general. For the most part these workers performed their duties and waited, knowing that only by a long chance would they ever be able to pick up really significant information. After all, the espionage manual pointed out that intelligence work was ninety-eight percent just waiting for something to turn up.

And now, tonight, Shoji had the first bit of information he'd so far deemed worth reporting.

He didn't suppose Wataru would praise him or attempt to give him credit for this, but that didn't matter so much: Shoji would find a way to let it be known in Party circles just who had done this thing. He smiled again. Two years ago he would have been much more naïve about it. He would have reveled in the idea that he had selflessly done something to help the world revolution. That was when he was all full of doctrine: the things that had attracted him to communism in the first place. Not that he still didn't believe in the basic precepts—a synthesis had to come, after all; that was natural law, as Marx had demonstrated—but he'd learned by now that idealistic sentimentalists got nowhere. In the Party, as anywhere else, a man had to look out for himself now and then. You could find this difference in the faces of the Party men if you looked sharply enough. The two students over there in the corner—they were still filled with dewy visions. Just as Shoji had once been. Useful, of course, because of their devotion, but tricky to handle sometimes—just a little unreliable if the task were critical.

Wataru came out in a *yukata*, still tying his obi. He was a small, solid man with a square face and a completely bald head. He had scars on his head. Shoji had heard that the scars came from leading strikers' brawls in the factory districts of Kobe. Wataru said, "You got me out of bed. I hope it's important."

Shoji tried his flat stare. Wataru met it strongly, and it was Shoji who looked down first. "Shall we talk here?" asked Shoji.

Wataru looked around. "Sit down. And speak in a low voice. Everybody here can be trusted, but—well, just the same, don't speak too loudly."

The barmaid came back and put a cup of hot green tea before Wataru. He nodded, she bowed, and disappeared again. He brought the teacup to his lips with both hands, sipped noisily, and looked at Shoji over the cup. When he took the cup down again he said, "Well?"

"They have a new kind of radar."

"Is that what you came to tell me? They have twenty new kinds of radar."

"No, this is really new. I know these things. I was trained in it, after all. I know what they've had before, and I know this is something pretty exciting."

"All right. What are the details?"

"It photographs at night. Apparently makes a three-dimensional effect by a double signal out of phase."

"What are you talking about?"

"Call it an artificial shadow if—" Shoji cleared his throat politely—"the technical details are a little too much for you. I assume it would be used in a reconnaissance plane."

"You assume," said Wataru. "We're only interested in what you know."

"How else would it be used?"

"Why ask me? You're the expert."

"All right. Let me give you a short course in these matters, Wataru-san. They've been taking night photographs with flash bombs—magnesium bombs dropped from RB-26s over the area they want to photograph. When these bombs go off they trip a photo-electric cell and activate the camera. They take good reconnaissance pictures, but their disadvantage is that the People's Army knows when it's been photographed. Now radar give a perfectly good flat outline of everything below, but because of that flatness it's very easy to camouflage against it. This new idea ought to make photographs that can be studied later to pick out the camouflaged items. Shadow, you know, makes all the difference in the world in camouflage. This way, the men on the ground will never know whether a secret installation of theirs has been detected or not."

"What proof have you got of this—this gadget?"

"I heard Pendermeyer talking about it."

"Frankly, it sounds like a wild tale to me."

"All right, Wataru-san. Suit yourself. I've told you the facts. If you can't see the importance of them there are others who can."

Wataru raised his sparse eyebrows just a little then. It seemed to Shoji that the scars on his head became a little paler against the brown-yellow skin. Wataru said, "Could it be that you're getting ambitious these days, Shoji-san?"

"Only to serve the Party," said Shoji, smiling sarcastically. "In the same devoted way that you do, Wataru-san."

This time he didn't lower his eyes away from Wataru's stare.

CHAPTER SEVEN

1

MAJOR PETE RONSDALE walked into Colonel Straker's office, marched smartly to the desk, saluted, and stood at attention.

"As you were, Pete," said Straker, smiling. "Sit down."

Ronsdale said, "Thanks. You'll have to excuse me for looking like this, sir, but I got your message when I got off the plane, and I figured it might be important, so I came right over."

"Well, you didn't have to be that quick about it, Pete—though I might have known you would. But as long as you're here we might as well go over this thing."

"Certainly, sir."

"Have you called your wife to tell her you're back?"

"No, sir." Ronsdale looked at his watch. "It's nine-thirty, and she'd be over at the commissary shopping now. I'll catch her later."

"Have breakfast?"

150

"Yes, sir. Had a bite in the lunchroom at Haneda before we left Tokyo." He smiled engagingly. "I could use some coffee, though."

Straker ticked the switch and said into the communicator, "Worrel, have them send some coffee over here."

"Right away, Bill," said Colonel Worrel.

"Well," said Straker, leaning back, putting his fingertips together, "I guess you're all ready to take over command of the 109th."

"Raring to go, sir."

Straker chuckled. "Thought you'd be. It's not an easy job, commanding a basic tac outfit. You've got all the combat worries of a pilot—plus your administrative difficulties."

"Well, at least it'll never get dull."

"No. No, indeed." Straker laughed. "I'll tell you frankly, I have utmost confidence in you, Pete."

"Thank you, sir."

"And that's why I called you over this morning. I need some frank answers. I need some information you might find it difficult to give me."

"I'll do my best," said Ronsdale, striking exactly the right note of sincerity. He was glad, now, that the colonel had summoned him. He could always behave very smoothly in front of the colonel, and he needed a small triumph of some kind to restore his confidence. It had been shaken in Tokyo. He'd been displeased with himself ever since waking up in that hotel and finding that girl—what was her name?—gone, and knowing he'd failed. Well, he could forget that now. More important things on hand. He said, "Just what is it you want to know?"

"I understand you're pretty well acquainted with Captain Tindle," said Straker.

"Why—yes. I guess so."

"Went through cadets with him, didn't you?"

"Yes."

"What was he like in flying school? Did he ever show any signs of cowardice there?"

"Cowardice? Why—not Dick Tindle. He was always a very cautious pilot, of course, but—"

"Ah-hah!" said the colonel.

151

"But I don't think he was ever exactly afraid of anything."

"Loyal of you to put it that way, Pete."

"No, sir. It's not just loyalty. I don't think Dick Tindle's a coward, that's all."

"Well, probably you don't. Friendship can pretty well blind you to things like that."

Ronsdale cocked his head. "What's Dick done?"

"Let's say he's in a difficult position. Now, I'm not an unsympathetic man, Pete, as Tindle probably thinks. I genuinely want to help him, And helping him will be your job, too, as his new squadron commander."

"Can you fill me in a little?"

"We took a mission yesterday. Troop concentration on a hillside. I'll admit it was a little tough to get into firing position—there was a high ridge right in front of our approach—but everybody but Tindle seemed to manage it."

"Well, maybe he's a little rusty. He hasn't been flying for some time."

"Oh, there's more to it than that. It's the things he says —the way he worries about killing the enemy. I'd always been led to believe a soldier's job was to kill the enemy. But then perhaps my military science is a bit outdated by now."

Ronsdale laughed with appreciation, though not entirely with sincerity. He said, "Well, Colonel, I don't know just what to say. I won't know until I see Tindle on a mission myself."

"A sensible attitude." Straker nodded. "I wish Tindle would use a little more sense. His attitude's pretty bad. Surly. Of course, I suppose it could be guilt feelings from his cowardice that makes him that way. I'm afraid he's not much good to the Wing in his present state. On the other hand, while there's still a chance of salvaging a pilot, I think it ought to be tried. Pilots cost the government quite a bit of money, after all, and they're not too easy to come by out here."

"I don't know exactly what I can do about it, sir."

"Take him under your wing. Both figuratively and literally. Let him fly behind you on missions, and keep an eye on him. Keep talking to him. Bolster him up, if you can.

152

You see, he'll probably listen to you, especially if you approach him in an intelligent diplomatic way. I'm sure you're capable of that. Unfortunately, there's a personality clash between Tindle and myself—we seem to strike sparks. I'd never let that stand in the way of my judgment of the man, of course, but it does make it impossible for me to reach him where I want to."

"I understand."

"Good." Straker rose, and Ronsdale rose, and Straker held out his hand. "Good luck with your squadron, Pete. I have an idea the 109th'll be piling up records from now on. I want to see troops killed. That's the Wing's special job in this war from now on."

"We'll try."

"Go to it, Pete," said the Colonel, and Ronsdale left.

2

This mission was a road reccy.

They took off in the early morning, when it was still dark; Ronsdale led the flight, Tindle flew his wing, and Captain Kingsley and Lieutenant Harold made up the second element.

They were already past the bomb line and cleared by Icicle Control when Tindle broke radio silence. It was just becoming light. The sun was far to the east, somewhere beyond the Sea of Japan, its disc magnified by the humid air. The mountains below trailed long, dark shadows in the valleys and on their western slopes. Chalk-blue morning mist gathered in the low places. Only a few minutes ago a searchlight, whose beam had been reflected from the overcast to light up the battlefront, had been switched off, and just before darkness melted away there had been several artillery flashes. Once, over Pyongyang on the western horizon, flak had shown for sixty seconds: it looked like a lawnsprinkler sending up watery fire.

Tindle said, "Candy William Leader, this is William Two. We're a little off course."

"Uh—just a minute, William Two, I'll check," Ronsdale answered.

Tindle said, "You don't need your map. That snake

curve of the Imjin's a check point. Better take about a five-two heading and we'll cut back. We should be on course again in about three minutes."

"Okay, roger, we'll do that," said Ronsdale. He gave the turn-warning necessary for formation flying at jet speeds. "Breaking right—now."

He turned, and the rest of them followed.

In Ronsdale's voice Tindle had sensed a certain embarrassment, and now he was almost sorry that he had called attention to the check point. It might have been better to let Ronsdale work the thing out on these maps for himself. Except that—well, he didn't have complete confidence in Ronsdale's skill with a map. Pete Ronsdale had never been very strong in pilotage, not even back in flying school. But he would have to be careful with Pete, now that Pete was a squadron commander. A few innocent, but badly chosen words could easily make it seem that Tindle was jealous; seeking to discredit Pete.

Colonel Straker would be quickest to believe that. Rotten break, getting a man like Straker for C.G. At least once in a man's service career, Tindle supposed, there'd be a personality barrier between him and his superior officer. The trouble was he couldn't establish communication with Straker in order to explain. They didn't speak the same language. The words Tindle chose simply had different meanings as far as the colonel was concerned.

Oh, he might bull it through, if he thought that would do any good. He might insist on his seven days' leave, quote the regulation authorizing them, and carry it to the Chaplain and the Inspector General. He might win a skirmish over Straker that way. But a queer pride kept him from doing that. There would be something childish in it, he felt. . . .

"Candy William Flight, this is Candy William Leader," said Ronsdale. "We'll take a heading of three-four-nine."

The four of them banked lazily into a new compass direction.

They flew for another several minutes and Ronsdale called, "Eighty-eight percent, and let's go down."

The spiraled toward the deck.

They had no specific target today: they were to follow

154

a Communist Main Supply Route to where it joined a railroad and then skim along the tracks for a while, looking for targets of opportunity. In the briefing Major Goff had said that probably they wouldn't spot any troops on this one, but just the same the colonel would be obliged if they'd keep their eyes open.

"There's the M.S.R.—about two o'clock," said Ronsdale. "Level off."

They began to follow the road at about a thousand feet, dipping now and then for better visibility of the terrain.

As on the last mission, Tindle now felt perfectly confident that he would be able to do what was required of him. He knew that he was a better-than-average fighter-bomber pilot. It was the only thing he did really well, in fact. It was the craft to which, in his life, he had devoted the most time. Not his idea, that. There were twenty other things in this world he would have liked to try. He began to wonder now just what, given a choice, he would pick for a life's work. In what field would he really like to become an expert and a specialist? And then he reflected that if he must devote his life to one thing, he *still* hadn't much of a choice. No freedom to dabble in a number of things—or plain loaf, if he chose. But if everyone had such freedom, there'd be no order among men. It was possible that absolute freedom of choice was immoral, inimical to the survival of the breed. It was possible that there would always be limits and that man should be content to move freely within these limits. But the limits became narrower all the time. . . .

"There's the tracks!" called Ronsdale. He banked toward them.

"Smoke!" said Kingsley. "Smoke over there—eleven o'clock!"

A ribbon of steam hung along a row of poplars two miles ahead. In the early morning steam dissipated less quickly. The Reds could never quite resist the temptation to keep their locomotives going till sunrise and a little beyond. This was why tracks were scouted in the early morning.

"There's an engine under me! I'm coming over it right now!" Ronsdale said.

155

"Roger, boy! Roger, I see it!" Lieutenant Harold called back.

"I'll make a one-eighty—stay with me," said Ronsdale.

Tindle saw the bulky shapes behind and beside the locomotive, looking at first like shadows. But he had seen shadows like this before. Then, for a bare instant, he caught the glint of a gun barrel. "Watch it fellas! Flak cars on this train!"

"Stay with me," said Ronsdale again. He made a steep, climbing turn, winged over, and came down again. The rest followed in his flight path. As Ronsdale began his shallow dive, the bright golf balls began to stream up from the ground. White puffs dotted the air. Orange lights winked from the shadows under the poplars. It seemed incredible that Ronsdale's ship could go through that cat's cradle of fire without being struck; he was surrounded by the stuff; it was passing over and under his wings.

Tindle, close behind him, could see all of this. During this part of a second Kingsley and Lieutenant Harold were still climbing and turning.

It was Tindle who saw Ronsdale jink.

The sudden terror was painfully clear in the very movement of Ronsdale's ship, in the almost animate way that it shied, flipped away and began to climb again. His rockets flashed, and exploded far beyond the target. The poplars, the shadows, the elusive bulk of the locomotive—all suddenly swung into Tindle's sight reticle. The balls were coming up at Tindle, now, seeming to float lazily for all their speed . . . coming toward him from the depths of the long, dark tunnel into which he was diving.

There were no men to kill down there; there was only the dark place from which the lifeless missiles came.

Tindle tripped his own rockets. He saw them whoosh away, and he watched them go halfway to the target before he flared out from his dive. He banked hard to the right as he climbed, looking down upon the target. But he had known as soon as the rockets left his wings that they would strike close to the locomotive if not directly upon it.

There was an explosion below him. The explosion tossed his plane upward like a charred fragment from a trash fire, and he fought the stick to keep the ship under control.

156

He caught glimpses of the target. Steam now squirted out in all directions from the area of the dark shadow.

Kingsley and Lieutenant Harold came along and poured their rockets in. There were other explosions.

The return fire dwindled to a puny line of tracers that tried to follow the jets and fell always far behind.

"Nice goin', boys, nice goin'!" yelled Lieutenant Harold.

A secondary explosion below grew like a century plant stepped up in time. White smoke with a black core billowed into the air. Bits of curved metal plate came lobbing up through it. The single machine gun stopped firing.

"Two of 'em!" screamed Harold. "They was two locomotives down there!"

The F-80s were already high above the target. Tindle, Kingsley and Harold followed Ronsdale's soaring circle; they were all staring down now.

"Nice shooting, Pete," said Kingsley.

Ronsdale didn't answer.

Tindle lifted his eyebrows. Hell, yes. He should have known they'd give Ronsdale credit for those locomotives. They hadn't seen Ronsdale jink. And they'd all watched Tindle on a mission before; they knew about where *he* stood. Tindle looked at Ronsdale's ship ahead and saw the small red dot of the major's helmet under the canopy. The red dot didn't tell him much about what was on Ronsdale's mind now. . . .

"Come on! Let's go in and get 'em again!" Lieutenant Harold's voice.

"This is Candy William Leader," said Ronsdale. His voice was unruffled. "No need for it, Candy William Four. Only be wasting ammunition. We'll drive on home now."

"Reckon you're right, William Leader," said Harold, with a note of apology in his voice.

"Good thinking, buddy," said Kingsley.

Ronsdale led the climb, then found his compass course and led them home. Tindle kept staring at the red helmet. Tindle didn't know whether to admire Ronsdale's cleverness or despise his gall. He'd worked this whole situation so beautifully to his advantage. But Pete Ronsdale had never been like this before . . . or had he! Had he really been this way all the time, but never before in Tindle's

157

presence encountered the sort of crisis that would expose him? Maybe that was what they meant when they said you never really knew even your closest friends. Maybe it took a good crisis to bring it out, and without the crisis, because they were your friends, you always managed to overlook the little indications of weakness that might catch up now and then.

And now Tindle and Ronsdale would have to face each other when they were on the ground. It would be painful and embarrassing; out of an empathy for Ronsdale, Tindle dreaded to go through with it. But this was no small thing Ronsdale had stolen from him. Pete was taking credit for those locomotives at a time when Tindle could use that credit to reinstate himself with the Wing. Pete deserved no relief from embarrassment; if anything he deserved any hurt Tindle could now inflict upon him. He would well deserve it, for instance, if Tindle now tried to use him to his own underhanded advantage—

Tindle suddenly permitted himself to consider openly what had been lying for some minutes like a sleeping winter serpent in the bottom of his mind.

He envisioned suddenly how he would be able to use Ronsdale. In his mind he went through a little imginary scene, hearing the dialogue quite clearly. Then he shook his head suddenly and with his lips formed the word, "No." He frowned and thought about this thing some more. A dirty trick, he thought. Not the kind of dirty trick he ordinarily permitted himself to use. But under the circumstances, well—well, he wasn't sure whether he'd pull this trick or not. He would have to wait and see.

At Akuni they wound down to a thousand feet, roared over the landing strip in formation, and then broke sharply away, one after the other. This maneuver strung them out in single file for the final approach.

Tindle came in close behind Ronsdale, so close that he could see the shimmering jet exhaust from the major's tailpipe. They both flared out at about 125 miles an hour; Ronsdale bounced twice and Tindle greased his own ship in. When Ronsdale turned from the runway to the short taxi strip, Tindle bumped his throttle and came up alongside. Ronsdale didn't look; Ronsdale kept his eyes straight ahead. Tindle rode with him to the parking place. He saw Ronsdale scramble hurriedly from the cockpit, then he stepped from his own plane, leaving the engine turning and calling to MacInnes, who had flagged him to the hard-stand, "Flush her for me, will you, Mac?" MacInnes nodded and swung into the cockpit in Tindle's place.

Tindle caught Ronsdale a few yards from the line. Ronsdale had been walking fast, looking over his shoulder several times, and now he stopped, as though finally giving up. He thrust his hands into the pocket-like side opening of his flying suit. Before Tindle could speak he said, "Wait a minute, Dick. I know what you're thinking."

"You do, eh?"

"I know you think I'm pretty much of a heel, Dick, and—and well, I am."

Suddenly Ronsdale's polished, precise diction was irritating Tindle. It never had before. Tindle said, "More than anything I'm puzzled, Pete. I keep wondering why you'd do a thing like that. You did *know* that I got those loco-motives, didn't you?"

"Dick—listen to me. Try to see it my way. It was—I couldn't help myself, Dick. It was as though somebody else—somebody I didn't have any control over—sat there and refused to say anything. I'll make it up to you, Dick. I'll see that the favor is returned with interest if you don't make a rhubarb out of this. Dick, this is the only time I ever asked you a really big favor. You've *got* to do this for me. . . ." Ronsdale was talking too fast. The words were stumbling all over each other. His face was bright red; his eyes were a little wild. He looked suddenly much younger. His voice was higher. He was a schoolboy, a fright-ened schoolboy.

Tindle said quietly, "What in the hell are you talking about, Pete?"

"Don't tell them. Don't tell them I pulled off. Let them keep thinking I got those locomotives. It's for the good of the Squadron, Dick—they've got to have confidence in me. I'll see that you get credit for other kills later on, but *this* one's important to me, Dick."

"For Christ's sake," said Tindle. He stared.

"You—you won't spill the beans, will you?"

159

"I'll make a bargain with you, Pete."

"A bargain?"

"I need my leave. The seven days Straker chiseled me out of. If—"

"I'll see that you get them, Dick. I can swing that for you easily. If you'll just play along with me this one time, I'll—"

Tindle's voice tightened. "You'd better shut up now, Pete."

"What?"

"I can't take much more of this conversation. I'm not only thinking you're rotten, I'm disgusted with myself, too. Maybe some of you rubbed off on me."

"Dick, what are you saying? You know you're the best friend I've got, Dick." Ronsdale put his hand on Tindle's shoulder. Tindle yanked his shoulder away viciously and turned and walked off. He didn't look back, but he felt that Ronsdale must be standing there, staring at him with wounded deer's eyes.

Just before chow that evening Colonel Worrel summoned Tindle from the barracks to his headquarters office. The chubby exec looked up mildly when Tindle came in and said, "Oh—uh—there you are. There are some leave orders for you down in A.G., Tindle."

Tindle nodded. "So the old man changed his mind." He looked at Straker's office. The door was open and he could see that Straker was not there.

"Yes. I guess Major Ronsdale must have gone to bat for you. Ronsdale was in there with him quite a while this afternoon."

"Okay. Thanks, Colonel. I'll go pick up the orders."

"Well—uh—just a minute. I've got a little errand for you. That's why I called you you in."

Tindle waited dutifully while Colonel Worrel unlocked a safe beside his desk and took out a large manila envelope. He looked right and left before he handed it to Tindle. "I forgot to get this off with the A.G. courier this morning. Keep that under your hat, will you? You know how Bill Straker is."

"Sure," said Tindle.

Worrel handed him the envelope. "It's highly classi-

160

fied stuff, so you better be pretty careful with it. I know you will be."

Tindle glanced at the envelope, then at Worrel again.

"It's poop on this new secret radar photo equipment the recon outfit's been using. There are a couple of top secret negatives in there they took. So deliver this by hand, personally, will you? And you'd better wear a pistol when you do. Make it look better."

"Okay," said Tindle. "Who gets it?"

Worrel nodded at the envelope. "The address is on there. Tech Intelligence up at FEAF. You can give it to an officer there or to that tech rep they've got working with them—Mr. John Pendermeyer's his name. He's cleared for top secret."

"Okay."

"You'll be sure to do this now before you go off having a good time?"

"No sweat," said Tindle.

"Well," said Worrel, getting up, extending his chubby hand, "have a good time."

"I'll try," Tindle said. He was suddenly, unaccountably weary. He wanted to sleep, now, and forget.

3

It rained the following day in Akuni. It was the first of the summer rains, gray and gentle, clinging, seductive.

Though no missions were mounted this day the routine jobs of the base were performed as usual. The Air Police guard was changed near midday, and the old Officer of the Day turned it over to the new one. The maintenance shops worked away at engines, radios, guns and airframes. The staff at headquarters raked through the never-ending paper work. Special Services fought to have the star players on the Akuni Panthers ball team released from duty for practice—there was an important game with the undefeated Combat Cargo Haulers next week. Public Information fought with the mess and billeting section for preferential treatment for several correspondents who had arrived that day. The dean of them, Herb Oscott, wanted to do a special story on the 66th Wing for a national magazine—something about this new nickname, "The Man-hunters."

Major Pete Ronsdale was listed as Airdrome Officer that evening. On most bases he would have merely left his telephone number—wherever he happened to be—with Base operations, so that he could be summoned in case something required an officer's decision. But Colonel Bill Straker didn't look upon the duty that way. He believed that an A.O. should stay upon the line, base himself in the ops shack, and make an inspection of the hangars and the airstrip every four hours.

Ronsdale ate supper early and at about six 'oclock he sat at the dinner table in his cottage, finishing his last cup of coffee. Essie sat across from him. She was having coffee, too, with brandy on the side. She wore a smart navy frock this evening; she was scrubbed, groomed and perfumed. She smoked her cigarette in a coral holder.

The purr of the rain came through the stripped bamboo blinds. Essie said, "Of all nights for you to pull A.O."

"Hm?"

"I'm lonely tonight. Rain always makes me lonely."

"Well, it only comes about once a month."

"The rain?"

"No. A.O. duty."

"Pete—"

"Yes?"

"Couldn't you get someone else to take it tonight?"

"You know I couldn't do that."

"You could trade off with someone. Take his trick later."

"Why? Why tonight?"

"I don't know, Pete. I'm—I've got the willies tonight. It's this rain. I feel like getting mad, mad stinko or something. Why don't we have a party right here, just the two of us?"

"Now, Essie—"

"You could ask Dick Tindle to take A.O. for you. He'd do it."

"Dick's in Tokyo. He took off on the courier plane. Seven-day leave."

"Oh." She drank some of her brandy. "I wish I were in Tokyo."

162

"Why?"

"Just to get away. Just to miss this every-day's-the-same feeling here."

"I thought you liked it here. You said you did. You've said lots of times we could never live like this, with servants and everything, even on a major's pay back in the States."

"I know. I know. But, good God, there's never any excitement here!"

He smiled. "I had a little yesterday morning over Korea."

"Yes. You've got a war to play with. You men—you've always got something like that. And what have women got? God, I wish I were a man."

"Essie, really."

She mocked him, drawing out her face to match his expression. "Essie, reahhly."

"Oh, hell," he said, and got up. "I'm going to work. I'll see you in the morning."

She followed him to the door. "Pete."

"Yes?" He turned.

"How do you think you'll feel when you come back in the morning?"

"Feel? Tired, I guess. What do you mean?"

"You know what I mean."

"All right, darling. I'll try not to be too tired."

"Make it good tomorrow morning, Pete. Make it wonderful just once. You can control yourself if you really try."

"Esise, look, I haven't got time now to—"

"Pete—" she cocked her head abruptly—"did you ever cheat on me?"

"Now what kind of a foolish question is that?"

"I don't know. I just wondered. If you ever do—don't let me know, Pete. Just don't let me know. Don't ever make any foolish confessions."

"Essie," he said, putting on his blue raincoat, "sometimes I just don't understand you."

"I know, I know." She sighed and finished her brandy. "Sometimes I just don't understand myself."

She puffed her cigarette in the coral holder and stared at the smoke hanging against the light rain outside, as Ronsdale disappeared into that rain.

163

She wasn't sure what she would do tonight.

One thing was certain: she wouldn't just sit around and then go to bed. She was damned sure of that.

4

Technical Sergeant Frank Braith sat on the edge of his cot and stared morosely at the two dozen men who were milling around inside the long barrack building. He held a canteen cup half full of whiskey and Coca-Cola in his hand.

It was a noisy party—a damn fool party to Braith's way of thinking—and they were celebrating tonight one Larry Dugan's promotion from tech to master. Leave it to that dumb Irishman to make master sergeant. Leave it to him to fall into a spot where the opening was, and get that third rocker after a lousy six months in grade. That was the way it always happened.

The bunch of them were singing. They stood in a knot at the far end of the room, most with their backs turned, and they were trying to sing "Nobody's Darlin' But Mine." While that spick, Marquez, played the guitar. They weren't bothering with Braith, any of them. Which was just fine. It suited Braith not to be bothered right now. So he told himself. He had other things on his mind besides a lot of nonsensical getting drunk and singing. He took a deep gulp of whiskey and Coke. Felt good.

They finished "Nobody's Darlin'," and there was an argument about what to sing next. Somebody said, "How about 'Workin' on the Railroad'?"

"Okay, that's swell," said Dugan. Master Sergeant Larry Dugan was a tall, red-faced lad. He held a bottle by the neck and drank his whiskey straight. He had a light, pleasant voice, which he seldom raised, and he was nearly always smiling, even when he bawled somebody out. He turned now and looked at Braith. "Hey, Frank—you can sing barry, can't you?"

"He used to be wit da Metropolitan," said someone.

"Yeah—but he never sold no insurance."

Much laughter.

"Up yours, you bastards," Braith said to all of them.

They laughed again, and then began to sing.

164

Braith took another gulp.

Feeling warmer in the chest now. Earlier in the evening he'd decided he wouldn't drink at all—the memory of that binge at the Cho-Cho Club in Tokyo, and its head-splitting aftermath was still with him. But they'd coaxed him into joining them in a toast to Dugan's promotion, and now he was glad he'd taken at least a little. Loosened him up; helped him relax. He could think more easily this way.

Well, all in all, everything was working out pretty good. He had Major Ronsdale just about where he wanted him now. Ronsdale wouldn't want him spreading the word around about how he'd gone for the panic button in that thunderstorm. On top of that Ronsdale owed him plenty for turning that Jap dame over to him. He wondered, in passing, how the major had made out with Terry. The works, no doubt. He'd tried to pump Ronsdale for the salacious details on the way back to Akuni next day, but the major had been in a pretty sour mood and hadn't talked much. Probably just a hangover. At any rate, Braith *had* mentioned the transfer to the jet maintenance squadron, where there were more openings for master sergeant. Of course he hadn't given *that* as his reason for wanting this transfer. "I'm anxious to work on jets," he had said. "They're the coming thing." The major had said he'd see what he could do. . . .

Braith finished his drink.

He got up. They were through singing for the moment, and Pfc. George Marquez and that crazy Polak corporal, Lensky, were arguing about something. Lensky was blond, hard, and shaped like a small milk bottle. He always went slightly apey when he drank. His eyes got pink and wild. Braith sidled up to the refreshment table, splashed more whiskey and Coke into his canteen cup and stood there with the rest and listened.

"Listen—what's a guitar got to do with it?" Marquez was saying. He had put the guitar aside and was looking up at Lensky with his motionless, licorice eyes.

"Anybody plays a guitar's a goddamned nancy," said Lensky.

"I think you are drunk," said Marquez.

"Go play your goddamned guitar," said Lensky. "Lemme see you."

"Lensky, why don't you be nice? Why don't you be quiet so we can have a party?"

"Frig you," said Lensky.

"Go on to bed," said Marquez. "Maybe you need some sleep."

"Frig you, you goddamned greaser," said Lensky.

Marquez rose swiftly from the chair. In Braith's now slightly fuzzy vision he made only a blur. His fists pummeled into Lensky, driving the stocky man back, catching him by surprise.

Master Sergeants Dugan and MacInnes stepped in and separated the two: Dugan on Lensky, MacInnes on Marquez.

"He don' know how to fight!" Lensky screamed. He was touching his cheek. Marquez had accidentally scratched it. "All them goddamned spicks fight with a knife! He stuck a knife on me!"

"Shut up, shut up," said Dugan wearily.

"I will fight him. I will fight him anytime." Marquez was breathing hard.

"Fair fight!" yelled someone.

"Yeah—that's it! Fair fight!" Several took up the cry.

"I'll rassle him! I'll break his goddamn back!" said Lensky.

"I will rassle you. I will rassle you anytime," said Marquez.

They cleared the center of the barrack room. Dugan suggested the six mattresses that they laid out on the floor to form a square. "I'll referee," said Dugan. And he glared about, waiting for somebody to challenge that. Nobody did. He said, "Here's the rules. No punching or eye-gouging or biting or using your fingernails or anything like that. You got that straight?"

Marquez nodded. Lensky just kept glaring.

"No kicking in the balls, either," said Dugan.

Lensky wiped his nose.

"You hear me, Lensky?" Dugan asked.

"I hear you."

166

"By God," said Dugan, "either one of you tries any funny stuff I'll personally take care of you."

"Yeah," said Lensky, uninterestedly.

"One fall," said Dugan. "'One fair fall. First man gets his shoulders pinned, that's it. He's had it. And, by God, the other man better move off fast when I tap him on the shoulder."

MacInnes stepped forward. "Look, Larry," he said to Dugan, "maybe we'd better skip the whole thing. Make them shake hands and let's get on with the party."

"Aw, let the dumb bastards have it out," said Dugan.

Braith had finished another drink. All this time he had been sipping and watching Marquez, who stood there, stripped to the waist. Hell of a good kid, this Marquez, even if he was kind of stupid, like all Mexicans, and Braith had always liked him. Braith would try to do something for him someday: see that he made corporal, maybe, once Braith was transferred over to the 79th. The kid was really built for a little guy. He had an evenly tanned olive skin, taut over smooth muscles, and these muscles rippled like snake-flesh whenever he worked his arms or shoulders. He had the flat, slabbed chest of a boxer and a small, well-formed head on a muscular neck. Those large, dark eyes were really something. They were so dark that you couldn't see the pupils, and you never knew exactly what Marquez was thinking. But the little son of a bitch could sing like a goddamned bird, that was for sure, and when he sang it was enough to bring tears to a guy's eyes, it was that good.

MacInnes and Dugan continued their argument. In this touchy situation—in the volatile alcoholic atmosphere all about—they were overpolite with each other.

Somebody called, "Are we gonna fight, or aren't we?"

"Aw, hell, let's sing another song."

Nobody was quite sure how it all ended—faded away. There was a great deal of talk, all right, and a great deal of milling about. Presently someone noticed that Lensky had disappeared, and a few minutes later somebody else reported that he was sound asleep in the next barracks, snoring his head off.

"Play that song, 'Eye-eye-eye,'" said Dugan to Marquez.

167

"Yeah, go ahead, Pedro," said Sergeant Uline, the cross-eyed redhead from the food service squadron.

"My name is George," said Marquez, and sat down and took his guitar again.

He played and sang "Cielito Lindo."

Braith sat down again, nearer the gathering this time, and watched Marquez. He scarcely heard the song. The room was rocking gently for him now, but he told himself that nevertheless he was not drunk, because he could still think clearly. He knew everything that was going on, by God. But a great, warm wave of emotion was coming up from his feet and sweeping over him. By the Christ, he felt good. His eyes were beginning to moisten. He looked around quickly to be sure no one was watching him, then wiped them with his big hand. Marquez had finished "Cielito Lindo." Jesus, but that was a nice song. And this whole gang, they were really a good gang, even if he did have a hassel with one or two now and then. It was great to be a part of them. It was great to belong this way, and have friends like this. The service life, when you got right down to it, wasn't really such a bad life after all.

Marquez was now playing "The Rose of San Antone." Everybody was singing loudly.

Braith joined in, harmonizing.

"Attaboy," said Dugan, and patted Braith upon the back.

The celebrants had formed a half-circle around Marquez now, their arms over each others' shoulders. Braith sang along in a strong baritone, liking the sound of his own voice. He kept his eyes on Marquez. Marquez was still stripped to the waist, and there was utter fascination in the flexing of his arm and shoulder muscles as he played the guitar.

After a while several of the men began to drift away. There was still plenty of liquor left, and Dugan and Uline were drinking most of it. Uline was glassy-eyed; out on his feet. Dugan was oblivious to everything except his own singing and his own remarks, which were largely meaningless, but at which he laughed each time loud and long. MacInnes was in bed, the blankets pulled over his face.

Marquez got up.

168

"Hey!" said Dugan. "Don't stop! Don't stop playin' now, boy! And you know why? This just ain't no time for it!" He shook with laughter at his punch line. He clapped Uline on the shoulder blades. Uline blinked.

"I got to go out," said Marquez.

"Why?"

"I got to get some fresh air."

"Okay," said Dugan, "but don't fall in!" He whooped at that one.

Marquez went out.

Braith finished his drink quickly and went out after him. Dugan and Uline then began to face each other and sing, nose to nose: "In the eeev'ning by the moooon-light . . ." They didn't notice Braith leaving.

Outside, Braith was surprised to find that his steps were a little unsteady. He still didn't believe that he was drunk. Tired, pooped-out a little, maybe, but not drunk. Hell, he could drink anybody under the table. Russians, or any-body. He began to invent a fantasy in which he met some Russians and started to show them how to drink vodka. Have to tell that to somebody. Marquez maybe, when he caught up with him. Marquez was pretty good at listen-ing to stories; he didn't try to interrupt all the time with sarcastic remarks. Marquez was just ahead of him now, walking down toward the hangars and the flight line.

Funny kid. He wasn't going to the latrine, after all. He really did want some fresh air.

Marquez came after a while to a stack of crated empty napalm tanks and sat on one. He lit a cigarette.

Braith walked up. "Hi, George."

Marquez was startled; he turned his head quickly, saw Braith, then nodded and said, "Hello."

"Get fed up with the party?" Braith sat down heavily beside him.

"Yes." Marquez looked at the ground.

"So did I. Too much partying is too much. I had enough of it when I was in Tokyo. Plenty, in fact. You wouldn't even believe the things I did up there."

Marquez nodded.

Braith had been weaving a fine tale of exotic debauchery in his mind, but he saw suddenly that Marquez wasn't in

169

a mood to listen this time. Something bothering the poor kid. Jesus, he was really a good-looking kid, all sad and moody like that. Braith said, "What's eating you, kid?"

"I don't know."

"Homesick?"

"Marquez laughed. "For what?"

"For—well, for home."

"Why do you think I got in the Air Force?"

"Search me."

"They don't treat Mexican people so good where I come from." He laughed again. He looked at the red tip of his cigarette. "You know, sometimes I think I want to stay here in Japan. These people don't care if I'm a Mexican."

"Well, hell, now, George—you don't think any of us care, do you? You haven't got a better bunch of friends than right here."

"Don't kid me."

"I'm not kidding you. Honest to God. Everybody thinks you're one of the nicest guys around here." Braith put his arm clumsily about Marquez's shoulder and squeezed.

Marquez stiffened a little.

"Listen, buddy," said Braith, leaning toward him somewhat unsteadily, "you just stick with old Frank. You'll make out all right in this man's Air Force. How'd you like to be a corporal?"

"It don't make a damn to me," said Marquez.

Braith let his hand fall from Marquez's shoulder to his buttocks. "You know it makes a damn. You can get to be a master sergeant, like Dugan, easy, if you play your cards right and know the right people."

Braith was thinking how lean and hard was Marquez's body, how wonderfully lean and hard! And there was a seed of excitement, a hot seed somewhere in the very central depth of Braith's stomach, and he remembered having this feeling before, and he was at once ashamed of it, and carried away with it. Maybe, by God, he was a little drunk, after all. Just a little. Sure, that was it; he wouldn't be acting this way if he were sober. But it was so wonderful to have your pals, your friends, around, the fellows that would be your gang and really stick by you and really under-

170

stand . . . and you could talk to them anytime about anything, which you couldn't do with most women. That was what was so wonderful about it. The tears were coming to Braith's eyes again. He put his other hand on Marquez's thigh.

Marquez looked around. "Hey, what the hell are you doing?"

"Nothing. Just talking to you, George. You need somebody to help you out. You know that."

"You better get your hand off my leg."

Braith took a deep breath. "What do you mean, George?"

"You know what I mean."

"What are you trying to insinuate?"

"I just say you better get your hand off my leg."

"What do you think I am? I don't like that kind of talk, George."

"Then take your hand off my leg."

It seemed to Braith that his mind was a little out of control now. It was clicking back and forth involuntarily. There was only dim remembrance from one moment to the next. Something was wrong. Marquez—who was his friend till now—was turning on him. The lousy little spick was turning on him, trying to give him a hard time. Braith said, "Goddamn it, are you trying to accuse me of something?"

"I don't accuse you nothing," said Marquez. "I just don't like the way you're fooling around."

"What do you mean—fooling around?" Braith raised his voice ominously.

"Nothing, nothing. Why don't you just go away?" Marquez moved along the crate.

Braith yanked him back by the shoulder. "You just better explain what you mean, goddamn it!"

"I don't have to explain nothing!"

"By God," said Braith, rising, "you'll explain to me! You'll explain or know the reason why!"

"I don't ask you out here. Why don't you go back? Why don't you leave me alone?"

"I asked you a question!"

"I'm not gonna answer any questions."

171

"You better tell me what you're saying! You better tell me!" shouted Braith.

He saw Marquez now as an elusive form, as a shape under water. The little rat was trying to get away. Couldn't let him get away. If he did, he'd talk—he'd try to ruin Braith's reputation. He'd tell lies about Braith to everybody—

Braith grabbed for Marquez and missed. Marquez struck at him. Braith felt a sharp pain along his forehead. He swung his arm heavily then; the force of the blow carried him forward and off balance. Marquez struck him in the face again, but this time Braith didn't seem to feel it. He caught Marquez about the torso and tried to force him to the ground. Marquez's knee moved, and Braith suddenly felt a dull and terrible pain in his groin.

"*Try to ruin me! Try to ruin me for life, will you?*" Braith was screaming now.

Marquez stepped back. Braith threw himself bodily at the slender, wavering shape. Marquez went down. Braith grabbed his ears and started to pound his head upon the ground.

Presently Braith realized that for some moments a hand had been jerking at his shoulders. He heard a voice:

"*Braith! Stop it! Braith!*"

He looked up and around. Major Ronsdale stood there; Major Pete Ronsdale with the blue A.O. brassard around his arm, and the webbed pistol belt around his waist. Braith got up shakily. Mind clearer now. Head aching. Chest tight —he was panting. Marquez was still down there, not unconscious, but twisting and moaning and sobbing.

Ronsdale bent swiftly, talked to Marquez, got a whispered answer, and then helped him to his feet. Marquez kept on sobbing.

Braith stood off to one side and stared. He was feeling a little frightened now.

Ronsdale turned to Braith. "That was a hell of a thing to do."

"Sir?"

"Picking on a little fellow like that."

"It was a personal argument, Major. It was just a personal argument."

172

Ronsdale said to Marquez, "What's your name, soldier?"

"Pfc. George Marquez."

"How did this happen?"

There was mistrust in Marquez's eyes. "I don't know, sir."

"You'd better tell me exactly what happened."

"Nothin', sir. Nothin'."

"See?" said Braith. "Just what I told you, Major. A personal argument."

Ronsdale said to Marquez, "Did he hit you first?"

"I don't know, sir."

"It wasn't George's fault," Braith cut in. "It wasn't really anybody's fault. It was just one of those things."

Ronsdale said, "Braith, I saw this. You were trying to kill him. That was no friendly little fight I was watching."

"Well, he isn't hurt much, is he?" Braith sensed a certain lack of conviction in Ronsdale's voice. Braith was sure he had the upper hand, now.

"I'm going to have to report this whole thing," Ronsdale said.

Marquez's face widened.

Braith said, "Now, wait a minute, Major. Wait until you hear our side of it."

"I'm not hearing sides," answered Ronsdale. "I'm just taking you in. The A.P.'s will investigate it. There's something funny going on here."

"Well, Major, if you report this to the A.P.'s we're sunk. You know how A.P.'s are. They're not like flying officers—they just don't understand. And you know in the Air Force flying personnel have to stick together. Because sometimes they need each other when they're flying." Braith watched Ronsdale's face closely as he spoke. It looked thin and pale in the diffused moonlight; its handsomeness was weakness now. And at Braith's words Ronsdale's eyes seemed to move for a moment into shadow. Good. Ronsdale must understand. He must realize that Braith was referring now to the major's behavior in that thunderstorm. . . .

Ronsdale frowned and fingered his pistol holster self-consciously, and said, "Well . . . I don't know just what to do about this."

"Well, sir—" Braith assumed a look of earnestness—

173

"I'll be frank with you. We'd been doing a little drinking —a little promotion party for one of the boys—and I guess we just kind of lost our heads, both of us. It's the first time it's ever happened, Major. I'm sure you understand things like that. After a while a guy's got to let himself go."

"Braith, I'm supposed to report all disturbances. You understand that, don't you?"

"Yes, sir." Braith narrowed his eyes, and spoke more slowly. "But sometimes, Major, certain things are better if you just don't report them. Sometimes a man does a little drinking and goes off half-cocked, and it's a perfectly natural thing. But certain people—a lot of women are this way, a lot of married women, especially—just don't understand that kind of thing. Know what I mean, Major?"

After a moment Ronsdale said, "I see."

"Can we go now, Major?"

Ronsdale took his time getting out a cigarette and lighting it. He blew a thick cloud of smoke. He cleared his throat. He was scowling deeply, and his cigarette was moving up and down in senseless motion. "Well," he said finally, "I suppose this kind of thing does actually happen all the time—"

"Every night, sir. I can assure you of that."

"And since no one was really hurt." He looked at Marquez. "How do you feel?"

"I'm okay," said Marquez moodily.

"Well, since that's the case, I guess the best thing to do all around is to forget the whole business." He took another draw on his cigarette. "But don't let it happen again."

"Oh, we won't, sir," said Braith. "I'll give you my personal word on that." He was beaming. He had the major, now. He'd be a jet crew chief before the week was out.

Marquez said nothing. The cloud had thickened and a light rain had begun again.

5

The rain irritated Colonel Bill Straker, at his desk in his cottage in the housing area. He could hear it hitting gently and without let-up on the plant leaves in the window box.

He looked at it distastefully, then at the effectiveness reports on his desk again.

He sighed, ran his hand through his cropped, graying hair, scratched the back of his neck with his pencil, and finally and suddenly arose and began to pace the room.

Skies soggy with cloud always meant at least several days' loss of operations. And the men were never quite the same the day after they'd been grounded. And it was getting on toward the middle of the month, and he'd counted upon the record this month to startle everybody.

It irritated him further to be irritated.

Not right. When Harriet had been alive he'd taken setbacks like this in stride. Seemed things had never really gone right since she died. He had classmates who were brigadier generals now . . . a couple well on their way to the two stars of major general . . . and while he didn't like to cheapen himself by saying they were inferior men, it was perfectly true that luck—the pure shuffling of circumstances—had entered into their advancement.

Or maybe they had their Harriets. If he were given a gift now he would call for Harriet to come back to life . . . or if not Hariret herself, a woman that could take her place. A quick emotional surge of loyalty caused him to revise that a little: no one could really take Harriet's place, but it would be nice to find someone sometime who came close to it.

He sighed again. A walk . . . a walk in the rain might help. He didn't like rain, and it would therefore be good character exercise to make himself walk in it. Perhaps, too, this would help his subconscious mind to work out a solution to the problem of his bewilderment and dissatisfaction.

He donned his blue raincoat, filled a pipe, lighted it and turned it upside down against the fine rain.

He walked down the street of the cottage area, toward the airfield. He came to Major Ronsdale's cottage and by habit—since this was his action every morning—he glanced at his watch. Then he laughed a little, remembering this was not morning. He looked at Ronsdale's house. A light was on in a second-story window. As he watched a figure crossed that bright frame. Essie Ronsdale. Completely unclothed. She walked languidly, smoking a cigarette in a long ivory holder, making with this what Straker could only think of as flourishing gestures.

For a moment he did not quite believe what he had seen. *Completely* naked, she'd been. That fool cigarette holder making her look nakeder. She had evidently been quite oblivious to the window. Carelessness; sheer carelessness. She really oughtn't to be that careless . . . she was the wife of an Air Force officer after all, and as such it was her responsibility to—

As he watched, she crossed the bright space again.

This time she had a drink in her hand—a tall glass. She stopped—right in the oblong frame—and took a long sip. The lifting of her arm, the movement that followed along her torso . . . it was not without a certain grace. Womanly, extraordinarily womanly it was. A tingling started in Straker's insteps and seeped upward through the rest of him. When he was completely aware of this sensation he damped it off hurriedly, and in shame.

He turned his head away quickly, feeling dry heat in his cheeks. He thrust his hands deep into his raincoat pockets and walked on, swiftly.

This Essie Ronsdale could be a problem. She could, indeed. In fairness, he could not allow her to influence any decision he might make regarding Pete Ronsdale, and yet he had to admit that such a consideration would always be in the bottom of his mind.

Well, here was another case where circumstances undid some of the good a man had fashioned. Ronsdale was a superior officer, no doubt of that, and though it was still too early to say how he'd handle a tactical command—like the 109th Squadron—Straker would still bet upon him. A man with Ronsdale's integrity and self-discipline could hardly go wrong on any job. Come to think of it, though, he hadn't seen Ronsdale at any Sunday services. Perhaps he was a Catholic. Have to look into that. If Ronsdale was missing services because he'd simply fallen out of the habit, it wouldn't be hard to josh him back into attendance in a good-natured man-to-man way. Straker flattered himself that he was rather good at that kind of thing.

His pipe went out, and at first he thought he would tap

it empty and stuff it into his pocket, but then he realized that this impulse was born of laziness. There was still tobacco in it; he would make himself light it again. He moved in under a tree and did this. The rain was a bit heavier now and the light wind had come to drive it into his face. He did not like this wetness. He walked, and kept his chin tucked away from it.

He was passing the Officers' Club now. There were the usual bright lights, the noise, the cheap music, and the tinkling of glassware.

He turned back toward the cottage area.

Before setting out he had told himself that he would walk for twenty minutes. Perhaps ten had elapsed now. But there was nowhere in particular to go, and by turning back in this way he would never use up his twenty minutes. He might walk more slowly. On the other hand, that wouldn't sufficiently dull the edge of his mind; that would bring him back to the mixed-up state that had forced him out into the rain in the first place.

He found himself on the street where his own and Ronsdale's cottages were situated. He didn't know quite why. He passed again the tree where he had re-lit his pipe.

The rain was abating; the cloud cover had worn thin and through it the fuzzy shape of the moon could be seen.

It was warm; it was too warm for his raincoat. He unbuttoned it.

That was better.

He looked up. The light in the second story of Ronsdale's cottage had gone out. He frowned. He hadn't meant to come back this way; he'd meant to circle and enter the street at its opposite end. Just habit that brought him this way. He'd have to turnbuckle a bit—a man ought to keep himself complete master of any habits. Well, he told himself, no harm done this time. . . .

Ronsdale's porch light came on suddenly. Straker stopped, looked, realized that his pipe had gone out again and fumbled for his lighter. Essie Ronsdale, wearing a black silk kimono now, was on the porch, lowering herself into one of the rattan chairs. She still had that tall glass in her hand.

Straker began to turn away; he would have to go in the

177

other direction and take a circuitous route back to his own cottage now. But just before he turned, he saw Essie look up. Although he couldn't quite see the set of her eyes at this distance, he knew somehow that she had seen him.

He took a deep breath and walked forward, in his original direction. Couldn't make a fool of himself, after all—

"Hi, Colonel!" Her voice seemed a little too loud in the misty night. "What are you doing out in the rain?" She rose and came to the porch rail, still holding her drink.

"Just a walk. Just an evening walk." He stopped and took the pipe out of his mouth.

"Come have a night cap. It'll keep you dry inside."

"No—no, thanks."

"Then come sit a while. I haven't had anybody to talk to all evening."

"Well—" said Straker. He cleared his throat. Be mighty rude of him to refuse. He couldn't let personal feelings interfere with his manners—that wouldn't show very much self-control. Besides, this might actually be an opportunity in disguise. He might be able to get across this evening, skillfully and tactfully, of course, that Essie Ronsdale's general demeanor was perhaps not the best thing for her husband's career.

As a matter of fact, it was his moral duty to have a stab at that.

"Well," he said, "just for a few minutes." And he smiled and walked to the porch.

"Sit down, Colonel." She made a place for him in another rattan chair, patting the cushions.

"Thank you." He sat down rather stiffly.

She sat down, smiled a bright smile, and he returned the smile, and then somewhat awkwardly put his pipe into his mouth again and finished lighting it.

She held her drink in one hand, the ivory cigarette holder in the other. She was not really a bad-looking woman, he thought. She had a nice, fresh, filled-out face—not quite as artificial as some of the younger women in this day and age. Not quite as boyish and bony as they all seemed to be currently. She was a very soft, very feminine woman, the colonel reflected.

178

She said, "You know, Colonel Straker, I never knew before you smoked a pipe. I like it."

He laughed a little. "I don't use it often. Just at home once in a while. You need leisure time to smoke a pipe. You need that to keep it lit."

She laughed as though he had said something immensely witty. He stirred a bit. Perhaps he had. Well, he couldn't say it wasn't pleasant to be thought witty. Fact was, he'd once enjoyed a small reputation as a maker of quips. But since Harriet had died, he—

He drove the thought of Harriet from his mind almost angrily.

Essie said, "I didn't know you smoked at all."

"Well, I don't really. I just puff."

"That's not what I meant. I mean, I thought possibly you had something against tobacco."

"Really? Do I seem *that* stuffy?"

"Well—" she cocked her head—"not really. I've always suspected a real heart pumped away under that stone face."

He chuckled. "I suppose I must give a false impression. In all honesty, I don't try to. In all honesty, I—well, I try to be honest, that's all."

"Of course." Essie looked sympathetic.

"It's not easy to run a command and pay attention to your personality."

"I know," said Essie. "You can't ever allow intimacy. I know that much. It must make you very lonely sometimes."

He smiled. "Yes—I'm afraid it does." She was not unintelligent, this Essie Ronsdale; he would say that for her. She had an instinctive grasp of things.

"I often wondered." She was smiling at him oddly.

"About what?"

"About what the *real* Bill Straker is like. That's your first name—Bill—isn't it?"

"I haven't been called Bill much lately."

"If you don't want me to—"

"No, no. Please do. I like to hear it."

"All right, I will. And my name's Essie."

"Fine. Fine." He didn't know exactly how to fill in the pause here.

179

"We'll make it a pact. Whenever you feel like being called Bill you come on over here."

"All right."

She looked at her glass suddenly. "You know what? While I was sitting here talking to you a mouse came and drank my drink!"

He rose. "Can I get you another?"

"It's a Tom Collins. I'll have to mix it."

"I can mix a Tom Collins. A rather good one, if you don't mind my blushing modesty."

"Colonel—I mean, Bill—you continue to amaze me. Don't tell me now that you even *drink* these Tom Collinses you mix."

"Oh, I take a drink now and then. Whatever gave you the idea that I didn't?"

She looked at him with an open-eyed look. "May I be frank?"

"Of course."

"I thought you had—well—religious scruples."

"Just because I go to church?"

"I suppose so. I suppose it's because you go to church. That is a little rare, nowadays, you must admit. Over here, anyway."

Straker smiled. "Yes, it is."

"I've tried to get Pete to go—he was quite the Episcopalian at one time—but, well, Sunday morning, and we're tired—you know how it is."

"Of course." It made Straker feel warm to know how it was. The ability to understand was an important part of being a commander, after all. And Essie Ronsdale was certainly surprising him—there was quite a lot of solid stuff in this girl in spite of her occasional misguided actions. He was sure she wouldn't be difficult to handle at all. In fact, she was amazingly easy to talk to. He hadn't felt this much at ease for a long time. Not since Ha—

He went into the cottage, found the icebox and the gin all by himself, and made two Tom Collinses.

"Two!" said Essie, raising her eyebrows, as he came out again.

"Just wanted to prove to you I'm not an old fuddy-duddy."

180

"Well, perhaps I did think you were a little fuddy—but I never accused you of being old."

"I'm forty-four."

She took a sip of her drink. "I've always preferred mature men. In their prime, you might say."

He laughed, sipped his own drink, and said, "I don't really think age makes much difference. I honestly don't feel a whit different than I did at thirty-six. Or twenty-six."

"I know." She took a longer sip. "Why, Bill—these are marvelous! When you retire from the Air Force you can be a bartender." She drained her glass to about the halfway mark. "And yet," she said, as though she had never left her previous direction of thought, "some men never seem to grow up outwardly either. Some of them stay boys all the time."

"What do you mean?"

She put a new cigarette into her holder. Carefully. Her kimono slipped apart at the throat a little as she leaned forward to take the cigarette from the pack on the table, and Straker glimpsed the roots of her breasts. He frowned and looked away. She said, "I don't suppose I ought to talk to you about *him*. Since you're his commanding officer and everything—"

"You mean Pete?"

"Yes."

"Well, I'm sure you can discuss Pete with me. I'm very fond of Pete. I think he's going far in this man's Air Force."

She stared at him blankly for a second. Then she said, "Yes, I sincerely hope he will. And I'm glad to hear you like him."

He lit his cigarette. He cleared his throat. "I'm glad you brought Pete up tonight." He sipped his drink. Nearly gone already—he'd drunk faster than he'd meant to. Didn't feel anything, though; nothing more than a slight warmth in the chest. "I wanted very much to talk about him—and about you, Essie."

"About me?"

"Well, perhaps this is a little difficult to say. One of those things you call a 'delicate subject.'"

"But you can be frank with me, Bill."

181

"I'm sure I can. It's still difficult."

She handed him her glass. "Why don't you go make us a couple more drinks?"

"All right, I will."

He came back with the new drinks and saw that she now had her leg thrown over the arm of the chair. The kimono skirt fell away to show some of her thigh. Damn, that was an annoying habit of hers—showing herself like that all the time. He supposed the way to treat it was simply to take it in stride, not let on that it bothered him particularly. He didn't look away this time. But he took a deep draught of his new Tom Collins.

He settled into his own chair. "Well," he said, "there's no question of it; Pete is one of my best officers."

"He thinks a lot of you, too," said Essie. "He said you're the first wing commander he's ever seen who really deserves the job."

"That's flattering—if a little strong," Straker said.

"You hadn't had a command before this one, had you?"

"Not for a long time. I'd had minor commands—junior officer stuff—but that was before the last war. They've kept me mostly in staff work up until now."

She smiled. "And you do enjoy this, don't you? You really like having a tactical outfit best, I'm sure."

"I suppose I do."

"Not all wing commanders would get out and fly missions the way you do."

He shrugged. "I just do that to find out what problems there are in the field. An old principle, really. Besides, I don't have anything like the cumulative risk the boys who fly every day have."

"I admire it just the same," said Essie. "I always admire a man who's a real man."

It sounded as though she had some hidden significance behind that last remark, but he couldn't imagine what it might be. He said, "I'm afraid you overestimate me a great deal, Essie. I'm just a rather dull, middle-aged widower who doesn't know much, except some tactical aviation theories."

"Do I hear a note of wistfulness there?" She cocked her head in that curiously attractive way again.

"Possibly. But not enough for you to be sorry for me. I'm afraid I enjoy my assignment out here."

"But you do get lonely." She was watching him steadily.

He shrugged. "Everyone does. Everyone gets a little lonely once in a while."

"Yes," she said. "Everybody."

They looked at each other, then, neither knowing quite how to move his eyes away gracefully.

Essie said abruptly, "This time you'll have to show me how you make those Collinses. I want your secret formula."

He laughed as he got up. "It's no formula. I don't measure a thing—do it all by ear."

"Honestly."

"Of course. Come on, I'll show you."

In the kitchen she stood next to him and every once in a while, as though by accident, she brushed against him with her shoulder or her hip. She smelled very good. Straker felt warm and relaxed now; he was enjoying himself thoroughly.

But somewhere in the lower darkness of his mind his conscience burned like a hall night-lamp . . . but it was already distant; it had been, and still was receding. He drank his third drink, and he was pleased to believe that he was quite in control of himself. He had always been able to hold his liquor. Back in Washington that had been an important social asset. Essie finished her drink and insisted trying his method herself on the next batch. . . .

He glanced at her in the kitchen. Wonder where she put it all. Been drinking before he'd arrived, obviously. But her stance was good; her gait and coordination were fine. The only small sign that she'd been drinking was the flushed look of her skin and the brightness of her eyes.

Now, her hair, he noticed, still had its look of being carefully attended to. That was good: most women managed first thing to muss up their hair when they drank. There was, indeed, a certain admirable fastidiousness about this wife of Ronsdale's . . . it showed in her well-kept living room and spotless kitchen. You could always tell a lot about a woman by looking in her kitchen.

"More lemons in the icebox," said Essie, turning.

He had been standing at right angles to her. She turned

183

into him. Her shoulder bumped his chest, and for an instant it seemed she might be off balance. He took her by the arms to steady her.

It was not Straker's idea to kiss her.

He told himself that afterward.

He admitted that the impulse indeed came to him—but he insisted that he himself was not about to obey that impulse.

He was going to break away in the first moment or two. He really wanted to. But her lips were incredibly warm . . . they were astonishingly soft and just a bit moist . . . her breath was fragrant. The feel of her, her substance in his arms—well, that was a superb feeling. She was soft, but firmly soft. Most womanly; altogether a woman.

As she pressed herself to him she curved her body forward, happily molding it to the shape of his own.

CHAPTER EIGHT

1

AS Captain Richard Tindle entered the Meiji Building, waves of Air Force officers and civilians came out, and he had the feeling of bucking a tide. It was almost five p.m.—seventeen hundred hours, as the military liked to say. Although these people quitting the day's work did not specifically hurry, there was an air of urgency to their pace. They all looked vastly relieved.

The white-gloved A.P. guard saluted Tindle. Tindle pushed through the swinging doors.

He stood for a moment in the marble vestibule examining the painted directory on the wall, looking for Tech Intelligence. He gripped the large envelope under his arm with a kind of annoyance. He had landed at Haneda Airport a little over an hour ago and jeeped into Tokyo with several others. Most of them had gone to their billets, and Tindle had been tempted to find himself a sack, first thing, but the secret material he carried was something of a live coal in his hands. At least that was the way he felt about it.

184

A lieutenant colonel and a stout secretary-type with an upswept hair-do paused for a moment near Tindle and he caught a bit of their conversation.

"Well, he's no more than a six," said the woman. "I don't see why he should be allowed to make decisions at a policy level."

"I don't either," said the lieutenant colonel. "That was what was behind that whole flap this afternoon. I keep telling them again and again you can't go out of channels."

"We've got the same situation in our shop. And it's not as though we were just some ordinary agency. After all, we deal with *internal* rather than external coordination."

"I know," said the lieutenant colonel. "I know just how you feel."

It seemed to Tindle awfully remote from the war. And it brought him back, in a momentary flash, to the corridors of the Pentagon. Americans not only brought their hot dogs and hamburgers and malted milks and juke boxes with them wherever they traveled, but even their Federalese. It was probably all an important part of the language by now.

He found the listing for Tech Intelligence, noted the floor number, and stepped to the elevator. He hoped someone would be manning the office. He'd hate to have the responsibility of keeping the brown envelope overnight. He rode upstairs, stepped out to a gloomy corridor and paced it for a few seconds, watching the room numbers until he found the one he wanted. On the door it said:

DIRECTORATE OF INTELLIGENCE
Evaluation Division
Technical Branch
Electronic Section
Mr. John Pendermeyer, Project Representative

He could hear a bustling inside; someone still in the office. That was a break. He opened the door.

A little man with wall eyes, a man round as ball of butter, was arranging a couple of paper sacks on his desk, obviously preparing to leave. He looked up and smiled as Tindle entered. "Hi, Captain."

185

"Hello. Mr. Pendermeyer around?"

"That's me, Captain. What can I do for you? Got a problem?"

"Well—not a big one." Tindle walked over to the desk. He put the envelope down. "Just want to get rid of this."

"What is it?"

"Classified stuff. Some radar photos from Akuni—I don't know much more about it."

"Oh, yeah—the out-of-phase stuff. Been waitin' for that!" Pendermeyer picked a half-smoked cigar from the ashtray on his desk and popped it into the corner of his mouth. "I can't make the recommendations they want, unless I see the results they get, hey?"

"I really don't know much about it, Mr. Pendermeyer—"

"Call me Johnny. Everybody calls me Johnny."

"Well, I'm just the messenger boy on this deal."

Pendermeyer looked at Tindle appraisingly for a moment. He grinned abruptly. "Bet you're more than a messenger boy down there with the 66th. You fly the 80s?"

"Well, yes."

"How many missions you got?"

"Eighty-one."

"No foolin'! Here—lemme shake your hand. I always want to shake the hand of the boys out there doin' the dirty work."

Pendermeyer's hand was warm and fat. Tindle said, "Well, I'll have to be getting along now—"

"Wait a minute, Tindle. You're the fellow brought that report back, ain't you?"

"What report?"

"That long one on effectiveness on the ground. The one you brought back from your tour on forward control."

"I didn't bring any report back."

"Hell, I heard them reading from it at secret briefing just this morning. Colonel Straker sent it up and signed it. He's some boy, that Bill Straker, ain't he? There's my idea of a wing commander."

"I don't know anything about it. Straker's office must have put my remarks into a report and stuck my name in there somewhere."

"Well, it was good stuff. Good, solid stuff. And I'm glad
186

to see they send a fellow like you up to Tokyo for a little fun once in a while. Where you goin' for supper tonight, anyway?"

"Well—I hadn't—I mean, no place special."

"You ever eat real Japanese food?"

"Well, I had *tempura* couple of times. But—"

"Look—why don't you tag on home with me for chow. I got a little place out in the boondocks—and a gal to go with it. She used to be a baroness, no foolin'."

"I don't think I ought to put you to all that trouble. And besides—"

Pendermeyer grinned salaciously. "You got ideas about what to do later, hey? Well, maybe I can fix you up on that, too. By God—that gives me a hell of a good idea. Sachiko's been wanting to go out. That's my girl, Sachiko. Why don't we make it a double-date? I'm kind of in a mood to make noise tonight."

"I don't have a date, and I was thinking more of a quiet evening," said Tindle. "Want to do a little shopping tomorrow, and—"

"Hell, nothing opens till ten o'clock anyway. And don't worry about a date. I know just the one for you—a knockout. Kid named Terry, works in a wholesale parts place I do some business with. You won't have to spend a lot of dough and go wasting your time with hostesses in clip joints like the Cho-Cho Club."

"I don't think I'd better, Mr. Pendermeyer."

"Hell—come on and have chow, anyway. You might not get a chance for real home cooking again."

"All right," said Tindle, wearily. Line of least resistance. "But I'd better check in at billeting and get a bed assigned first."

"No sweat, no sweat," said Johnny Pendermeyer, and took Tindle by the arm and led him out of the office. Johnny had the brown envelope under his other arm.

"Are you taking that secret stuff home?"

"Sure. Safer there than with this bunch of muddleheads in FEAF. Anyway, I want to look at it in peace and quiet, not down here at the office. Gets to be a madhouse here sometimes."

"I imagine it does," said Tindle.

187

Sometimes when Teriko wished strongly it appeared later that she had made things happen—controlled the future according to her wishes. Tonight she was wishing that this foolish young man would go home.

And that the rain would stop outside.

And that a wonderfully handsome American officer would appear from nowhere and take her off to a place of bright lights, music and dancing.

"Teriko!" said Oka-san.

"Yes?" Teriko came out of her wishing dream.

"Ichiro-san's glass is empty."

"Very well." Teriko poured beer for Ichiro. The young man beamed at her with a buglike expression. That was what he reminded her of—a grasshopper. When she'd been a child she'd always had in summertime a little singing grasshopper in a cage of split bamboo. Well, Ichiro-san looked like that, all right: the way he sat there at the low table and said very little, and chewed with much motion of the jaws, forcing her to make practically all of the conversation.

It would be better if he could at least rub his hind legs together and make a singing noise—that, at least, would amuse her.

Ichiro bowed stiffly as she filled his glass.

"Don't mention it," she said.

They were in the second-story room where Teriko and her mother lived. It was a small room—six mats to be exact —and it perched over a vegetable store owned by a second cousin of Oka-san's, which was why they were able to rent it fairly cheaply. At that it took nearly all of Teriko's salary from Yamamoto Wholesale Parts, Ltd. Oka-san had a small pension from Father, and the second cousin helped out a little with the food. For her clothes, or occasional luxuries, Teriko had to rely on boy friends: she didn't like doing this too much, but she didn't see how else it could be. Even her profits from the black market didn't come often enough to be relied upon.

Living—just everyday living—was uncomfortable and complicated enough. There was no bath in this house; she

188

had to spend ten yen at the public ofuro every day. The kitchen, downstairs, was used by four families. Teriko's and her mother's few belongings were stuffed impossibly into a small closet with their sleeping mattresses. The street outside was noisy until nearly midnight with shoppers and merrymakers and street cars clanging by, and nearly all the time drunken Australian soldiers from the near-by camp. Even the quiet of deep morning was lanced by the shrilling of the noodle vendor's charumera.

Teriko had tried to put off Ichiro's visit by saying it would shame her to bring him to this place. Oka-san had said, "Don't be foolish. These are bad times. He will understand that even good-family people can live in a place like this."

And so Ichiro had come, bearing gifts. He had brought Oka-san a box of scented toilet soap and Teriko a stuffed silk doll. The doll sprawled in a corner now.

"Sake, Ichiro-san?" asked Oka-san.

He bowed, but held his palm out in refusal.

Oka-san nodded. "That's wise. A man has good character who can refuse sake on a rainy evening."

Ichiro beamed.

"Teriko!" Oka-san always spoke her daughter's name sharply, as though it were a rebuke in itself. Oka-san was a small, wiry woman, very brown and agile. She had a low, strident voice.

"Yes, Oka-san?"

"Ichiro-san has nothing to eat."

Ichiro began to go through the same polite protest, but Oka-san interrupted.

"Some egg and green pepper, Teriko. I'll help you make it."

Teriko understood. Oka-san wanted to talk to her downstairs in the kitchen—and she could easily guess what Oka-san wanted to talk about. She sighed, rose, excused herself, and followed Oka-san downstairs.

In the kitchen they began to scramble an egg and cook some chopped green pepper in soy sauce.

Oka-san said, "He won't like you. You don't act like a woman."

"Not like a Japanese woman." She was petulant.

189

"What are you? Chinese? A Korean garlic-eater? Maybe you're the goddess Kwannon, herself."

"Oka-san, you don't understand. These are different times."

"I understand what's right. I haven't taught you to be like this, Teriko-chan. You're rude. You have the manners of a north-country savage. I went to a great deal of trouble to arrange this meeting with Ichiro. He has a good job, he comes from a very fine family, and—"

"But, Oka-san, I don't want him. I don't want any Japanese boy."

"What do you mean? Are you ashamed of being Japanese?"

"No, no. But since Giichi—I don't want any other Japanese boy. Can't you see that? I loved Giichi. Now—"

"You're a fool, Teriko. Giichi is dead. I sent you to the country to forget him—when we really couldn't afford it. I sold most of the furniture so you could go to the country."

"I know, I know. But Mama, I can't love him."

"Love!" Oka-san snorted. "You see too many movies. You'd learn to love a fine boy like Ichiro if you married him. And he's not bad-looking."

"He looks like a grasshopper."

"He has fine features. He has a very good head."

"I don't like him."

"What would you like, Teriko? Some red-faced American soldier to come home drunk every night and beat you?"

"Not all American soldiers have red faces. And they don't beat you."

Oka-san snorted again.

"And they always have enough money. You don't have to worry, worry, worry. Oh, Oka-san, I'm so sick of hunting for little pieces of money every day, like somebody looking for grains of rice in the sand—I—I can't stand it any longer."

"You're a very lucky girl, and you don't know it. You're pretty, and you have nice clothes, and there's always something to eat."

"I'm not lucky. I'm a Japanese girl."

"You are ashamed of that, aren't you?"

"No. No! I'm simply sick of it. I'm not a pig or a dog

to be owned by a man. I'm a woman. I want to be treated like a woman."

"You see too many movies. There's the trouble. The movies try to show us too many American ways. We're Japanese—we can't live in American ways."

"You're an old woman; that's why you talk like this."

"Yes, I'm an old woman. I've seen enough of things to know what's true."

"I don't care what's true. I just want to be happy. Why can everybody else but me be happy?" Tears were coming into Teriko's eyes.

"Teriko-chan," said Oka-san, speaking a little more tenderly now, putting her hand on her shoulder, "when I speak to you like this, I want to make you happy. I know you'll only be happy with a fine Japanese husband. I know you don't believe this—but why don't you give it a chance? Be nice to Ichiro tonight. Do at least that much for me."

"All right," she said, "I'll try to be pleasant to him. I'll try."

Oka-san glanced at Teriko obliquely. "If—if he cares to stay here tonight, I can go visit your aunt in Shibuya-ku. It's only a short ride on the street car."

Teriko turned widened eyes upon her mother. "Well! You never spoke like that before! You always scolded me when I came in late!"

"You'll like Ichiro." She pretended to be very busy with the egg. "He's very fond of you already."

"I don't think I want to sleep with him."

"If you decide to, let me know. You can make a signal. As a matter of fact, I think I'll go visit your aunt anyway."

"You'd better stay here, Mama."

"No, I'll visit your aunt. I'll get ready now. Take Ichiro's food up to him."

Teriko shrugged and said, "Whatever you wish, Mama," and went upstairs again.

She watched Ichiro as he pecked delicately with his chopsticks at the scrambled egg and green pepper. She filled his beer glass several times. It had been rather an expense to buy these six bottles of beer, but Oka-san had insisted.

Ichiro's face seemed a little flushed from the beer, now.

191

Teriko would have liked a sip or two, but Oka-san had definitely cautioned her against showing Ichiro that she would drink anything stronger than the bland soft drink the Japanese call "cider."

Well, at least he is not impossibly gross, thought Teriko, staring at him.

But Oka-san's outspoken suggestion—

And yet there might be something in what Oka-san said. Teriko would never admit that in the heat of argument to her, of course, but when she could look at it coldly (and in Ichiro's presence she could certainly look at everything coldly), it was evident that her only future happiness lay in getting a good Japanese husband. She knew instinctively, too, that if she slept with Ichiro she would be able to get out of him anything she wanted after that. She'd be able to show him pleasures he'd never dreamed of, she was sure. Funny that her mother should encourage this, and should lecture her so strongly about sleeping with GIs just to get a little money or some presents when she needed them. Essentially there didn't seem much difference between the two acts, in Teriko's estimation.

But these were strange times and right and wrong had always been maddeningly interwoven, unfathomably mingled, ever since Teriko could remember, and so she could at least endure—if not fully accept—certain contradictions.

"Are you comfortable?" Teriko asked Ichiro. It was all she could think of to say.

"Yes, thank you," said Ichiro.

"Of course we haven't very pleasant surroundings. You must be used to much better things."

"Oh, no. It's a very happy house. I always look for the inner feeling."

"That's wise. You must be very intelligent."

Ichiro blushed. "Oh, no, no—I'm afraid I'm quite stupid. But I learn to look for the inner things from the teachings of Jesus Christ."

"Oh! You're a Christian."

"Yes, I'm a full Christian. I've been baptized."

Teriko had been ready to unearth (with pick and dynamite, if necessary) something attractive in Ichiro—but this was a great disappointment. She'd heard that some of the
192

Christian missionaries were very noble people, and possibly this was so, but most of the Christians she'd known had been very dishonest, bad people. Foreign traders and soldiers and such who professed strong Christianity—they always seemed to her extraordinarily addicted to lying. She could remember at least three who swore they weren't married (supposing she wouldn't sleep with them if they were) when all the time they had both wives and children—one of them even had a family right here in Tokyo.

"I suppose that's very lucky," said Teriko. "I am not a Christian."

Ichiro showed, for the first time, a look of animation. He lifted his head. "Would you like to come some time with me to church?"

She winced a little. "I've been to a Christian temple. I—well, it seemed very sad to me."

"Sad?"

"Everybody looked very sad."

"But they couldn't have been. Surely, if they knew the joy of God—"

"They were all afraid God was going to punish them. They'd all been very sinful and they were just waiting for God to hit them with lightning bolts, or something."

"No, no, Teriko, that wasn't it. They weren't sinful."

"They kept saying they were."

"You don't understand, Teriko. In everyone there is sin. Man is born with it."

"So it's not their fault that they're sinful?"

"No. Of course not."

"Then why does God wish to punish them for it?"

He spread his hands in mild exasperation. "He doesn't. He wishes to save them."

"Then why are they afraid of Him?"

"They're not afraid!"

"They seemed so to me. Afraid and very sad." She shrugged, filled his small beer glass again, and said. "We'd better not talk of this now. I'm sure I don't really understand enough about it."

"That's it, of course," said Ichiro beaming. "And you're very intelligent to recognize that fact."

"Would you like to sleep with me tonight?" she asked.

He drew back. "What?"

"Oka-san says you may stay here and sleep with me to-night."

"Teriko—I—" he was blushing furiously.

"It's up to you."

"You know I'm very fond of you. Teriko! I really am!"

"Then you should enjoy it."

"Oh, Teriko—I would! I would, indeed!"

"Of course you'll have to go to church and apologize for having a good time."

"Now, Teriko—you don't understand." He moved toward her, and was about to put his arm around her.

When she saw that she lost courage. "Are you sure this won't be too sinful for you?"

Ichiro frowned. "It's not good for everyone—or just anyone. But with you and me, Teriko—"

"I don't see the difference."

"It's hard to explain. If you and I can love each other—"

She shook her head. "Ichiro-san, it simply doesn't make sense."

He looked helpless. He twisted his eyebrows into a knot, squatted back, and said, "I will try to explain."

There was a hammering downstairs on the door of the vegetable store.

"Hey, Teriko! Hey—you still up?" bawled a raucous voice, in English.

Ichiro stared toward the window in astonishment.

Teriko rose swiftly and went to the window. She looked out and saw Johnny Pendermeyer's barrel-like figure in the street below. Pendermeyer was looking up, grinning, his cigar uptilted between his teeth. A taxi purred at the curb.

"Hi, baby!" said Johnny.

"Johnny-san! Why you come here?"

"Wanted to see you, kiddo. Had a hell of a time finding the place—only drove you here once before. Trouble is, these Tokyo taxi drivers don't know their way around their own town."

"Johnny-san—I can't see you tonight. I have a customer."

"A customer?"

She shook her head irritably. "No, not that word. That

194

is business word. Some other word. Somebody comes my house."

"You mean a *guest*, hey?" Johnny roared with laughter. "That's a hot one—a customer! Look, come on down for a minute, will you, kiddo?"

"I cannot, Johnny-san."

"Somebody here I want you to meet. A fly-boy. A real good-lookin' captain in the Air Force. Looks almost like Gary Cooper, this character."

Johnny-san had obviously been drinking, and she was both shocked and startled that he should come here like this, and that he should try to make a date, sight unseen, for her. Ordinarily she would have turned him away firmly. She could be even firmer with American men than she could with Japanese—they seemed to expect it from a woman.

But tonight—

She turned and glanced at Ichiro again. Ichiro was blushing furiously and staring with his bug-eyes. He looked more than ever like a grasshopper. She knew that he spoke English fairly well, and he must have understood what Johnny had said. She knew, too, suddenly, that she never wanted to see him again. And she knew how to insure that once and for all.

Oka-san was right: her manners were those of a Hokkaido hairy one. But she couldn't help herself. She could act no other way.

She said out of the window, "Wait, please. I'll be right down."

"Teriko!" said Ichiro, in a shocked tone.

She picked up her handbag.

"Good night, Ichiro," she said calmly and pleasantly. "*Oyasumi nasai.*" She scurried down the narrow stairs. In the vegetable store she slipped on her shoes and went outside.

3

Tindle, in the back seat of the taxi, was both impatient and nervous. Somewhat embarrassed, too. The whole thing had seemed like a marvelous idea back in Pendermeyer's

195

Japanese house an hour ago. They'd both drunk a little too much after that remarkable supper Sachiko and Pendermeyer's houseboy had fixed—but now he had sobered up a great deal. Now he could see that the situation, at best, would be awkward, and that neither he nor this girl of Johnny's would quite know what to say to each other.

She was coming out of the vegetable store now. She seemed to have a good figure—and a decidedly sensuous walk.

The walk was exciting.

Tindle was uncertain of his own feelings right now. Pendermeyer had said, "You understand, I don't *guarantee* nothing. It's up to you how you make out with this broad. But she's cute as a bug's ear, I can tell you that."

Tindle had told himself at first that he didn't particularly want a woman tonight, that all he really wanted was the chance to talk and dance and laugh a little. And then he'd had to admit to himself that he probably wouldn't turn any opportunities down. Funny he hadn't done something like this so far over here. It had been kind of a matter of pride that he hadn't been unfaithful to Martha. Why, he didn't know. After all, they'd both been very intelligent at the parting—"I don't suppose you'll just sit at home and twiddle your thumbs while I'm gone," he'd said to her, and she'd answered, "And I don't expect you to spend your spare hours listening to the radio." And they'd both laughed. But tacitly they knew that this was a trial separation. Nothing less. Therefore they owed no faithfulness. Yet all this time Tindle had been queerly pleased to be celibate.

Johnny and the girl were piling into the back seat of the taxi. He couldn't see the girl too clearly at first in the dim light. He had the impression of slender features, and a face that was an inverted isosceles triangle.

"Terry, this here's Dick I told you about."

It seemed impossible that anyone should be able to curtsy sitting down, but somehow she did it.

"Hello," said Tindle.

"I didn't hear name," said Terry.

"Dick. Dick Tindle."

"Dick-san, neh?" She turned to Johnny for confirmation.

196

"That's him," said Johnny. "That's the boy." He said to the taxi driver, "You take me home first. Me home first number one, okay? Wakarimashitaka?"

The driver looked baffled.

"Same-o place you pick us up," said Johnny, getting a little angry.

Teriko laughed and said, "I'll tell him." She told the driver in Japanese.

The cab started off and they all settled back, and Teriko looked at Tindle and smiled, and he smiled back at her stiffly, and tried desperately to think of something to say. Johnny took over the conversation. He bubbled. "Yes, sir, only the best for old Johnny Pendermeyer's friends, and old Dick here is a friend o' mine. Who's the best-lookin' gal in Tokyo, I ask myself. Not hard to figure that out. Terry—I think—and I'll just bet she's lookin' for something to do tonight."

Tindle wondered why Pendermeyer hadn't brought Sachiko along. That had been the original idea. But there'd been one of those tight, whispered squabbles they thought, of course, Tindle didn't notice, and Sachiko was still home. There'd probably be an even bigger scrap after Johnny got back.

Well, it wasn't quite eight o'clock. He wished he didn't feel so weary. He'd like to talk to this girl beside him—if Pendermeyer would stop babbling—she had a decidedly interesting face. And an odd charm in the way she tossed her head and moved her shoulders; a ballet grace.

Johnny leaned forward suddenly and called to the driver, "Here! Right here! Hey—chotto matte!"

They were at Johnny's house. They had been riding a good twenty minutes, and Tindle had as yet barely spoken to his companion for the evening. No matter. Nothing he did in Tokyo mattered, really, as long as he kept himself sort of numb for a few days and gave himself a rest from all the mix-up and hopeless complication of his soul. There was a short argument about who should pay the taxi, and Johnny, being louder of voice, won.

The taxi pulled away, and the driver turned and said something to Teriko, and she said to Tindle, "Where you want to go, Dick-san?"

"Well . . . I hadn't thought."

"You want go dancing?"

"All right."

She stared for a moment, then smiled. "You don't want go dancing."

"How'd you know?. . ."

"I know from your face, neh?"

"Okay." He laughed.

"You want drinking beer?"

"Not especially." He turned toward her. He had to admit that he was both pleased and flattered by her wide-eyed attentiveness. "Is there something more Japanese we could do? A party or a festival or something? What do they call these local dances they have—*bon odori*, isn't it?" He'd seen one once. Colorful.

"Ah, so. But no *bon odori* tonight."

"How about just walking in the park or something?"

"I have idea," she said. She spoke to the driver again in Japanese.

The driver crossed the Ginza and took them to a small boat landing on one of Tokyo's canal-like rivers. A sign said: ROW BOAT. Y 300 FOR THE ONE HOUR PAY.

"Wonderful!" said Tindle. He led her by the arm from the taxi to the boat landing. To touch her excited him.

This, he was thinking, might have been the early minutes of a date back in schooldays. The externals were all the same; the girl herself followed the standard physical pattern. But there was an odd, intangible seriousness that underlay her laughter and most trivial remarks. An illusion, perhaps: a stereotyped reaction on Tindle's part that made him regard all orientals as smoldering and inscrutable.

But then again, maybe not so much an illusion—

He helped her into the rowboat. He held her by the waist to do this. She was decidedly slim and compact; she continued to move in a series of dance movements, and he found himself almost unable to stop watching her.

The canal had graystone banks ten or twelve feet high and he rowed against the current. There were numerous other rowers, plus several motorboats that rocked them with a wash when they passed. Along the banks there were both electric lights and lanterns. Tindle felt suddenly not

198

weary. Indeed, he felt an abrupt surge of energy, and he was happy with this chance to expend it in rowing.

"You like Tokyo?" Teriko asked. She had the faintest uvular roll to her pronunciation of the letter "L," so that the word was almost, but not quite: "rike."

"Haven't seen enough of it to know," he said. "They shipped me down to Akuni almost as soon as I got here."

"You are in Japan long time?"

"Only since last November. But I haven't really seen enough of Japan, either."

She cocked her head. "Why Americans come here don't see Japan?"

"Well—some are too busy. I was, I guess." He trailed the oars for a moment. "Or was I? Maybe just too lazy." He laughed. "Maybe just too mixed up. Maybe too busy sitting and feeling sorry for myself to get out and see the country. The sketches I've wanted to do—the water colors. I never have gotten around to the damn things."

"You can paint water color?"

"Look," he said, facing her suddenly, "I'm talking in circles. Funny—for a moment I had the feeling you knew all about me, and there wasn't anything left I could tell you."

"I feel also same," she said.

"Also same what?"

"Also feel you know me. Know me long time."

"Really?"

"Honto."

"What's that mean?"

"Really."

The short exchange of words had merely been cover for the silence of spoken ideas while they stared at each other. For this was clear: they both knew—without having to say it—that they suddenly each felt warm in the other's presence. An odd thing. Not love, surely; nothing so ridiculous as classical love. A physical attraction as much as anything, Tindle was sure. His blood was champagne of a sudden.

She said, "You have wife, America?"

"Yes."

"Children?"

"No."

"I am always meet married man," said Teriko.

"Really? I mean—*honto?*"

"*So. Honto.*" She laughed. "Why I am always like married man better? Maybe I like older man."

"Do you think I'm old?"

"You are not old. But same time not young, *neh?*"

"Sometimes I'm not so sure."

"Many American man—even old man—seem young. Like little boy. *Doi-sh'te?* Why?"

"Maybe because it's a virtue in America to be young. Everybody always wants to be young. Maybe the meanest failure thinks he always has a chance as long as he stays young."

"I don't want to be old. How about you?"

"Well, I don't suppose I ever thought about it very much. But come to think of it, I never liked being young when I was. You read a lot about happy, happy childhood. It's the bunk."

"Bawnk?"

"Lie—not true."

"Ah, so." She thought for a moment. "American people tell *takusan* lie, I think."

"No—no more than anybody else." Tindle was surprised to find himself leaping into the breach. He never admired shallow, hair-trigger patriotism, but he felt here a definite emotional need to defend his own kind. Funny. "People are pretty much the same all over the world," he said.

And then he realized that he'd done something else that ought to be below his pride. He'd uttered a fatuity. People were not—repeat not—pretty much the same all over the world. Or in different cities, or even on different sides of the same street. To say they were the same was simply a vast oversimplification that could sometimes be used to strongarm bigots into silence. But she—with or without intent to wound—had attacked—and he had had to parry.

He felt suddenly a strong desire to prove to her that Americans were not all the loud, shallow, adolescent sort she must have mostly seen; that there were many who were sensitive, empathetic, kind, strong, noble—even wise.

"But sometimes American man," she continued, "always
200

say to Japanese girl, 'Love you very much'—but he's not love her. Only wants sleep with her, neh?"

"It's a custom," said Tindle, with some amusement. "Hardly seems right to sleep with a girl without saying you love her."

"But just same not really love her?"

"I suppose not. Not in the sense I think you mean."

"So, neh? Americans tell takusan lie."

He laughed. "Teriko—we're getting nowhere, you know that don't you?" He laughed again, and kept on rowing.

They passed a long block of Japanese-style house half-concealed behind a garden with a bamboo fence around it. The sound of laughter and a popular recorded song came from within. It was a Japanese song Tindle had heard before—something about the moon and the river. Teriko started to sing. She had a remarkably easy voice, essentially low, but at home also in the higher notes. He watched her as she sang. She was looking out over the water. They were past the lights now, in a darker stretch of canal bordering a large park. He shipped the oars and the boat drifted to the stone bank, and stayed there, bumping gently.

He lit a cigarette. Silent now; she had finished her song. And in the silence it seemed to Tindle that he and this Japanese girl said all manner of things to each other, without speaking.

He felt like a damned schoolboy.

"Dick-san—"

"Yes?"

"I have favor."

"Of course. What?"

"I am tired tonight. You not ask me sleep with you tonight, neh?"

He stared, then broke into laughter. "What on earth made you think I was going to ask you to sleep with you?"

"Always happen," she said blithely.

"Yes, I suppose it does. We're the conquerors, aren't we? Pretty fine and pretty just—the most benevolent occupation in history they call this. We call this. Maybe so. But maybe we do it this way because it suits us, not because it means any overwhelming sacrifice on our part. And our soldiers still take in the victor's spoils, don't they? You'd

201

be out with some Japanese boy who could some day offer you a good home, instead of me, tonight, if we hadn't moved in."

"I don't understand, Dick-san. My English not—"

He leaned forward and took her hand. "Never mind. I've got an awful lot of words I've been keeping in me. Got to get them out sometime. Forgive me. And Teriko—I wasn't going to ask you to sleep with me. I suppose if you'd made the offer I wouldn't have turned it down—but honestly I wasn't thinking along those lines. And not because you don't excite me, either."

"*Honto?*"

"*Honto.*"

She studied him for a moment. "You are very different man, *deshoo?*"

"Maybe." He shrugged. "But tell me something. Do you always sleep with whoever asks you?"

"Oh, no. Sometimes not like somebody."

"You only sleep with somebody you like?"

"Only if like *takusan*—very much."

"And how often do you decide you like somebody *takusan?*"

"I cannot tell. Sometimes my body is get very excited, neh? But sometimes don't like somebody even if body is excited. Funny—some man kiss my neck, maybe, but if I don't like him, not excite my body."

He shook his head and smiled thinly. "East is east and west is west, and so on," he said. "I guess the bromides are true sometimes—maybe because they were drawn from life in the first place. Look, Teriko—is this a Japanese custom, sleeping with everybody like this?"

"I don't sleep with *everybody.*"

"All right, all right. Let's say sleeping with a lot of people. Were you taught to do it like that?"

"If I like somebody, and he wants sleep with me, we can do." She looked puzzled, and her look implied that all this to her was simplicity itself.

"What I mean is this," said Tindle. "You dress western style, speak English, probably dance western style—and so on. Do you think American girls sleep with a man automatically every time they go out on a date?"

"But some man get angry if they don't sleep with him, deshoo?"

"Is that what these damned ambassadors of good will of ours have been teaching you? Teriko—good Lord—this is terrible. You don't know, and I can't explain, how terrible it all is."

She frowned. "Not understanding you, Dick-san." She looked up. "Ah—I know. You are Christian, deshoo?"

"Well, I went to Sunday School as a kid. I'm not a churchgoer."

"But you are Christian."

Now he frowned. "I don't know. I don't know exactly. I believe in something. Only it doesn't seem to be what the rest of the people around me have to offer. I keep feeling the idea is right, but it's been muddled somewhere along the line. I'd like to have a faith I could share with a lot of other people—but I can't just make myself have it by snapping my fingers in front of my eyes."

He knew by her blank look that again she didn't understand.

"I'm sorry," he said. "I'm not speaking to you. I'm just speaking to myself."

"But I like your speaking to me. Not like baby—Johnny-san always speaks funny, like talk to baby. You always talk good English to me, neh?" She sighed. "I want very much speak good English."

He held her hands now (when had that happened?), and on a sudden impulse he pulled her forward gently and kissed her on the mouth. For a moment they merely touched lips. And then abruptly she rose from the seat and threw herself into his arms and began to kiss him passionately. Her arms encircled his neck, and her fingers ran lightly over his ear and around the back of his collar. She was warm; her breath was sweet.

Tindle sensed suddenly that the boat was far off balance. He yelled, "Hey! Look out!"

She seemed oblivious to the danger.

The boat turned over.

The water was cold; it made him gasp. He went under for a moment, then scrambled to the surface. She was in front of him, her hair plastered down over her face. She was sputtering. He grabbed her about the waist, held her with one arm, and clung to the overturned boat with the other.

They stared at each other for a moment—and then both of them broke into uncontrollable laughter. It was some minutes before he righted the boat again.

At the dock, the boatowner was properly sympathetic. Especially when Tindle paid him double. He bowed and bared his gold teeth, and provided them with towels and the relative privacy of his boat-office. Teriko dried her face and arms and legs, but her dress, soaked, clung to her heavily. She looked helpless as a newborn rat. "What we do now, Dick-san?"

"I'd better get you home in a cab."

"Oh, no—not go home."

"Why not?"

"Mother come back, I think. Maybe Ichiro telephone aunt. Big fight."

"Fight? About what?"

"Difficult explain. But big fight—*honto.*"

He frowned for a moment. "Well, I suppose I could get you to a hotel. Maybe you can phone for some clothes in the morning—or dry these by then."

"How about you?"

"I've got a bed waiting in one of the billets. The one Johnny Pendermeyer's supposed to use at Army Hall. Don't worry about me."

Teriko gave the cab driver the address of a hotel. They were there in a few minutes: it was a two-story building in a small alley, with the usual frosted-glass sliding doors in front. The hotelkeeper, summoned by the driver, came outside to assure them that there was room.

Teriko opened the door and started to step out, then turned suddenly.

"Dick-san—"

"Yes?"

"You come with me, please."

His heart began to pound and he said, "Yes," and followed her.

204

CHAPTER NINE

1

OF COURSE he knew that it had to end. But it was astonishing how, being aware of this, he could nevertheless refuse his mind to it and truly feel sometimes that this thing could not possibly end . . . not unless all time and the earth were also to disappear.

Days passed, and until later Richard Tindle did not know how many.

There were a few clear moments, like unexpected breaks in an overcast. Then Tindle could see himself in perspective. Then he would be both puzzled and startled, and he would tell himself that surely he could not be in love with this wanton, this extraordinary child.

Most of the time he whispered that he did love her, and believed it himself. This, most of the time.

He could not remember which of them had first acknowledged love. Teriko, perhaps that first morning in the hotel. That morning the place looked sordid, like all hotels in the morning. He did not care especially. And Teriko probably didn't say in so many words that she loved him then, but there must have been a certain look, a certain tilt of her head and shoulders that told him. He must have shown something, too. He was sure that both felt this rapport, and that to both of them it was something almost new.

For that first night had been eminently successful, in all respects. They did not want to leave each other the next morning. . . .

Tindle took her home to change her clothes.

"Mother angry—but I don't care now," she said.

Mother was wooden-faced. Tindle didn't understand the sharp, quick, whispered conversation between them. He waited patiently until she changed, and he noticed that she walked out of the house quickly and with her head high and angry.

They returned to the Ginza and began to walk the big street and look into the store windows. Tindle presently bought her a new cashmere sweater in a British shop. "This is nice and plain," he told her. "Natural color. Wear just one small string of pearls with it. And roll the sleeves up on your forearms a little."

She smiled. "I know, Dick-san. I reading American magazine."

He felt a little ashamed then that he had patronized her.

All that afternoon, as they traversed the busy shopping avenue, laughing, touching together, holding each other's arms, looking at the same things and often making the same remarks simultaneously, Tindle was happy.

"I don't know when I've enjoyed being with somebody so much," he said to her. "Hell—I don't want to leave you for a minute."

"I am same." She pressed his arm to her bosom.

"Don't go to work tomorrow. Or the next day. Stay with me. Stay with me all the time I'm in Tokyo."

"Yes, Dick-san."

"Where could we go? To stay, I mean. I don't want to be just in any cheap hotel—that doesn't seem right for us."

She laughed. "I am think same last night. Not with Dick-san in hotel. But when you are must go, I think—no, don't want you are going. Want you stay with me. Takusan. Maybe I am not such good girl, neh?"

"You are. Don't let anybody tell you you're not."

He thought at this point how in his own land this wondrous little she-animal would definitely have been labeled a tart. And back there that might have been true: probably there she would have slept with all the men she had known for much different reasons. Here she had done this simply because she had been taught that there was nothing basically wrong with gratifying her natural appetite, and she had been further led to believe that sleeping with one's companion of the evening was merely the mutually satisfying climax to a social engagement. She regarded sexual intercourse as casually as most American girls regarded petting or the good-night kiss.

Well, he had enjoyed her tremendously last night in the hotel; his head still swam with it. And now he was enjoying her quite as much. Every word, every gesture, every tiny graceful movement that she made.

206

Ten years ago Tindle would have been sure he was in love.

"I have idea," said Teriko.

"What?"

"Why don't we go country. I know nice place. Maybe four hours on train."

"Can you get away?"

"I call Yamamoto-san, say I am not feeling good. Go visit aunt."

"That's a handy aunt you've got," said Tindle.

The arrangements took the rest of the afternoon. He had left his bag at Johnny Pendermeyer's and he caught Johnny at quitting time at the Meiji Building, then rode out with him to pick up the overnight case.

"Fast work, fella," said Johnny, chuckling lasciviously. "Before you know the kid twenty-four hours you got her trotting off to the country with you, hey?"

It was an effort for Tindle to be pleasant. But he managed—mostly by changing the subject. "Look, Johnny, just so I don't disappear completely I'll call up from this place when we get there and give you the phone number. No need telling anybody where I am, but you could call Akuni and tell the A.G. there that you can get in touch with me in case anybody needs me."

"Why the hell bother?" asked Johnny, rolling his cigar in his mouth.

"We're supposed to keep in touch."

"Okay, anything you say," said Johnny. He sighed. "Wish *I* could get off a few days with some gorgeous dame."

"You've got a pretty good set-up where you are," Tindle reminded him.

"Maybe," said Johnny. "Maybe. But a guy gets tired of the same hunk of woman night after night, night after night. . . ."

Tindle changed the subject again.

Later it was exciting to walk with Teriko through the crowded Tokyo station. He held her arm close to his body, and they pushed forward through the narrow gateways and then to the stairs that led upward to the train platform. He held her by the waist in the crush to board the train.

The second-class coaches tonight were even more crowded than the third class.

"Are the trains always this crowded?"

"Hai. Always—itsumo."

"Why don't they put on more trains?"

"Always make more trains. Always more people just the same."

He didn't bother trying to unravel that one. They pushed forward, and laughed together at all the discomfort. Men elbowed and body-blocked and kicked each other. They rushed madly for empty seats, the loser usually losing his balance and sprawling. When this happened their angry faces changed with insane abruptness and they bowed and smiled and pardoned themselves to each other. When Tindle and Teriko—who entered the car with somewhat self-conscious dignity—obtained no seats they stood contentedly in the aisle and looked into each other's eyes. They talked. It seemed that there was an inexhaustible supply of things to talk about.

The electric train hurtled southward . . . Tokyo, Yokohama . . . and then the candy-mountain countryside blurring past the windows. Sometimes on the left they had glimpses of Tokyo Bay, flat as slate, with an evening drizzle giving a faint tooth to the surface. Holiday mood. Their fellow passengers (who before had been fighting for seats) now laughing and smiling at each other. Two doll-faced Japanese children with their noses pressed in wonder to the window. A distinguished-looking Japanese gentleman in British tweeds who was very drunk, and who stared at everyone both foolishly and malevolently, like a squid.

Then it became dark, and somewhere along the way they changed trains, rode for another half-hour, and got off at a little, dirty station in a ramshackle town.

But the air was clean and exhilarating. A station wagon met them and took them to the hotel, which was on a steep hillside.

Tindle would never forget that little country hotel upon a Japanese hillside. Their large, mat-floored room looked out upon a garden of carefully clipped, twisted shrubs that nested in flower beds surrounded by tiny bamboo fences. There was a small rivulet with several natural flat boulders

208

carefully arranged into a kind of abstract sculpture. In the early morning the mist rose from the garden, and the gardener came through, raking with his split-bamboo broom, and the housemaids tripped through the sequined grass in their wooden *geta*, carrying other trays of breakfast, eminently graceful as they walked. And just beyond the garden the mountainside swept down into a puddle of silk-blue mist in the valley.

Then the sun would gently, yet inexorably warm the mist away, with the same loving determination of a mother sending her procrastinating child to school. And the sky would flush blue overhead, but shreds of cloud would cling like live, unraveling cocoons to the mountaintops. The rocks of the mountains were of all colors: blue-green, vermilion, ochre, pastel in their intensity and quite unreal. Sometimes a soft, passing rain would draw a light veil over all of it. When this rain fell Tindle would sit by the fully opened sliding Japanese window, smoke quietly, and look into the rain. Teriko would gather her legs under her supple body and sit at his side, letting her arms rest on his knees, and for the most part watching him as quietly and contentedly as he watched the landscape.

Tindle did call Johnny Pendermeyer the first morning to give him the number of the hotel. After that he forgot Johnny Pendermeyer and the Far East Air Forces. And indeed the outer, the practical world. . . .

Then there was the day they bicycled to the lake in the valley. It was hot that day, and on impulse they swam, naked, from a rock by the lakeside. Teriko was a water-creature, clean-limbed and elusive. On their way back to the hotel they drank a liter each of Japanese beer. The best beer, Tindle reflected in some surprise, is not made by the Teutons and their kin, it is made by the Mexicans and Japanese. When they returned to the hotel they went into the western room where there was an electric phonograph and a stack of popular records only nine or ten years old. They danced to Artie Shaw's "Begin the Beguine."

Was he . . . was he possibly in love with this female human in his arms?

The record ended. Teriko said, "Please. Dance more."

"No, no," he said, laughing. "I'm an old man. I can't

209

take all this exercise. Let's go sit and watch the sun go down."

"All right, Dick-san." But she pouted faintly.

"Okay, you physical-culture fiend. One more dance. A slow one."

Why did he want to please Teriko this way, in every little thing? If Martha had said all right, he would have stopped dancing, thanked her for being considerate, and patted her without passion upon the shoulder or the arm.

Teriko, he thought, was so natural, so easy, so unaffected; so devoid of really complicated workings of the mind. Even the slight selfishness she showed in the little flashes from time to time—like her pouting a moment ago—was a frank and open thing, a part of her ingenuous charm.

There—he had his finger on something. Martha, in her very self-effacement, in her fierce pursuit of Good and Honor, in her impeccable behavior, expressed an inner motivation essentially smug and selfish. There was always the implication that she was morally superior to him. While he would have admitted this cheerfully, he did not like having it constantly suggested. . . .

And then in bed, even when she achieved apparent ecstasy, there was always with Martha the underlying sense of grim compliance. Husband, husband, lord and master; husband, husband, I will do.

Martha would always do her duty.

Later that night, Teriko looked at Tindle and said, "You miss home?"

He was caught off guard, and it took several moments for him to develop an answer. "Well—I don't know. Some things yes, some things no."

"But oku-san—wife—you want see her sometime?"

"I—I don't know that, either."

"One time you did love her, neh?"

"Yes. Yes, I suppose one time I did."

"So. She have something good for you. I have something good for you, but oku-san have, too, desho-o?"

Tindle said, "What the hell kind of conversation is this, anyway?" and then they were silent for a long period.

After a while she said, "How long we stay here?"

"I'll have to leave in—well, maybe four more days."

"So."

"You'll go back to work then, I suppose."

"Who can know future?"

He laughed a little. "That's a handy philosophy."

"Not understand."

"Never mind, darling. Kiss me."

When they had kissed and fondled each other a bit on the grass mats, she said, "Sometimes I want baby. Not now, but if I am more old."

"How much older?"

"I don't know. Some time future."

"You're twenty-four now. You'd better get started sometime." He sat up, squatted cross-legged, and studied her. "Why don't you marry some nice young Japanese man and stop fooling around like this? You're only going to be all mixed-up and in bad shape when you're thirty-five or forty. Nowhere to go, no one to latch on to."

"Who can know future?" she said again.

"Who *wants* to know the future?"

"I don't want know." She shook her head vigorously. "And sometimes think I don't want all time happy. Because if happy, neh?, afraid for losing happy."

He thought about her attitude—on the surface irresponsible and by western ethics highly immoral—but she had not fashioned this attitude for herself. She had been there, impotent, and it had been fashioned for her. Was it not the same with Martha? Martha had not chosen the nineteenth century Anglophile family into which she had been born, and from whom she had acquired the ideas that were now, in this twentieth century, antiquated. You could not blame Martha. You could not blame Teriko. You could not blame the cheat and the thief and the murderer and the rapist and the men who made war upon each other . . . you could not blame. Yet, if you could not blame, then nothing was wrong—but it was necessary to decide what was wrong so that you would have a reference point for what was right.

He sensed abruptly that he was inviting all these complicated thoughts in order to justify himself should he sud-

211

denly decide that truly he was in love with this woman creature beside him.

She said, "You like drink sake now?"

"Yes. I think I'd like a drink now."

She studied his face. "Something inside trouble for you?"

"Do I show it that easily?" He smiled.

"Easy for me, I can see. Before is different—but now I can know you."

"Why was it different before?"

"American face difficult tell what thinking. Not like Japanese face."

He restrained some of his laughter. "You mean we Americans are inscrutable?"

"Nani?"

He pointed out the word in her pocket American-Japanese dictionary. Inscrutable.

"Ah, so!" she said with great fervor. "American people this way, neh?"

"They'd be surprised to hear it," said Tindle. "But maybe you're right."

"So. But—you don't tell me—what is trouble you?"

"Well . . ." he shifted on the mat floor, not yet quite at ease crosslegged . . . "a lot of things. The fact that this has to come to an end sometime, for one. Do you realize we've been here three days already? I have to be back in Akuni pretty soon."

"I know." She pouted a bit. She rearranged the flowers in the vase on the table, appearing for a moment to be deeply engrossed in this. "And you must fly. Kill Chinese man, neh?"

He had told her how he felt about killing. "Maybe that's mainly what's bothering me. Maybe." He got up, stretched his legs and began to pace back and forth. "But I have to do it. There's no way I can get out of it, and still be myself, don't you see? It would be a lot easier if I could be strongly idealistic—or religious—like Colonel Straker, for instance. Then all I'd have to do would be convince myself that war, or killing, or shady dealing, or corrupt politics, or whatever, was in line with God's will and the common good. That would be the clever thing to do. Most people

212

are clever these days—they're too goddamned clever for their own britches. . . ."

Teriko got up, went to the sliding door, looked at him impassively, and said, "You better have drink now."

The soft days . . . the green rain mountain and the clean mist. The delicacy of the bamboo garden. The free clouds, the gentle sky. When she sat on folded knees before the mirror of her floor dresser and combed her black hair he watched her contentedly.

Did not God, making the lotus, mean it to be plucked?

For there was this girl, this woman-child, this natural body out of the generous and loving earth, the first whole and heavenly fulfillment he had known. There was something gloriously honest in her attitude toward sex. Doubtless she thought herself not particularly unique, but to Dick Tindle—Occidental, American, Christian (in his broad ethics if not in his faith), all this was quite new. With her there was no shame: there was only now and then the residue of his own pre-impressed shame. He enjoyed, for a change, their passion not because it was forbidden, but because it seemed fine and just and even ordained that it should exist—

"I love you, Teriko."

In the heat of his loins he said this many times. But he did not know yet if this was true.

Then, on the fourth morning, the telephone rang. The telephone seldom rang in this hotel, and twice before when it had rung Tindle had been surprised to find himself stir uneasily. They were eating osushi when it rang. She had introduced him to osushi. He'd playfully imagined how he might describe osushi to someone back home, and convince this person that it was truly delicious. The moment he'd say "raw fish" he'd set up an automatic negative reaction. And probably he'd never be able to overcome this first reaction by explaining that the fish was delicate and tender, and arranged skillfully with pats of cold rice and blankets of thin, nutty tasting seaweed. He liked best the brick-red tuna, and after that the silvery white flounder and kingfish. The boiled crawfish and smoked eel and the spotted herring came next—he didn't care too much for

213

the tough white octopus or squid. He was dipping a piece of tuna into the soy and mustard sauce when the phone rang that morning—

One of the maids shuffled to the door and piped: "Gomen-asai!"

"Do-ozo," called Teriko. The maid opened the door; they chatted for a moment, and then Teriko said, "Telephone is for you, Dick-san."

"For me?" It could only be Pendermeyer. No one else knew he was here.

He felt a little light-headed as he picked up the phone out in the hall. The connection was bad; full of static noises. "Hello, Dick? Johnny Pendermeyer. How you doin'?"

"Pretty good. Having a wonderful time. Wish you were here. No—on second thought, it's better alone."

Johnny laughed a lot at that one. "Well, I wish I was there, too. Anything to get away from that Sachiko a while."

"What?"

"Sachiko. My moose. Always yapping for more dough. I'm getting rid of her. To hell with her. She's more trouble than she's worth. Besides, you can't trust these Japanese dolls any more than you could fly to the moon."

"Something else on your mind, Johnny?"

"Well, yeah. They called up here today from Akuni. I think they want you back there."

"Back to Akuni?"

"That's right. Some big deal going on. I think we're probably going to make a max effort somewhere. I know they've been fussing a lot over those radar photos of Tinju."

"Of where?"

"Tinju. Big Red build-up there. Only we shouldn't talk about it on the phone."

"You're talking about it. I'm not."

"Okay, okay. What the hell, they know everything before we do it anyway. No sweat. Anyway, Dick, you're supposed to get on down there."

"All right. I'll try to make it."

Pendermeyer must have sensed the disappointment in
214

Tindle's voice. He said, "If you don't want to go, I'll call Akuni back and tell them I couldn't get a-holt of you."

"I'll take the first train back in the morning," said Tindle. It surprised him that it was easy to say this. And that, in some odd way, he *wanted* to go. If the Wing was making a max effort, he wanted to be in it. A sentimental idea—but there it was. Why? He knew suddenly now that he could leave Teriko for this thing easily, and although she affected him profoundly he was *not* truly in love with her. He knew this, now. "Look, Johnny. Call Haneda or Tachikawa Air Base and see if you can set up a plane ride back to Akuni for me, will you?"

"Sure, buddy, sure. Will do."

"And thanks for calling, Johnny."

"Forget it."

"So long."

"So long."

Tindle hung up and turned to walk from the phone. Teriko had been standing behind him. She said, "You are going back, neh?"

"Yes."

They looked at each other for a moment; and then he took her arm and led her back to the room.

Later that night, when they had come together, then parted, then lay side by side, wonderfully exhausted, she turned to him suddenly. She clung to him. "Oh, Dick-san! I love you! I love you!" She wept. He turned the small floor lamp on and saw the short black lashes of her oriental eyes wet with tears. She said, "Please don't leave me, Dick-san! Please don't leave me!"

"Listen, Teriko." He held her bare shoulders and looked into her eyes. He was going to tell her that he did not love her, that he had a profound affection for her, and that he would never forget her wherever he might go, and that—but, hell, how could you tell a woman something like this?"

"What, Dick-san?"

"Listen, you must understand. I'm a soldier. I have to obey orders." That was rather cheap, he thought.

"Dick-san—I want come to Akuni with you."

"You want to come to Akuni?"

215

"I want be near you."

He turned that over in his mind. They could have a small house in the town at very little cost. He would only have to stay on the base about once every week. He could have his wondrous Teriko; he could enjoy all the time the peace he had found in these past several days. But what about Teriko herself? What about that future of hers? He would make it even more uncertain by taking her south with him—

"Teriko, it might be difficult."

"I don't care, difficult!" (What a strange sight—that still face, with the tears streaming unheeded down her cheeks!) "I want be with you, Dick-san!"

He could not say no. He wondered what had happened to him that he could not be truthful and strong. He did not admire himself as he made the arrangements for her to follow by train. . . .

Later he was strong again, or at least there was the illusion of strength. He held her upon the grass mats with their sweet hay smell; he held her there in the dark, but it was as though he carried her inexhaustibly in a great climb to the crest of one of the peaks they saw in daylight. It was the best of all, that night.

2

In Tokyo that evening Johnny Pendermeyer waited until after supper to break the news to Sachiko. It had taken him several days to make this decision, but now he was firm in it.

After Shoji cleared away the dishes and Sachiko brought his beer, he squatted there in the soft evening sunlight. She lit his new cigar for him.

She said, "Something wrong, Johnny-san?"

He looked at her. He looked at the fat of her jowls and the gold teeth on the side that showed through her parted lips. He looked at the wrinkles about her mouth and eyes. Starting to fall apart. She'd go fast in the next few years; those Japs went fast, like spicks, when they went. Well, she'd still be able to find some sucker to take care of her—though probably not as well as Johnny had done. Anyway, she was no dumb, wide-eyed schoolgirl, and she

216

ought to know by now that sooner or later all good things
had to come to an end.

"Nothing's wrong," he grunted. "I just been thinking,
that's all."

"Yes?" She was attentive.

He gestured inclusively with his fat arm. "This layout's
costing me a hell of a lot. Almost fifty thousand yen a
month. And I'm not saving much over here. The smart
boys are putting away a fortune."

Sachiko smiled. "You spend most of your money on beer
and whiskey, Johnny."

"Look," he said sharply, "I spend that anyway. Whether
I keep this layout or not, I buy my beer and whiskey. I'm
over twenty-one. I guess if I want to have a little beer and
whiskey—"

She sidled toward him, lowering her eyelids. "You're
cute when you're angry, Johnny-san."

He grunted.

She touched his bare thigh.

"Not now."

"Just a little. Please."

He pushed her away roughly.

She stared at him for a moment, then said, "Are you
thinking of home, Johnny-san?"

"Hell, yes, I'm thinking about home. Who wouldn't
in this crummy place? Sister, when you boil it all down,
there's nothing like the good old U.S.A."

She sighed a little.

"Yes, sir," said Johnny, looking out of the window. Out
there the leaves of the banana palm glistened in the late
sun. "I should have been saving a little nest egg all the
time. Putting something aside for when I get back. And
that—that brings me to something I got to tell you."

"What, Johnny-san?"

"Where's Shoji?" He looked around. "I don't want him
around if you're gonna raise a big fuss now."

"Shoji went home."

"Well, he went home too damned early. He's been going
home too damned early every night. Hell, he's supposed to
live here, isn't he? He's too damned expensive to keep, by
God, for what good he does. And if you think I don't know

217

he steals me blind, you got another think coming."

She shrugged. "Fire him."

"I got to do more than that. I got to get rid of more than just Shoji."

"What do you mean?"

"We got to give up this house, kid."

She cocked her head. "You mean live some place else?"

"No—I mean give up everything. I can't afford the set-up any more. You and me are just gonna have to say sayonara."

She stared at him for a long, long time.

"Well, you heard me, didn't you?" said Johnny. "You understood what I said."

"I understand."

"Well, what do you think?"

He could tell nothing from her face. By God, they could wear a mask, these orientals. Had no feelings, by God; just like niggers or animals. Only two things could ever get a rise out of them. Fighting or frigging. He chuckled. Not a bad one; have to tell that down at the shop tomorrow. Frigging or fighting—

"Johnny-san—"

"Yeah?"

"When are you leaving, Johnny-san?"

"Well—" he scratched the fat of his neck—"day after tomorrow's the end of the month. The rent's due. I thought maybe I might as well pack up tomorrow." He was uncomfortable in her presence now; he felt the weight of their sudden double loneliness. He felt a sudden need for noise and laughter. There would be noise and laughter at the bar at Army Hall. "In fact, maybe tonight I better get over to the billets," he said, "and get everything ready. Yeah. I better get out tonight."

"Johnny-san—do just one more little thing for me, will you?"

"What?"

"Say you'll do it."

"How can I say I'll do it if I don't know what it is?"

"Don't go tonight. Wait until tomorrow. That's the favor."

"Now, look, kid. We better just make a clean break, huh? No tears, or none of that stuff. I'll leave you some

218

cash so's you don't get left out in the cold. You can go stay with that sister of yours till you find somebody else, can't you? And you won't have any trouble finding somebody. Hell, there's a million guys would take care of you." He laughed, and tried a clumsy joke. "Not everybody can have a baroness for a girl friend, hey?"

She said evenly, "Stay with me tonight."

"Now, Sachiko—"

She was coming toward him. She was like an animal, creeping upon him. He felt the shock of her stare. His wrists and ankles suddenly began to prickle. He was panting—

And then she touched his hairygoat chest.

He grinned, and said, "You little bitch," and pulled her to him. She jammed his head against the swollen fleshbuds of her breasts, and said, "Oh, Johnny-san, if you leave me, I'll kill you! *I'll kill you, Johnny-san!*"

He heard it. He thought not much of it. He laughed and said, "You bitch. You sweet little bitch."

She got him very drunk that night. Johnny did not remember going to sleep, but he recalled vaguely being totally exhausted, and drifting away into something gray and soft. In his hazy dream Sachiko was completely mad— a madwoman in a madhouse, filthy and screaming and unkempt, running through a grove of upstretched naked legs . . . for there were thousands in this mad place, all screaming, all with the wild moon upon them . . . and he was one of them.

He awoke, and the moonlight came through the open window. He was not sure why he had come to life like this—suddenly, and with his body cold and wet. His head throbbed. Good Christ, he shouldn't have drunk so much; he—

And what was this shadow in the room?

"Sachiko!"

Sachiko, all right. The naked shape of her, dark in the corner there. But she didn't answer.

"Sachiko. What the hell's the matter with you?"

The shadow came toward him.

"You walking in your sleep now? Is that the latest?"

219

She spoke very softly. "You go back to sleep, Johnny-san. You close your eyes."

"Damned if I don't want to. Come on to bed." He patted the mattress beside him. "Come on."

"Close your eyes, darling."

He saw now that she held her hand behind her back. "What've you got there, you bitch?"

Her shadow expanded suddenly in the frame of his vision, and it took him an instant to realize that she was springing toward him. He opened his eyes wide in surprise. A heavy thing in her upraised hand. A bottle? Was it a bottle? Was it one of his own goddamn bottles of whiskey he'd brought here?

He saw it come crashing down toward him.

At first there was blackness—a void that flashed by, letting him have but a glimpse of infinity—and then it was again much like his last dream, where he knew that he was not conscious, but had no control over it; could not break from this curious state. He could neither see nor hear. But he did sense everything about him in a way much beyond his everyday ordinary senses.

Well, now, only yesterday he'd been a hustling kid in South Philadelphia, turning four bits here and four bits there . . . he sometimes wondered where all the years had gone . . . Ha, ha, ha, ha! Oh, Jesus Christ! . . . sure, this being a tech rep was really a soft touch . . . but when you boiled it all down there was really nothing like the good old U.S.A.

Good God—he'd better hurry to the office!

Had to see that kid in the comm-supply about selling some more tubes on the black market.

Had to get rid of Sachiko, too. Getting to be too much. Acting more and more like she owned him or something. Wait till after supper to break the news. Bitch. Sweet bitch.

But Sachiko was here. She was bending over him.

What the hell for?

She was doing something. She was busy as hell doing something.

She was squatting beside him, on her knees, Japanese-
220

style. Just like a bunch of squatting monkeys, these Japanese.

He knew there was a knife; now, how the devil did he know that?

There was only one sharp electric instant of pain. And in that instant, before the utter nothingness came, he knew what she had done . . . and he knew that part of him, at least, was now hers.

CHAPTER TEN

1

AT FIRST, in the morning, there was a low, cool cloud over Akuni, but by eight o'clock the sun had swept this away. Now there was a blue May sky: a little bluer, perhaps, because it was getting on to June. There was only the lightest breeze from the Sea of Japan, and this came directly down the runway from the west. It was a steady breeze; perfect for take-off and landing.

This was mission weather.

Nearly everyone on the base knew something was brewing. They'd watched linesmen grooming the F-80 fighter-bombers all yesterday afternoon, tightening their guts and sleeking down their mirror flanks. The lights in the maintenance sheds had been on all night.

Twelve correspondents had arrived from Tokyo; everybody knew this, too. They were staying in a cottage especially assigned to them in the housing area. And among them was this Herb Oscott who had recently been doing a column called "It's This Way—," which the *Stars and Stripes* had been carrying, and which some people said was like Ernie Pyle's old column last war. The men didn't know much about the other correspondents, but they were all anxious to see and talk to Oscott. They figured there must be something pretty big going on if a man like this came down to Akuni to see it.

There was another bit of evidence: the Officers' Club had been relatively quiet last night. Most of the pilots tried not to drink too much the night before a big one.

Technical Sergeant Frank Braith, however, had tied rather a beauty on last night. All on account of the correspondents. Two of them had descended upon him while he was more or less minding his own business out on the line, and they'd asked him for technical data on the F-80. After assuring them that he'd played a major part in the development of this airplane ("Back when I was a designer at Lockheed," he'd said), he had given them this data. The ungarbled word, too, because he'd actually been studying the damned airplane ever since his transfer to the maintenance squadron, and he'd always been able to study and retain things pretty quickly. They'd presented him with a bottle of whiskey.

So now, with his head aching slightly, and his belly full of breakfast, he wandered toward the maintenance shack on the line. The night crew was gone; the day crew hadn't come on duty yet. It was quiet here. The quiet made Frank Braith somewhat restless.

He stood before the hangar, drinking some sun. The parked jets all along the line looked like so many silvery, sleeping beetles. One of them would be his own baby pretty soon. He hadn't been assigned to a specific airplane yet, but he was working under MacInnes. O.J.T., which is what the initial-loving service calls "On-the-job-training." He didn't too much care for the status of trainee. He'd be glad to get away from MacInnes, whose quiet, penetrating eye always seemed to see through him and despise him. And this MacInnes, for all his snotty, superior air hadn't done too damned well for himself when you boiled it right down. He was crewing this Captain Tindle's plane—and there was little chance that Tindle would ever distinguish himself. Kingsley was the man to watch. Kingsley already held the record on enemy tanks and locomotives destroyed. Braith would like to get the assignment as Kingsley's crew chief—or maybe even Colonel Straker himself. When a crew chief had a good pilot, he could share in the honors —and in the publicity. Braith would have to work on Major Ronsdale now for a good airplane assignment. That would be the next move.

He hitched his trousers on his wide middle, lit a cigarette, and puffed it contentedly.

222

A three-quarter-ton truck, the type called a Weapons-Carrier, rolled by. Corporal George Marquez sat in the open back with some ammunition cans. The damn little spick had finally made corporal, he had. As the vehicle passed Braith saw Marquez turn his head quickly, avoiding Braith's look. Marquez, he knew, had been staring at him lately, whenever he thought he didn't notice. Staring with those burnt-coffee eyes and planning God-knew-what in that simmering Mexican brain. He'd have to watch Marquez . . . he'd find a shiv slipped quietly between his ribs some night if he didn't watch out.

Maybe the best thing would be to hop Marquez quick and fast—push him around and dominate him a few times; let him know he wasn't about to be afraid. That was the way to handle these dark types. Psychological warfare.

Braith watched the armorer's truck wheel to the line and stop by one of the parked jets. He dropped his cigarette, toed it, and casually began to stroll in that direction.

Not far from Braith, among the parked Shooting Stars, Sergeant MacInnes was busy polishing the fuselage of aircraft number 3861. He was using a dry gauze cloth to make the alloy skin shine like a mirror. You could get a few extra knots out of a shiny airplane—less wind resistance at five hundred miles per hour—and Captain Tindle might like a few extra knots today. Something big going on today; MacInnes didn't know what, exactly, but the quiet around here this morning was the kind of quiet that you could feel in your bones—

MacInnes heard a sudden whirring sound behind him. He turned abruptly. A man in fatigues had a movie camera pointed at him. There was a square blue and white patch that said U.N. WAR CORRESPONDENT on the man's shoulder.

The man looked around the camera. Thin, hollow-cheeked, nervous sort of guy. "Don't look at me. Keep on polishing like that."

"Okay," said MacInnes. He polished, and puffed his large black pipe.

The whirring went on, intermittently, behind him for a while, and finally the man said, "Okay. Thanks."

"You're welcome," said MacInnes.

The man pointed toward the end of the line. "What's going on down there?"

MacInnes looked. The armament section's three-quarter-ton truck was at the nose of the first F-80. "Loading the guns," said MacInnes. "The bombs and napalm are already strung on."

"I see. Thanks, again." The newsreel man moved off.

MacInnes resumed his polishing and hummed something tuneless in a flat, contented voice. Without self-conceit, or smugness, he thought to himself how strange it was that so many people knocked themselves out to do things, and got all in a flap about whatever they tried to do. Like the nervous newsreel cameraman. Like Braith, trying so hard to be something he wasn't. Like Major Ronsdale, trying to keep on being something he already was. And even Captain Tindle, who seemed to MacInnes the most even of the lot, got that strained look around his eyes sometimes, that tendency to fuss tautly—probably worrying because his record hadn't been too good since he got back from forward control. Funny that people worried so much about themselves. MacInnes never did this, and it wasn't exactly that he was without personal ambition—it was just that he figured no long range goal was important enough that you should make yourself and everybody around you miserable trying to achieve it. MacInnes had a gift. . . .

At the first jet on the line Corporal Marquez unbolted a nose plate and removed the large aluminum can that would hold the clips of fifty caliber bullets. He took the cartridges from an olive-drab ammo box and noisily rolled them into the can. He replaced the can, pulled the charging handle on the guns, and fastened the nose plate once more.

He was getting pretty good at this. He could arm a plane faster than just about anybody in the section now. That was how he'd made corporal, finally. Felt pretty good to be a corporal—took you out of the private class, so to speak. Might not be too hard to make buck sergeant in a few months now, with the war going on and everything. If he were a buck sergeant he could send a little money home. The family—Mamacita and Chico, the kid brother—

could use it. They didn't have it too easy since he'd signed up with the Air Force to keep from being drafted in the army. But now maybe it would be the best thing to stay in the Air Force and make a career of it, the way the recruiting posters and pamphlets always said. He had this much of a start anyway. All he had to do was figure on the war lasting a little longer, because, like the older fellows back at the barracks said, you practically never got promotions in peacetime; you just sat.

A motion at the nose of the plane caught his eye. He looked up and saw Tech Sergeant Frank Braith standing there. Braith was staring at him—almost, but not quite smiling.

At first Marquez was going to scowl and look down again. But something prompted him to meet Braith's stare. Funny, his feeling toward Braith—he didn't like him much any more, but at the same time he didn't especially hate him. He just plain didn't care one way or another about him. Braith had been pretty drunk the night he'd made so much trouble for Marquez, and Marquez could understand how a man could lose his head once in a while when he was pretty drunk. Well, anyway, he just didn't want anything to do with Braith.

Braith put his hand out and leaned on the nose of the airplane.

Marquez did frown this time. "You better not get near those guns, Sergeant."

"Why not?"

"They cock off sometimes."

"Look who's telling me."

Marquez shrugged. "You want to get killed, that's your business."

"You'd like to see it happen, wouldn't you?" Braith still held that cold, partial smile.

"It don't make nothing to me—but if you don't want to get killed, you better go off the line."

"Look, Pedro," said Braith, "I was hanging around airplanes when you were still playing with yo-yos."

Marquez shrugged again. He started to replace the nose plate.

A thin man with a motion picture camera came up and

225

said, "Hey, soldier—hey—do me a favor, will you?"

Marquez looked at him. "Sir?"

"Do that again. That business you were doing with the ammunition."

"Do it again?"

"I want to get a couple of shots of it." The man waggled the camera.

Marquez said, "But I'm not supposed to do it again." He was mildly puzzled.

Braith, at the nose of the airplane, snorted. "You crazy bastard, the guy wants to put you in the newsreel. If you don't want to do it for him, I will. I helped them develop this gun installation back at Lockheed when I worked there."

The newsreel man looked at Braith and said, "I want the kid to do it."

"It's okay with me, if he wants to," said Braith airily, in a way that implied that he was in charge. He was a little disappointed. He'd like it fine to be in the newsreels—maybe later on he could work himself into a picture if this guy kept shooting around the field.

Marquez said, "Okay, I'll do it for you, mister."

There was more activity all along the line now. Fuel trucks were rumbling up to the aircraft, topping the tanks with JP-1. Radio maintenance men were giving VHF and radio compass sets final checks. Crew chiefs were peering into scoops, wheel wells and tailpipes, testing canopies and surface controls. The curved basket antenna of the ground control radar trailer out near the center of the field was shifting and turning.

In the Group briefing room, just off the line, Colonel William A. Straker, Commanding General of the 66th Fighter-Bomber Wing, was holding a press conference. He stood before a huge map of Japan and Korea and looked at the correspondents seated before him. Behind them were several members of the staff, Captain Gorgas, the public information officer among them. Gorgas' job this morning was to ride herd on the correspondents and be sure they filed no copy until after the strike was successfully accomplished.

"By now, gentlemen," Straker began, with a hard white
226

smile, "I'm sure you suspect something's in the wind."

He drew a chuckle. Fine. Good start.

"I'm going to give you the whole story right now. Military security, of course, keeps this material from being released until the mission is over. I know you'll cooperate on that score."

Funny that he did not feel at ease today. He'd always felt quite natural addressing a group before—prided himself especially on his poise back in that pulpit in the mission in Virginia—but his timing, or something, was a little off today. Maybe that was because he had so much on his mind. Or maybe, more accurately, because he had one bothersome thing on his mind—

That Ronsdale woman. It seemed now perfectly incomprehensible to him that he had behaved the way he did. The alcohol had done it, of course; he should have known better than to let her tease him into drinking that much.

And yet he must not entirely blame her. Even though she was in many ways misguided, there were still a lot of fine basic things about Essie Ronsdale. No, he must be courageous and blame only himself. And he must have enough inner discipline to keep it from affecting his job. Only that was more easily determined than done. Even now he found it difficult to keep his mind on the press briefing he'd planned. He must drive . . . drive a little harder . . . he must use every ounce of strength now. . . .

He picked up a pointer and tapped a spot on the map near the Yalu River. "Tinju, gentlemen," he said. "You haven't heard of it much before, because we haven't talked about it much before."

The correspondents stirred with interest.

"And today every available plane in the theater—with all the armament they'll carry—is going to Tinju."

He paused to let that sink in.

"We call this a max effort, gentlemen. It's the first really big strike of the Korean War." He sat on the edge of the desk. "We haven't talked much about Tinju because we didn't want the enemy to know we were watching this place closely. But we've been photographing it every night by means of an advanced radar photo technique—I can't give you any more details on the equipment than that."

Pencils raced.

Straker turned to the map again. "The enemy has been making a tremendous troop build-up here—obviously for a big spring assault. As you know we've been hitting their roads and rail lines making day movement almost impossible for them. Now they've picked out a new route to bring troops down to the east central front, above Seoul. You can see how this natural valley line runs east of Pyongyang, and into Kaesong, which is their forward jump-off point. This time they're planning to move a horde of troops quickly—within the space of a few nights, we believe. They hope to expose them to aerial attack for a shorter period that way. But, of course, as you can see, the Red is putting all his eggs in one basket by doing this. Gentlemen—today I think we're going to upset that basket of eggs!"

There. That was better. The correspondents laughed and scribbled. They'd quote that one.

He went on. "The 66th Wing—forgive my pride in it—plays a leading role in the show today. As you know our pilots have something of a reputation for eliminating enemy troops. They like to call themselves 'The Manhunters.' Well, this job is tailor-made for them. Roughly speaking, the operation is going to work like a large game hunt. Other outfits will go in and flush the game—and the 66th will bag it."

They were still scribbling. He waited until most of them had stopped, then said, "Any questions, now?"

Herb Oscott looked up. He was a sallow, deceptively mild little man with pale blue eyes and steel-rimmed glasses. "I was just thinking," he said in a dry, cracked voice, which he appeared to produce only with great effort, "what's the big game going to be doing all this time you're flushing it?"

Straker laughed politely, but he was inwardly annoyed. "He'll be too surprised to do much of anything," he said.

"Hope so," said Oscott.

"You can bank on it," said the colonel. "You can quote me on that."

"What about air opposition?" Oscott persisted. "You're near the MIGs up there. Judging from the map they'd
228

almost be able to see you coming from across the Yalu."

"Don't worry too much about them, Mr. Oscott. We'll have our own fighter cover of F-86 Sabres keeping an eye on us." He wished the man wouldn't needle him like this. He wished, in fact, he didn't have to go through this nonsense with these correspondents—they all seemed to have what he could only think of as disbelieving eyes. Probably a Godless lot, too. And certainly a sloppy bunch, in their dress, in the very way they sprawled rather than sat upon their chairs. He understood most of them had been enlisted men in the last war, rather than officers. Easy to see why. Not that he actually had anything against enlisted men—nobody could say that Bill Straker wasn't as tolerant as they came, and the way he could overlook Essie Ronsdale's mistakes and weaknesses was certainly proof of that. After all, everybody wasn't fortunate enough to be thoroughly self-disciplined. With a little time and a little effort he could straighten out Essie Ronsdale so that you'd never know she—

Why the deuce couldn't he stop thinking of her?

Seemed his mind always wandered back to her no matter what subject he put it to.

He'd have to drive a little harder; concentrate a little more. He frowned unconsciously with the effort.

"Who do you think's flying the MIGs, anyway?" asked Oscott, almost languidly. "Russians, or what?"

"We don't know." Straker's voice became a little snappish. "Naturally, we have instructions to find out if we can. Shoot a MIG down some time and have our rescue helicopters go in and pick the pilot up."

Captain Gorgas was staring at him in a strained way.

Straker remembered then that this was classified information; this came under the heading of secret plans, and it was nothing to be handing to the press. He saw that they were all writing again.

"You can't print that," he said hastily.

Oscot's eyes were mild. "Why not, Colonel? Surely the enemy figures you plan on doing it."

"It's not up to me to guess what the enemy is thinking. It's classified information and you can't print it. If you try

229

to put it into your copy it'll be censored out. I'll make it my personal business to see that it is."

"Why don't you just leave that up to the censors, Colonel?"

Damn this Oscott! thought the colonel. He felt the steam pressure build up within him. He clenched his fists and held it back. Easy . . . easy, now, don't lose control . . . been working a little too hard lately, that was the only trouble . . . he should have taken time off for an hour or so of meditation in the chapel . . . to do that had crossed his mind yesterday, as a matter of fact, but somehow he'd felt a little too tainted for the chapel after that business with Essie; he'd had the idea the guilt might wear off a little in time . . . oh, damn, now his thoughts were getting confused. He didn't ordinarily allow them to get confused like this.

His hands were still clenched. He opened them and straightened his shoulders. With tremendous effort he forced a smile. "Because, Mr. Oscott," he said, "sometimes the censors make mistakes—just as I did a moment ago in bringing the whole darned subject up."

He got a good laugh out of that one.

He felt better.

But he was still anxious to get into the air, and fly, and be away from all this nonsense for a change.

2

In the briefing room Major Pete Ronsdale sat quietly by himself, a little off from the rest, and scowled at the mission data card in his hand. The briefing proper had ended, and Chaplain Heyden was up there praying for all of them. The colonel's idea. The chaplain droned a bit. *Keep us, we beseech Thee, from harm as we pass through the Valley of the Shadow of Death. . . .*

Why did he have to remind everybody of it? thought Ronsdale. It was bad enough to sit here and know it was coming, without having to be reminded of it.

He noticed the smoke from his cigarette wavering as it went upward in a spiral ribbon. His hand was shaking. He took a deep breath to control the shaking. That wouldn't do. Wouldn't do at all. None of them knew yet how frightened he was on these missions; they thought instead he was great; they thought he was a hero.

Sometimes it was just too much to keep up the front. Sometimes he wanted to scream out the truth and be done with it. But he couldn't; he couldn't really do that.

Anyway—two people knew the truth. Dick Tindle was one. Dick had been cold and impersonal ever since the day Ronsdale had begged him not to reveal his cowardice. That was painful, losing Dick's friendship like that. But losing Essie was even worse. Yes, he'd definitely lost Essie now, and he couldn't very well kid himself that he had not. Oh, they still lived together, and they still smiled at each other and said good morning . . . they still kept up all the pretenses . . . but in the last week he'd sensed that they were further apart than ever. Essie seemed to have some kind of secret. As though something had happened to her, and it suddenly made all the difference in the world. She no longer showed the same signs of affection—obedient devotion was perhaps a better phrase—and she no longer wanted to be loved at night in that insatiable way. . . .

He sensed that sooner or later it would have to end in divorce. He sighed.

The prayer ended.

Then they all left the briefing room and Ronsdale picked up his chute and helmet and strolled out to the line. A movie cameraman took a shot of him walking across the sunny ramp.

"Don't look at the camera, Major!"

Ronsdale didn't.

The movieman said, "Thanks," and dashed off somewhere.

Tech Sergeant Braith had been greatly interested in this movie cameraman for the past quarter-hour. He had followed him after he'd left Corporal Marquez; he'd lumbered alongside of him as he strolled down the line. He'd asked the sizes of the three lenses on the camera's turret and then began a discourse on how he, Braith, had helped this Austrian physicist develop the Zoomar lens that was so popular at sports events now. Only a few weeks ago Braith had read an article on this in a photography magazine and his immensely clever mind had retained most of the details.

The movie cameraman was professionally taciturn and noncommital about the whole thing. Braith felt about this man much the way he often felt about Sergeant MacInnes: the man could see through him. He'd felt that way about that heavy-lidded Lieutenant Cohen, too.

But Braith was not to be put off so easily. They came to Major Ronsdale's airplane. Braith talked a little about the major, explained what a great guy he was and how they were buddies—like this—and he held up his fingers, entwined.

"Mm," the newsreel man had said absent-mindedly.

"That's him now," said Braith.

"Who?"

"Major Ronsdale. Coming across the ramp."

"Yeah?" The movieman squinted.

. ."*Looks like a pilot, don't he? Brother, there's one officer's got everything.*"

"Ngh," said the newsreel man, and nodded. He left Braith abruptly and trotted out across the ramp toward Ronsdale walking, twisting and squatting for his angles.

Ronsdale came up to the airplane then and saw Braith. Braith was startled to see that the major's face was somewhat pale. His lips looked thinner today. But maybe that was just the way he'd trimmed his neat mustache.

"Hello, Braith."

"Hi, Major." Braith grinned and waved.

Ronsdale turned away hastily, and then Ronsdale's crew chief came running up and the two of them held a short, muttered conversation about the airplane. When Ronsdale climbed into the cockpit the movieman backed off and photographed that, too.

The crew chief came around to the front of the airplane and saw Braith. "Let's clear, Sergeant," he said briskly.

Braith scowled and moved off toward the edge of the wing.

The movieman made a wide circle to photograph the airplane from the front.

Hell, Braith was thinking, these pictures would be in every damn movie theater in the States. And on television, too, probably. He would sure like to be in them. As a matter of fact, as soon as that damned crew chief moved

232

out of the way he would get into 'em. Damned if he wouldn't. . . .

In the cockpit Major Ronsdale made his check nervously. He hated the narrow confinement of the cockpit; he wanted sometimes to beat his fists against the canopy after it was closed, break through, and then run as far as possible from the airplane. From this alien thing. This machine, this insect . . . this bloodless thing, whatever it was . . . this weapon, this fine-edged weapon . . . this product of all the hard minds, the squint-eyed minds, the beings that fought each other, not by reason, but by instinct, indeed—by compulsion! He felt apart from them always. He stood aside and watched as they banded into groups . . . and the groups fought . . . and within the groups, the individuals fought. Fight upon fight, wave upon wave, node upon node. And Ronsdale off to one side—

He had always felt off to one side in his choir days. Way back, long ago that was: in those days of heavenly sound and the sweetness of the white flowers on Easter morning. He had been happy then. He had never really been happy since. He knew this now.

But all the others would swear he was happy. He had so much.

He was leading a flight today. The controller in Group ops called him on Charley channel. "Candy Zebra Leader —you'll take off in about five minutes."

"Roger," said Ronsdale. "I'll hold at the end of the runway. Going up to twenty-five percent now." He spoke to the other three pilots of his flight. "Rest of you got that?"

They rogered back.

He advanced the throttle slowly and felt the airplane break reluctantly from its stand. He steered the nose wheel with the rudder pedals in order to swing the ship out to the ramp. He had made his final check—chest harness locked, oxygen on NORMAL, gyro caged—the sun, coming through the plexiglass was quite hot upon his face and shoulders; where the rubber oxygen mask pressed tight against his cheeks there was profuse sweat. The cockpit smelled, somehow, of metal.

This machine: it would be more beautiful in flight, but

233

it was hard and squat and ugly now. It was a monument to the squabblers. It was a—

He had only a momentary glimpse of the figure that seemed to come suddenly toward the nose of his airplane as he turned. He tromped on the brakes. Damn—he should have looked before turning. But this man shouldn't have been out there on the ramp either.

It was too late.

Good God, yes—truly—it was too late!

There was a slamming noise; there was a choking of air pressure and a scream that was audible even above the whining from the turbine blades.

Ronsdale yanked the throttle back and heard the loud VROOM! of flame-out.

But of course it was too late. Lord, it couldn't be . . . it couldn't be real, yet it was; the thing was fact now, it had already happened.

In the last instant he had recognized the man that had been sucked with terrible force into his air scoop. He shoved the canopy back and tumbled from the airplane. The crowd was already gathering. They were running this way from all directions. As they arrived they were queerly silent; they said nothing and stared, horrified. Ronsdale stared, too, at the half-body hanging from the air scoop. *There is nothing quite so red as blood,* he thought. . . .

After that things were blurred for a while. He remembered trying to pull the body out, and he remembered someone saying there wasn't any use trying that now. He didn't remember exactly when Colonel Straker arrived. But here he was, of a sudden; here was Straker facing him, looking with odd intentness into his eyes. They were standing off to one side. An ambulance truck had come.

Straker said, "How do you feel, Pete?"

"I'm all right." His voice (the strange, faraway voice that came out of him) was steady enough, thank God.

"Not shaken, are you, Pete?"

"No, no. I feel rotten about this, of course. But—"

"It wasn't your fault. This man—what was his name?"

"Braith. Tech Sergeant Frank Braith."

"—Braith. He should have had better sense than to stroll around the line like this with jets taxying. Lord knows,

234

we've put out enough information on ground safety."

"Yes, sir. I suppose so."

"Are you *sure* you're all right?"

"Of course I'm all right, sir."

"Well," said Straker, "after something like this you ought to rest. But I know how anxious you are to be in on today's show."

"Yes, sir."

"You still want to go along?"

"Of course, sir." *Had he said that? Was it really his own voice saying that?*

"All right." Straker put his hand on Ronsdale's shoulder, and smiled his hard, white smile. "I'll yank Lieutenant Harold out of my flight. You can take his airplane and come along."

"Thank you, sir," said Ronsdale.

He had wanted courage many times, but never before had he wanted it this much. He would have given anything now for the courage to admit his cowardice.

When Straker walked off he again felt cold, miserable and alone.

3

Tindle, heading for his airplane, saw Colonel Straker approaching him. He did not particularly want to speak to the colonel. But Straker saw him first, and came toward him. Tindle shifted the parachute he carried over one shoulder, and the soup-bowl helmet under his other arm.

The sunlight was bright on the concrete ramp, forcing him to squint. This light overwhelmed everything today; it was unreal. Tindle, in fact, had been under a queer sense of unreality ever since returning to Akuni night before last. He had ridden the air courier down from Tokyo, sleeping most of the way, and the rest of the time thinking of Teriko ... trying in his mind's eye to recall her elusive beauty, her dancelike motion, the sound of her voice. He knew now that he was not truly in love with her—not, for instance, as he had once been in love with Martha—but he still wanted her very badly.

Well, in about twenty-four hours he would have her again. They had made all the arrangements in Tokyo before

235

he left: he'd bought her train ticket to Korokua, the town near the air base, and he'd made a reservation in a hotel for her yesterday. She'd find a little house, possibly on the shore, where they could live together down here and have all the time the ecstasy they'd found together in the country town south of Tokyo.

He'd tried to do something about that pricking of his conscience. He'd said, "Teriko, darling, you shouldn't be wasting this best part of your life as somebody's mistress. You ought to be finding yourself a good husband."

She'd given him her wide, dark-eyed look and said, "But you love me, neh, Dick-san?"

"Of course," he'd said. He hadn't known how he could explain if he'd said no.

"So," she said. "Nothing else important, desho-o?"

That was when he should have had the strength to end it. But he hadn't.

And here was Colonel William A. Straker, salt in his wounds.

Straker stopped, looked Tindle up and down, and half-smiled. "Well, Captain, I see you made it."

"Did you think I wouldn't?"

"I wasn't sure. But, well—frankly, I'm glad you did. This is going to be another chance for you. I hope you'll appreciate it properly."

"I don't think I know what you're talking about, Colonel."

"Let's put it this way." Straker changed his stance. He looked younger—even somewhat dashing—in his flying clothes. He had a bright blue scarf tucked into the neck of his poplin coverall. "I was possibly hasty in condemning you for your poor showing after you came back from forward control. Some people need time to adjust themselves to flying again. And, in honesty, Tindle, I must admit that I was emotionally angry. A commander shouldn't allow himself to become emotionally angry."

Dutch uncle, thought Tindle. Big brother. Nuts to him. He said, "Go on."

"Your record's good, Tindle; I went over it again after you left. I don't think an innate coward could have made a record like that. I'm sure you've got the basic stuff in

236

you somewhere, and I'm sure this difficulty of yours was only temporary. Possibly personal troubles. Isn't that so?"

"I don't know," said Tindle. "Maybe you know. You seem to think you do."

"Sometimes it's easier for another person to see what's wrong," replied Straker. "Another person has more perspective, you see."

"Colonel," said Tindle wearily, "if you don't mind—" He started to move off.

"Just a minute, Tindle. I'm not through yet. And I think you'll want to hear what I have to say. I told you, I went over your record. I was interested to see that you'd had experience in staff work—plans and operations, wasn't it?"

"I worked at it a while in 'forty-three."

"You must have done more than just work at it. Your rating shows superior. Good staff men are always scarce, Tindle. And now that Ronsdale's commanding the 109th, our Wing ops section could use a little bolstering. How would you like to work in ops?"

Of course he would like it. He would like anything that didn't require him to drop bits of hell on living human beings and watch them shrivel, watch them burn. But he'd be damned if he'd let Straker know he could be pleased. He said, "A job's a job, Colonel."

"You know you don't mean that." Straker laughed; thinly and somehow not whole-heartedly. "Look here, Captain, if you'll try to be frank and honest with me, I assure you I'll reciprocate."

"Do you mind unraveling that a bit more?"

"Not at all. The fact is, Tindle, I'm not one hundred percent certain of you, yet. As I said, I have an idea you can be useful in my operations section, but I want to see, first, what you'll do on today's mission."

"What's that got to do with staff work?"

"Even a staff man ought to be a man who can come through in a pinch. Do you understand?"

Tindle stared back for a full second, then nodded slowly. "Yes. I understand. I understand perfectly. You're a great big important bird colonel now, aren't you, Straker? The big boss. The word nobody can question. Those chickens on your shoulder make you all-wise, don't they? Enough
237

to be judge and jury on anything. Maybe they make you God himself—"

"Watch your language, Tindle!"

Tindle could feel the dry whiteness of his face. "You're a religious man, aren't you, Colonel? You probably think of yourself as a good Christian, and a fine, compassionate soul. An understanding soul. But let me tell you this, Colonel, you don't even begin to understand what goes on in a man's mind and in his guts. You don't know what it's like because you've anesthetized yourself with all the surface techniques of goodness. You're a technician, like all the rest: you're very clever and skillful at what you do, but you don't do anything worth being clever and skillful at."

Tindle was wound up now. He went on: "I'll bet you can quote a dozen passages on forgiveness from the Bible —but can you bring yourself to forgive an enemy shooting at you from a hillside? You can lead a whole wing of jet pilots in battle—but can you lead them in real morality? In absolute integrity? Could you be clever and skillful at that? Could you—oh, hell, forget it."

Straker said, "I'll do more than forget it." He was calm again. Calm and cold. "I'll ignore it. And I'm not backing out on my promise, Captain. Show me what you can do today, and that staff job's yours."

In spite of himself Tindle felt a curious admiration for the man. He tried not to show it. He said, "Is that all, sir?"

Straker glanced at his wrist watch and said, "That's all."

They both walked off, toward their respective airplanes.

4

At twenty thousand feet Candy Baker flight was still climbing; the Shooting Stars were already over Korea, over the cutting edge of the peninsula just north of Pusan. They came to a layer of cloud. "Let's close it up," called Captain Kingsley, who was leading the flight. They tightened the formation. Now, in the milky cloud, they could barely see one another. It was hot in the cloud: the tiny droplets magnified the sun.

Tindle flew on Kingsley's right wing. The feeling of unreality had passed; his head was clear. Always was, in the air. He was thinking now that he ought not to have lost his

238

temper with Straker that way. Odd that Straker took it without slapping him in the guard house, or at least dropping a fine formal reprimand in his two-oh-one file—probably part of Straker's vanity to feel that he was above such petty reprisal. Anyway, it had done no good. Made not a dent in the Colonel's stone mind.

In a way, the colonel was lucky to be so inflexible. He had a fine set of yardsticks for his behavior; he had a Standard Operating Procedure—an S.O.P. Anybody who had an S.O.P. was fortunate. He could act, then, in any given situation, according to the neatly laid out instructions. It saved the agony of making constant decisions. And it could even be convenient: if you wanted very much to do something that seemed to conflict with S.O.P. you could usually rationalize and make it fit. For instance, Straker, the humble Christian, must really abhor killing—but he could always believe that in these just and holy wars he was killing for the eventual Good.

The cheap and easy way, this S.O.P.—and yet if you were without any set of principles, you were in Tindle's shoes. You were almost constantly in dilemma.

Where? Where?

Somewhere . . . somewhere here, thought Tindle, looking at the glowing milky cloud all about . . . watching it shred at the bite of his wings. Somewhere there is an S.O.P. for myself upon this earth and in this time . . . for all who must feel this same bewilderment . . . for those who have watched the stupid as well as the vastly intelligent fail to make a really habitable dwelling of this world.

He wanted Martha, of a sudden. He wanted her again, and all the difficulties of their union. He wanted and needed that double strength, now. This time it would work, because he would expect and accept the things that occasionally came between them. Dependent travel to Japan would be open again shortly; he could send for her. If he had that staff job it would all be easy.

He felt this way, now—but would he feel this way when he had come back from this mission?

And Teriko: if he had Martha, he could not have this most exquisite pleasure he had ever known. There could be at least another year with Teriko if he didn't send for

239

Martha. He was sure that Teriko would want that year, also.

So he could still not make a decision. He still had no S.O.P.

"*Let's go down on the eighty-eight*," came Kingsley's voice, breaking into Tindle's thoughts.

Tindle looked. They were almost to the target area. Ahead, and far below, he could see the etched pattern in a small, bowl-like valley that was the village of Tinju. Other jets, making rendezvous, had already begun to join them. No one had struck the target yet. There had been a last-minute change in plan, and the F-80s of the 66th Wing were to go in and help knock out the flak positions, in addition to their main job of catching the troops. The pilots had frowned and shifted uncomfortably in their seats upon hearing this change of plan.

And now it was quiet, in the sky, on the ground below. Not so much as a column of smoke rose anywhere in sight.

It was an eerie quiet, and Tindle's scalp began to prickle.

CHAPTER ELEVEN

1

TINJU was a target much more to everybody's liking. It was behind the lines—which was where air power ought to operate. The specialists had fine theories on this.

When the Korean War had begun—nearly a year before —Air brass had been involved for half a decade in a congressional fight for an air arm built around heavy bombers. Nobody foresaw anything like the queer situation in Korea. The words "air power" meant for most professional minds images of aircraft like the six engine B-36. The B-29 Superfort that thrilled a nation with its range and size in the last war was now classed as a "medium" bomber. It was occasionally referred to as obsolescent. A nice big word, that, and the military enjoys big words—(it never uses, it utilizes; it never just goes some place, it proceeds)—and in this case the word "obsolescent" came in handily as a tag for something they privately believed obsolete, but didn't quite dare to call obsolete.

240

At any rate, they had been thinking in terms of long range bombardment, and here came the Korean War with its accent on short range, pinpoint strikes near the actual ground fighting in the early days. A specialized job, this: it called for different skills and different equipment. The Air Force was caught with its flaps down.

Nor was this wholly the Air Force's fault. A short-sighted nation had kept not much of a military establishment in Japan and Korea, and only a few airplanes were available there. Most of them were World War II types, obsolete— obsolescent, if you will.

The first attack upon enemy troops was made in late June, 1950, by an F-82, a postwar development of the Mus- tang fighter, with two bodies set upon one wing. This air- plane was painted black, carried radar equipment in the nose, and had been designed as a night fighter. It was there for the defense of Japan. There were also, in those early days, a few F-80 Shooting Star jets available, but most of the work was done by F-51 Mustangs.

Now, the Mustang had been designed as a high-altitude fighter in the days when twenty-five and thirty thousand feet was high altitude. It was a high-speed fighter when four hundred miles an hour was considered high speed. It was a ferret-nosed, liquid-cooled fighter, and amidship on its belly was a large air scoop for cooling the oil system. The liquid cooling system and the air scoop were both extremely vulnerable to enemy ground fire. One rifle bullet could, on occasion, bring down a Mustang.

As fast as the F-80 jets came from the United States they were put into use. The F-80 proved a fine ground support airplane, but it aged quickly. Some of these jets, like one- hoss shays, fell apart all at once after constant, steady use.

Meanwhile, the experts turned hastily from the study of long-range bombardment to the new job of ground support. Actually, they didn't care for the word "support"—it im- plied a secondary role. They didn't like being looked upon as a kind of flying artillery. The Air Force was still fiercely jealous of its newly won autonomy. But there was no other really satisfactory term, and so, ground support it was. They were careful, however, to make a distinction between actual front-line strikes and those at supplies and communications behind the lines. These last came under the heading of what was called "interdiction."

Yes, the fine theories were spun.

The function of air power was all carefully outlined into an overall doctrine. This gospel was widely printed, widely discussed, and widely taught its members by the Air Force. It was the word; the ungarbled word. The first job of air power, said the word, was to isolate the battlefield. The next job was to attempt to destroy the enemy upon this isolated battlefield. (It was admitted that the ground forces might have some part in this phase.) And while all this was going on, longe-range bombers would be eliminating the enemy's vital nerve centers far, far behind the lines.

But there could be none of the third phase in Korea. The United States was not officially at war with Russia or China. Ground support and interdiction were the only jobs left.

The specialists and the technicians, individually and for the most part, did these jobs well. Combat crews demonstrated so much heroism that heroism—as in any war—presently became commonplace, and behind the fighting, staff officers often rode their swivel chairs so furiously and for such long hours that they courted nervous breakdown.

Still, the Yalu River border of Manchuria could not be crossed, and this led to a certain frustration on all levels. To be able to strike at Tinju, today, which was at least at the outer limit, was something of a great relief to everyone concerned.

There was a tacit feeling that everybody had been waiting for this show for a long time. . . .

2

"I'll lay a couple of rockets first," said Kingsley, leading the flight. "Keep a sharp lookout. Stay close behind, Candy Baker Flight."

He half-rolled, changing direction, then curved down suddenly upon what was apparently a cluster of rice paddies in a bowl-shaped valley. They looked like scales.

Tindle followed—surprised to find himself quite relaxed in his flying. The other two jets of Candy Baker flight came along in Tindle's wake.

A little rice-bowl valley, thought Tindle, watching it grow in the frame of his windshield. A green valley that someone planted among the harsh mountains of this peninsula. A road winding through it, and the tall poplars lining the road like flagstaffs at a county fair. Now some thatched huts: one or two larger houses with roofs of gray tile. And around the bowl the red-earth hills dotted with bottle-green shrubs.

Not a sign of life on those slopes—but here the troops were bivouacked. He wouldn't be able to see them until he was right down upon them; he wouldn't know the exact locations of the anti-aircraft guns until they opened fire. And they wouldn't open fire, giving away their positions, until they were certain that this was a genuine attack.

Kingsley, in the lead, wouldn't pull flak this first time. Anyone after him might.

Tindle, plummeting through the silence, wondered now if he was afraid. Probably a part of him was. His stomach felt hollow and his forehead was clammy. His mouth was dry. And yet he could not say that he knew any sort of terror. It was not especially difficult to keep on diving and wait for the flak that surely would come in the next few seconds.

This was the essence of air war, he reflected. Down on the ground, on the grubby, crawling surface of the planet, you could see and hear so much more clearly and immediately the forces that were hellbent to send violent pain or death upon you. There, your senses were gripped—here, only your intellect. And the intellect was braver than the senses. Here, too, you felt that if death should come it would be quick. And here you seldom looked upon the face of the man that killed you.

And so it was not difficult to be brave in the air—at least in these fighter-bomber missions they were now flying. There was even a feeling of superiority brought about by the altitude. Men in the days before machines must have felt like this when they mounted a horse and looked down upon the foot-creatures.

No, he was not afraid; he was really not afraid. If anything, he was indifferent.

All this in his mind, his thinking mind. But in a few

243

seconds another part of him would take over: the part that could not bring itself to kill. Then, perhaps, in spite of himself, he would pull out of his dive too soon, or he would miss with his rockets, or he would jink shamefully to the side.

Straker would be watching.

Straker was leading the flight behind them—Candy Dog flight—and he would be smugly watching.

Well, to hell with him. To hell with his staff job and his role of the great, kind father. And to hell with his finely machined and unidirectional mind. To hell with all of them, and what they thought—

But he knew he didn't mean that. He wanted desperately to exist in relation to others . . . that he could not quite achieve this was the basis of his perpetual, gnawing loneliness.

Ahead, Kingsley's rockets suddenly broke from his wings and floated earthward, trailing foxbrushes of smoke and flame. His ship pulled up, curving to the left. The rockets exploded in a clump of thatched huts and flat-topped trees. There was a moment of orange flame, then smoke.

Tindle slid the crook of his finger to the stick trigger. He glanced at his rocket switches: they were armed. And then several lines of bright grubworms began to stream up toward him from a green embankment to the right of Kingsley's rocket hit. Tindle sticked and ruddered a sixteenth of an inch, and swung his nose toward this flak position. The grubworms passed far to his left, seeming to curve. Now suddenly there were black puffs in the air around him. They slammed by as he flew through them. Through the black orchard . . . through the dark-seeded grove. He held the embankment in his sight, and within that illuminated circle it seemed to rock gently for a while.

An embankment, and curious bright missiles coming from it. An inanimate thing. No men. No human beings to cut in half or roast alive.

Crazy idea! You thought crazily at a time like this—

He squeezed the trigger and the rockets went off and the ship nosed up slightly after they left. In the instant that he pulled away he saw his rockets strike a short distance in

244

front of the embankment. He had missed—but not by a great deal. The important thing was: he had been able to fire. *He'd been in control of himself.* The ship curved into its climb, and the centrifugal force crushed him to the seat. The carbon dioxide bottle in the packed life raft on which he sat dug painfully into his buttocks, but he didn't care.

He laughed. Even though his mouth would not open easily, he laughed.

And then, when he came out of his climb at about three thousand feet, and leveled off to swing around for another pass, he saw with some surprise that the air in every direction was thick with these glowing streams and flak puffs. He frowned. They hadn't predicted this at the briefing. They'd said the flak would be both light and inaccurate. A bright flash to his left—he swung his head. He saw a jet grow a sudden skin of flame, stumble in the air, then spin abruptly toward the ground. . . .

"Candy Group, this is Candy Leader!" That was Colonel Straker's voice, "Don't let it bother you! Stick with it! Keep that flak down!"

There was a curious hidden elation in the colonel's voice. As though he were glad that there was unexpected flak; that the job would not be so easy after all.

And now the colonel's flight of four airplanes, two thousand feet below, was going through a concentration of all that flak. Toy planes, bobbing and weaving over a green carpet someone had laid there in order to simulate the earth.

Tindle went back in. He laid a second brace of rockets on the embankment. Right into it this time—possibly because it was already smoking and flaming, and was thus a more visible target. The automatic fire no longer came up from there. He climbed again, in Kingsley's wake, feeling much more at ease now. Kingsley led them to a different target on this third pass: a clump of trees halfway up a hillside. Tindle's tracers went directly into this target on the first pass.

"Keep it up, buddy—you're doing fine," said Kingsley's voice. Tindle knew it was meant for him. He wished Kingsley hadn't said anything. It was better not to recall; it was better not to think in any way; it was better to be only in this vacuum.

He laughed again, and this time rather wildly.

3

Major Pete Ronsdale flew number four position in Colonel Straker's flight. When the colonel himself led the first pass in, Ronsdale was chilly with fear. He felt a sudden numbness in his lower lip, and then realized that he had been holding it too long snagged by his upper teeth. He let it go and felt warm blood upon his chin. His green rubber oxygen mask, tight about his mouth, was wet with condensed breath and perspiration.

Ahead—to his right—there was a bright flash in mid-air. He saw a jet lob off toward the ground. "Oh, God, oh, God," he said.

Straker was barking some nonsense or other. A pep talk. Ronsdale couldn't absorb it. His hearing was frozen; he was all frozen with fear.

Now it was his turn. That green embankment down there. He forced himself to hold his sights upon it, and as he triggered off his rockets he shut his eyes. "Oh, God, oh, God," he breathed as he pulled away. His headsets were thick with chatter now; he could understand none of it. He was violently ill in his stomach. On the pullout of the third pass he was unable to control his sphincter. At this ultimate shame he reddened with embarrassment, and then cried aloud—a wordless animal cry of despair.

On the fourth pass it all became just too much for Major Ronsdale.

He had been diving and turning, following the others in. He had been looking directly at the target. Abruptly burning lights began to come toward him—a new gun position near the poplar-lined road, one that hadn't begun firing until now. He knew that in a tenth of a second his sights would swing about and encompass this new target, and then, with only a touch of his finger, he could send bright deadly things back into it. He could not hold his dive that much longer. He sobbed, and his sob became a gasp as he pulled away.

Now, out of the welter of talk, one voice began to
246

emerge. He didn't know why he caught this one, but he did, and it was sharp in his ears. He wasn't sure to whom the voice belonged.

"*The colonel's hit!*" it said. "*Watch it! Watch that new battery!*"

Somebody else said, in a ridiculously calm way, "*Roger.*"

Ronsdale was at three thousand. He dipped his wing and looked down, and a moment later he saw the tiny white plane that curved toward a hillside and trailed black smoke. If Ronsdale had fired on that new gun position this might not have happened. He realized this suddenly and icily. He was gripping the finger-molded handle of the stick as though he would choke it. His fingers were numb.

He kept watching. A heavy speck flew from the colonel's plane, tumbled in the slipstream, and then a moment later a parachute appeared, like a suddenly flowering white blossom.

"*Cap him, Candy Able! Cap him till those choppers get here!*"

Somebody must have called for rescue helicopters. Ronsdale hadn't heard it. He swung now to a heading that would take him across the hillside where the colonel's parachute was still falling. The parachute looked like a white handkerchief blowing gently over the green carpet now. There was no flak in the vicinity of the hillside. In a second or two Ronsdale would be there. He felt a tremendous wave of relief; his eyes misted over with happy tears.

Over the hillside the three remaining planes of Candy Able flight began to make a wide, continuous orbit. They were about two thousand feet high. Ronsdale, looking down along his lower wing could see everything on the ground in sharp, tiny detail.

"*Delicious Control, this is Candy Able Two.*"

"*Delicious here. Go ahead.*"

"*Candle Able Two. We have a man down here. Parachuted down. We're capping him now. Can you get a chopper up here?*"

"*Uh—roger, understand, Candy Able. I'll put it through Jig Oboe Charley. Give me your coordinates. . . .*"

Some moments later: "*Hello, Candy Able Two, this is Delicious Control. We have two choppers in the vicinity returning from an abort. They're headed your way now."*

"Roger, and thanks. We'll stand by. Candy Able out."

"Out to you, Candy Able. Good luck."

The parachute had landed and collapsed. Ronsdale, searching carefully, could presently make out Straker's figure below, moving in the vicinity of the parachute. Couldn't quite tell what he was doing.

Then Ronsdale wondered if the colonel had seen him jink fearfully when that hidden battery opened up. If the colonel knew about this, he wouldn't be able to pretend any longer. The colonel would hate him for it, of course. Maybe even find grounds for court-martial. Desertion in the face of the enemy, or something like that. God . . . that would shame Essie terribly; that would all but shame her to death. Funny—he loved Essie, he really did. Maybe more than ever now. She'd always been a good wife; she'd always made a nice, shining, orderly home for him, but in the past week there had been something more desirable than ever about her. Maybe because she'd always been so dutiful before; maybe in his heart he'd always resented that a little. Maybe there was a kind of bitchiness about her now, and maybe he liked that better. He was suddenly sure that he *hadn't* lost her irretrievably: that there was something he could do about the whole situation after all if he'd only try . . . try hard. . . .

Oh, God, more than ever he wanted to live now; he wanted to live successfully and be admired by all about him. No one could blame him, of course, for Braith's accident; no one could have possibly known how he had hated Braith. Furthermore he must stop imagining that he might somehow have avoided that accident by reacting more quickly. He must not even begin to think that he had unconsciously murdered Braith.

He must get back to Akuni whole and safe. And this time he must work it so that he wouldn't have to fly missions any more. There'd be a way. Only the other day the colonel had been saying that the staff was weak without him, that good staff men were hard to find. He'd present it to the colonel as though he were making a sacrifice. "Naturally, I want to fly missions, sir—who wouldn't? But if going back to staff work is for the good of the Wing, well, I'll do it."

248

If he was courteous and careful and used the right phrases he would be able to swing it.

Bits of smoke began to feather away from the top of the hill where the colonel's parachute lay. At first their significance escaped Ronsdale.

He looked back toward the valley where they had attacked. The air immediately over it was dotted with gray flak. Drops of India ink settling in a glass of water might look like this. And there were cross-hatchings of white yarn where the tracers sprayed up from the ground, and there were the small metallic planes, the toy planes, spinning and weaving through all of it. He saw another jet lose control and wing crazily into a hillside, exploding when it struck, sending up thick black smoke after that. Someone had certainly slipped up on this one. Almost seemed the enemy had known they were coming, had set a trap for them.

He was over the ridgetop now, in a vertical bank. He glanced down casually at first—and then his eyes widened. There a mass of mustard-yellow figures, seemed to ooze from the ground, and began to move toward the white marker of the colonel's parachute further down the slope.

He thumbed the mike button on the throttle. "Candy Able, this is Candy Able Four. Troops near the colonel— right on top of the hill there! Maybe five hundred yards from him!"

"This is Candy Three. I see 'em. Let's clobber 'em!"

"Hold it—hold it. I'll try to call in a flight that's got napalm."

"Yeah, roger. That's better." There was acquiescence—a kind of respect—in the man's voice. They still looked up to him, thought Ronsdale. In the quick heat of everything it was doubtful that anyone had noticed how he'd shied from that automatic weapons fire. They wouldn't blame him for Straker's accident, then. He was still in the clear . . . in the clear . . . just get back from this nightmare, now . . . just get back, that was all he had to do. . . .

He used the radio again. "This is Candy Able Four. We're capping our flight leader here, about ten miles northwest of Tinju. He's got troops around him, and we need napalm. Anybody got napalm? Over."

An answer came and Ronsdale recognized Major Goff's

flat, nasal voice. "Roger, Candy Able Four. This is Candy X-Ray Leader. Just got here. Fat with napalm, buddy. Fat with it."

"Northwest, X-Ray. We're northwest about ten miles."

"I have you in sight," said Goff, and clicked off with two audible blips of the mike button.

Seconds later Candy X-Ray flight came in. The four jets, twisting, came down from the higher sky, dove, then threw their chins upward and climbed again. Yellow, elongated eggs tumbled away. Flame appeared, then grew upon the hillside; oval spots at first, and presently the smoke poured away from each spot and fused into a great black cloud.

Ronsdale spiraled down a thousand feet and skidded into place behind X-Ray flight. He saw figures on the ground, some scattered and sprawled, others scuttling from the burning areas. He said, "Nice work, X-Ray. Beautiful job."

"Thank you," said Goff. "That'll cost you one bottle of scotch."

"Get it from the colonel."

"Looks like I might. There's the choppers, at nine o'clock."

Ronsdale looked and saw the two helicopters waterbugging over the earth far to the south. He smiled. Everything was fine now; everything was going to be all right. He might even get a damned medal for capping the colonel like this—

"This is X-Ray Leader. The colonel's still got trouble. That's a tank down there!"

"Where? Where? I don't see a tank."

"Edge of the road. Near the bottom of the hill there!"

Ronsdale saw a tiny dark blob with the giveaway length of a gun barrel showing. A machine gun winked. Near the white parachute Straker was no longer visible.

"That's our meat, that tank," said Candy X-Ray Leader. "Let's go."

Ronsdale was sweating again; he was dizzy, drunk. He heard himself say, "Follow me in, Candy X-Ray. Make it evasive. Keep moving."

"Right with you, skipper," said X-Ray. That faint note of admiration in his voice. It gave Ronsdale no pleasure this time.

He led the attack. His body seemed not his own. The

real Pete Ronsdale seemed to float a small distance above that body, watching it perform, and having no real control over it. With fascination and with some awe he saw this strange being move stick, throttle and rudder pedal. He saw a hand click the toggle switches and arm the remaining rockets.

Just this once. Afterward everything will be all right. One more time, that was all.

A sheet of flame showed for a moment where the tank lay. Something jolted his wing and nearly snapped the airplane into a vertical bank. He righted it, and backsticked. He knew that his rockets had missed, but he didn't really care about that: in his excitement he realized that he'd made this pass without flinching, *and without fear.* It could be done! It could be done after all!

Suddenly he knew the secret of doing a terrifying thing without fear—or, more accurately, in spite of fear. It had to matter; it had to matter terribly to you.

He swung around for another pass. He looked down. The other two planes had both made their passes, and the tank still squatted there.

"Let's get him this time. You hear? Let's get him."

He didn't know whether they heard. The air was full of chatter now; everybody trying to get a word in. They were having a rough time over the Tinju valley—the whole sky was smoking over there. There were airplanes at all levels and there were bright lines and bright flashes throughout the sky.

Just this one time and everything will be all right.

Laugh. What was funny?

Well, it was all funny. The whole damn thing was funny. It was funny as hell that you should take a choir boy and make a fine figure of major and a fighter pilot out of him. What would Dad have said? Dad would have been proud, of course—but secretly Dad would have envied him. Dad would have made a much better fighter pilot. Instead Dad grew paunchy and proper in a brokerage office and played golf on Sundays.

The tank in his sight, now . . . the long gun swinging toward him. . . .

He would get it. Only that tank stood between himself

251

and no-pain, and it must be struck away. Hold it there: hold it smack in his windshield, and in the glowing circle of his sight. Abey his fire . . . wait . . . wait . . . oh, the son of a bitch, the rotten son of a bitch, and all the sons of bitches that fought each other and filled the world with fighting. The dirty sons of bitches.

But it was not enough to press a trigger and watch a missile fly. He wanted to feel the blow: he wanted his heart to feel the strength of it and know it had been struck.

He began to sing.

He knew this was madness, and he didn't care. He could feel his sanity slip away as a man feels a heavy load ease away. An emotion of tremendous joy came over him, suddenly replacing the terror that had been with him so long. He sang, and he could smell the lilies in the great, quiet church on Easter morning.

We praise Thee, Oh God. We acknowledge Thee to be the Lord. All the earth doth WOR-ship Thee. The Father ever-lasting!

He was in fine voice this morning.

He was forgiven. He knew he was forgiven. He was forgiven his weaknesses and his sins. Even having murdered Braith was all right on the books now. With forgiveness came strength. *Heaven and earth are full of the majesty of Thy glo-o-ry!*

And for an instant he saw the white hot blaze that covered everything. He kept his eyes open as the airplane struck the tank and exploded.

4

Colonel Bill Straker was surprised when he found himself floating earthward in a parachute. He did not remember being struck, nor did he remember bailing out. But something like that must have happened, for here he was —and some miles to the southwest, the air battle was still raging. Inky dots all over the sky down there. He could hear the crump of anti-aircraft and the heavy stutter of aerial fire.

He saw that he was coming down upon a long, sparsely vegetated hillside. He checked his own person. Still had his pistol in its shoulder holster, and the white escape belt with its sewn-in contents around his middle. He must remain cool now, he told himself. Others had walked out of North Korea, and so could he. It was even possible that a helicopter might come for him. He remembered how he'd insisted on thorough briefings for everyone on escape tactics, and this gave him a rather warm feeling of satisfaction, not at all lessened by his predicament.

The roar of near-by jets caught his attention. He looked up and to the southwest saw a formation of three jets in file swinging toward him. That would be the remainder of his flight. Probably Ronsdale leading them—it would be like Pete Ronsdale to take over at a time like this. They appeared to be deploying in order to fly cover.

Good thing, he thought, smiling, that he'd substituted Ronsdale for Lieutenant Harold this trip. He felt better with a man of Ronsdale's skill and judgment running the show.

He looked down again. Near the ground. It came toward him with increasing swiftness. He looked away from the ground and held his legs together with the knees slightly bent—that was what the manuals on jumping always said to do. He grasped the risers and waited.

The landing was hard. The pain came up through his legs and into his hips; his teeth jolted together. He hadn't known that you would hit this hard. He grunted in spite of himself, then collapsed and rolled quickly. Part of the parachute settled quietly to the earth beside him, and he scrambled upright again, and pulled on the lower shroud lines to bring the billowing remainder down. He slipped the cotter pin, punched the round harness lock, and the straps fell away.

Now he looked around him.

A quiet hillside, this; it seemed not an insect stirred here. The earth was reddish, rock-strewn and dry, and dwarf trees with twisted, corded limbs were scattered over it. There was a dirty yellow outcropping of rock at the crest, and the crest itself looked like the edge of an old flint arrowhead against the sky. Perhaps three hundred yards below the hillside flattened gently to become a broad valley. There were rice paddies and several huts in the valley; there was a narrow road—little more than a wagon trail—that ran at the foot of the slope.

Very well. He would make for the hilltop; first, because there was more likelihood of meeting the enemy in the valleys and on the roads, and second, because from the hilltop he'd be able to spot his rescuers more easily if they came.

He took the precaution of cocking the barrel of his forty-five, putting a cartridge into the chamber, and then he started to climb. He had been climbing for less than a minute when he heard near-by small-arms fire. He brought his head up sharply. He saw a wisp of gray smoke on the hillcrest, and then abruptly he heard a whining ricochet behind him.

Vrrrrr-WHEEEEEEEEENG!

Straker dropped, and rolled to the cover of a small, eroded trench. He drew his pistol.

Strange, finding troops in this remote spot. The enemy must have them scattered all over this area. What the deuce had happened to Intelligence, anyway, sending them into a hotbed like this one? Their strike would be a complete surprise the planners had said. But Straker would swear that the enemy had been sitting there waiting for them. And laughing all the time.

There must have been a leak somewhere. That seemed incredible with all the precautions they had taken, and with the tenets of military security subscribed to all the way—but the evidence of a leak was strong. One would almost think that somebody—somebody in his own Wing, perhaps—had been deliberately supplying the enemy with information about this strike. That sounded melodramatic, of course, but such things *did* happen. Might very well be some Comumnists around. After all, you could never tell who was a Communist and who was not. Or could you? Sometimes he'd come close to suspecting certain people of—well, pretty radical thinking. Take Captain Tindle. There was a man who might easily think along those lines.

He'd have to remember to look into Tindle a little further.

If he got out of this mess.

The firing on the ridgetop increased, and the bullets began to slap the ground around him. Then abruptly he
254

heard shouting up there and the firing stopped. At first he didn't know why. He lifted his head cautiously and looked. There were khaki-clad figures moving cautiously over the lip of the outcropping, lowering themselves, and then sliding downslope toward him. Ridiculous, squat, monkey-like figures. Baboons— that was what they reminded him of. And he would bet they were coming toward him because someone had given the order to capture, not to kill.

He sighted his pistol carefully, holding the sight just below one of the advancing figures. He steadied his right wrist with his left hand. He squeezed and fired. He ducked back again before he could see whether or not his bullet had struck.

Then Colonel Straker closed his eyes and held his hands—one still gripping the pistol—lightly together, and prayed.

"Our Father," he said confidently, "which art in heaven—"

The sound of a jet overhead drowned out the words in his mind. He rose, twisted about and looked. The jet curved from its dive and began to climb. Others were coming in behind it. He thought at first that this would be Ronsdale's flight, and then suddenly the hillside above him erupted with flame. Napalm. Ronsdale didn't have napalm. Well, whoever had dropped it, there it was. The flame was a great rolling mass and the brightness hurt his eyes. An instant later the heat struck his face, making him wince. The air was hot; he gasped when he tried to breathe. The oil smell clawed at his nostrils.

He wanted to pull his head away, to duck into the eroded trench, but somehow he could not. He stared. In the brightness of the flame he saw a human figure, black and silhoueted. It shriveled into a crazy rag-doll shape. Other humans were running—and at least a dozen of them were screaming. He could feel those screams in the pulp of his teeth.

The second jet passed overhead and more yellow eggs came down. There was another great whoosh of flame, to his right this time. He saw men engulfed by it. One ran out of the holocaust—God knew how he still lived—

255

screaming and slapping at his burning clothes. Another, some distance from the flame, fell to his knees and held his meat-raw face in his hands. One man near the whooshing curled and became black and then shrank, like overcooked bacon, into virtual nothingness.

Now, mingled with the oil and gunpowder smell, Straker could detect the awful stink of charred flesh.

The third and fourth planes came in, doing the whole thing over again.

After the planes had gone it was ponderously quiet. Straker looked dazedly about him. His face was raw from the heat, but he barely noticed that. The hilltop was smoking and burning, and now a figure stumbled out of the smoke, looked about, and suddenly fell.

"Dear God," said Straker.

There was a drawn-out, terrified moan some distance up the hillside.

"Thy will be done," Straker said.

His hand was shaking. It looked whiter than it ought to be. He opened and closed it, watching the veins in his wrist bulge and fall. He shook his head to clear away some of the daze. He tucked his pistol carefully and slowly back into its holster. Then he took a deep breath and began very slowly to walk once more toward the crest of the hill.

Scarcely fifty yards further on he almost stumbled over a Chinese soldier. He stopped, gaped, and saw that the man was lying on his back, staring into the sky. Some of the man's flesh was still smoking. He was an older man with a wide, round face. The man's eyes moved suddenly and met Straker's. Fright widened them.

"Well, what else did you expect?" Straker heard himself say.

The man stared at him, still with that frightened look. Something awfully steady and unchangeable about that look. It took some moments for Straker to realize that the man was already dead.

Then, suddenly, the ground on Straker's right began to erupt with small geysers of dirt, each about a foot high, and there was the drumming of a machine gun from somewhere. He threw himself face down. He squirmed, then

256

lifted his head and looked down the hill. He saw a dark tank sitting near the edge of the road. He could just about make out the figure that stood in the hatchway.

The machine-gun fire came again, in bursts, none more than a second long. It came and it moved the scrub trees away, and the slugs sang from the rocks with a banshee wail. Several struck in front of him sending stinging dirt particles into his face. He heard a growling noise—almost as loud as the drone of a bomber—as the tank gunned its engine and maneuvered to another position.

His hands began to tremble again. His teeth ached where he had been pressing them together. His forehead was cold and wet. His larynx seemed suddenly too large, and though he wanted to swallow the dryness in his throat he was unable to. His stomach ached.

"I am afraid!" he whispered, in a surprised tone. He looked down at himself. "God in heaven—I am afraid!"

Another burst. The ground shook.

Straker stood where he was, clasped his hands together tightly before him and began to move his lips. He gave no voice to the words but they were sharp and clear in his mind. *Almighty God, deliver Thy servant from this peril. If Thou seest fit to deliver him now he will serve Thee for the rest of his natural life in the ministry of Thy gospel. . . .*

It was really no surprise to Straker when, some moments later, airplanes began to attack the tank that was firing upon him. He watched three jets make their passes—he watched them calmly. He caught the fuselage number of the third jet.

"Ronsdale," he thought admiringly, and smiled.

Then Ronsdale's ship circled and came in for another pass. Straker continued to smile. The plane came down . . . down . . . never wavering, and the bursts from the tank's rifle fell far behind it.

Straker's smile disappeared slowly and unbelievably as he watched Pete Ronsdale fly his airplane into the tank and die.

CHAPTER TWELVE

1

THERE were other flights and squadrons. There were airplanes wherever Tindle looked. And the chatter in his headsets:

"Superman Charley, this is Charley Leader. Going down."

"Uh-roger, Charley Leader.

"Superman Charley Leader, this is Candy William. Is that you just north of Tinju?"

"Roger. We're shooting up some tents, old lad. Want to come along?"

"You soften 'em up, Charley. We'll finish 'em."

"Eggnogg Three here—look sharp, everybody, look sharp!"

Tindle was circling high, following Kingsley. They had suppressed the flak positions assigned to them, and now they would circle and reconnoiter, looking for flushed troops. They had not much more time. Even with tip-tanks of increased capacity, designed here in the theater, the Shooting Stars could spend altogether not much more than a quarter-hour at the target.

Tindle, looking down, could see the jumbled groups of yellow tents on nearly all the hillsides; he could spot the blemishes of freshly dug earth where foxholes and bunkers had been constructed. Occasionally he could see a scuttling feather of dust as a vehicle tried a short, desperate run in the open. And new flak positions. Dozens of them, it would seem. They were seeding the air with flak. Kingsley said, "Stick with me, Candy Baker—"

"Roger," said Tindle.

"Roger . . . roger," said the others.

"I'm looking for something to clobber," said Kingsley. "Something where we won't get in somebody's way."

"Like Times Square around here," said somebody.

"You ain't just a-whistlin' 'Dixie,' " said somebody else.

"Stick with me—"

Tindle knew from Kingsley's voice that he was not enjoying this one. More men than had been counted upon would cream in today. Many would buy the farm. Those were the slang words, the words that whistled in the dark. . . .

"The colonel's hit! Watch that new battery!"

Tindle wasn't sure who said it. He rubbernecked, trying to find Candy Able flight in all that melee—

"Candy Able—cap him till those choppers get here!"

"Keep it quiet, fellows," said Kingsley. "Let them call those choppers in."

They kept circling. Tindle still could not find Candy Able flight. He heard the call for the rescue helicopters and he heard Candy Able flight taking as it capped the colonel. Then he heard someone scream, "No! No!" and for a moment wondered why. There was a short silence.

Finally somebody said, "He dove right down on the bastard, did you see that?"

"I saw it."

"That Ronsdale—what a guy!"

"He's gone now. Come on. We've got work to do."

Ronsdale—gone in? It was hard for Tindle to believe. Somehow he'd had the feeling that Ronsdale would never get close enough to death to have it reach out and take him . . . a brave man, maybe, but not Ronsdale. . . .

Kingsley called again. "Candy Leader here. Time for our second target. I'm breaking left—stay with me, now—"

Kingsley led them across two more ridges. There in a rocky valley, along a sinuous stream, there were dozens of thatched huts. They looked lifeless, innocent—but the reconnaissance photos had caught foot and vehicle tracks about them night after night. One print had even shown clearly a line of soldiers' laundry hanging out to dry.

"Count the Chinks you get," said Kingsley. "They'll want the box score."

"I can't count that high," said somebody, and laughed.

They started down, each half-rolling, then falling lazily into a dive from the top of the roll. Tracers began to come up from the valley immediately. Tindle ignored them, stared at the thatched huts, and wondered when, precisely, he would see human beings run from the huts and then

259

be cut in two by their fire. But maybe they'd stay hidden; maybe he wouldn't have to watch this time.

"*Bandits! Bandits! Three o'clock high!*"

The call caught Tindle completely by surprise. No one had predicted enemy planes. They'd said maybe there would be some—but they'd said it in a way that indicated they didn't really believe there would be any. He wasn't sure who'd made the call—might have been the F-86 Sabrejet pilots flying cover for the whole operation, or it might have been one of the other fighter-bombers near the ground. He snapped his head upward and to the right. Something flashed in the sun. He squinted, and just barely made out the silhouettes of airplanes far above them. The Sabres maybe—but these silhouettes seemed to be diving, coming toward them—

"*Stick with me, Candy Baker,*" said Kingsley's quiet, easy voice.

Funny how in an air battle time drew itself out. It was difficult to realize that in only a few seconds they had dropped a couple of miles. They were continuing their attack on the huts below—bandits or no bandits. Kingsley, about three hundred yards ahead, was already spraying the structures. Everything in Tindle's windshield glass was clear and tiny, unreal in its solidity, like the view in a stereopticon.

Kingsley pulled up and away. Tindle squeezed his own trigger. His six guns, all firing at slight inward angles, made the slugs converge upon a hut by the stream, one he'd selected as a bull's eye. It looked remarkably like the hut where long ago he had found a dead woman and a glossy-haired child playing with the corpse's fingers. But of course it couldn't be the same. His missiles struck. The wall blew away, powdering into dust. Three—no, four small figures broke away and ran; then threw themselves into the water. He kept up his fire. High spurts appeared in the water, walking toward these figures. . . .

Then Tindle backsticked, was pressed into the seat, and at the top of his climb he rolled gently to the left.

He frowned. He had no emotion. He had felt no compassion for those terrified, scrambling figures. He was sure that he could come around again and strafe them, make

260

pulp of them, stain the waters of the stream—and not even shudder.

What had happened?

Scratches of light in the corner of his eye caught his attention. He turned his head and saw tracers going by. *Coming from above.* There was another airplane somewhere near by, and it was firing upon him. Firing upon the living consciousness that was Dick Tindle, wanting it destroyed. *I must not die now,* he thought; *there's too much yet to be discovered.*

He dropped his wing tanks.

2

This was the feeling of the hunted, a marrow feeling that the hunter, unseen, was there and watched. And you might flee, but there were uncountable avenues. Which one? Or best be still? Here? There? If the heart would stop pounding, and you could think—

And why did they hunt; and why had he become quarry? Why Dick Tindle who would affect very little the lives of most people if he went on living. Or if he died.

Of course it was impersonal. Of course none of it was directed toward him by name, or by the mark of his soul. That was the external reality. But it must be important to the hunters that he be destroyed: they would not take such trouble to destroy him otherwise. In their minds—according to whatever *inner* realities drove them— he was not unimportant. He was himself an excellent machine of destruction. He had permitted himself to become this, and this was now his function among men. Somehow, now, there was little other reason that he should exist.

You had so little to say about it all; you couldn't even pick your own nightmare.

He laughed nervously. He was startled that all of this could pass through his mind in so short a time, and in so incongruous a place as the cockpit of a jet fighter-bomber in a whistling scimitar turn.

And now he saw the hunter.

The MIG-15 at first was only a speck high above the line of the horizon, but almost instantly it swelled into a fat silhouette as it came toward him. It was to his right. He turned right instantly; he turned toward it. Turning away would only present an easy target and put the MIG into position on his tail. For a shuttered instant he saw merry, winking lights upon the MIG's nose before it slammed by, and went out of sight again. The cannon shells—looking like hot embers thrown at incredible speed—lobbed by a hundred yards ahead of him.

The talk in his headsets was jumbled and continuous, and he wished that he could shut it off. He continued to turn, trying to coordinate stick and rudder, and he realized that his hand shook slightly. Apparently he was afraid. He hadn't noticed that at first. His mouth tasted of bile.

Again he searched the sky somewhat frantically, and this time he did not see the MIG coming. A stream of embers passed overhead, seeming to float for a moment just above his canopy. A shadow blurred past on the right. The shadow flirted with the edge of his sight ring. He tripped his guns, but the line of his fire curved far to the left.

He fought the centrifugal force as he came about in another tight turn.

He checked his fuel counter. Low. But still enough to land at one of the Korean bases if he could keep working southward. He swung his head continuously, until his eyes ached from currying the empty sky. Where the devil had everyone gone? He glanced at his compass. One thirty degrees. He's evidently drifted far to the south of the big fight.

A second time the glowing projectiles came out of nowhere and curved by his wings. Closer this time. They didn't really curve, they only seemed to. And when one could travel this fast, what else might not be illusion?

Easy. Easy there. Crazy ideas again. Hang on. Pay attention. Stay with the business at hand.

A second time the shadow went by and began to climb a short distance beyond him. Where was the bastard's wingmate? The bastards usually traveled in pairs. Maybe the bastard has lost his wingmate in the shuffle and decided to get himself a little lone glory. The bastard. Tindle fired a burst, but it fell away short. He turned to the right immediately.

262

He thumbed the mike button and said, "For God's sake, this is Candy Baker Two—listen—I've got a MIG on my tail—I'm south of Tinju somewhere—"

He was not directly answered. He did not know whether, through all the jumble of voices, anyone had heard.

A large drop of sweat, cold as sleet, fell from his overhanging brows where for a moment it had been caught, and trickled down the side of his nose.

The MIG was coming at him head-on. He started to turn left. He had no idea whether the enemy pilot was skillful or clumsy. He would have to be in an airplane more nearly equal to the MIG in performance to know that. He knew clearly enough, however, that the MIG was a much better airplane, and that he himself had only one small advantage—with his lesser speed he could make narrower turns. This was defensive advantage only; it gave him a small chance of escape, but virtually no chance of inflicting return damage.

"Candy Baker Two, this is Cleveland Three."

The words came out of the jumble.

Again:

"Cleveland Three here—do you read me, Candy Baker Two?"

"Hello, Cleveland. I'm Candy Able. Where the hell are you?"

"Got you in sight. Got the MIG in sight, too. Hold on, boy!"

Cleveland would be an F-86 Sabrejet; Tindle knew the call-sign. He said, "I'm holding." And he looked and saw the MIG coming toward him again, head-on once more, with terrible closure speed . . . and Tindle was frightened enough now that he wanted to scream, but he hadn't the physical strength to scream. Where the devil had his strength gone? This was like a dream in which you were pursued by an unspeakable being somewhere behind you, but you ran on a treadmill and stayed in one place as the being came closer and closer. But he had strength to press the trigger. He saw his tracers fly away, and they seemed to strike the MIG, seemed to be swallowed by it, but he was not thoroughly certain. The MIG's nose was covered with winking orange-colored lights again. He stopped firing his own guns for a moment, and in that moment he heard a sound like that of large stones coming down a tin chute. He had never heard this sound before but he knew instantly somehow that it was the sound of slugs striking his plane. He took a deep breath. He waited for oblivion, wondering if he'd really know when it came—

Not that it would matter. He would be pretty quickly forgotten, this mind and flesh that had been tagged Dick Tindle for convenient identification, and at the longest someone—Martha perhaps—might remember him vividly for two or three years. Did he flatter himself? Well, even five years would not be long. A man, he reflected, could not have lived more uselessly. In his time he had become skilled only in destruction, and it was even possible that in his time he had destroyed someone, somewhere, who might have mattered.

But with all this conviction strong and bitter in his mind, he still did not want to die.

A second passed, and nothing happened.

He looked at his right wing, and saw several holes near the tip, with sharp strips of metal peeling away in the airstream.

"Got him! Got him!" someone was yelling excitedly. He recognized the voice of Cleveland Three. The same voice said, "Where the hell did he go? Anybody see him?"

"Hey, boy," said another voice, "you get yourself a MIG?"

"I don't know. I hit him—saw him smoke. Can't find him now!"

"We're up at forty thousand, just south of Tinju. Where are you?"

"Down here. Down below you."

"Roger, I see you. Better get on up here, boy."

"I'm coming. But what about that MIG? Where's that goddamn MIG?"

Tindle kept going south. He trimmed for gradual climb; he would use less fuel at higher altitude, and if he ran dry he could coast into one of the Korean fields—Taegu with its long P.S.P. runways of linked metal might be the best bet. He glanced at the terrain below, looking for a checkpoint. A river running at a right angle to his course looked

264

as though it might be the Chongchon—he checked one of the sections of his book of glassine-enclosed maps and compared a few curves. Seemed likely. That would put him to the east and slightly north of Sinanju.

Then a white dot caught his eye. Down there . . . a parachute falling earthward, moving before the wind. Far beyond, on a steep mountainside, a patch of flame and a column of black smoke still climbing.

Tindle stared for a moment, then switched channels on his radio. "Delicious Control," he said, "this is Candy Baker Two."

"Go ahead, Candy Baker."

"Look, I'm in a Fox-eighty—just east of Sinanju, I think. About Yoke Dog five three seven four coordinates. I have a parachute in sight. Going down. I think he's a MIG pilot—you understand?"

"Stand by one," said Delicious.

Okay, Tindle would stand by for a minute. Delicious he knew would be getting instructions on this from higher up. From way higher up. He nosed down, and made a sweeping pass toward the parachute. He used his dive brakes—flaps that came down from the belly of the ship— to reduce his speed. He curved past the parachute. He thought he saw the flash of a white, upturned face, but he wasn't sure. He did see a bright green uniform or coverall.

Delicious called in again. "Candy Baker Two—"

"Candy Baker here. Over."

"Do you have a gun camera? I say again: do you have a gun camera? Over."

Tindle said, "I have a gun camera."

"Jelly Central wants pictures. They want you to get pictures of that enemy pilot—do you understand, Candy Baker Two?"

Tindle said, "Roger. Understand."

He switched his sixteen millimeter gun camera into the circuit, and took his guns out. He widened his turn and came back toward the falling parachute. He held his sight steady upon the small figure there and started his camera. He throttled back and mushed in, but still he went too fast for a clear look. The chute and its passenger blurred

265

by. All he saw was that the pilot covered his face with his arms.

That wouldn't do at all. "He's covering his face, Delicious," Tindle reported.

"Roger. Try it again."

He made a second pass. The same thing happened.

Delicious said, "Hello, Candy Baker—"

"Roger. I'm here."

"They want that pilot, Candy Baker. They're diverting a helicopter now in the Yoke Dog area to pick him up. Can you cap the pick up?"

"I don't know. I'm a little Josephine." Josephine was the code word for a shortage of fuel.

"Understand. At your discretion, Candy Baker Two."

"Okay. Okay, roger." Tindle was weary of the whole business.

"It's very important, they say, Candy Baker."

"Yeah. Okay."

"If there's any way to detain that pilot, they want you to use your own judgment."

"What's that?"

"I say again: if any way to detain enemy pilot you are to use you own judgment."

"You mean they want me to shoot him?"

"I just pass on the orders," said Delicious Control.

It was clear enough. Some brass-encrusted character wanted that MIG pilot, and wanted him bad. Wanted to see whether he was a Chinaman or a Russian or a German or a North Korean or maybe a bear that walked like a bogieman. But said brass-encrusted character didn't want to come right out and issue orders to shoot the poor bastard, there where he swung under his fat white parachute. Not that such orders wouldn't be legitimate. This was war, after all; this was war with the new silhouette, and the chivalry crap went out with Fonck and Von Richthofen—or was Sir Lancelot the last? No, there wasn't any reason why the MIG pilot shouldn't be clobbered with a few fifty calibers just to make sure he didn't get away when the helicopters came along; there was no good reason at all. But you could never let it be known such an official order had been given. The howling press would tear that

266

one apart in no time at all. The Communists would mill bushels of propaganda out of it. It would be the inspiration for a million atrocity posters from Vladivostok to East Berlin.

And then suppose Tindle—who hadn't been given an order, mind you—simply decided not to detain (as they delicately put it) the enemy pilot in this way. They could hardly court-martial him for disobedience, could they?

He did not deceive himself. There were other ways of punishing a man in the strong state within a state known as the military service. All you had to do was find out what he wanted most—what he was working for—and then make damn sure he didn't get it. In Tindle's case they'd probably draw his overseas tour out unto the next century and make him a file clerk in a communications outpost somewhere in Korea. The most difficult man to injure in the military service, he reflected, was the man who didn't particularly want anything.

And now, having made a swift mental examination of these matters, he looked to himself. How did he feel about shooting to death the poor, helpless bastard under the parachute there?

He scowled, trying to find out. He was presently a little shocked to discover that actually it didn't make much difference to him one way or the other.

But this wasn't Dick Tindle—this wasn't the name and the mind and nerve and flesh he'd known so well for nearly three decades. This wasn't himself at all.

Why?

Why so sudden a change?

Now that he thought about it the change had already begun back there at Tinju when he'd been able to strafe those huts and their scattering erstwhile occupants with a certain amount of ease.

Something had happened to him. Dick Tindle—who hadn't wanted to kill—now didn't care.

(He was diving toward the MIG pilot again. He could just barely begin to make out the shape of this man. Again, the other was holding his crossed arms over his face.)

Was it because it was so easy? Was this why he didn't care?

Sure . . . easy. Finger on the trigger built into the stick handle. Move that finger maybe a thirty-second of an inch, with perhaps an ounce of pressure. Then it would be done. Then he would have fulfilled himself—hell, yes, that would be the moment toward which his whole life (without his having much to say about it) had been directed.

Only this wasn't why he didn't care. It was nothing external, it was something burned into his belly. It was something that had begun, perhaps, even before his attack on the targets at Tinju.

Maybe it had begun in the open doorway of a taxi when he'd decided to go into that hotel that first night with Teriko. Maybe it had begun on the sun-bleached ramp at Akuni when he'd cheaply blackmailed Major Ronsdale into arranging his seven-day leave. Maybe it had begun when he'd left Martha, running from his trouble and not fighting it. But maybe even further back. Maybe the first time he stole a cookie from the tin box in the kitchen.

A man knew; a man always knew. Call it built-on, or built-in, whatever, a man always knew right from wrong. Nor knew how he knew. He tried to give this feeling form sometimes: he became an artist or a philosopher or adopted a religion. He usually sneered at the attempts of others to do this thing by their different means.

And then, having authored or borrowed his Standard Operating Procedure, a man began to depart from it whenever it was slightly more convenient. Not in big ways—that would make him too obviously a fraud. In little ways. Always in little ways that didn't really seem to matter. Mostly there was little wrong with the systems—the S.O.P.'s—the trouble was in a man's inability to follow them consistently. Straker was a Christian and believed in mercy, but he had permitted himself to be cruel. Ronsdale was a gentleman and a fine figure of an officer, but he hadn't followed his code and accepted the blame for his cowardice. Essie believed in love, and allowed herself too much passion. Johnny Pendermeyer believed in the superiority of the White American, but couldn't accept the responsibility that must go with leadership.

268

And Tindle himself had believed individual man a sacred thing, but he had let his own sacred individuality slip away. In little ways, of course, and only now and then. But that was what had happened to him. *That was why he had changed.*

His jaw ached; he had been holding his teeth together too tightly.

And many seconds ago he had blurred past the falling parachute without firing his guns. He pulled the stick back suddenly, pressed his trigger, and shot off his remaining ammunition into the empty sky.

CHAPTER THIRTEEN

1

TINDLE awoke into fright. He knew he had been crying out in his sleep: he knew he had been dreaming of yesterday's mission. He was wet with perspiration.

He looked along his own rumpled length upon the cot, across the dark soaking of the sheets, and through the window of his room at Akuni. The sun was edging over the candy mountains; the flat-topped pines along the ridges were in sharp outline. The sun was red. It would be a hot, hazy day; it would be perhaps the first really hot day of the season.

He looked at the alarm clock on the dresser and saw that it was twenty minutes after seven. He had not set the alarm last night; he had undressed quickly and carelessly and fallen into bed.

Now there were things to be done—and things to be faced.

First he must call upon Essie . . . she, of course, had heard by now of Ronsdale's death, and he hadn't called upon her yesterday because it was better that she get the news briefly and impersonally the first time. Second, he must explain how the MIG pilot had escaped. He'd explained that tersely at the de-brief yesterday, but there would be others today who would want the details. And who would pass judgment upon Tindle after they had

269

heard the details. He would tell them the simple truth, of course, and they would neither believe nor understand—but he could not help that. He knew he faced some kind of tacit punishment—in a half masochistic way he was objectively curious to know exactly what kind. They would punish him for seeming like one of them all this time, and turning out not to be one of them after all. That was what they would forgive least—the masquerade.

He arose, stretched, yawned, gathered up his towel and shaving kit, and then paused, before leaving for the washroom, to look at himself in the mirror. He looked tired, though he must have slept ten hours or more. His exhaustion was somewhere behind his eyes, like the emptiness of a bombed-out house whose front still stands. . . .

Shave, shower, breakfast, coffee. That would help some.

After his bath he dressed carefully in clean khakis. He walked the short distance to the officers' snack bar which was in a wing of the club building. There were twenty or thirty people already there, sitting at the small tables, finishing coffee, talking, reading newspapers. One or two glanced at Tindle as he came in, and then hastily glanced away. He noticed several of the correspondents who had come to Akuni to cover the max effort. He picked up coffee and doughnuts at the counter and went to an empty table.

There was another unpleasant chore this morning. Teriko would arrive on the eleven o'clock train. He had played with the idea of sending someone else—the Japanese jeep driver perhaps—to tell her what he had to say, but he had dismissed that as cowardly. He would meet her. He would do his own talking—

Someone came to his table and sat down across from him. Tindle looked up. His new companion was a thin, gray-faced man of about forty, who wore a blue and white UN correspondent's patch on his shoulder.

The man said, "You're Captain Tindle, aren't you?"

"Yes."

"I'm Oscott."

"Oh. Yes. Herb Oscott. I've read your column."

"Mind if I join you for a minute?"

"No." Tindle almost shrugged. He looked at the reporter

270

rather warily. In this man's mild eyes there was mixed astuteness and skepticism—and maybe even a bit of arrogance.

Oscott said, "Guess you heard about Colonel Straker."

"I heard he jumped."

"The Air Rescue boys got him. Not a scratch. They brought him in on a special flight last night."

"He's all right?"

"Good as new, I guess. They wanted to keep him in a hospital for observation, but he wormed his way out of that somehow. You know Straker."

Tindle nodded and said, "Yes, I know him."

"Have you seen much of him—at close range, I mean?"

"Why?"

"I thought I might do a little background piece on him. I just want to round it out with what his men think of him."

"I haven't talked to him much."

"But you've been under his command," said Oscott, with a slightly persistent tone. "What kind of a commander would you say he was?"

Tindle took a long sip of coffee and then, looking over Oscott's shoulder, said, "He's a good commander in every way. A good leader and a good soldier. He's a man of—how do you say it?—unimpeachable integrity."

Oscott smiled dryly. "That's not how I say it."

"But you know what I mean."

"Yes. And I don't think you believe it."

"Isn't it what you wanted to hear?"

"I'm a reporter. I want to hear the truth."

"Then you better ask somebody else. Better ask somebody who'll say what I just said, and believe it."

"I think I understand," said Oscott.

"What you mean, you think you understand?"

"You and Straker struck sparks, didn't you?"

Tindle stiffened. "If we did, it was private business."

"Not exactly. Straker's a public figure now. Anything that has a bearing on him is public business."

"Mr. Oscott," said Tindle, "I didn't ask you to come over here."

Oscott was still smiling, and now he said, "Still hating

yourself after yesterday, Captain? Better calm down. You'll feel better. Nobody really blames you for getting buck fever."

"Buck fever?"

"They asked you to shoot that MIG pilot in his parachute, didn't they?"

Tindle simply stared back.

Oscott waited for a moment, then leaned back in his chair. "Okay," he said. "I didn't make the grade. I thought if I got you stirred up you'd let some information slip. It's an old reporter's trick—sorry I tried to pull it on you."

"It's a cheap goddamn trick, Oscott."

Oscott sighed and nodded.

"Okay," said Tindle, "maybe I didn't exactly mean that."

Oscott leaned forward. "Look, Tindle, you don't have to admit it, but I know you were asked to shoot that MIG pilot. And I'm not reporting now, I'm just curious. I won't print what you say, either. Why *didn't* you shoot him?"

Tindle frowned. "I don't know exactly—"

"You don't have to be cagy. This is just between us. I'll even let you buy me another cup of coffee to show my good faith."

Tindle smiled a little, then said, "All right, I'll give you an honest answer. It seemed damned clear to me at the time why I didn't—and now I'm not sure. Maybe your first guess was right. Maybe it was just buck fever."

"Maybe it was," said Oscott. He got up, and took both coffee cups. "Here, I'll go against my principles this time. I'll buy the coffee."

Afterward Tindle went out into the bright sun and walked with quick, stiff strides toward the dependent housing area. Now that the morning had taken hold the air base all about was coming to life. Jeeps, trucks and weapons-carriers rumbled along the streets, raising dust, and on the line jet engines were roaring intermittently. A transport circled overhead in the landing pattern. Japanese laborers worked at a roadside ditch, and in a sandbagged revetment helmeted men swung a twin mounting an anti-aircraft guns in dry practice.

272

Busy lives all around him—only adding to his loneliness.

He turned on to the street where the Straker and Ronsdale cottages were located, and he saw again the tailored lawns and neat houses; the symbols of order and stability in a volatile world. There was fresh dew smell on the grass, and the leaves of the trees were cupped to retain the dew. Three children, swinging book bags, waited at the far corner for the school bus. All of it looked as though it would surely be there forever.

He walked to Essie's door quickly and slammed the knocker at once, as though hesitation might make him forever unable to do either of these things. Essie's Japanese maid opened the door.

"Mrs. Ronsdale in?"

"Missy Ronsdale, she—"

Essie's voice came from inside. "Dick? Is that you, Dick? Please come in."

He went in. Essie, in a navy blue suit and crisp white shirt, came across the room to meet him. She was perfectly turned out, and she smelled again of powder and the bath. She was pale. Then Tindle looked beyond her and saw Colonel Straker standing by the window. Straker looked tall this morning—and a little awkward.

Tindle glanced at the colonel only briefly, then stepped toward Essie. He took her hands and pressed them. "Hello, Essie."

"Hello, Dick."

"I—well, you know why I came."

"Yes."

"I don't have to tell you how I feel."

"Yes, Dick, thank you. Everybody's been very kind."

"You're taking it wonderfully, Ess."

She lowered her eyes, let go of his hands, and turned away. She walked to the coffee table, picked up a cigarette and put it in her mouth. Colonel Straker lit it for her. She sat down on the sofa then.

Tindle shifted his stance, looked at Straker and said, "Glad to see you back, sir." He felt that both of them looked extremely awkward. He admired Essie for being the only one who did not.

"Yes," said Straker absently, folding and unfolding his

273

hands. "Yes." He walked to the window, then back again.

Tindle turned to Essie. "Is there anything I can do?"

"No, Dick. Thanks." She was looking at the floor. "Julie Gorgas is coming over in a minute. She'll help me with everything."

"Well, if anything comes up—I mean if later I can do anything—" Tindle looked at Straker, and made a broad, clumsy gesture.

Essie rose suddenly. Tindle saw the sudden widening of her eyes; he watched the moisture well up. For a moment he thought she was going to put herself into his arms to be comforted. Then, abruptly, she turned and ran with several quick steps across the room to Straker. Straker put his arms around her and she rested her head on his chest and began to weep quietly.

Straker said, "It's all right, Essie. It's all right. Don't worry . . . it's all right."

Tindle said, "Well, I guess I'll run along."

"Wait," said Straker. "I'll go with you. Wait just a minute, Tindle."

They left together when Captain Gorgas' wife arrived. Leaving was awkward, too. Then Straker and Tindle walked down the street side by side and for some moments neither spoke.

Straker finally took a deep breath and broke the silence. "She's a fine woman, Captain. She's a fine, brave woman."

"Yes," said Tindle. He almost added, "I suppose so," but checked himself in time.

"And Ronsdale was a brave man. One of the finest officers I've ever known. I owe my life to him."

"Yes," said Tindle again.

"It's given to some of us to be brave," said the colonel.

Tindle said nothing. He felt that Straker wanted to say more, but wanted exactly the right words for it. Straker now seemed to be trying to see how much distance he could find with his eyes. Tindle recalled now how Essie had turned to Straker for comfort, and he remembered how tenderly Straker had comforted her. Well, it was not illegal that widow and widower should seek each other now. A good thing, possibly; very probably a better combination than Pete and Essie had been. He wondered how

274

long Straker would consider a decent interval before proposing to Essie.

"About yesterday," said Straker abruptly.

"Yes?"

"You were out of ammunition when you found that MIG pilot, weren't you?"

"No, sir. I wasn't out of ammunition."

Straker looked at him coldly. "I think perhaps you were. I think it's better that way. I don't want any discredit reflected on the Wing. I think we'd better put it in our report that you were out of ammunition."

"Colonel, I don't want to lie about it. I don't want anybody covering up for me."

"I don't think you have much choice in the matter. As for your attitude, I think you'd be grateful to escape punishment."

"I'm relieved," said Tindle. "I'm not grateful. Let's be frank, Colonel—this isn't exactly mercy or compassion on your part. It isn't even understanding."

"All right, Tindle, let's not have one of your soap-box orations again. I'm very tired of you, Tindle. I'll be relieved when you're out of here."

"Out of here?"

"First I'm grounding you. Then I'm sending you over to the air base group on the other side of the field. The housekeepers. They need administrative personnel. I won't be with the the Wing much longer, but I don't want to wish you on to my successor as a fighter pilot."

"You're leaving?"

"I have enough points for retirement if I want it. I'm going with the church, Tindle. Not as a minister of the Gospel, of course, but in an administrative capacity with their headquarters. They've approached me about the thing several times. I—I made a promise with myself to that effect out there on the ground after a prayer of mine was answered. If you ever doubt the efficacy of prayer, Tindle—"

"Is that all you learned out there?"

"Listen to me, Tindle. Listen to me. You need strength, Tindle. I advise you to seek it in the church. I say that in all seriousness. If you could humble yourself some time

275

to ask God for His help you'd solve a lot of your problems."

"Well, Colonel," said Tindle, sighing, "in a way you're right, and in a way I'm right. It's a complicated business."

Straker shook his head and said, "I'm sorry for you, Tindle. Really sorry for you."

"You don't have to be," said Tindle. "I'm a happy man, now. Yes—" he nodded thoughtfully, and raised his eyebrows in some surprise—"I think all of a sudden I'm a happy man."

They had reached the road that led to the airstrip. Straker went on toward headquarters, and Tindle turned and headed for the barracks.

In the hall there he picked up the telephone and called the railroad station at Korokua. He had one of the housemaids handle his query in Japanese. The morning train from Tokyo would arrive on time. It would be at the station in half an hour. He called a jeep taxi from the motor pool and told the driver to take him to the station.

2

The station at Korokua was dirty and crowded. A female voice on a loudspeaker called out the train and its connections a few seconds before it arrived. The voice was shrill and the volume was full on—the Japanese are infatuated with sound amplification. People surged forward, jostling each other, toward the lip of the platform as the electric train slid metallically to a stop.

Tindle stood near the center of the platform with his back against a pillar, and his hands in his pockets. As the passengers came out of the train doors he moved his head this way and that, looking for Teriko. He was disturbed that he could not picture her fully in his mind; he remembered the details, but not the whole of her. Once, a woman in a green coat stepped from the car some distance down the platform and from her shape, or perhaps her step, Tindle thought for a moment she might be Teriko. When she turned and he saw her face, he saw that she was not.

The waiting passengers, having let the others off, began to crowd into the train now. The loudspeaker shrilled again. A laborer in a short blue cotton jacket with a huge

276

chrysanthemum design on its back was arguing fretfully with the uniformed platform official. The official was trying to outshout the laborer and waving his tightly rolled red flag for emphasis. Tindle frowned, and darted his glance here and there.

Perhaps she hadn't come. Changed her mind, perhaps—or even found someone else. That would make it all very easy. But in a perverse way he didn't want this to be easy—what he was about to do was too symbolically important to him to be easy.

Then he saw her, toward the rear of the platform, carrying a suitcase and walking toward him. Seeing her now he wondered how he had ever forgotten that graceful figure, that dancing walk. He skirted the crowd and pushed toward her. He could see her smile now; he could see how she quickened her steps.

She came directly toward him, dropped her bag, pushed into his arms, and lifted her face to his without a word. He bent and kissed her. He wanted to make this a warm kiss, but he felt that it was not. She clung, her eyes tightly shut, and for many seconds she would not let go.

She broke away finally and said, "Oh, Dick-san, Dick-san."

Tindle said, "Hello, Teriko."

Her eyes went from side to side as she scanned his face. Her expression changed suddenly, and became puzzled. "Is trouble, Dick-san?"

"No trouble, Teriko." He was still holding her in his arms. "But I must tell you something. I must try to make you understand something."

Her eyes widened, and he thought again how utterly false the fiction of the expressionless oriental. "Dick-san," she said quietly, "you don't loving me now. Something happen."

"Look—we can't talk here. Let's find a coffee shop."

"But you're not loving me. True, neh?"

"It's not exactly that, Teriko. It takes more explaining than that."

The loudspeaker blasted away again.

"Tokyo train coming," said Teriko.

"Let's not stand here."

277

She fumbled in her handbag and lifted a small square of cardboard. She smiled wanly. "You see—I buy ticket go back."

"But not now. Not on *this* train."

"I think better, neh?"

"Listen, Teriko, I want you to know how I feel. I want you to know the reasons. It's for you as well as me, Teriko—"

She shook her head in a hasty but stubborn way. She was still smiling, but a large tear had gathered and was poising before the drop in the corner of each eye. "Talking no good. Please, Dick-san—don't talking. Please going away now. Please *quick!*"

"Teriko, I—"

"Please going. Don't see me go train."

"Teriko, it was my fault for asking you down here in the first place. The whole thing was my fault, do you understand? It's not that I'm sorry for anything we did—I'll never forget those few days—that soft rain, and the mountains, and you, darling—everything. But I mustn't keep you down here. They're giving me a ground job which means I'll be in Japan a pretty long time finishing out my tour. I'm going to send for Martha. We're going to make it work, I know we are. If I lived with you down here, Teriko, it would be another of those little slips—the ones that add up. Damn it, I *can't* explain this standing out here with all this noise. I wish that woman on the loudspeaker would shut up!"

"Sayonara, Dick-san. Please good-bye."

She was right, of course. She didn't want and didn't need an explanation. That would only broaden the wound. He believed suddenly that she must have almost expected something like this all along, and he knew that throughout their affair she had been altogether wiser than he. "Teriko," he said abruptly, "maybe you love me—maybe you still do. I don't know. I certainly don't want you to tell me, one way or the other. But if you do love me— if you have any regard at all left for me after this heel's trick I've pulled—do something for me. Please do something very important."

"Do something?"